ALSO BY LENA JEONG

And Break the Pretty Kings

THE
WITCH OF
WOL SIN
LAKE

THE WITCH OF WOL SIN LAKE

LENA JEONG

HARPER

An Imprint of HarperCollinsPublishers

Dedicated to Na-Young

THE
WITCH OF
WOL SIN
LAKE

Chapter
ONE

Normally when Mirae heard the palace women call softly into her chamber just after sunrise and heave in a surasang spread of steamed fish, twelve side dishes, soup, and scorched rice tea, she would rise bleary-eyed out of bed and devour her breakfast. In the year since she'd ascended the throne, she'd quickly learned that she needed all the energy she could muster to make it through yet another rigorous day as Seolla's youngest and most inexperienced queen.

But this morning, Mirae had already been up for hours and sat fully dressed in the garments left out for her the night before, specifically chosen for that day's ceremony. While her attendants set up the various tables for her meal, Mirae finished fixing a large braided wig to the top of her head, a heavy adornment she always wore when conducting official business. As soon as the palace women were finished, Mirae nodded for them to leave. Although it was an unconventional thing for the High Queen to ready herself in the morning, the palace servants had become accustomed to her way of doing things, and no longer protested her deviances from tradition.

As for Mirae, being at the entire queendom's beck and call at all hours of the day had made her protective of whatever alone time she could steal.

When she was by herself again, Mirae turned her attention back to the spread of ddeoljam before her. She'd spent nearly half an hour just trying to choose which of the vibrant hairpieces to pin to her wig, a decision that never usually took this long. She was still undecided when a familiar voice echoed down the hallway outside her chamber.

"Three hours to herself and she still isn't ready?" she heard a man outside groan to the guard at the door. "Does my noonim realize she isn't just a crown princess anymore? She can't be late to these royal engagements! Lollygagging is *my* job now."

"It is exactly as you say, Seja jeoha," the Wonhwa responded obligingly, as she did almost every morning.

"Really, I don't know what she'd do without me," Hongbin huffed, and then waited for the soldier to wryly reply.

"You are utterly unappreciated, Seja jeoha."

"Indeed, I am!"

Mirae didn't even turn around when she heard the silk screen doors to her chamber slide open and Hongbin's feet stomp indignantly across the bamboo floor.

"What's taking so long, noonim?" her younger brother practically bellowed as he approached. "The oracles will be here in just a few hours, and you're not even dressed!"

Mirae raised an eyebrow and gestured to the resplendent hanbok draping her body, replete with a pale green dangui and deep plum chima. "Calm down. It's not like I'm sitting here naked."

"I wish the same could be said for your hair," Hongbin said

with a grimace. His own dark tresses were pulled into a smooth bun. Capping it was a small golden coronet pierced with a dragon-tipped binyeo that complemented the golden flecks of his deep blue hanbok. In short, Hongbin was, as usual, perfectly put together.

"My hair has been a bit of an ordeal this morning," Mirae admitted, and gestured to the slew of ornaments glittering in front of her. "I could really use your discerning eye."

Hongbin let out a dramatic huff before collapsing next to her. "Well, what choice do I have? We can hardly trust you to manage this simple task on your own."

Mirae ignored his jab, knowing full well it was all a performance for the benefit of the palace women and guards listening in. This was hardly the first time her younger brother had swooped into the queen's chambers uninvited when he suspected that Mirae needed his "rousing support." Sure enough, as soon as he could speak at a normal volume without being overheard by anyone outside, Hongbin finally dropped his charade.

"Rough morning?" he asked quietly. He gestured to Mirae's uneaten breakfast.

She nodded and let out a sigh. "I can't say I'm looking forward to today."

Hongbin nodded sympathetically. "One thing I've learned recently is how tedious royal duties can be."

"It's not just that," Mirae whispered. She was extra cautious that someone might eavesdrop on her next words. "This will be the first time since last year that I've interacted with any oracles except for Areum."

Hongbin's eyes widened. "Oh, I see."

While Mirae sat in her chambers, paralyzed by a seemingly small decision concerning hairpins, the palace courtyard was being prepared for that day's ceremony, the first one she'd be taking part in since her disastrous Sangsok Ceremony. Today, she would once again be surrounded by Sacred Bone Oracles, who were still recovering from that fateful night when many of their own were slaughtered. Now Mirae was tasked with anointing the new Kun Sunim of the holy women's order, knowing full well that their last one died only because Mirae couldn't fulfill her duty as protector of Seolla.

Sensing the dark direction of Mirae's thoughts, Hongbin cleared his throat before her anxiety could spiral any further. "There's nothing to worry about, noonim. Didn't Lady Areum say that the oracles don't blame you for what happened?"

Mirae nodded. It was true, her longtime friend, now serving as the court liaison between the oracles and the palace, had assured Mirae on several of her visits that the oracles she was training with blamed the massacre of their order on the anciently prophesied nemesis of Seolla—the Inconstant Son. A villain fated to destroy the entire queendom unless the gods-ordained High Daughters stopped him.

A man whom everyone believed Mirae had defeated.

Hongbin, seeing the look on her face, scooted closer and wrapped her in a hug. "You're doing it again, aren't you? Wallowing in guilt?"

"How could I not?" Mirae choked back a sob. "I told everyone that the Netherking was gone. Then I covered up what happened to Minho, and the Josan king's plot against Seolla. I've made everyone think the queendom is headed toward a golden age of peace."

"You did what you had to," Hongbin reminded her. "As Mother said, if the Hwabaek had learned of the Josan king's act of treason, there would have been war, the likes of which we've never seen. You had no choice but to blame Minho's abduction on the Netherking so all the political messiness would 'die' with him. Now you can finally push the Josan king to create a united peninsula. It's the least he can do after you covered for him."

"Even so, I lied." The ornaments below seemed to glitter more brightly as tears glassed Mirae's vision. "If everyone knew the truth—"

Hongbin waved away Mirae's words like night terrors that perished in daylight. "The Netherking can't hurt anyone anymore, not since you cut off his magic, decimating his mindless dark army. Thanks to you, everyone is safe."

"Not everyone." Mirae's head, heavy as a stone, slipped forward until all she could see was the floor, dewdropped with tears.

Hongbin sighed and took Mirae's hands. "We'll find a way to get Minho back. You, me, Mother, Father, and Kimoon. We made a pact. And, honestly, if you look at our combined skill sets, we're pretty unstoppable."

Hongbin reached up and wiped away the streaks of water on her cheeks. "You lied, yes, but that's the reason you get to sit here poring over jewels instead of battle maps. The fact that you can't see that as a blessing makes me sad. You have no idea how noble and greathearted you are. Which is why," Hongbin said, puffing out his chest, "I'm going to have to start telling you how amazing you are every day, morning and night, until you start believing me."

Mirae sighed as she brushed away the remaining wetness pooled up in her eyes. "You mean you're going to burst into my room like this all the time now, and bully your queen into seeing things your way?"

Hongbin shrugged. "For all your virtues, you can be quite thickskulled sometimes, noonim. It takes a lot to change your mind once you've decided to believe something."

"I could say the same for you."

"Yes, but I'm always right, so it's different." Hongbin stroked an imaginary beard. "I am your moral compass. The heart and soul of Seolla. Crown prince extraordinaire."

Mirae chuckled despite herself. "Well, oh wise one, how about you put that exceptional mind to work and help me finish getting ready before Captain Hanyoung comes to drag me out of here?"

Hongbin clapped his hands and rubbed them together. "Your wish is my command."

Without further ado, Hongbin leaned forward until he was nearly parallel to the shimmering pins. Moments later, he pointed at a pair of round ornaments. "How about these? They're quite pretty."

Although the pins he'd chosen were lovely—each had a round white jade base topped with garnet beads and gold butterflies—Mirae couldn't help but giggle. "Do you know what those are enchanted to do?"

Hongbin frowned and leaned closer, as if trying to read a minuscule script. "Hm, I know garnets are often associated with the heart, and butterflies are associated with beautiful women. Perhaps these ddeoljam make you extra attractive to the person you wish to court?"

"Not quite," Mirae said softly, conscious once more of not being overheard by anyone outside. "Don't use your head to figure this one out, Hongbin. Use your magic."

Her brother's eyes widened as they shot up to Mirae's. "You want me to use magic *here*? In the palace? You made me promise never to do that, or else you'd stop teaching me!"

Mirae shrugged. "I guess you've made me feel brave today."

It had been only half a year since Hongbin had confessed to Mirae that the mark at the base of his neck suppressing his Sacred Bone Magic—the ability to wield all three of Seolla's magic systems—had dissolved when the Netherqueen submerged him in a tub of black water, a change that the high collars of his hanboks had hidden from view. Since then, he'd been secretly trying to train himself in the ways of magic, but was soon forced to admit that he needed an instructor if he was to learn to use his powers safely.

At first he'd been afraid that Mirae would rat him out to their mother, especially after seeing firsthand what Sacred Bone Magic could do in the hands of a man like the Netherking. To Hongbin's relief, however, Mirae had agreed to mentor him. It was time, she'd decided, that Seolla stop suppressing magical men out of fear of the Inconstant Son's rise to power. After everything Mirae had seen, she couldn't help but feel that by trying to thwart the Inconstant Son, Seolla had only created him. So it was that Mirae had become determined to break the cycle of cultivating monsters, starting with her brother.

But first, Mirae had sworn Hongbin to secrecy. They both knew that it would take some time before the Hwabaek would be ready to condone this massive break with tradition, even after Mirae had declared that the Inconstant Son had been defeated. Since the inception of Seolla, its citizens had believed that the gods themselves were against men using magic. But after hearing the true story of the Deep Deceiver from the Netherking after his capture a year ago, Mirae had begun second-guessing a lot of what she'd been told about the gods' will.

"Are you sure about this, noonim?" Hongbin asked nervously. But after Mirae gave him an encouraging nod, his excitement finally won out. Hongbin reached forward, cupping his hand over one of the glimmering pins. Mirae stayed quiet as she waited for Hongbin's magic to connect with the subtle power emanating from the ornaments.

"Hm, let's see," Hongbin muttered as his eyes squeezed shut. "I'm sensing a thread of the enchanter's intent. The red garnet was chosen to emulate blood. But it was specifically enchanted to increase its wearer's circulation. The butterflies on top were enhanced to bring out the generative properties of gold that mesh with the transformative power of butterflies. Together, the enhanced flow of blood and the invocation of rebirth were combined to enchant these pins to . . . oh."

Hongbin's eyes flew open. "Are these, um . . . fertility pins?"

Mirae couldn't help but laugh at the mixture of emotions

on her younger brother's face. Pride in his successful exercise of magic, coupled with chagrin at what he'd suggested his sister bewitch her body to do that day. Cheeks lightly flushed, Hongbin cleared his throat. "Well, I think we can rule these out. I don't think there's use for them today."

"No, not particularly," Mirae said, the corners of her lips still twitching.

Once his embarrassment subsided, Hongbin smirked as well. "Let's try this again, shall we?"

Still smiling at his gaffe, Hongbin closed his eyes and hovered his hand over the remaining ddeoljam, pausing over a pair of amethyst discs piled with multicolored pearls. Seeming to quickly work out the enchantment exuding from them, a calmness that would soothe the stomach of its nervous wearer, Hongbin pointed at the pearly pins triumphantly.

"These will be perfect for you, noonim. I know how grumbly your stomach gets when you're anxious."

Grateful that they were still speaking too quietly to be overheard, Mirae nodded in agreement. "Right you are. I think you've made a fine choice."

Hongbin lifted his chin proudly as he helped Mirae finish adorning her hair. Just then, another familiar voice echoed outside the chamber, right on time. "Your Majesty, I have come to escort you to the Garden of Queens."

Captain Hanyoung slid open the screen doors and bowed before entering. When she straightened, the older woman raised an eyebrow. "I see you're running a little behind."

"My noonim was just suffering from a small bout of indecision!"

Hongbin quipped, once more putting on his charade of boisterous aplomb. "But fear not, our lovely queen is finally ready, all thanks to me."

Captain Hanyoung glanced at Mirae's untouched breakfast. "Perhaps I should come back after you've had a chance to eat. That's more important than your daily walk to—"

"No, no," Mirae said, a little too quickly. "I can't skip today."

"As you wish, Your Majesty." Captain Hanyoung didn't push any further. She knew how important it was to Mirae to light incense in honor of her older brother every morning. Captain Hanyoung's unfailing dutifulness, so like her young predecessor's, sent a pang through Mirae's heart. She was yet again reminded of the courageous, fiercely loyal young woman who had been like a sister to her—Captain Jia.

It didn't help that Captain Hanyoung was her late friend's aunt, and shared many similar features. The same high cheekbones and slim nose graced both their faces, though the veteran woman's freckled skin was far more tanned and weathered.

"I'll pack up your breakfast and bring it to the garden," Hongbin offered cheerfully as he rose to his feet and held out a hand to help Mirae up as well. "We'll have a picnic."

Mirae nodded her thanks before smoothing her chima and straightening her silk jacket. Then she followed the waiting captain outside to begin their morning trek.

The walk to the dragon gates was brisk, leaving Mirae somewhat breathless as she and the captain hurried past the colorful offices of the palace, leaving half-moon dents in the sand behind them.

Once they neared the courtyard, where preparations for that night's anointing ceremony were in full swing, Mirae was glad for the soothing magic emanating from her pins; the churning in her stomach might have been too much for her otherwise.

Thankfully, Captain Hanyoung interrupted her thoughts as they rounded the main hall. "May I offer you some advice, Your Majesty?"

"Of course," Mirae said as she eyed the magnificent building beside them, strangely satisfied to see that the paint of its green and red supports was beginning to fade for the first time in centuries. It had been some time since Mirae had cast the routine embellishing enchantments over the palace to keep it jewel bright and radiant. Ever since her excursion into Josan, where she'd seen the beauty and ease of a magicless existence, she'd gotten a new perspective on what her queendom's magic "should" be used for.

"I've noticed recently," the captain said carefully, "that you've been struggling to balance your desires for reform with the Hwabaek's strict adherence to tradition. While I support your mission to change outdated conventions, I think there are a few ways you can ease your stress."

"Such as?" Mirae asked.

"Choosing your battles more wisely," the captain said. "I know you abhor gaudiness, but instead of agonizing over what to wear this morning, you could have just donned the traditional ornaments passed down to you. Surely our beloved dowager queen would not object to you wearing her fineries, given that she's still convalescing in the southern isles and cannot wear them herself."

Swallowing back distaste at the lie she was forced to maintain about her mother's whereabouts, Mirae shook off memories of the wooden chest in the corner of her chamber where her mother's ceremonial attire was hidden away. If it weren't for the palace women's constant tidying, it would be covered in a thick layer of dust and cobwebs.

The last time Mirae had even looked at her mother's vestments had been the day the world she thought she knew and loved had shattered, and the truth about Seolla's dark history had been unearthed. Although Mirae had tried hard as queen to ensure that the unsavory mistakes of her foremothers lay as impotent as their heirlooms did now, it was no small task to shake off the shadow of a time when secrets were as bonded to the Sacred Bone line as their own blood.

"I'm sorry if I misspoke, Your Majesty," Captain Hanyoung said after a moment, mistaking Mirae's silence for a reprimand. "I was just trying to help."

"It's all right," Mirae said quickly. "I just—I'm internalizing your words. Thank you for your concern."

The captain nodded and said nothing more as she and Mirae entered the sandy courtyard just ahead of the dragon gates. Mirae, too, fell silent as she looked around the clearing, and at all the preparations already in place for the anointing ceremony.

Palace women with long rakes were drawing intricate designs along the outer reaches of the sandy plaza. At the very center of the enclosure was an enormous stack of pine logs and bundles of sage, ready to be lit at sundown. What caught Mirae's eye most, however, were the countless ribbons, as multicolored as the sky at dusk, streaming from wooden poles secured around the perimeter. The last time Mirae had seen such flourishes, oracles had been murdered, and a forest set alight by Sacred Bone fire.

Mirae's eyes darted away from the cheery decorations, and anything else that reminded her why a new Kun Sunim needed to be anointed. Instead, she kept her gaze fixed on the dragon gates, and the Wonhwa guarding them.

When she and Captain Hanyoung finally reached the palace exit, Mirae slowed to a stop while her companion approached the guards standing at attention. After walking up and down their ranks, thoroughly examining the scale armor of the Jade Witches and the silver-embroidered black robes of the Ma-eum Mages for any sign of errant enchantments, Captain Hanyoung finished her perusal by exchanging passwords with the Wonhwa as an extra security measure. When she was satisfied, she returned to Mirae and bowed.

"All is well. We may proceed."

Mirae nodded and headed out the gate with her ever cautious escort. Captain Hanyoung took Mirae's security very seriously, never letting her outside the dragon gates unaccompanied, especially since Mirae's mother was "away" and the crown prince was too inexperienced to take over should anything happen. Mirae's fateful foray into Josan had been over a year ago, and there hadn't been much word since of trouble brewing in Seolla's sovereign nation, despite the fact that Mirae had made a fool of their king, and even stole one of his most trusted sons to her side. But Captain Hanyoung's instincts told her that no news was bad news. Silence meant scheming was happening in the shadows. Hence, even though Mirae craved alone time now more than ever, her protector allowed as little of that as possible.

But Mirae didn't complain. After all, the captain was righter than she knew, even without an inkling of what Mirae was actually on her way to do.

Mirae breathed in the crisp, late morning air as she padded down the path leading away from the palace, the grass as deeply teal as the hilly ridges on the distant horizon. Together with her eagle-eyed companion, whose hand never left the hilt of her jade sword, Mirae slipped into the forest where, not long ago, her Sangsok Ceremony had gone horribly wrong.

There was no trail to follow to the Garden of Queens, but Mirae had walked this path hundreds of times, enough to know each root and protruding mound by heart. Soon enough, she and the captain broke through the sun-dappled trees and entered the resting place of queens.

Before entering the hallowed clearing, Mirae turned to her companion. "I'd like some privacy today."

The other woman nodded. "As you wish, Your Majesty. But I must insist that you not take more than an hour, as the oracles are scheduled to arrive by noon. I will come fetch you if you have not returned by then."

"Understood." Mirae waited until Captain Hanyoung moved to stand guard at the edge of the trees before she finally entered the Garden of Queens, passing swiftly through the grassy domes of her ancestors' restored tombs. She slowed only when she neared the shrine on the far side of the garden, obscured from Captain Hanyoung's sight by the hilly graves.

Mirae stopped and knelt at the low table. Then she conjured just enough fire to light a stick of incense in honor of her deceased relatives. Beside the golden burner rested the sacred heirloom of one of her High Daughter ancestors—the jade dagger of the Silver Star. Mirae wasn't concerned that the sacred Seollan treasure would be stolen out here in the open, given that it would instantly kill anyone who touched it except for Mirae and the new gods-appointed Kun Sunim. But the blade reminded her every morning why this was the last High Daughter relic in her possession.

Initially, there had been three High Daughter relics. But Mirae had shattered the seong-suk of the Deep Deceiver, forcing the spirit of her ancestor to save the Netherqueen instead of imparting the vital message she'd waited hundreds of years to share—an act of mercy that Mirae still wasn't sure was worth the cost. Mirae's own black bell, bestowed upon her as the final High Daughter, who was also cryptically titled the "Unnamed Dragon" in prophetic records, had been left in the care of the man for whom Mirae had spared the Netherqueen. Siwon, who still mourned the loss of the woman he had once loved as a mother. The soul of the Netherqueen, known to Siwon as Suhee, still coated the black bell, making it safe for him to touch.

That also meant Suhee's soul was blocking the bell's extraordinary power—the switching ability Mirae had relied on to rescue Minho. She'd tried several times since her return to Seolla to ring the bell and activate its power, to no avail. But she had a plan to remove the Netherqueen's soul soon. If all went well, then Minho's liberation would quickly follow.

After offering a quick prayer to her ancestors and bowing, Mirae approached the doorway of shadows suspended between the two closest trees, a muddle of writhing tendrils of darkness beckoning her closer.

The dark portal to the cage created by the Deep Deceiver looked less sinister than the first time Mirae had seen it, especially now. It was guarded by a pair of grinning haetae statues, lionlike sculptures that would let no one pass without her permission. Facing the shadowy gateway, Mirae raised her arms until her long, pale sleeves hung like moth wings off her shoulders. The jade statues, sensing that the blood beating within her was harmonious with the subtle rhythm vibrating from their own manes, began to glow. As their light grew, the inky darkness between them began to churn.

Mirae shot a quick glance back in Captain Hanyoung's direction, making sure the sharp-eyed woman hadn't left her post. Satisfied that she was alone, Mirae slipped into the swirling void.

Chapter
TWO

The newly strewn, enchanted sand on the other side glimmered faintly, softening the stark, clawlike silhouettes of the surrounding trees. Though Mirae had tried lacing their branches with beautiful autumnal leaves and summoning birds to sing in their boughs, none of her cheery spells had lasted long enough to fend off the haunting memories she had of this path to monsters and poisoned magic.

So, Mirae wasted no time in bidding the morning chill to surround her. Once swathed in glimmering mist, she gathered the icy wind into the silk bellies of her hanbok until it lifted her off the ground. Then she floated through the sunless trees, her hovering golden shoes drawing soft lines into the freshly replaced sand. Draped in twilight chill, Mirae sped as quickly as she could toward Wol Sin Lake, feeling like one of the ghosts who haunted the wintry woods she'd nicknamed the Gwisin Forest.

Within seconds, she noticed that she wasn't alone. Up ahead, the restless spirit of Sol, daughter of the Deep, drifted onto the moonlit path. As always, the gwisin brought rolling fog to hide her legless lower half, and her long black hair lay wetly over her pale, featureless face. The gwisin didn't have to speak for Mirae to know what she wanted—the same thing she silently pleaded for every time they crossed paths.

Justice against the man who had destroyed her people.

Mirae had done what she could to bring the gwisin peace; she spared Sol's mother and thwarted the Netherking's vile plan. Sol had even come to Mirae's aid during her battle against the Inconstant Son, proving that their wills were aligned. And yet, after everything, the gwisin couldn't find rest. Not until Mirae finished what she'd started—something she wasn't ready to do.

Mirae regretfully swept past the pale, haunted woman and continued on her way. She couldn't give Sol what she needed, not yet. *Soon*, she promised, *soon my brother will be free, and your father will get everything he deserves.*

I swear it by the gods.

Mirae was coming close to the end of the trail. She slowed her gale and dropped lightly to the ground so she could cross the final few steps between her and the bone-white pebbles of Wol Sin Lake. With the grace of practice, Mirae strode toward the inky loch, a lidless eye gazing eternally at the stars. She braced for the shock of the paralyzing cold and dense, oily pressure of the spelled water to envelop her, heedless of its own strength.

And then, taking a long, deep breath, Mirae sank into its depths.

Sinking wasn't quite the right word for it. The pull of the giant green hand that caught her, guardian of the entrance to the Deep, had become gentle over the months. A spot of warmth in her descent, proffered by the creature that had memorized a path through the darkness.

They had gotten used to the frequent ferrying, both the bohoja and Mirae. As they neared the end of their journey, she felt its grip loosen around her wrist, her cue to relax her body. Then the bohoja released her, sending her sliding smoothly across the floor of the lake. Mirae reached out just in time to plunge her hand through the gelatinous border between the inky water and the hidden kingdom below.

As soon as she made contact, the barrier let her pass through its gripping midst until her body broke free on the other side. Mirae summoned wind to slow her fall, though she balked at the musky air in the Deep that wafted the hint of mildew and fish up her nose.

"Mirae." Her name echoed through the cavernous chamber. As she floated to the ground, Mirae glanced down at the man waiting below.

For a second, the sight of him sent a jolt through her body, making her blood pound as if she were about to rush into battle. In the dim lighting of the Deep, her greeter's long black hair and towering height made him look like the Netherking, who had stood in the exact same spot back when Mirae first plunged carelessly into the Inconstant Son's cage.

But the man's eyes, yellow green in the gloomy glow of the water above, calmed Mirae's racing heart. This man was not the Netherking, but rather the trusted steward of her enemy's cage. By the time her feet touched the ground, Mirae had recovered enough to nod calmly at the exiled prince of Josan.

"Kimoon," she said. "I see you were expecting me."

"Of course," he said with a nod. "The oracles are arriving today." With each word, the shadows beneath his pronounced cheekbones shifted, making his face look even more gaunt than it did in sunlight. Kimoon had always had angular features, but their sharpness had grown more pronounced over the past few months. "I figured you would stop by before the anointing ceremony in search of good news. I expect tonight will be difficult for you."

Mirae hid a grimace at Kimoon's frankness. While the Josan prince was a different man now than he had been when she first liberated him from the Josan king's tyranny, some things never changed, like his lack of tact when discussing sensitive topics. "And do you have any good news for me?" she asked. "How is my orabeoni today?"

Unfortunately, Kimoon's candid, straightforward demeanor served him even less well when he was delivering an unfavorable report. "Our latest concoction had no effect. I'm afraid the dowager queen and I will have to reexamine the formula."

"I see." Mirae felt her shoulders slump. "I swear it feels like we've already tried every variation we can think of."

"There is still . . . one other option," Kimoon ventured, his detached tone slipping briefly. "If you're finally willing to hear me out."

Mirae crossed her arms over her chest. "We've been over this, Kimoon. The answer to that is, and always will be, *no*. I refuse to stoop to the Netherking's level."

"We both know nothing else is working," Kimoon pressed.

When Mirae frowned, he held up his hands placatingly. "What I mean is, it may be time to at least consider the possibility that thinking like the Netherking is the only way to reverse his spell."

"As I've said before," Mirae retorted, "the second we debase ourselves is the moment he wins. Exploring dark magic is out of the question."

"I understand that," Kimoon said, inclining his head, his voice tinged with impatience. "But like *I* said last time, I'm willing to handle everything on my own. I just need your permission. Neither you nor the dowager queen need sully your—"

"This isn't about keeping our hands clean," Mirae interrupted. "This is about sacrificing the unwilling, as the Netherking once did. Something we will never do."

"But what if we limited ourselves to criminals, or other people undeserving of—"

"Enough." Mirae held up a hand. "I've already said no, and that's final. I'm tired of having this conversation. Do not mention the harvesting of that revolting dark ingredient again, or I will have you removed as warden of the Deep. Am I clear?"

The shadows on Kimoon's face seemed to seep into his eyes for a moment before he wiped his face clear of any expression. An unsettling skill he often used when Mirae irked him. "Yes, you are perfectly clear," he said, voice neutral. "My apologies, Mirae."

Although it had been some time since Mirae had given Kimoon permission to continue calling her by name, instead of using her royal title, she still wasn't used to the way it sounded coming out of his mouth, especially when laced with resentment. Uttering a queen's name was an intimate thing, something granted only to parents, siblings, close friends, and her eventual lover. Kimoon wasn't any of those things, but the bond she and he had built on their shared guilt over Minho's predicament, and their commitment to finding him a cure, didn't fit under any existing labels.

Reminding herself that she and Kimoon wanted the same thing, however much they disagreed about how to obtain it, Mirae breathed out all her pent-up frustration.

"No, *I'm* sorry," she relented. "I told you your help would be welcome here, but I tend to veto more of your ideas than I entertain. Even the good ones. I'm sure it's irritating."

At Mirae's softened tone, Kimoon's expression relaxed as well. He waved away her apology. "No more irritating than I can be when I latch onto an idea. I'm not exactly good at letting things go." Kimoon cleared his throat and looked down at the floor. "It's difficult being down here, seeing no results week after week. Watching Minho deteriorate while we get no closer to curing him. It weighs heavily on the soul."

Mirae swallowed back the guilt clotting in her throat. She knew full well that Kimoon was shouldering a burden she couldn't, and he did so willingly, resolutely, which, unfortunately, made him the best person to remain sequestered here with her mother, under conditions little better than those their prisoner endured. Mirae didn't want to forget that Kimoon was trapped down here so she didn't have to be.

"I know this hasn't been easy," Mirae sighed. "But it'll be over soon. Tonight, I'll solicit the help of the new Kun Sunim in creating a cure."

Perhaps it was just a trick of the light, but the corners of Kimoon's mouth seemed to twitch. "Are you absolutely certain you can trust an outsider not to expose the truth about what's happening down here?"

"Of course." Mirae nodded, feeling completely sure of her words for once. "The oracles are sworn to serve the High Queen unfailingly, even above the needs of the queendom. That is their calling. They will keep my confidence, as they have for all my ancestors."

Kimoon snorted delicately. "Yes, your people's penchant for keeping royal secrets buried is truly unmatched." Before Mirae could chide him for his snark, he quickly added, "But in this case, sealed lips will be most appreciated. I do hope the Kun Sunim will be able to help us." Kimoon rubbed his face tiredly. "If not, I'm afraid you may not like our remaining options."

Not knowing what else to do, Mirae reached out and patted Kimoon's arm. When he raised an eyebrow at her uncharacteristic show of affection, she cleared her throat and awkwardly returned her hand to her side. "In the meantime, if there's anything you or my mother require for your work, you need only ask."

"Thank you, Mirae." Kimoon offered a rare albeit strained smile. "On that note, we should go check in with the dowager queen. When I left, she was buried under a pile of heavy books. I'm sure she's eager to regale you with her findings."

Mirae returned Kimoon's tepid smile and gestured for him to lead the way.

Every time Mirae made her way to the deepest, darkest corner of the Inconstant Son's cage, she was forced to recall the evil event that kept bringing her down here.

After defeating the Netherking on the shores of Wol Sin Lake, with the help of a vengeful army of gwisin, Mirae had dragged her brother's unconscious, stolen body back down into his possessor's longtime prison, and sent out a desperate Sacred Bone call to the only person who could hear it—her mother. As soon as the queen arrived and saw what had happened, she and Mirae fashioned a set of magic-suppressing chains, much like the ones that had incapacitated Mirae in Kimoon's fortress. They'd used them to shackle their foe into a place farthest from the black water above, which the Netherking had become too good at manipulating to be trusted anywhere near.

From there, they had made the difficult decision to keep Minho's predicament a secret while they figured out how to save him. As far as the rest of the queendom was concerned, Mirae had obliterated the Netherking in battle, tragically sacrificing Crown Prince Minho in the process. It was better, she and her mother had decided, to let everyone believe Minho was at peace, and that the Netherking—and his dark army—was soundly defeated. The painful, horrible truth would only incite the very war Mirae had fought so hard to prevent; for if the crown prince's plight was brought to light, the Hwabaek would undoubtedly investigate and discover the Josan king's treasonous role in Minho's abduction, as well as the fact that Mirae had covered everything up to keep the peace. She couldn't allow all her efforts, or Minho's suffering, to have been in vain, so to secrecy she was sworn.

Of course, not all of her story was a lie. With their united powers, Mirae and her mother had been able to ensure that the Netherking had become nothing more than a dormant threat—soon to be a deceased one, as soon as a cure for Minho could be found.

Now, as Mirae entered the murky cavern where her brother was imprisoned, she did her best not to react to the awful sight, one that widened the crack in her heart with every visit.

The first thing she saw in the purple, bruised light of the dim orb her mother had cast above were the pearly toes of Minho's feet. Then the glittering black silk of his possessor's hanbok. As Mirae drew closer, she looked past her brother's long, messy hair and into his gleaming eyes, willing herself not to react to the look on his face, as steely as the iron that kept him there. The Netherking, in Minho's body, sat calmly on the cold floor as if he were a meditating scholar, not a prisoner. Mirae came to a stop just outside the shackled man's reach.

"Hello, orabeoni," she said, forcing herself to smile. She did this every time, hoping that Minho's soul hadn't been buried too deeply for him to hear her.

"Queenling." The Netherking's low, oily voice sounded especially noxious oozing out of Minho's throat. "My, how bleak you look. Care to talk about what's troubling you?"

Mirae ignored the Netherking's taunts. As much as she wanted to muzzle him, her mother had forbidden it. If Minho's soul ever retook control, he would need some way of alerting them.

Thankfully, Mirae didn't have to shut up the Netherking

herself. Behind her, a voice, high and commanding, echoed through the chamber. "Say one more word to her, and all you'll be eating is larvae for the rest of the week."

The Netherking scoffed. "You wouldn't do that to your son's precious stomach."

"Actually," Mirae said, turning toward the reverberating sound of her mother's voice, "beondegi is one of orabeoni's favorite snacks."

"Indeed." Mirae's mother finally emerged from the shadows, carrying a stack of books. "Far be it from me to deprive my son of a source of joy, especially at your expense."

The Netherking's smirk straightened into a thin line of disgust as he shrugged off the threats, causing the heavy chains around Minho's wrists to clink against the floor. "You can hardly blame me for trying to make a little conversation, especially since our queenling will soon be off, busily carousing with those pathetic vision hags."

"You will address Mirae as 'Your Majesty,'" her mother said with a glare. "Unless you actually *do* want a little extra crunchy protein for dinner."

The Netherking rolled Minho's eyes. "Am I to address the queenling by her proper title, or not converse with her at all? Which is it, Noeul?"

"I think I speak for all of us," Kimoon interjected, "when I say we'd prefer the latter."

To Mirae's surprise, the Netherking didn't hurl any barbed words at the bastard prince of Josan. Usually, he was quick to torment the traitor who had turned on him and his wife. Mirae didn't get to dwell on that peculiarity for long, however, for her mother soon walked up beside her.

"I'm glad you made time to visit," the former queen said, smiling tiredly. Mirae noted the way her mother's arms wobbled under the pile of thick tomes. From the deepening bags under the other woman's eyes, it was clear that sleep was as elusive as the answers she sought. "And before you ask," her mother continued, surprisingly cheery, "we have plenty of food and supplies; no, we don't need a break from all this; and yes, we'll be fine even if you end up attending to royal duties for a few days."

Mirae couldn't help but chuckle at the one-sided dialogue. Her visits to the Deep usually ended with her asking the same rote questions, given that she was the only one who could enter and leave freely. "I'm glad to hear it, and to see that you're unusually chipper this morning."

"Well, I think I've had a breakthrough." Her mother's smile widened and, for a moment, she looked like the woman who had taught Mirae to enchant jade turtles to fly around the palace library.

"Oh?" was all Mirae had time to say before her mother nodded for Kimoon to come take the books from her. As soon as her mother's hands were free, she pulled a vial out of the silk pouch tied to her waist and held it up triumphantly, its oily contents as dark as the lake above.

Taken aback by her mother's excitement, Mirae shot Kimoon a look, but he seemed as perplexed as she. They both watched curiously as her mother strode up to Minho. "I have a good feeling about this one," she said as she uncorked the small flask.

Mirae did her best not to exchange another look with Kimoon. They'd heard the dowager queen say similar things before, only to walk away sorely disappointed. The Netherking, however, found the confidence of his old rival nothing short of laughable.

"What ancient, mythical remedy did you research this time?" he asked smugly. "Did you throw in some mugwort? Ginseng?" The Netherking turned his nose up at the dark vial. "It better not have any sanghwang in it. I don't like the taste of it."

Ignoring the Netherking's taunts, Mirae's mother gestured to Kimoon. "Hold his mouth open."

Kimoon, who didn't possess any Sacred Bone Magic for the Netherking to poison—as he'd once done to Mirae's mother, driving her to madness—was the only person allowed to touch Minho. He moved forward obediently, but before he could approach, the Netherking let out a low chuckle. "No need to put your hands on me, princeling. I'm curious to see what the False Queen has concocted this time. I will drink it willingly."

With that, he tilted his head back and opened his mouth, the edges of his lips creased with barely contained laughter. Undeterred by her opponent's mockery, Mirae's mother tipped the vial's contents into his waiting mouth.

True to his word, the Netherking swallowed.

Chapter
THREE

Mirae waited warily beside Kimoon. The warm heat of hope began expanding through her chest, despite all the times past experiments had let her down.

At first, nothing happened, except the Netherking grimaced at the potion's taste. But after a few seconds, the frown on Minho's face deepened, his expression turning from one of amusement to confusion.

"What's happening?" The Netherking doubled over, grunting with pain. "What did you give me, Noeul?"

Mirae's mother didn't answer. Mirae didn't speak, either; she just stood there, eyes wide, watching Minho's body shudder and shake, the hope within her warming into something searing, eager to boil away all the guilt she'd been holding on to for so long.

Is this it? she thought with a thrill. *Did we actually find a cure?*

No sooner had she had that thought, however, than Minho's twitching stopped. She couldn't see her brother's face; he was still bent over, breathing heavily. But then she heard it. A sound that swept through her like daggers in her veins. A small, pitiable voice, agonizing in its familiarity.

"W-Where . . . am I?"

Mirae gasped as her older brother straightened and looked around, his brown eyes and gentle, bewildered voice softened by their true master's return. "I-Is anybody there?"

"Orabeoni," Mirae whispered, at the same moment her mother tearily spoke his name.

Minho's head whipped around. "Mirae?" His voice quavered. "Mother?"

Breaking the most important rule of the Deep, Mirae's mother fell to her knees before Minho, wrapping her arms around him. "Yes, I'm here, my darling son."

"Mother," he murmured. "I was having a terrible dream." Minho leaned into his mother's warmth. "I was trapped in a starry void, with no warmth or food. All I could see or hear . . . was *him*." Minho shuddered. "He kept saying such awful things."

Unable to stop herself, Mirae, too, rushed up to her shackled brother, falling beside him and grabbing his hand. "You're safe now, orabeoni. Back with us, where you belong."

Minho's eyes had adjusted enough that he could finally see her. "Mirae."

It was really him, not some cruel trick of the Netherking's—a man with a soul so noxious, he could never impersonate Minho's gentleness. Mirae could practically feel it, the ebbing away of the evil that had tormented Minho for so long. His face, once creased with sneers and glares of hatred, was smooth and open, just as before.

He's back, Mirae thought, overcome with relief. *My orabeoni is really back.*

"My beautiful boy," Mirae's mother cried, soaking Minho's matted, overgrown hair with tears. "We never lost faith, not for a moment. We always knew you'd return to us."

But Minho didn't seem to share their joy. Eyes fixed on Mirae, his expression haunted, he whispered hoarsely, "He made me watch as he killed Jia over and over again. I saw her die a thousand times, a thousand ways." Minho's voice broke. "He told me her death was my fault for resisting the Netherqueen, and that you would be next if I didn't give in to him now."

"No, you were right to fight them both." Mirae squeezed his hand. "Captain Jia did not die because of you. Do not listen to the Netherking's lies."

"But why is he in my head?" Minho asked, trembling. "What happened to me?"

Mirae opened her mouth to answer, but her mother quickly interrupted. "We'll tell you everything, later." She stroked the sides of Minho's face. "First, we should draw you a warm bath, and get you some real food. Maybe even let you walk in the sunlight a little."

"I'm not sure that's a good—" Mirae began, but her protest was silenced by a look from her mother.

Oblivious to the tension between the two women, Minho nodded tiredly. "I think I need some help standing up, though. It feels like there are rocks tied to my . . ." Minho's voice trailed off as he lifted his arms and blinked at the manacles around his wrists. His mind, fuzzy from pulling out of a deep sleep, suddenly seemed to sharpen.

"What's this?" Minho looked around. "Where are we?"

"It's a long story," Mirae's mother soothed, reaching for the shackles. "We'll tell you everything, I promise. But first, you need some proper rest and nutrition."

Alarmed at what her mother was about to do, Mirae grabbed her hand, nails biting into the other woman's skin. "We can't release him yet," she spluttered. "We don't know if he's been cured permanently. For now, we should keep him under observation."

Minho looked between the two of them, his brow furrowed. "What do you mean *cured*? Cured from what?"

Mirae's mother shook away Mirae's hand like it was an annoying moth. "I will not treat my own son like a criminal. If the Netherking resurfaces, we'll curb him, just as we did before."

Minho's face paled. "Is the Netherking here? What's going on?"

As much as Mirae hated it, she latched onto her mother's wrist, holding on firmly this time. "I want to believe he's cured just as much as you do," she said slowly, emphasizing each word, even though they felt like needles prickling her throat. "But we must be certain that the Netherking is truly gone. We cannot underestimate him."

"I agree." Mirae had forgotten Kimoon was with them until she heard his voice. "I am as delighted by this breakthrough as anyone, but given the depravity of our enemy, we cannot afford to be anything other than abundantly cautious."

It killed Mirae to see all the happiness drain away from her mother's face as the grim reality of their situation sank back in. Mirae knew her mother could feel it, too: the dark magic still lingering inside Minho that couldn't be purged so easily.

"Kimoon?" she heard Minho say. Her eyes snapped back to her brother, who was straining to see through the darkness. "Is that . . . you?"

Mirae's heart skipped a beat as Kimoon emerged from the shadows, where he'd remained during her family's reunion. As soon as Minho could make out the other man, the prince who had tortured him with black water at the Josan king's behest, Minho's muddled, perplexed expression melted into something else. Something Mirae had seen on her brother's face only once before.

"*You.*" Minho clenched his fists, and his lips pulled back into a snarl. "What are you doing here, *bastard*?"

"It's all right, orabeoni," Mirae said nervously, placing her hand on his arm. "Kimoon helped me save you, remember? He turned against his father. He's with us now."

"With us?" Minho turned to Mirae, the disbelief and rage in his eyes blistering hot. "You allied with the man who chained me up and experimented on me with—"

Minho's voice suddenly choked up as his eyes shot back down to his shackles, and the empty vial in his mother's lap. His eyes widened with horror. "Oh no," he whispered. "This . . . this isn't real. It must be another nightmare." He turned to stare at Mirae as if she were a specter conjured up to torment him. Struggling against his chains, his muscles bulging through the Netherking's black jeogori, he stammered, "This is just another one of his vile tricks, isn't it?"

"No, orabeoni." Mirae grabbed one of Minho's arms while their mother clutched the other, desperate to calm him. "This isn't what it looks like. I can ex—"

A sudden stab of pain throttled Mirae's reassurance. Minho had driven his shoulder into her, shoving her to the ground as he yanked at his chains, bruising his flesh in his eagerness to be free of them.

"*Orabeoni!*" Mirae cried, but when her brother turned to her, his eyes were black with rage, his face contorted with fury.

"I don't know who you are, but you're not my sister," he snarled. "She would never cage me like an animal, or experiment on me, joining hands with"—he shot a scalding look at Kimoon, whose face had paled to a ghostly white—"a *monster*. This is just another one of the Netherking's cruel delusions. I won't fall for it!"

Shocked into silence by her brother's hateful words, Mirae just sat there, paralyzed at the sight of Minho so desperate to get away from her, confusing reality with torture.

What has the Netherking done to him?

"Mirae!" Her mother's shout jerked her back to the present. "We've got to take these off him—it's the only way to calm him down!" Her mother grabbed a manacle. "Help me!"

"Get away! Don't touch me!" Minho shoved their mother away as he had Mirae, slamming her backward. His eyes shot around the room, which was almost completely swathed in shadows, much like the cell he'd spent several days in, suffering at Kimoon's hand. "Not this . . . anything but this . . . I'm begging you. I can't go through this again. Send me back into the void . . . I won't complain anymore, I *swear*."

Minho's head rolled back as he beseeched the darkness around them, a place he believed his tormentor was watching from, laughing at his pain.

"Orabeoni," Mirae gasped, her cheeks hot with tears. "We're real—this isn't a trick. Please, you're safe now . . . you have to believe me!"

"Take me back to the void," Minho begged again, heedless of the women who loved him more than life itself. "*Please.*"

"It's all right, son." Mirae's mother crawled back to Minho, breathing shakily from the pain of her bruised chest, and reached for his chains. "I will take you away from this awful place. He won't hurt you anymore."

"Mother, no!" Mirae lurched forward to intercept, and heard Kimoon rush up to do the same.

In her haste, Mirae practically tackled the other woman, successfully swatting her hands away from Minho's shackles—but not swiftly enough to fall clear of Minho's reach.

It happened too quickly for her to react. One moment she was colliding with her mother, and the next, she felt Minho's arms wrap crushingly around her shoulders, yanking her toward him. Before she could so much as scream, she felt a shock of pain explode from the side of her neck as something sharp sank into it.

Mirae tried to whip her head back, but Minho had latched onto her, and the pain of ripping away from him sent white-hot stars into her vision. A second later, she felt Minho's jaw unlock, releasing her.

Mirae fell backward, stunned by the violent, ferocious push of teeth that sent shocks of pain through her body, from her temples down to her chest. Lying on the floor, dazed, she barely heard her mother scream her name, or felt the hands that pressed against her neck.

All she knew was that the cold ground around her head was becoming warm and sticky.

"Mirae . . . I'm so sorry," she heard her mother sob. The words sounded muffled, as if spoken underwater. "I don't know what I was thinking. Please get up—*please*."

Moments later, the searing pain in her neck subsided, replaced by a dull, aching throb. Mirae's vision cleared, but her ears still rang from shock. And yet there was one sound that cut through all the noise, echoing menacingly.

Laughter, low and evil. A sound she could never forget.

"I had rather hoped you would be foolish enough to unshackle me," she heard the Netherking cackle. "But alas, I guess I'll have to settle for the despair on your faces instead."

Mirae felt hands pull her into a sitting position. Kimoon sighed with relief that she was all right. But Mirae was staring at her brother, her heart sinking. Gone was the tenderness, the benevolent gaze of her orabeoni. Now his dark eyes were ebony beads glittering wickedly, his full lips smeared with her garnet blood.

The Netherking's smugness lit a fire deep in her core. Fury, unlike any she'd ever felt before, grew like the flames in her palms, racing up her spine, eager to wreath her entire body. But the Netherking only continued to smirk as she lit the Deep with the fires of her rage.

He knew she wouldn't hurt him, not if it meant harming a hair on Minho's head.

"Mirae." Kimoon, who had stumbled back from her scorching blaze, quickly moved to fill her view. "This is what he wants.

Don't give him the satisfaction of watching you suffer."

As intended, Kimoon's words raked through Mirae like cold water on hot coals. *He's right*, Mirae admitted as her boiling rage subsided. *The Netherking is enjoying this, relishing what little power he has over me and Mother.* Willing herself to calm down and deny her enemy the turmoil he so craved, Mirae closed her eyes and bid the flames disperse.

"Tell me, Kimoon," she said as soon as she was composed enough to speak. "Did my mother's remedy work, or was everything we just saw a ruse?"

"The latter, I fear," Kimoon said grimly as the other man laughed.

"Of course the False Queen's little potion had no effect!" the Netherking crowed. "You think a handful of herbs will subvert my spell? Mark my words, queenling," the Netherking spat, cracking his heavy chains against the ground like thunderous whips, "I am never leaving this body until I get what I want. I promise you that, and words cannot be false in the Deep."

Mirae didn't realize her hands were shaking until Kimoon grabbed them, steadying them. His yellow eyes bored into hers, as if to bolster her with his own strength. "Don't listen to him. He cannot fathom a world where anyone is more powerful than he is, but his arrogance will be his downfall. You are going to beat him, in the end. That is *my* promise."

Calmed by Kimoon's undaunted spirit, Mirae let out a breath, releasing the rest of her anger. "Yes, you're right," she said, steeling her shoulders. "It's only a matter of time before we figure this out. His days are numbered. And soon we'll add the knowledge of the Sacred Bone Oracles to ours."

She heard the Netherking scoff. "You'll get nothing from those useless vision hags who couldn't even foresee my rebellion in the Deep. Face it, queenling, there's only one way to end this; you're just too much of a coward to do it."

Mirae felt her hands curl into fists as she pulled away from Kimoon. "Muzzle him," she said, jerking her head in the Netherking's direction. "I think we've all had enough of his poison for one day."

Kimoon moved to obey. As he rushed off, Mirae touched the tender scar on her neck and searched for the woman who'd healed her, but her mother had disappeared.

"If you're looking for the False Queen, I suggest checking her study," the Netherking jeered. "That's where she usually goes to lick her wounds."

Mirae gritted her teeth as she turned to leave, trying to block out the Netherking's parting words, to no avail.

"Take it from me, queenling," he said, his low voice rumbling. "You think you're so noble, laying siege to Minho's body under the guise of saving him. But if you believe that the ends justify the means for you alone, and not for me, then you're a fool. All monsters loved someone once. Love is the greatest calamity, and it will be your undoing."

Back in the main chamber of the Deep, Mirae looked up at the late morning sky, its rosy glow dimmed by the dark belly of Wol Sin Lake, which made the world above appear to be draped in every bruising hue of twilight. For a moment, she stared up at the phenomenon, struck by how aptly it represented the state of everything that spent too much time in the Inconstant Son's cage—like her mother, who'd locked herself into her study, refusing to come out. As much as Mirae hated leaving her mother heartbroken, she knew Captain Hanyoung would come looking for her soon, and she had an anointing ceremony to officiate that was becoming more imperative by the moment.

"I hope everything goes smoothly," she heard Kimoon say, startling her. When Mirae turned around, she could barely make out his face, sickly pale under the lake's green light. When he was close enough to touch her, he instinctively reached out and smoothed the sides of her hair, slicking it back to meet with her halo wig seamlessly. Then he tightened her hanbok ribbon into a perfect bow, and finished off by rubbing the peaks of her collar. When his hand pulled back, the tips of his fingers were smeared with blood.

"You should clean that off before anyone sees you," he urged, reaching into his purple jacket to pull out a handkerchief. When he leaned closer to carefully rub what redness he could off her clothes, Mirae felt the warmth of his body, a sun in the endless chill of the Deep. His long fingers worked deftly, occasionally tugging her closer as he scrubbed the fabric, his brow furrowed in concentration. Had anyone else been around to observe this intimate moment, Mirae would have pushed Kimoon away. No men except her own family, or a lover, were allowed to touch her like that. But she and Kimoon were alone, and the rules of tradition had always been a little blurred between them.

When Kimoon finally finished, he crumpled the soiled

handkerchief into his palm. "There we go. You're much more presentable now."

Mirae nodded her thanks and turned to leave, but Kimoon stopped her with a hand on her arm.

"Before you go," he said softly, "I wanted to ask if today's unfortunate event has made anything change between us."

"Between us?" Mirae asked, unsure why her cheeks started flushing.

"My offer," he clarified. "Have you reconsidered it?"

Realizing what Kimoon was talking about, Mirae felt all the warmth drain from her face. "I told you not to speak of harvesting that dark ingredient anymore."

"But you've seen what the Netherking is doing to Minho," Kimoon insisted, the muscles in his jaw tightening. "How can you let him suffer like that without doing *everything* you can to save him?"

"I'm not failing him by making sure he's freed the right way," Mirae said, her words as icy as the air between them.

"The *right* way?" Kimoon said, barely biting back his contempt. "And what happens when you finally realize there was no right or wrong way all along, just the *only* way? How long must Minho wait for your moral superiority to fade? Do you really think he has that kind of time?"

"I know he would never accept the idea of harming someone else for his sake," Mirae shot back. "You may not care about my family's principles, but I do. I have to. I can't just do whatever's easy, or entertain every path presented to me. There must be boundaries I will not cross, because I have an entire queendom watching me. One that seeks to do good no matter how difficult, and even took you in despite your crimes against us."

"Yes, you took me in," Kimoon said quietly. "Now you expect me to obey you unquestioningly. Just like my father."

Mirae took a step back, offended at the comparison. "Where is this coming from?" she demanded, bewildered at the change in Kimoon's face. Before he could respond, a shadow passed over the sun, reminding Mirae of the duties she needed to return to, and quickly. She didn't have time to address whatever dark internal crisis Kimoon was dealing with.

Mirae took a moment to compose herself before locking eyes with Kimoon. "Look, I don't know what's really going on here, but we'll talk about it when I get back. Just please do as I've asked. No more talk of dark magic until we have the new Kun Sunim's guidance. Then I'll hear you out. Until then, have faith in me a little longer."

Thankfully, Kimoon's ire also deflated, at least enough for him to nod curtly. Then, still only barely appeased, Kimoon reached back into his hanbok and retrieved the milky-white pearl that allowed the magicless to come and go from the Deep.

Despite the tension simmering between Mirae and Kimoon, she couldn't help but take in the unparalleled beauty of the relic glowing warmly in his hand. Once she had thought it nothing more than a key to the Deep, guarded by the spirits of the Gwisin Forest. But, in the year since the pearl had lent her its aid on the shores of Wol Sin Lake, she'd learned what it really was—no mere artifact but a Yeouiju, an orb of power once wielded by dragons. Creatures that had been dead for over a thousand years.

Where once it had held omnipotent power, the extinction of all dragons had left this last pearl with a mere fraction of the magic it used to hold, the depths of which Mirae hoped to tap into someday, when she had time and energy to dedicate to such things.

For now, it continued to serve as a key to the Deep for those, like Kimoon, who did not possess Sacred Bone Magic. Raising the pearl above his head like a palm-size moon, Kimoon waited until the shadow of the lake's bohoja obscured the sunlight above, summoned by the orb's power, before retucking the shimmering pearl into his clothes. Then, offering Mirae a brusque bow, Kimoon turned and retreated back into the darkness.

Hoping that she and Kimoon would be able to talk through their disagreement with clear heads later, Mirae summoned wind to carry her up to the world above. As soon as she was close enough, she reached through the barrier and wasted no time clasping the green hand waiting to ferry her back to the shores of Wol Sin Lake.

Chapter

FOUR

When Mirae burst back through the portal, she half expected to see Captain Hanyoung standing there, hands on hips, eyes narrowed. Thankfully, what she saw instead was Hongbin sitting cross-legged before the incense altar, stuffing his face with her breakfast.

"Noonim!" he exclaimed, spraying bits of chewed rice on the ground. He quickly lowered his voice. "You were gone longer than usual. I thought the gwisin might have gotten you this time."

Mirae's eyes darted toward the tree line, where Captain Hanyoung was still, hopefully, standing guard. "Don't worry," Hongbin reassured her. "I told the captain to leave us be while I forced you to eat. It was the only way to keep her away as long as possible."

"Good thinking." Mirae collapsed next to Hongbin and snatched the chopsticks out of his hand. Her trek to the Deep had made her ravenous. "Has Captain Hanyoung not come to check on us yet?" she asked between mouthfuls of sprouts and cucumber kimchi, savoring the spicy saltiness bursting on her tongue.

"No need," Hongbin said proudly. "I make sure to laugh

loudly every few minutes to make it seem like we're having a blast. She'll stay away until we're out of time."

It was easy to imagine her brother chortling to himself to keep prying eyes away. After all, it was imperative no one find out where Mirae was disappearing to every morning—or the truth about the Inconstant Son. After shoving several more bites into her mouth, Mirae heard the captain approach at long last, her boots thudding across the ground.

A second too late, Mirae realized that she'd been too distracted by Hongbin and her breakfast to remember to clean herself up. She hastily magicked the dampness out of her hair, dispelling it onto the ground just as Captain Hanyoung rounded the corner of the nearest tomb.

"A messenger has sent word that the oracles are nearly at the gates," Captain Hanyoung reported. "It's time to head back."

Mirae froze as the captain's eyes flitted over her frizzy hair, wrinkled clothes, and the bloodstain by her neck. For a moment, no one spoke until, to Mirae's relief, Captain Hanyoung sighed and walked over without saying a word. She immediately began restraightening Mirae's hair and clothes, finishing off by expertly drawing the red stains out of her once stark-white collar. Then she silently gestured for Mirae and Hongbin to follow her out of the Garden of Queens. Mirae was grateful that the captain understood there was no point in asking questions that Mirae wasn't going to answer. Instead, the captain performed her duty, trusting her liege in ways Kimoon clearly couldn't.

Presentable at last, Mirae grabbed the Silver Star's dagger and followed her escort back toward the palace.

As soon as the dragon gates were in sight, Mirae lowered her shoulders, elongating her neck so that her silks draped prettily and her stiff white collar pulled away from her throat. It was time to look and act like the queen that the crowd gathered at the gates expected her to be.

The True Bone royals and members of the Hwabaek awaiting the oracles all bowed as soon as they caught sight of Mirae. As she approached, she marveled at how her cousins and aunts looked very much like a festive array of rainbow lanterns with their voluminous skirts and bright but sensible gems. There had been a time when the entire court had been a truly dazzling sight, teeming with enchanted iridescent silks and luminous, sparkly jewels. But those days were a thing of the past.

As soon as Mirae had taken the throne, she'd asked for a detailed report on all the things the Hwabaek and True Bone royals were using their magic on, as well as every official capacity in which the Seollan queen's powers were to be wielded. After determining that much of the royals' skill sets were being spent on glorifying the monarchy with elaborate homesteads and galas, rather than improving the queendom, Mirae had drafted several decrees rectifying that. Her creeds were wildly unpopular at first, but now, nearly a year later, few in her court could argue that diminishing their assets and showpieces wasn't worth the higher-yielding crops and healthier livestock Seolla had gained in return—especially once the people's increased happiness was credited to the royals who were now focusing solely on their subjects. The gratitude of Seollan citizens had quickly made reluctant hearts grow soft.

Still, there were several women bowing to Mirae whose obeisance was performed stiffly, their bodies barely bent enough to be polite. While Mirae found herself missing the smiling faces of her friends Jisoo and Yoonhee, who were off assisting their True Bone mothers with constructing more gateways between Seolla and Josan, Hongbin rushed off to change into fresh clothes, and Captain Hanyoung left to rejoin the surrounding palace guards.

Taking a deep breath and securing a smile to her face, Mirae approached one of the impudent, minimally bowing women. Sangsin Bada, the head of the Hwabaek and an unsurprising adversary, given their fraught history together.

Although Mirae didn't need to show deference to anyone as queen, she still inclined her head courteously as the older woman straightened and fixed her sharp eyes on Mirae. "I appreciate you gathering everyone in my absence, Sangsin Bada."

"I live to serve, and fill the voids of your reign, Your Majesty." Sangsin Bada raked her eyes up and down Mirae, as if looking for clues as to what had delayed her liege.

Hoping the elderly woman wouldn't notice anything incriminating, Mirae cleared her throat. "You are nothing if not dependable. I saw the courtyard when I passed through earlier, and all the preparations appeared to be in order."

"Of course they are," Sangsin Bada said gruffly. "I remember well when the former Kun Sunim was anointed. Of course, I never imagined that I would have to arrange yet another such ceremony in my tenure, but your sovereignty has yielded many firsts."

Mirae forced her smile to remain fixed on her face. "The gods work in mysterious ways, don't they?"

"Increasingly so," the old woman said, shaking her head. The movement sent ripples down her customary jade robes, making the bloodred ribbons securing it slice across her body like fresh wounds. Hoping to change the subject, Mirae glanced around the gathered crowd, which had straightened after showing their queen proper respect.

"I see the new Josan dignitary hasn't arrived yet," Mirae noted.

"Nor is he likely to." Sangsin Bada's eyes cut away to stare at something in the distance. "Especially since the last dignitary was shredded to pieces on our watch."

Mirae choked back the bits of her breakfast rising up her throat at memories of the former dignitary's horrific fate. "Well," she said thickly, "I hope the Josan king will accept that things are different now, and that I truly want to foster peace by establishing a new open-door policy between our nations. I'm hopeful that by sharing more of Seolla's important events with our sovereign state, they will do the same with us."

"Yes, I'm sure he's planning on taking full advantage of your decision to lift the ban on monarchs entering each other's lands," Sangsin Bada said stiffly, eyes still fixed on the horizon. "Though likely not in the way you intended."

"Well, we have to start building trust somehow," Mirae said, turning to see what the other woman was staring at. A large group of blue-robed travelers was slowly approaching. The oracles were drawing near.

"There's only one thing you can trust when it comes to Josan,"

Sangsin Bada said coolly. "The past will never die until Seolla lies beaten and bruised at their feet. They do not want peace, Your Majesty. They want restitution. And that is a price this great nation cannot afford to pay."

With that, Sangsin Bada strode past Mirae, making her way toward the procession without saying another word. Before Mirae could swallow her pride and patiently follow, the call of a bright, familiar voice stopped her in her tracks.

"Noonim, I'm here! I made it!" Mirae turned just in time to see Hongbin dashing madly toward her, the pale pink sleeves and baji he'd swapped into whipping behind him like cherry blossoms trailing from the boughs of a windswept tree. When he finally reached Mirae, Hongbin collapsed against her, chest heaving. "I think I set a new record with that one!"

"That was your fastest outfit change yet," Mirae concurred, patting his sweaty back as he did more coughing than inhaling. "Did you by any chance forget to bring your scented pouch?"

Hongbin's eyes widened as he patted himself down. "Oh no, do I stink? Am I going to lose my title as the Alluring Flower Prince of Seolla?"

"No one calls you that," Mirae muttered as she pulled out her own hidden pouch. "Here, you can borrow mine. I can always just enchant my clothes to smell nice."

Hongbin made a face at her scented satchel. "No, thank you. I like light, uplifting florals. You always pick the heavy, overpowering smells."

Mirae frowned and took a whiff of her dangling pouch, the spicy aroma emanating from it rich with cinnamon and ginger.

"What's wrong with my taste in perfume?"

Before her brother could answer, another familiar voice interrupted from behind. "Hongbin, where are your manners? Haven't I taught you to never insult a lady's aroma?"

Mirae whipped around and smiled at her father, who hobbled over to them across the sweeping grass bordering the dragon gates. Even though he was clearly doing his best to turn his pained limp into a playful gait, it was refreshing to see the dowager queen's consort well enough to join in on royal duties.

"Ah, so nice of the oracles to show up on one of my good days," her father quipped as he reached his children. "Sometimes I feel like a captive dragon hidden away while you two have all the fun without me."

"Father, you know the reason we can't take you with us outside the palace," Hongbin whispered conspiratorially. "Once our people realize rumors about your growing handsomeness are true, they'll only invite *you* to visit them, and the rest of us will die in obscurity. I'm sorry, but we must keep you secreted away, radiant as you are."

Mirae's father shook his white-streaked head. "Oh, the sacrifices I make for you children. It's not easy being the most handsome man in the kingdom."

"Someday, I will know what that's like," Hongbin said wistfully.

Mirae's father laughed and stroked the swooping ends of his mustache. "Don't think you'll get rid of me that easily! I'll be around long enough to see you both grow a headful of gray hairs."

Based on the way their father's legs trembled with the effort it took to remain on his feet, Mirae and Hongbin both knew his bravado was false, but they smiled and said nothing.

After a moment, Mirae's father took her hand. "I wish Minho could be here to see you right now, all grown up and magnificent, ready to officiate your first ceremony. He would be so proud."

Mirae did her best to hold the smile on her face, but as she took in her father's silver hair, his face lined with the toll of having his ki, his life force, slowly leeched from him, the muscles in her face struggled to hold back from expressing her sorrow. It was no secret that her father's body was failing, his body and mind ravaged by the pain of nearly losing a son; and from the zodiac beads—which Mirae had since drained of power—that had siphoned his life force as fuel. Even though Mirae had returned as much of her father's ki as she could, enough had been spent that years, perhaps even a decade of his life, had been lost forever.

"How was Minho today?" her father asked quietly. "Is he eating well? Is he staying warm?"

Somehow, telling her own untruths was far easier than listening to her father's unfailing optimism. Making sure her expression was unchanged, Mirae let the lies spill easily from her lips. "He's looking healthier every day."

Her father smiled. "That's my little earth rabbit for you. Timid and harmonious on the outside, but shrewd and determined when he's got something to fight for."

"He's always had a strong will," Hongbin agreed. "Hyungnim will be out here keeping you company in no time, Father."

Mirae's fingers dug into her bruise-colored chima as she reminded herself that it was better to let her father and brother believe a lie than burden them with something they couldn't live with or change. Her father hadn't been there when the Netherking forced Minho to stab a jawbone crown into her chest. Hongbin hadn't been around, either, when Minho's eyes darkened, his lips spewing only vile words. Neither of them had witnessed how the kind, gentle man they all loved had become twisted by the Netherking's corruption.

And that was for the best. After all, how could she allow the most tenderhearted members of her family to face the horrible truth that she'd let their brother, their son, become little more than an animal in a cage? The Netherking may have given Mirae no other choice than to be cruel, but Minho was the one who continued to suffer.

That was her and her mother's guilt to bear alone.

"The oracles!" Hongbin exclaimed, shifting everyone's attention back to the approaching women. "They're here!"

Mirae turned to face the entourage of light blue robes and shiny bald heads. One face in particular caught her eye. Traveling at the front of the procession was the only oracle Mirae had seen regularly over the past year—Areum, her longtime friend and the official liaison between the Temple of the Sacred Bone and the palace. Her True Bone upbringing had made her a natural choice for that calling, with the added benefit of being able to frequently return home.

As soon as Areum was close enough, she smiled and bowed. Although this wasn't the first time Mirae had seen her eonni shaven-headed and stripped of True Bone fineries, she still found her friend virtually unrecognizable every time she saw her. Not just because of the change in her everyday wear, but also the new lightness in her step and the knowing gleam in her eyes that had deepened ever since she'd begun learning how to harness her rare power of Horomancy—the ability to forge a connection with the gods themselves and unravel their will for the future.

"Your Majesty," Areum said, her eyes crinkling with a smile. Mirae was pleased to see her friend looking well. Her cheeks were pink as peaches, and her skin was dewy with good health.

"It's wonderful to see you," Mirae said, her voice loud and clear for the benefit of all the gathered royals. "Come, Sangsin Bada has prepared refreshments for you, our welcome guests, as well as everything else required for the selection of the new Kun Sunim."

"We are grateful," Areum said, though the cheeriness in her voice seemed to dip a little. After clearing her throat, however, she sounded like her old self once more. "If we may, we would like to pray before we begin the anointing."

Mirae inclined her head. "You are welcome to do as you wish. The palace is as much your home as it is mine."

For some reason, Mirae's words seemed to dim the light in Areum's eyes for a brief second, until she smiled brightly and gestured for Mirae to lead the way into the courtyard. Mirae nodded and turned back toward the palace, marshaling everyone—oracle, royal, and family member alike—through the columns of Wonhwa lining the dragon gates, their eyes watchful of all who entered into the heart of the queendom.

Well-practiced at assembling themselves for prayer, the oracles wasted no time spreading themselves out into a grid on the courtyard, leaving plenty of room for the pine-and-sage bonfire at their center. As soon as all were in position, the blue-robed women knelt and bowed as low as they could before beginning to chant.

Mirae stood respectfully to the side, knowing that until the anointing ceremony was completed, it was her duty to attend to the oracles while they were still leaderless and under her hospitality. Thankfully, Hongbin soon scurried over to join her, a reliable distraction as always.

"Father went to get some rest," Hongbin whispered as he sidled up next to her. "But he said he's looking forward to the feast."

"I think we all are," Mirae whispered back. "Far more than the trial."

"Trial?"

Mirae nodded. "I'm supposed to hold an audience with the three Kun Sunim candidates. If I find them all worthy, then they will present themselves before the gods, who will hand select the new Kun Sunim from their midst."

"Interesting," Hongbin said lightly, clearly distracted by something else. "Though not as interesting, I must say, as whoever that stunning young man is."

Mirae looked where Hongbin was not-so-subtly gesturing and noticed the figure he was referring to. A soldier standing at the far end of the courtyard.

Unlike Hongbin, Mirae recognized the other man immediately, even though she'd never seen her former traveling companion with his hair tied up in the Seollan style, or wearing brass armor with a sword dangling at his side. Though his head was partially bowed out of respect for the praying women, Mirae could still see the familiar angular cheekbones and suntanned skin of the man who'd been her guide in Josan . . . before betraying her to the Netherqueen.

"Is that Siwon?" Hongbin asked, finally figuring out where he'd seen the handsome stranger before. "I didn't know he was working for the oracles. Did you, noonim?"

Mirae nodded. "I specifically asked that he be present."

She'd heard from Areum months ago that Minho's former manservant had approached the oracles, begging to serve them as penance for his role, however small, in the slaughter of their order. He'd vowed to protect the holy women with his life, and, to his relief, the oracles sensed that his intentions were pure. So, they allowed him to become their guardian, the only man in their ranks. According to Areum, Siwon had kept his promise many times over, not only by serving as a bodyguard whenever any of the oracles needed to leave the temple but also by shouldering all the backbreaking work that needed doing at their sacred site. Whatever physical labor was demanded of him, Siwon always took it up without complaint.

The awe with which Areum always spoke of Siwon, and the perfect trust that the prescient oracles seemed to have in their new little brother, had inspired Mirae to send her friend back with the black bell coated with his mother's soul, making Siwon its guardian as well. But what had stood out even more to Mirae than Areum's admiration of Siwon was the way her eonni spoke of the Netherqueen's son, with a look of deep fondness in her rich dark eyes.

As if sensing Mirae's thoughts, Siwon lifted his head and noticed that Mirae and Hongbin were staring at him. At first Siwon offered them an uncertain smile that only grew bigger once Hongbin started beckoning enthusiastically. Emboldened by Hongbin's dramatic insistence that he join them, Siwon made his way over, his grin continuing to blossom.

Mirae felt her own expression soften as the other man came closer and she got a better look at him. Although her former guide had amber eyes just like Kimoon, his were warmer, more like sun on honey than a star twinkling coldly. The armor Siwon wore suited his muscular frame far better than baggy servants' garb ever did. As he strode forward, Mirae could hear his vest of brass plates clanking like muted chimes, their quietness almost like a show of deference to the black bell hanging from his neck like a glossy dark star.

But most of all she noticed the new confidence in his step, both humble and self-assured, which made her observe how sturdy and broad his shoulders were. Even the way his hair was pulled up into a topknot seemed to accentuate the strength of his jaw and the height of his cheeks, features that Mirae had never given much thought to before. Seeing now that every flattering thing Areum had said about Siwon was true, Mirae started to understand why her friend always spoke of him with such . . . enthusiasm.

"Siwon!" Hongbin nearly jumped into the other man's arms, embracing Siwon with his customary overzealous style. "It's been far too long! Don't tell me you've already forgotten this handsome face."

"Of course not." Siwon chuckled. "I never forget a face, Seja jeoha, especially one as striking as the Alluring Flower Prince of Seolla's."

Hongbin shot Mirae a triumphant look as he pulled away and finally gave Siwon some breathing room. Mirae shook her head at her brother before meeting Siwon's gaze, his light eyes, playful like his smile, practically glowing in the late morning sun. She couldn't wait to see how much brighter his face would beam when he learned why she'd requested his presence at the palace. "You look well. I trust the oracles haven't been working you to death?"

Siwon bowed so low that he folded into a tiny mountain. As he straightened out, he said good-naturedly, "The oracles have been unfailingly kind, Your Majesty, but doing dishes for dozens of people can be a little time-consuming. Not to mention quite frigid in the cold mountain water. Fortunately, I think I'll survive."

Hongbin put his hands on his hips. "Dishes can't be *that* hard to do up there. What do holy women even eat—plain rice juk for every meal?"

Siwon held up his arms defensively. "Hey, they put a little salt in their food every now and then. If I'm lucky, I'll even get a few slices of orange for dessert."

Hongbin cringed. "I don't think I could ever be an oracle."

"Thankfully, you'll never have to worry about that," Mirae said wryly. Then, before Hongbin could veer the conversation off topic again, she turned back to Siwon. "Were you told who the three Kun Sunim candidates are?"

Siwon nodded and gestured toward the oracles chanting at the head of the kneeling throng. "The three in the center are the ones you'll be meeting with today."

Mirae followed the direction of Siwon's arm, taking in the three blue-robed women, each bowing so low their faces were obscured. Mirae squinted at the trio, particularly the oracle in the center.

Areum, perhaps discerning that she was being watched, lifted her head just enough to sneak a quick glance over at Mirae and the men flanking her. Then, before dipping her face back down, she shot a smile in their direction. Not at Mirae, but to the man on her right.

As soon as Areum ducked her head, Mirae turned to Siwon, catching the last glimmer of a reciprocal grin splitting his face.

Chapter
FIVE

Mirae wasn't used to seeing the throne room so empty. Typically when she oversaw state business, the hall was packed with members of the Hwabaek vying to be heard, all of them campaigning endlessly for their queen's attention.

Today, however, the enormous chamber felt empty. Instead of loud voices, Mirae heard the distant, monotonous chanting of the oracles just outside. Golden light streamed in from the open front doors and the paper screen windows latticed with wooden flowers. Soaking in the warm sunshine, the crimson pillars on either side of Mirae's throne seemed to glow as brightly as flames.

Mirae wished the peacefulness of the room would help her relax while staring down at the three women kneeling before her, but instead her hands trembled in her lap, as they often did when she felt as if she was sitting in a space her more experienced mother was supposed to be. Even though Mirae held all the power in the room, she somehow still felt as if she was the one with everything to prove.

"Your Majesty," Areum said from where she knelt, flanked by the two other candidates. Her youthful features offered a stark contrast to the more seasoned women beside her. "We present ourselves to you, and are ready to receive your judgment."

Per tradition, whenever a new Kun Sunim needed to be called, the Sacred Bone Oracles spent a year observing each other so they could select the most talented three among them, just as they had centuries ago when their order was first organized. Mirae's role was to confirm that the oracles, with all their foresight, had done as they said they would.

At the anointing ceremony, the gods would do the rest.

Mirae held her head high, hoping she both looked and sounded like the queen they were addressing. "Thank you for answering my summons. Shall we begin?"

The three women bowed and said together, "Yes, Your Majesty."

Mirae nodded and raised her voice to be heard by the Wonhwa guards at the throne room's entrance. "Bring him in."

Mirae had thought long and hard about how she would determine the fitness of the new Kun Sunim, not only to fulfill her duty but to ensure that the next leader of the oracles was the right woman for the job, someone who could help Mirae navigate her current challenges without ending up murdered like her predecessor. But never had Mirae imagined that her own friend would take part in the trial she'd designed. It made Mirae feel even more guilty for conceiving a selfish exercise meant to ascertain not only the candidates' aptitude for Horomancy but their ability to help her with her own trial—expelling the Inconstant Son out of her brother.

Unable to meet Areum's trusting gaze, Mirae watched the distant, masculine figure who'd entered the grand hall approach the small gathering around the throne. Every step he took echoed like a drumbeat around the chamber. When Siwon was close enough that Mirae could see the puzzled look on his face, she deepened his confusion by gesturing for him to approach her.

"Come," she said, nodding at the space to the right of the dragon throne, where only the dowager queen and crown prince typically stood. "I want you to see what's about to happen."

Siwon hesitated, as would any commoner who was invited to stand as an equal on the queen's dais, but after Mirae gave him a reassuring look, he moved to obey. Once Siwon stood where directed, towering over her, Mirae gestured toward the black bell around his neck. "Hand that over, please. It's time to see if we can set Suhee free."

The look in Siwon's eyes sent a thrill through Mirae—a hint of surprise, with a dash of excitement for a moment he hadn't expected to come so soon. Wasting no time with questions that were about to be answered, he whipped the bell free and returned it to Mirae.

It had been some time since Mirae had seen her relic, one of the three artifacts crafted by an unknown creator for the High Daughters of Seolla. The High Horomancer's bell used to grant Mirae the ability to switch places with her future self, a cryptic gift that often left her more confused than illuminated; but it had nonetheless aided her on her path to rescuing Minho from the Josan king. Even though the Netherqueen's soul now blocked the bell's power, Mirae hoped that today, the relic would once more be key in helping her thwart her old nemesis.

Once she had the dark bell in her hands, cold and powdery to the touch, Mirae held up the domed instrument as if to clang it for all to hear.

"The task that I wish you to perform," Mirae proclaimed to the three candidates, hoping her voice wouldn't shake and bely her anxiousness, "is to safely remove the spirit encasing this relic. Whoever helps with this feat will earn my commendation to the gods."

Once again, the two older women looked at each other before the more wizened oracle, gray brows furrowed, gathered the nerve to say, "Are you asking us to perform an exorcism? I don't mean to be insolent, but that hardly seems like a practical demonstration of our powers."

"Why shouldn't it be?" Mirae asked, lowering the bell lest her sweaty palms cause it to slip out of her hands. "The point of today's trial is to prove to your queen that you can, and will, serve this queendom unquestioningly."

"Yes, but we Horomancers do not deal with spirits," the elderly oracle said, clearly embarrassed to be offering a correction. "A Josan shaman would be more suited to this task. If you require one, we can arrange for—"

"A shaman cannot undo a spell performed by a High Daughter," Mirae interrupted.

"True," the other woman admitted. "However—"

"If you are indeed the most talented oracles," Mirae cut in again, ignoring the frown of disapproval creasing Areum's face, "then you are adept at communicating with the gods. You have studied divine knowledge at the Temple of the Sacred Bone. Surely your orders' most elite can perform a feat you deem accomplishable by a mere shaman."

Out of the corner of her eye, Mirae saw Siwon's body stiffen at her words discounting Suhee's former occupation, but he didn't interrupt. He, too, was eager for Mirae's test to proceed, for a reason all too similar to her own. While Siwon wanted nothing more than to bring his adoptive mother back from the brink of death, Mirae desperately hoped that the new Kun Sunim would prove, here and now, that she was capable of and unopposed to helping Mirae exorcise spirits from places they didn't belong.

"And what do we do after we succeed, Your Majesty?" Areum asked, her voice tense as her eyes flitted between Siwon and Mirae. "Once the Netherqueen's soul is removed, what do we do with her?"

Conscious that Siwon was listening, Mirae called once more to the guards outside. "Bring in the chosanghwa."

Metal-plated boots clanked in unison as the waiting Wonhwa entered the hall, carrying a mahogany tray between them. After depositing their load at the foot of the steps leading up to Mirae's throne and angling it so that everyone could see what rested atop it, the Wonhwa bowed before retreating to their posts.

As soon as the guards were out of hearing distance, Mirae gestured to the small silk screen propped up on the wooden platform. "This is where the Netherqueen will remain until we find a suitable replacement for the body she lost." Turning to Siwon, Mirae said softly, "I regret that we cannot do more than see if transferring her soul is possible, but I did my best to find her a comfortable home. One that captures who she used to be."

Every eye turned to study the portrait. Staring back at them was a white-robed shaman with round, full cheeks that tapered gently down to a chin as dainty as the point of a peach. Thick lips and a narrow nose rested beneath a pair of dark, wide-set eyes that even on silk seemed to peer into the souls of all who fell under their gaze. The deep black hair framing Suhee's pale, lightly freckled face was swept backward with artful brushstrokes into a thick, braided bun as satiny as the screen it was painted on.

The painted woman was astonishingly beautiful, betraying no hint of the monster that would one day lurk inside her bones. Mirae snuck a glance up at Siwon, the only other person in the room who had seen the Netherqueen in person, and was glad to see him smile.

"I thought you might like to take this back to the temple," Mirae said, "and set up a shrine to Suhee, knowing that we have the power to save her someday."

Siwon bowed as low as possible. "Thank you, Your Majesty." His voice quavered. "Your compassion is immeasurable."

Feeling her face begin to warm, Mirae cleared her throat and turned back to the business at hand before her cheeks noticeably pinkened. "I have relayed all the directives of your test, esteemed candidates. If you succeed, you will have my endorsement."

While I, Mirae thought as she rose from her seat and set the black bell down beside Suhee's portrait, *will be free to use my switching ability as High Horomancer, and acquire an ally capable of expelling a corrupted soul.*

After Mirae returned to her throne, an uneasy hush filled the hall while the three candidates stared at the items before them. While it was clear that none of the oracles approved of Mirae's test, they all knew that if they refused to do her bidding, they would lose their eligibility to be anointed Kun Sunim. Those were the rules of advancement, whether they thought Mirae's request was fair or not.

For several long, tense minutes, the oracles sat there wordlessly. Mirae heard nothing at all except the calming sound of Siwon breathing beside her, until Areum finally broke the silence. "We shall do as you command, Your Majesty," her friend said uneasily. "Please allow us time to discuss this . . . unexpected task."

Mirae nodded and leaned back in her throne. Of course, she couldn't help but listen in as the three women began to review their options.

"It is impossible to tamper with a High Daughter spell without possessing Sacred Bone Magic ourselves," the oldest woman muttered, shaking her head.

"But we have unparalleled knowledge that we can draw from," Areum said encouragingly. "And the power of the gods to assist us. I am sure they are watching this trial very closely." The sharpness of her words prickled Mirae, as if they were meant to feel a little pointed. "The calling of the next Kun Sunim is not something the heavens take lightly."

The oldest oracle sighed. "Do either of you have any ideas on how to proceed?"

"I do," Areum said, though her voice shook slightly. "But it could be dangerous. The chances of failure are high."

"Not as high as doing nothing," the middle-aged oracle grumbled. "Go on, child, speak."

Areum took a deep breath—as did Mirae—before laying out her proposal. "In the early days of our order, the rank of Kun Sunim was granted to the most senior, experienced oracle, while the youngest and most talented initiate was given a different calling."

"You speak of the shinmyeong," the eldest oracle said, a wary look in her eyes.

Areum nodded. "The existence of such an appointment implies that we possess the ability to serve as a vessel for another being, which could prove useful in accomplishing Her Majesty's task."

Shinmyeong? Mirae thought, frowning. *A vessel for the gods? What is Areum talking about?* She wanted to interrupt and ask for clarification, but Siwon, astute as always, read her body language perfectly and leaned down to whisper into her ear.

"I only know a little about this ancient practice," he said. His breath, smelling of honey and pine leaf tea, tickled her ear. "Similar to a kangsin shaman, the shinmyeong allowed deities to enter her body and possess it. Then they could speak or act through her. But there hasn't been a shinmyeong called in years."

"Why not?" Mirae whispered back, careful not to move her head as she spoke, lest she accidentally brush against Siwon's lips, which were distractingly close to her face.

"The gods have not always been mindful of the fact that they were inhabiting the body of a mortal," Siwon said delicately. "If they possessed her too long, or exerted her too much, their powers could result in the young girl's death. After many an innocent young oracle was lost this way, the order eventually banned the practice of divine possession."

Mirae swallowed thickly, horrified at the thought of what previous shinmyeongs had endured as an act of faith. Still, Mirae turned to thank Siwon for sharing his knowledge with her, but as soon as her eyes rested on him, the words got stuck in her throat.

The first thing she saw, directly at eye level, was the black headband securing the curly hair Siwon had pulled into a neat topknot. The embroidered bronze suns circling the manggeon seemed to reflect the glimmer of his bright amber eyes, the cloth as black as his midnight hair. Next she noticed the striking profile of Siwon's face, the elegant curves of his nose and lips, their shapeliness accentuated by his beautifully tan skin.

But what drew Mirae's eye most was what raced across his face. Up close, she could see the pale scars that veined along his cheek and half his neck like raised roots. Marks left by his own adoptive mother the night of Minho's abduction. Remembering herself, Mirae quickly looked away before her stare made them both uncomfortable, and reverted her focus to the discussion at hand, which had become a little heated.

"Drawing the Netherqueen into our own bodies is madness," the middle-aged oracle huffed. "We don't even know how to remove the Netherqueen's spirit afterward."

"If we do not act at all," Areum insisted, "then there will not *be* a Kun Sunim. We're here because our order desperately needs guidance. We are lost without a divine leader."

"A divine leader would acknowledge that the calling of a shinmyeong was banned for good reason," the middle-aged oracle thundered. "None of us can allow our first act as incumbent

Kun Sunim to be the reinstatement of a wretched, forbidden practice, let alone corrupting it by taking a fallen mortal spirit into us instead of a god."

After hearing why the calling of a shinmyeong had been banned, Mirae couldn't help but agree with the middle-aged oracle, and yet she also couldn't help but hope that this woman, a clear stickler for the rules, would not end up being chosen as the next Kun Sunim. On the other hand, it seemed Mirae's longtime friend, whom she never wanted to put in harm's way, was the one most aligned with her objective, something Mirae found equally troubling.

As if sensing that Mirae's resolve was waffling, Siwon placed a hand on her arm and shook his head. "Your words have already been set in stone," he said. "They cannot be amended, or else this trial will be forfeit, and become a stain on your name. The oracles feel commanded by the gods to return to the temple with a new leader. Be very sure of what you do next, so you do not cause them to fail, and betray their trust again."

Mirae was all too aware, from conversations with Areum, that the oracles were desperate to reclaim structure in their decimated order. They had not come here to fail, any more than Mirae had. And yet, she couldn't stomach the thought of allowing someone else, even temporarily, to become another Minho, enslaved to the monstrous queen of the Deep. Even though Siwon believed in his mother's goodness, Mirae had not forgotten Suhee's part in her brother's abduction, or how she had brutally murdered Captain Jia, Mirae's protector and friend, before her very eyes.

While Mirae warred with herself, Areum stood up, towering

over the other two candidates, and said something that made Mirae's blood run cold. "I will do it. I will allow the Nether-queen's soul to possess me so that we may complete this trial. Neither of you need put yourselves at risk." The other women fell silent, and Mirae watched, frozen in her seat, as Areum let out a breath and said, "We were all surprised when the gods chose me, a novice, as a Kun Sunim candidate. Now I understand why. This is what they brought me to do."

"To rashly resurrect the calling of shinmyeong?" The middle-aged oracle's eyes widened with disbelief. "You cannot truly believe that, *either* of you."

"These are dark times," the oldest oracle said grimly. "We have long felt that the peace Her Majesty brought to the queendom is shrouded in mystery. What lies hidden from sight troubles our order. The future is murky even to our strongest seers. We need the gods among us now more than ever."

"And with the High Horomancer by our side," Areum said, gazing up at Mirae, her expression guarded but hopeful, "the Kun Sunim and shinmyeong will be able to help steer our queen-dom toward its fated golden future. Besides," Areum continued, closing her eyes, "there is an ethereal presence here that approves of our plan. I can feel it."

"As can I," the eldest oracle said, nodding. "I move that we begin your initiation as shinmyeong with a little practice. Draw the Netherqueen's soul into your body, young one. Open yourself to your new calling as a spirit vessel. Show the gods they were right to choose you, and you will have their protection."

Mirae wanted to jump out of her seat and forbid her eonni from doing any such thing, but Siwon's hand tightened in warning. Remembering that any interference would not be looked upon kindly—by the oracles, or perhaps even the gods—and would annul what two of the candidates clearly considered a moment of sacred inspiration, she instead appealed to their conflicted rival. "Are you going to allow this?" she asked desperately.

The other woman sighed and shook her head. "As you said, no one without Sacred Bone Magic can reverse a High Daughter spell. Though I do not agree that the gods brought us here to call a shinmyeong, I will let my sisters enact this foolhardy plan, for I do not believe it will work."

Mirae started to protest, until Areum silenced her with a look, a pleading yet confident expression that deflated Mirae's terror, lulling her panic into a muted dread. *Please trust me*, her friend's eyes seemed to say. *I know what I'm doing.* As Mirae fell silent, Areum smiled reassuringly, her lips forming a heartening command.

"Have faith," she mouthed. Words Mirae had said to Kimoon just hours before, expecting him to be instantly mollified at her request. How presumptive that seemed now.

Mirae gritted her teeth, withholding any more objections as Areum and the eldest oracle dragged the mahogany tray toward them, careful not to wobble the standing portrait or the black bell. Once it was directly in front of her, Areum placed her hands above the glossy relic, hovering her palms over its gleaming metal. Eagerly serving as Areum's assistant, the elderly woman scooted to kneel across from Areum, her back facing Mirae, as she began bowing and chanting in supplication to the gods. Up and down her bald head rose, a pale moon rising and falling to the rhythm of her prayer.

Areum, eyes closed, remained stock-still until her shoulders began to relax, her breaths soon evening out as she entered a calm, well-practiced meditative state. Mirae, on the other hand, gripped the edge of her throne as tightly as Siwon held on to her arm.

After several minutes of silence, Areum finally lifted her head to the heavens, heedless of all the eyes fixed on her, and said, "Come, haggard spirit. Enter my body and unbind the High Horomancer's holy relic. I am willing." Then Areum leaned forward and pressed her forehead to the ground.

Mirae and Siwon waited breathlessly to see who was right— the skeptical oracle, or the two aligned in their conviction of the gods' will. At first, nothing happened. As Mirae watched, heart pounding with anticipation, the chamber fell into an uneasy silence, like the sudden lapse of rain during a monsoon.

Then, suddenly, Areum's body jerked into a sitting position, startling everyone as her head rolled backward. When she opened her eyes, they were as black as the bell.

"Eonni?" Mirae rose to her feet, wrenching free of Siwon's grip.

Areum stared unblinking up at Mirae. The ebony marbles in her skull gleamed with recognition but held no adoration in their dark, tortured depths.

"Suhee?" Mirae's eyes darted over to the bell, which looked no different than before, still darkly swathed in the Nether-queen's soul.

Too stunned to do anything else, Mirae looked down in horror as Areum's hands curled like talons and she began to slowly crawl up the dais steps. "You *swore*," Areum said hoarsely, "that you would end him. Free my people. But you *lied*. Like every other false queen."

"S-Sol?" Mirae stared at Areum, possessed not by the Netherqueen but by the forsaken gwisin Mirae had snubbed for far too long.

"He has not. Been idle. In his chains," Sol rasped as she crept up the steps. Her movements were slow, unsteady, as she struggled to recall how to command a body. "Now everyone. Even the heavens. Are in grave danger."

Mirae froze before her throne, too shocked to move. Siwon, too, could only gape beside her, unbreathing, as he heard the voice of his adoptive sister who'd perished in the Deep while he and the Netherqueen tried, and failed, to save her.

"S-Sol," Mirae stammered again, fighting for the will to do anything but watch the fuming gwisin lurch toward her. "I-I'm—"

"A *coward*," Sol choked out. "A fraud. Now he is coming. For his prophesied reckoning."

Areum had reached the top of the dais. Slowing to a stop, she craned her head upward, meeting Mirae's horrified gaze. "He is coming," Sol warned again, then shot out her hand to seize the hem of Mirae's chima as her black eyes flashed. "You need to *run*."

Then, just as suddenly as she was possessed, the shadows in Areum's eyes faded, returning them to their original warm brown. Her head fell forward as she collapsed at Mirae's feet.

Finally finding the strength to move her own limbs, Mirae fell beside her friend, gathering her limp body into her arms. "Eonni, are you all right?"

Areum's eyes rolled backward, lids shuttering closed as she whispered, "The Netherking . . . h-he's—"

Before she could finish, Areum shuddered and fell still, barely breathing. But Mirae could feel what Areum was trying to say. It was there, in the pounding of Mirae's Sacred Bone heartbeat, mirroring the thundering of her mother's far away.

Following the pulsing connection that bound all in her bloodline, Mirae soul-walked to her mother, her spirit racing to where the terrified woman hurtled through the Gwisin Forest, fleeing with all her might away from the Deep.

Chapter
SIX

As soon as Mirae's eyes snapped back open, she pushed Areum into the arms of the waiting oracles and jumped to her feet. But the moment Mirae stood up, her vision swirled, as if her soul had not yet adjusted to its lightning-fast return to her body.

"Your Majesty!" she heard Siwon call out.

Mirae swayed on her feet, struggling to remain upright. The colors of the chamber were whirling together, the bloodred pillars and bronze sunlight streaming in through the windows blurring into whorls of fire, as if the throne room were swarming with ravenous flames.

Mirae, her mother's voice echoed in her mind, frantic. *I felt your presence just now. I know what you saw. But you must not come. Stay away, for all our sakes.*

"No," Mirae breathed, shaking her head. "I won't abandon you."

Someone grabbed her hands. When Mirae looked up at the man trying to coax her back to the present, her vision finally cleared as all the blazing colors of the room seemed to be pulled into Siwon's burnished, golden eyes.

"I—I have to go," Mirae said, still swaying. The memory of what her Sacred Bone connection had shown her flashed back into her mind: *her mother, racing barefoot toward the shadowy portal that would take her back to the Garden of Queens, pursued by a thick black fog that glittered with green lightning. Terrified, stumbling, her ankle dark purple and swollen—*

"My mother needs me." Mirae shoved past Siwon as she raced toward the courtyard, dashing past the Wonhwa, who were caught too off guard to stop her. As soon as she was clear of the building, Mirae raised her arms to the sky and bid her dragon rise.

Though it had been a year since Mirae had summoned her magical steed, it answered her call effortlessly, for manifesting its master's will was as natural as breathing air. A creature born of equally balanced Jade Witchery and Ma-eum Magic, a feat only Sacred Bone heirs were capable of accomplishing, the dragon took form by whipping nearby elements together—wood from the oracles' bonfire, and stone from the bricks encasing it—but drew visual inspiration from the plethora of rich colors surrounding it. The red and green of the palace offices; the blue of the astonished, kneeling oracles' robes; yellow from the noonday sun overhead; the jewel tones and pastels of the Hwabaek and True Bone royals' garments, glittering like their stares; and even the pink of Hongbin's hanbok and the whites of his bright, wide eyes.

Every hue melded with the elements, whirling together at Mirae's command, coalescing into a long, slithering beast with rainbow scales that glinted as brightly as the sun-bleached sand.

Ignoring the guards sprinting her way, Mirae leaped onto her dragon's back and commanded it to fly. As it settled back onto its haunches, readying for takeoff, Mirae heard a shout, and the clatter of metal against stone. She turned to see Siwon, who'd thrown himself onto her dragon's tail, hold on for dear life as her Sacred Bone creature shot into the sky.

As her dragon zipped toward the Garden of Queens, sentient enough not to require any steering, Mirae closed her eyes and pressed a hand to her chest. Her heartbeat thrummed alongside her mother's, strong yet panicked.

She's alive, Mirae thought, relieved. *But what happened? Sol made it sound like the Netherking has escaped—but that's not possible. The spell on his chains is impenetrable. So, what is Mother running from? And why isn't she using her magic? What is she so scared of?*

Mirae didn't have time to puzzle out any answers, for the dragon had already reached the garden, and now zoomed toward the shadowy portal ahead—too narrow for the enormous beast to pass through.

Clutching one of the protruding ridges on its back, Mirae sent a silent command to her dragon. The creature obediently straightened its body into a rigid line and stretched itself out, shifting its width into length, like a cook shaping dough into noodles. Soon, the dragon had elongated enough that it was no thicker than Mirae herself.

Remembering that there was another passenger aboard, Mirae twisted around just enough to see that Siwon, who'd managed to inch his way closer to the front, had wrapped his arms around the scaly beast and was bravely holding on.

And then they were through.

The contrast between the world outside the shadowy door-way and the Gwisin Forest was instantaneous and stark. Where the sunny palace grounds were verdant and fertile, the other side of the portal yielded a land that was wintry and bleak. The sky here was deeply bruised with twilight, and the sun looked more like a veiled moon than a radiant orb.

As her eyes adjusted to the sudden darkness, Mirae scanned the sandy ground, searching for any sign of her mother. When she saw the other woman on the pathway up ahead, Mirae inhaled sharply. The pitch-black mist closing in had doubled in size. The immense ebony plume spilled through the trees like a cloud of eternal night, but instead of stars glittering inside it, green lightning slashed through its depths, crackling with ominous power.

"Mother!" Mirae urged her dragon to swoop in and scoop up the fleeing woman in its massive claws. But as her creature barreled toward its mark, Mirae heard Siwon shout.

"Your Majesty—watch out!"

Mirae's eyes snapped back to the front, but it was too late. A tendril of shadow had broken away from the thick, sparking fog, hurtling toward them. Fast as an arrow, it rammed into the dragon's head before Mirae could even blink, spearing it through.

It may as well have gored Mirae as well. White-hot pain exploded inside her chest as she screamed, her vision blanking while the dragon shattered beneath her.

Without thinking, Mirae reached for her creation as she fell. Protective to the end, the sole remaining sliver of the rapidly disintegrating beast cradled her and Siwon in its crumbling embrace. Encased in the dragon's dying remains, they crashed to the earth. Mirae noticed only the thud of their bodies, and an explosion of jeweled shards, before everything went black.

Queenling.

A familiar voice, a hated sound, thrummed like an itch between her ears. Yet all Mirae could do was lie there, the breath knocked out of her, as her vision slowly cleared.

I'm so glad you came. I've waited a long time for this.

Mirae sat up slowly, grateful to find that she hadn't broken any bones. Beside her, Siwon was also struggling to catch his breath.

Up ahead, Mirae saw her mother stumbling toward her, her twisted ankle buckling. Behind her, the mass of crackling fog had grown bigger still. It inched toward the clouded sun like a bruise blossoming beneath a wide, frightened eye. Green lightning flashed through the expanding mist, its electric branches arcing like poisoned veins.

Mirae's breath caught in her throat as she noticed a shadowy figure striding through the dense fog. A tall, gaunt man who walked leisurely, pacing himself in his hunt for Mirae's mother. His crown and garment were steeped with night, and in his hand was a twilight orb, from which the pitch-black mist was pouring.

How? Mirae's breath froze in her chest. *How is this possible?*

As the Netherking stepped out of the dark, flashing mist, he twisted Minho's lips into a sneer. The man she used to call her brother stood dressed in the shimmering black robes of a monster who should never have escaped. The ebony jawbone crown circling Minho's brow mirrored the jagged, overgrown locks of her brother's hair—both of which surrounded the prince's pale, ashen face like the night surrounds the moon.

"Queenling," the man who was not Minho said. He smiled cruelly.

"How" was all Mirae could say, still struggling to find her footing. Her lungs burned, and her bones felt as if they were slowly piecing themselves back together. "How did you—"

"Get free?" The Netherking stretched Minho's lips into an even deeper grin, one that bared his teeth. "I had a little help."

Mirae forced herself to meet Minho's eyes, glittering and malicious under their new master's control. As much as she wanted to obliterate the Netherking where he stood, he wasn't making any moves to harm her. Not yet. And if there was any chance of avoiding an altercation that would put Minho, Siwon, and her mother, who was still limping toward her, in harm's way, she had to take it. Thankfully, she knew just how to distract the Netherking. If there was one thing he enjoyed, it was gloating. "So, what now?" she asked, lifting her chin. "Is this where you make me an offer I can't refuse?"

"Oh, I already have what I want, for the most part." The Netherking inclined his head toward the dragon pearl in his hand, which she'd left in Kimoon's care. Once, it had been a gleaming, milky moon with no dark side, reflecting all the colors of the skies.

But in the Netherking's hands, the dragon pearl had become corrupted, a sinister new moon sitting in the palm of the Inconstant Son, gleaming as darkly as the robes of its wielder.

"I finally figured out how to unlock its true power," the Netherking crooned, eyeing the pearl like a newborn child. "And now my new plan cannot be thwarted."

Mirae's mother was close, hobbling only a few steps away. Mirae needed to stall only a little longer. "Where is Kimoon? You know that pearl doesn't belong to you."

"Nor to you." The Netherking inclined his head, the green lightning behind him flashing like a splatter of venom across his face.

"Mirae, don't try to reason with him. You have to run." Her mother was finally close enough to fall into Mirae's arms, but her words were sharp, staccato from shortness of breath and the pain of her twisted ankle. "You shouldn't have come. Why didn't you listen?"

But Mirae simply passed her breathless, weakened mother over to Siwon, who obligingly slipped under the dowager queen's arms to support her while Mirae stood in front of them both, locking eyes with the evil, grinning abomination wearing Minho's body. The fire she summoned into her palms was blistering, twin suns formed to combat his dark, wicked moon. She had defeated this monster once before, on the shores of Wol Sin Lake.

Today, she would beat him again.

"Oh, queenling," the Netherking sighed. The pet name he'd given her rolled like frosted air off his tongue. "I should thank you for being such a thorn in my side. I've had so much time to sit and think in the darkness, and recruit some unexpected allies. Now my bold new plan is far more sublime than anything I could have ever come up with on my own."

"Please, Mirae," her mother begged. "He can kill you with a thought. You have to get out of here *now*."

"If he wanted me dead, he would have attacked by now." Mirae held the Netherking's gaze. To her mother, she sent a hasty thought: *You're the one he blames for the loss of his family. You're the one he wants to kill. Get to safety with Siwon, and I will follow.* To the Netherking, she said, "But there's something you want from me, isn't there?"

The Netherking took a step forward and cocked his head. The dusky glare of the dragon pearl cast deep amethyst shadows under his eyes and cheeks. His smile was like the crease of a dark river on the horizon, stark and brimming with the unknown.

"Yes, there is a small favor I'd like to ask," he murmured. "It's the least you can do after holding me captive like a lowly animal."

"What is it?" Mirae demanded, hoping her mother was coming up with a way to clear out, with Siwon in tow.

"It's a small thing," he said with a wave of his hand. "All I ask is that you and all your kin abdicate, paving the way for a peaceful transition of power. If you do, I won't wipe out all the True Bone royals, Wonhwa, and magic-wielding citizens who get in my way."

"You expect me to just hand you the queendom?" Mirae asked, voice flat.

"In exchange for a chance to preserve the peace, yes," the Netherking said mildly. "I thought what you wanted was to prevent war. I'm showing you how."

He was enjoying himself. The way he held the pearl like a scepter, it was clear he believed he had absolute power over the

Daughters of the Sacred Bone in front of him, and that before the day was over, they would cower before him.

But he was forgetting one thing. Mirae had seen the future; she knew she would not die that day. All she had to do was protect her mother and Siwon long enough to find a way to put the Netherking down once and for all.

Even if it meant losing Minho forever.

"Surrender the pearl and face me without any more of your tricks," Mirae said, eyeing the gleaming orb that contained depths of magic more potent than she had ever imagined. "It's the least *you* can do after tormenting my innocent brother."

"Innocent?" The Netherking's false cheer wavered. "There are no innocent children of the Sacred Bone. All I want, all I've ever wanted, is your cooperation, queenling. There need be no war, no bloodshed. Despite what you think, I am not a villain but a restorer."

"Then restore my brother," Mirae said coldly. "Give him back to me. Then maybe I'll begin to believe the hot air pouring from your mouth."

The Netherking's smile soured. "My rule is inevitable, queenling. It's up to you to decide how many people will die just so you can cling to an illusion of power you never deserved. Just like every other false queen."

As he spoke, Mirae noticed something strange. The pearl was starting to grow more luminescent in his hand, shedding the twilight haze of corruption. As the sphere brightened, so did the sky behind the Netherking. Even the crackle of lightning began to fade away.

His spell was losing power—the dragon pearl was resisting the Netherking's corruption. Now was her chance to strike.

Wasting no more time on idle chatter, Mirae drew back her arm and hurtled one of the blazing suns in her palm, aiming for the hand that clutched the corrupted Yeouiju, the source of the Netherking's new and frightening magic.

But before her flame could reach its mark, one of the dark, smoky tendrils pouring out of the pearl whipped out and, instead of swatting her fireball off course, absorbed it entirely, like a serpent gulping down a mouse.

Mirae stared, shocked, as the tendril retreated as if nothing had happened. But the Netherking's hands curled tighter around the brightening orb.

"I thought we were having a nice, friendly discussion," he said darkly, like a predator no longer interested in playing with its food. "But fine, we can do things your way." With that, the Netherking brought the pearl up to his chin and opened his mouth. Black water spilled out of his throat, and the pearl's shell darkened once more to a deep, midnight purple.

Mirae cocked her arm back, ready to hurl her remaining fireball at the Netherking's face, but her mother grabbed her shoulder.

"It's too late, Mirae. You have to run, *now*."

One look into her mother's eyes, wild and terrified, and Mirae knew better than to disobey. But before either of them could move, the dusky light exuding from the pearl pulled together, thickening the smoky tendrils spilling out of it and bolstering the looming mist. Several of the pitch-black arms twined together and shot toward Mirae like a lashing whip.

She didn't even have time to scream, or dodge the attack. But her mother acted instinctively, pushing Mirae behind her and taking the blow in her place.

Instead of flinging her mother backward, the dark arm latched onto her face, like an enormous leech, pinning her in place. Though she struggled to get free, her hands passed uselessly through the twilit shadows seeping into her mouth, nose, and eyes.

"No!" Mirae would have lunged toward her mother, but Siwon grabbed her tightly from behind, restraining her with all his might. Mirae struggled, screaming for Siwon to let her go, but he ignored her, forcing her to watch helplessly as her mother collapsed and fell unmoving to the ground while the Netherking laughed. The tendril left her there, lifeless, and turned to Mirae next.

For once, Mirae had no idea what to do. She had nowhere to run, nothing up her sleeve, and no idea how to protect anyone from the evil man in front of her, or his new, confounding power that could obliterate queens and blast dragons out of the sky.

There was only one thing she could do, and that was to raise her hands and gather the elements around her in preparation for one final battle.

Right here, right now, either she or the Netherking would die.

With a scream of rage, Mirae lifted her starlit palms as her enchanted wind surged forward, successfully knocking aside one of the tendrils the Netherking shot her way. But he'd sent a dozen more, more than she could battle alone.

They would reach her, this she knew. They would latch onto her face, suffocating her. Then Mirae would collapse like her mother, and Seolla would be doomed to fall into the hands of the man who had spent his entire life plotting its ruin.

Just as Mirae had resigned herself to her fate, Siwon stepped in front of her, as her mother had moments ago. But he held something in his hands that he raised high.

Her black bell, gleaming like a cold jewel. Siwon held it in front of him as he would a shield, an offering to the Netherking's lashing whips. To Mirae's amazement, as soon as the foremost tendril grazed the surface of the bell, it and all the others stopped dead in their tracks. They hung in the air, frozen bands of shadows as rigid as prison bars. The Netherking's eyes widened as he recognized the substance that coated the bell.

Suhee's soul. All that remained of the woman he loved.

His hesitation gave Mirae the time she needed to launch her own attack. She sprinted toward the man who'd assailed her mother, stolen her brother's body. Her rage burst out of her in a cry as thunderous as the Sacred Bone pulse racing through her chest as she shot fireball after fireball until one of them hit its mark.

The Netherking howled as the pearl flew from his hand and lay smoking on the ground. He barely had a chance to cradle his scorched flesh before Mirae, emboldened by disarming him, gathered wind to push her forward, faster than human feet could run, just as she had the last time she'd fought the Inconstant Son on the shores of Wol Sin Lake.

Dodging as much of her unrelenting fire as he could, the

Netherking turned and bolted toward the pearl, scooping up the deadly instrument. Mirae gave him no time to charge up his powerful spell—not if he wanted to hold on to his precious cargo. Before he could straighten, she threw her arms in front of her, propelling the wind driving her forward to slam into him instead, sending him flying as she dropped to the ground.

To Mirae's dismay, the Netherking managed to maintain his hold on the dragon pearl. And, with surprising dexterity, stuck his landing. Still on his feet, the Netherking whipped around, compelling the shadows to cascade out of the corrupted orb once more. But before he could command them to do anything else, he looked behind Mirae, and his face paled.

Mirae didn't need to turn around to see what had unnerved him. She could feel the gwisin's presence in the sudden icy shift in the air. Sol, princess of the Deep, had come to curb her father's violence once again.

The fury in the Netherking's eyes faded as he took in the pitiful sight of his daughter's restless spirit, in whose name he had launched his vengeful campaign. A different, softer emotion took its place. Something that made Minho's face look something like its old self. Then, shooing one last, hateful glare in Mirae's direction, the Netherking lowered his arm and darted into the surrounding trees, fleeing the scene that pained him, dragon pearl in hand.

Taken aback by her enemy's retreat, Mirae prepared to follow him until a panicked voice called out, stopping her in her tracks.

"Your Majesty, the dowager queen . . . she's—" Siwon's voice faltered.

Mirae spun around to see her friend kneeling beside her mother, clasping her limp hand. Mirae sped toward the unmoving woman, barely catching sight of Sol's ghostly white dress disappearing into the wintry trees.

Mirae fell beside Siwon and reached out to check her mother's vitals, but what she saw made her gasp and throw her hands over her mouth.

She thought she had prepared for the worst, the possibility of finding her mother unbreathing, her skin ashen and gray. But the Netherking had done something far worse than merely slaying the woman he blamed for the loss of his people.

Mirae's mother lay slumped on the ground as if sleeping, but her eyes were wide and staring, her irises faded to a dull, watery blue. Her face was similarly blanched, her lips purple-tinged. Her hair, too, had changed into a bright, shocking white. It was as if all the warmth and color had been sapped out of her body along with her life.

But what horrified Mirae most was how sunken her mother's frame had become, her skin gaunt and paper thin, as if all the liquid inside her had been drained. The hollows of her face were deeply bruised with shadows, darker still from the lines of black water streaking from her eyes, nose, mouth, and ears. She looked more like a skeleton than a being of flesh and blood.

This was not her mother, the former proud queen of Seolla, but a withered, unrecognizable corpse desolated by the cold-blooded villain whose heartbeat was trailing farther and farther away. His pulse was fast and lively while her mother's was silent, gone forever. Snuffed out while Mirae had stood by and watched.

Whatever strength Mirae had left failed her as she took in what remained of her mother. The toll of everything she'd endured hit her all at once, but the loss of her mother, and her orabeoni, struck her harder than the agony of her dragon crashing into the earth.

As her vision swam with scalding-hot tears, a scream erupted from her throat. Mirae fell forward onto her mother's emaciated chest, her own bosom heaving uncontrollably. She barely felt Siwon's arms lock tightly around her, or the heat of his own tears dripping into her hair.

Held by someone who knew what it was to lose a mother, Mirae succumbed to the despair ravaging her heart and mind, and wept.

Chapter
SEVEN

The funeral procession for Mirae's mother began the next evening, after a day of washing the dowager queen's body in incense water and dressing her in white burial robes. Assisted by Hongbin and her father, Mirae silently wrapped her mother in several layers of silk. When the queen's body was ready, palace women placed her on the funeral bier waiting outside her chambers, which was then hoisted onto the shoulders of her personal guards, per tradition, as penance for allowing this tragedy to occur.

Mirae and her family followed the bearers to the palace entrance, where everyone who was to join the procession had gathered, dressed in the scratchy hemp garments of mourning, raised hats, and humble straw shoes. After everyone had taken their places, the bearers lowered the bier three times at the dragon gates before beginning the long, slow march down the hill toward the Garden of Queens. The final resting place of every Daughter of the Sacred Bone.

Mirae silently led what remained of her family toward the forest below. She kept her eyes straight ahead, focusing only on the sight before her as a way to calm her inner turmoil.

The pall-bearing Wonhwa had traded their armor for the

same coarse hemp Mirae wore, and instead of weapons they now bore an immense palanquin. Atop the wooden beams they held was a red-and-gold box, gabled in bright greens and blues just like the palace itself. A blue canopy, draped with a rainbow of ribbons, lorded over the entire structure like a sky full of kites, exuding a whimsical playfulness that Mirae knew would bring joy to her mother's spirit.

Mirae also knew that her mother, if she was watching, would be pleased that her favorite singer, one of the best in Seolla, was performing a traditional mourning song ahead of the bier, accompanied by a fleet of drummers playing in perfect unison.

Behind Mirae, the rest of the procession—composed of her immediate family, True Bone royals, palace workers, and councilmembers—loudly mourned the loss of their former queen, wife, and mother. They wept and wailed openly so that all who witnessed, be they living or dead, would know that the deceased had been well loved.

Mirae, on the other hand, was forbidden to show any emotion. She alone bore the death of her mother stoically, for she was a Daughter of the Sacred Bone, a divinely ordained woman who represented the gods' will. And gods did not cry over a queen's death. If anything, they celebrated the chance to elevate a deserving soul, raising her from the turbulent mortal sphere to their own bright and beautiful realm, where she would rest and feast for all eternity.

So it was that by withholding her tears, Mirae was publicly showing confidence in the gods' judgment of Queen Noeul, and her worthiness to ascend to the heavens. As impossible as it felt to walk impassively behind the bier, Mirae stared straight ahead, determined not to dishonor her mother's life by weeping at her ascension.

When at last the parade of mourners reached the large clearing of burial mounds, Mirae and her family gathered around her mother's freshly dug funerary chamber: a deep hole in the earth lined with stone and decorated with divine figurines, elaborate paintings, offerings of food, and the dowager queen's most prized possessions.

The notes of the mourning song grew louder, and the wails of sorrow grew into a clamoring chorus as the pallbearers lowered the bier to the lip of the gravesite. Then the Wonhwa retrieved their former queen's body from the decorative box and placed her slowly, reverently, onto a table in the center of her grave.

As the Wonhwa climbed back out, Mirae stared at the shrouded body. It looked too small to belong to her mother, an enchanted queen who had ruled the most powerful nation on the peninsula. Just as Mirae had that thought, an image forever burned into her brain clawed its way to the surface like a bristly insect—the memory of what her mother's corpse looked like on the forest floor. Gray and emaciated. Thin, withered flesh stretched over protruding bones.

Mirae squeezed her eyes shut, trying to block out the gruesome image. Thankfully, the mourning song ended, forcing Mirae to redirect her attention to the funeral before she lost control of her emotions. Opening her eyes, Mirae rested her gaze on her mother's body as it looked now, veiled by several layers of silk that had been folded to form crisp scales running from her head to her toes. It looked more like a cocoon than a shroud, a promise that death was not the end for Seolla's former queen.

Now that the procession was over, the crowd began to dissipate, for it was time for the family's watch to begin. The singer, drummers, True Bone royals, councilmembers, and palace workers respectfully withdrew while the Wonhwa bearers hoisted the bier away to be burned, leaving Mirae, Hongbin, and her father to mourn in private.

As soon as they were alone, Mirae took a deep breath and reminded herself that she still had a duty to fulfill—a night's watch over her mother's grave, meant to suffuse the air around her with her family's undying love before she was buried with those energies at dawn.

Mirae had a second responsibility that night as well, one she dreaded even more.

Hongbin had already entered the burial chamber, and was reaching up to help his father descend. Mirae quickly took one of her father's arms, helping to lower him into Hongbin's waiting embrace. Both she and Hongbin were careful with their father's frail frame. Grief had weakened him to the point of looking almost as brittle as his wife's corpse. Shaking away that heart-breaking thought, Mirae slid into her mother's tomb, joining her family on the packed, cold earth.

At first, no one knew what to say, so they remained silent, casting their eyes around the underground room. Surrounding Mirae and her family were various funerary items: elaborate pots, jewelry, and figurines of mythological guardians. But Mirae's eyes wandered over to the stone walls around her, studying the paintings on their surfaces.

Some depicted stories she knew by heart, like the tale of the three Go sisters, the original recipients of Seolla's magic systems. Others were sweeping, elaborate portraits of the gods and past queens. One of these featured a triptych of a story Mirae didn't immediately recognize.

Because of the way the pallid moonlight fell on the painting, stripping it of color, the only thing Mirae could see clearly was the figure in the center: a proud queen wearing the Seollan crown, decked out in all the fineries of her rank. But what caught Mirae's attention was the bloodred orb she held in her hands, the only part of the painting that seemed to maintain its bright hue. As she surveyed the landscape behind the queen's portrait, Mirae realized with a start that she'd seen it before: the stark lines of barren trees, and the gleaming white stones surrounding inky water.

The depicted queen was standing in front of Wol Sin Lake, the cage of the Inconstant Son where the Netherking was supposed to be trapped eternally.

That could mean only one thing: this woman was the Deep Deceiver, High Daughter of Seolla, and the guardian of her mother's reign. Thanks to the Netherking's penchant for spouting disturbing historical facts whenever Mirae visited Minho, she also knew this queen's name, which was forbidden knowledge.

Queen Sunbok. A woman whose spirit Mirae had met after shattering her relic over a year ago, and whose story, according to the Netherking, was an utter lie.

At first, Mirae had balked at the Netherking's impetuous

uttering of what he called Seolla's "true history." *The High Daughters were fallible, imperfect queenlings just like you*, he'd taunted, laughing at her discomfort. He'd been especially eager to dispel Mirae's beliefs about the Deep Deceiver, a woman who, according to legend, was an unrivaled wielder of Jade Witchery. It was said that she used her immense power to end a civil war started by the Inconstant Son without shedding blood. A feat that she was honored for to that day.

But the Netherking had told Mirae a different version of this famous legend, and what the civil war had truly been about. According to him, Queen Sunbok was no protector of the realm, but rather a corrupted, greedy usurper. The worst of Seolla's false queens.

According to the Netherking, Queen Sunbok's brother, Dasan, was the true hero of this ancient tale. When he was young, Prince Dasan began questioning the gods' instruction to suppress magic-adept men. He defied tradition in secret by removing his mark and nurturing his magic on his own. Allegedly, he even became powerful enough to rival his sister's abilities, to the point that he convinced himself it was unfair that he was considered unfit to rule all because of baseless rumors about a so-called Inconstant Son.

One day, he made the mistake of expressing his feelings to Crown Princess Sunbok. When he confessed that he had been secretly learning magic, Sunbok did not react well to the idea that her brother sought to become her competition, and take what was hers.

So it was that, rather than entertaining any talk about turning

Seolla into a merit-based monarchy, Sunbok convinced the Hwabaek that her brother was the Inconstant Son, destined to destroy the queendom. If he was not curbed, Sunbok warned, then Seolla would fall.

Forced to flee the palace or be tried for treason, all for embracing what he believed was his destiny, Dasan hid from his sister's guards, retreating to a remote town where he continued to explore his powers, and even began inviting other magic-adept men—and their families—to come and nurture their abilities as well. Soon, Dasan's enclave became a haven for anyone who believed Seolla was not the utopia it claimed to be.

In time, Dasan amassed quite the following of powerful magic users, large enough to potentially threaten the matriarchy of Seolla. Claiming that this was proof that her brother was indeed the Inconstant Son, Sunbok was given permission to deal with her brother and his disciples as she saw fit. So, Sunbok hatched a plan to end Dasan's insurgency. Using her considerable powers, which she, too, had been tirelessly cultivating, and soliciting the help of the equally formidable Hwabaek, Sunbok fashioned a dark cage that she lured her brother and his followers into.

Then, in what she considered an act of mercy, she trapped them all in the Deep, rather than executing them for treason. There they would stay, alive but cursed, until their numbers dwindled to nothing.

To Sunbok's dismay, however, her act of "kindness" soon became the bane of the queendom. Instead of a prison, she had created a breeding ground of undying hatred. Her captives, who called themselves the nether-fiends, declared themselves eternal enemies of Seolla, dedicated to deposing the false queen who had made wretches of them all.

For the curse she'd imbued into the very air of the Deep did something far worse than merely confining her enemies in a lightless abyss. Their very bodies began to change; their day eyes became accustomed only to darkness, and their hard-won powers became a source of excruciating pain. A sickness that eventually cost them their lives, as agonizingly as possible.

Princess Sol had been the last to die at Queen Sunbok's hands, and the Netherking had sworn that her death would be sorely avenged.

Staring into the dark eyes of the painted queen now, Mirae remembered the last words the Netherking had said to her in the Deep, before invading Minho's body.

This isn't any mere cage, queenling. It's a well of magic that's about to run dry.

"Noonim." Hongbin's gentle call pulled Mirae out of her reverie like a splash of icy water to the face. "Could you come here? Father's freezing."

Mirae tore her eyes away from the triptych, shifting her gaze back to her sole surviving parent, who leaned wearily against Hongbin. Her father looked utterly exhausted. His under-eyes were red and puffy, his cheeks sunken craters. It almost seemed as if the past day alone had aged him more than the last three years.

As Mirae scooted closer so she could warm her father's other side, she shot a look of concern over at Hongbin. But her brother refused to look her in the eye, as he had during the entire funerary rite. Although Mirae was hurt by how her brother had been avoiding her, she knew why Hongbin was upset. She'd left him behind at the palace when their mother was in danger, making him unable to help in any way. Now he would forever wonder if, had he been there, things would be different. However unlikely, his presence might have triggered a better outcome. It would be some time, Mirae knew, before Hongbin would forgive her for keeping him out of harm's way when their family was in trouble.

Biting back all the useless apologies she'd already inundated her brother with, Mirae curled up next to her father and took his brittle hand. Once more, the tomb was filled with silence, no one wishing to disturb the rest of the woman they'd all dearly loved.

As Mirae's fingers gently smoothed the paper-thin skin of her father's hand, she felt his pulse, slow and weak. So unlike the Sacred Bone heartbeat thrumming inside Mirae's body, connecting her to the Netherking. She could sense him, but his whereabouts gave her little comfort. Although he was far away, inexplicably heading northwest through Josan, every step he took filled her with rage. He was free, unpursued, while Mirae stayed behind to bury her mother. She couldn't even send guards to hunt him down, not while he had the pearl.

As it turned out, the Yeouiju's deadly power was even more sinister than Mirae had expected. After examining her mother, the royal physician had declared that the dowager queen hadn't just been killed, but completely drained of magic. A grisly process that had withered her body, shriveling her from the inside out. Her very soul, inextricably entwined with her powers, had simultaneously been torn from her body like wings from a moth. A horrible, agonizing death.

It seemed that instead of infusing the black water with a new, abominable spell, the Netherking had found a way to amplify its natural ability to drink from any soul it touched. Empowered to an extreme and guided by the Netherking's vengeful magic, the black water had instantly siphoned every drop of life out of Mirae's mother, extinguishing her like dying embers raked by cold wind.

And it wasn't even just Mirae's own family he'd left worse than dead. When Mirae had sorrowfully led Sangsin Bada and other senior members of the Hwabaek to Wol Sin Lake after her mother's death, admitting to all her lies, Mirae had found Kimoon floating facedown in the inky water, left to rot in its soul-feeding depths. He'd been pulled back to shore, alive but unconscious, his veins black and bulging. The royal physician was working to save him, to drain the black water from his body before he became yet another casualty of the Netherking's escape.

Fueled by her righteous fury toward the monster who had murdered her mother before her eyes, stolen her brother, and poisoned her friend, Mirae took a deep breath and uttered the words she knew her ailing father was dreading most.

"I'm going after him," she announced. "As soon as our watch is over I'm going to hunt down the Netherking. I've already ordered Captain Hanyoung to bring a horse and provisions at dawn. Hongbin, you will rule as regent in my absence. Please don't argue. There's nothing either of you can say to change my mind."

It took only a few seconds for the shock to wear off the men's faces. Eyes wide, they leaned forward and protested vehemently, indignant about two entirely different things.

"Are you out of your mind?" her father choked out. "That monster killed the most powerful woman in the queendom. Going after him would be suicide!"

"You're seriously going to leave me behind again?" Hongbin yelped.

Mirae sat there calmly, accepting the verbal onslaught. Only when Hongbin's and her father's censures trickled away did Mirae speak again. "I have to do this," she said calmly, taking a page out of Kimoon's book and keeping her tone carefully neutral. "I have to destroy the Netherking before he finishes what he's started."

"You mean you have to destroy *Minho*," her father said, voice breaking. "After everything we've lost, everything you've done to save him, you can't give up on him now."

"We don't even have the *beginnings* of a feasible plan," Hongbin added. "You've always been reckless, noonim, but this is plain insanity. The Netherking can kill you with a single spell. I'm not even sure he *can* be stopped anymore."

As Mirae stared back at the grieving, fearful faces of her remaining family members, she began to hate the Netherking even more for destroying not only her loved ones' lives but their unshakable optimism as well.

"So that's it, then?" Mirae asked, clenching her fists. "We just roll over when the odds seem insurmountable?" She gestured to her mother's shrouded, lifeless body. A woman who had died so Mirae could escape and fight another day. "I'm not letting him get away with this, and I *will not* allow him to succeed at whatever he's scheming up now. You're right, he took down the strongest of us, but think about what that means. With this new, terrible power, he'll easily be able to destroy the entire queendom, especially if I sit around and do nothing. I have to stop him. I'm the only one who can."

"Mirae." Her father shut his eyes. "Can't you just mourn your mother without running off to join her? Does her death, her last act to protect her child, mean nothing to you?"

"Of course not." Mirae blinked back sudden tears. It hurt to see her father so upset, so helpless, and to know that he thought her duty as High Horomancer was futile. "But she died so I could finish this. I won't let her sacrifice be for nothing."

"Yes, she saved you for a reason," her father said shakily. When he opened his eyes, tears slipped down his face. "It's because you are precious, and the queendom needs you. Do not run off and die at the hands of that vile man. Do not give him what he wants."

Mirae felt her shoulders slump, her chest deflate. "I'm not going to die, Father. I've seen the future, remember? I grow old. You don't need to worry about my death, but rather me *failing*. That is something not even the gods can protect me, or the peninsula, from. I have to do this, for all of us. It's my destiny."

"No," her father said, shaking his head. Tears splashed against the back of Mirae's hand. "Your only duty is to live and be loved by your family."

Mirae had known she would not easily persuade her father to let her go, not when he had already lost so much, but she also knew she couldn't stay by his side. She was no more willing to lose the rest of her family to the Netherking than her father was.

Mirae looked to Hongbin, who didn't seem any more swayed than their last living parent. It pained her to see both him and her father so forlorn when they used to be the light and heart of their family. But she had expected them to reject her decision. Wordlessly, she reached into the pocket of her chima and pulled out the relic she'd hidden there.

Both Hongbin and her father stared at the glossy black bell, coated with another woman's soul—except in one place. The spot where the Netherking's magic-draining spell had grazed it, and the original metal now peeked through.

"I don't want to leave without your blessing," Mirae said, meeting her father's teary eyes. "But if I can't convince you to trust me, then maybe you'll accept the word of my future self, who has seen and lived the things I'm telling you now. I will summon her so we can find out what the future holds. Then we'll make a decision together, as a family."

This time, when Mirae's eyes flicked over to Hongbin, he gave her an encouraging nod. She looked at her father next, who hung his head resignedly. Taking their silence as an agreement to accept whatever the gods revealed through her switch, she held the bell out in front of her and swung it resolutely.

The sound of a deep, booming gong rang out of the relic's depths, rumbling through the air, the ground, and Mirae's body. She closed her eyes, submitting to the familiar darkness that clouded her vision, and the searing pain in her hand that made her collapse into oblivion.

Chapter
EIGHT

It took a few moments for the pain shooting up Mirae's arm to abate enough that she didn't have to stifle a scream any longer. When the pangs were finally gone, her eyes fluttered open, and she looked around at the strange scene that awaited her.

The first thing Mirae saw was the night sky looming over her, looking closer than it ever had before. Bright lights—blue stars and red-tinted planets—flickered in the darkness, like flashing jewels in midnight-black hair. They surrounded her on every side, some small enough to fit into her hand, and others large as the dragon gates themselves, beaming too brightly for Mirae to stare at for long. But no matter where she looked, celestial orbs dotted her vision, orbiting her. It was as if she were a lost, untethered star, or a missing moon floating through the universe.

No, not floating. Her feet were planted on some kind of surface, one that had seemed invisible at first. But when Mirae examined the ground, she saw she was standing on an endless mirror stretching off infinitely in every direction. Its smooth surface reflected the light of the stars around her, making it blend in with the heavens. As Mirae took in the strange sight, she realized that it wasn't mere glass she stood on but a liquid plane, shallow enough that the crystal clear water coating the surface came only halfway up the sides of her shoes.

As for where this plane was, all Mirae could see both above and below was a dark sea riddled with starlight, as if she stood at the galaxy's core—higher, even, than the heavenly realm.

Mirae marveled at the stillness, the silent splendor of her surroundings, but she didn't let her sense of wonder distract her for long. She had come here for a reason—to find out what the future held, while the version of her that came from this unfathomable place convinced her family that she was following the gods' path.

But it seemed the answers Mirae sought would have to be earned. There was nothing, no clue or answers, written in the stars themselves. So, she took a few cautious steps forward, unsure if the depths of this shallow lake would change as she walked, but the water hardly rippled as she moved. Whatever this place was, it was clearly a vault of mysteries, a spellbound road to perhaps the greatest secrets in the universe.

Mirae strode forward, unable to ignore the urgency drumming in her heart. It was only a matter of time before this switch ended, and she didn't want to return empty-handed.

As her eyes adjusted to the relative darkness of her surroundings, her body began to feel the chill of the encircling void, riddled with stars that shone brightly but coldly. When Mirae wrapped her arms around herself to preserve some of her warmth, the movement caused her to notice something strange.

There was a red thread tied around the smallest finger on her right hand, arcing through the air in front of her like a kite string. Easy to miss in the darkness. Mirae held her finger in front of her face as she walked, studying the ribbon's rich vermilion color, and the way it disappeared if she looked too far into the distance.

The red thread of fate, Mirae thought, filled with wonder. She'd only read about it in stories; the fabled string was said to tie two people together, conjoining their destinies. *But to whom am I walking toward?* she thought. *Who is the person I'm predestined to meet? And why am I able to suddenly see the invisible tether that interweaves our fates?*

With a start, Mirae realized the answer was right in front of her. It was because she wasn't in the mortal world anymore but the cosmos themselves, where things like fate, gods, and planets were created. Forged from inexplicable power as ancient as time itself.

As she thought back on her previous switches, her intrepid jumps into the future were starting to make sense. The last two times she'd rung her bell, she'd found herself dancing at a festival for spirits with an unnamed lover, and climbing a staircase of swords to the heavenly realm. *What was it Hongbin said was our quest back then?* Mirae thought back to their conversation, dredging up the words he'd spoken:

We're trying to find your patron goddess before you lose your powers.

Mirae had been confused about what he meant at the time, but now, after having seen the Netherking suck the very life out of her mother with his vile new ability, Mirae realized with a jolt the unprecedented danger she and the heavens could actually be facing.

It was no coincidence that the Netherking had merged the Yeouiju and black water together, but an intentional part of his bold new plan. The pearl, once teeming with near-omnipotent power, was now little more than an empty vessel primed to be filled with another's magic. Magic that the Netherking's black water would sap out of his enemies, siphoning it all into an ancient artifact with a near infinite holding capacity.

Enough, perhaps, to even hold the magic of the heavens, the gods themselves.

Is that his plan? Mirae froze with horror, even as her heart nearly leaped out of her chest. *To drain all magic users, and store their power in the pearl for his use alone?*

If that was true, then her mother's death had been merely practice. A trial run. A prelude to a magical apocalypse where all magical beings would fall before the Netherking, leaving him the sole god of the entire peninsula. Perhaps even the world.

If I'm right about this, I must stop him quickly, no matter the cost . . . but how? Mirae thought desperately.

Up ahead, Mirae spotted something like an answer to her prayer—a shimmering structure that materialized against the horizon, breaking the starry, spotted monotony of the seemingly endless plane.

By its radiance alone, Mirae might have mistaken the apparition for the moon if it weren't for the looming pagoda's high, sharp peak. The semicircles of stairs at its enormous base and each of the seven levels' disclike roofs seemed to be made from glowing abalone, while the walls of the palatial building appeared to be coated with effervescent mist and liquid pearl.

From top to bottom, the tower of light dazzled Mirae with its luster and beauty.

Once she drew close enough that her shoes could touch the tip of its gleaming reflection in the water, she raised a hand to shield her eyes from the pagoda's glaring incandescence and noticed that the thread tied around her finger had grown taut.

Mirae blinked several times, letting her eyes adjust to the mysterious building's intense shine before following the direction of the bloodred string until she saw where it led—right into the glowing pagoda's depths. Before Mirae could investigate the palace further, a resounding boom erupted behind her, rumbling almost painfully through her chest.

Mirae whirled around, but couldn't see any signs of an attacker. Instead, the darkness of her surroundings began closing in, enlarging the space between stars until she could see nothing but the ever-expanding void signaling an end to her vision of firmaments and unfulfilled fate.

Mirae returned to utter silence. Half wondering if she had actually left the cosmos at all, Mirae opened her eyes and found herself kneeling before her father, with Hongbin close beside her. Her hands, and Hongbin's, were pressed together in the act of pleading, while her father looked down at them both as if he had never seen a more heartbreaking sight.

She had no idea what her future self had said or done while she was gone, but it seemed Hongbin had been convinced to take up her cause, and she could see her father's stubbornness relenting, even if it was only because he was clearly outnumbered.

"All right," her father finally choked out, his face creased with sorrow. "You may go, Mirae. I give you my blessing."

Beside her, Hongbin breathed a sigh of relief, but their father wasn't finished. "Just promise me," he said, eyes glistening, "that you will come home without losing yourself to this quest. This is not about seeking revenge, it's about saving Seolla. Nothing else matters."

Mirae reached out and squeezed her father's hands, her own shaking from the revelations she'd received in the heavens. "Protecting Seolla has always been my sole focus. That will never change, I give you my word."

While her father clung to her, Mirae looked to Hongbin, whose expression had changed. Instead of quiet resentment, his eyes seemed to have found a glimmer of light once more, rekindled in her absence. It appeared that her future self had indeed relayed the importance of Mirae's mission and the daunting road that lay ahead, which left Mirae wanting to know what all Hongbin had been told, the things she had yet to encounter on her quest.

"In my switch, I was walking among the stars," Mirae said, seeing the same glittering beauty of the heavens reflected in Hongbin's dark eyes. "Guided by the red thread of fate. My other self . . . did she tell you where I was going?"

Hongbin nodded, frowning as he tried to remember the exact words he'd heard. "You said you were on your way to see the goddess of time, your patron deity, to learn how to stop the Netherking. You told us what you could about the Netherking's 'new, bold plan' in the short time you had."

"He's going to slaughter the gods, isn't he?" Mirae asked quietly, relaying what she'd surmised on her own. "He intends to steal their power the way he did Mother's, and become the only source of magic on the peninsula, making him a god."

"Yes," Hongbin said grimly, confirming her worst fear.

Memories of her mother's last moments flashed back to her, a prelude of the horrors to come. Mirae breathed long, deep breaths to quell the rising rage and terror threatening to overwhelm her. She'd made a promise to her father not to let her anger get the best of her. The peninsula, and the gods themselves, were counting on her to keep her wits about her. When she regained a semblance of calm, Mirae gestured for Hongbin to continue. "What else did she say? Tell me everything."

Her brother readily acquiesced. "She filled me in on something you apparently already know, that the Netherking's pearl, combined with black water, can steal and hold an unfathomable amount of magic. Perhaps all the power in the heavens themselves. She also warned that as long as the Netherking continues to accumulate and hoard this stolen power, each murder will only make him stronger. We must stop him before he becomes indomitable."

Mirae swallowed back a swell of panic. "I guessed as much during my switch. But," she said, shifting uncertainly in her seat, "something I don't yet understand is why the gods aren't stepping in themselves, if they're in so much danger."

"They can't, as long as the Netherking remains in the mortal realm," Hongbin explained. "And by the time he reaches the heavens, he'll be too powerful for anyone to stop, especially beings made of pure magic. It'll be a massacre. The gods have no choice but to run or die." Hongbin sighed. "It was too long a story for your future self to tell me everything, but she said there are unbending rules about interfering with our world, set by the Jade Emperor himself after the Samsin gifted Seolla with magic. Unfortunately, he hasn't been seen in a thousand years, which is why the gods need people like you and the other High Daughters. The last thing you said about that is to ask Areum if we want to know more."

Areum, who, like Kimoon, was resting under the royal physician's care after valiantly trying, and failing, to follow her queen's command, battered and bruised over Mirae's relentless obsession with saving Minho, a quest she now knew had distracted her from her true duty, perhaps even allowing the Netherking to bring his new plan to fruition. A lump of guilt began to form in Mirae's throat. Thankfully, Hongbin resumed his report without any prompting.

"As far as where to even begin with taking the Netherking down, you told me that he's seeking out a hidden sect of seers known as the Dark Moon Oracles. They apparently have the forbidden knowledge he needs to enter the heavens."

"The Dark Moon Oracles?" Mirae frowned, certain she'd never heard of them. "Are they stationed in Josan? That's where the Netherking has gone. I can feel his presence there."

Hongbin shook his head. "They live in Baljin."

"I see. That makes more sense." Baljin, the nomadic, northernmost nation on the peninsula, was not hostile to magic or its users, unlike Josan. And it was remote enough to be an ideal hiding place for anyone wishing to stay out of the public eye. "Is the Netherking just passing through Josan, then? Making a beeline toward the Dark Moon Oracles?"

Her brother shook his head again. "Apparently he has a purpose in Josan. Something he needs from the capital. Which leads me to something else you relayed in your switch." Hongbin hesitated. "You insisted that Kimoon go with you."

Mirae raised her eyebrows. "Kimoon? But he's still recovering, and he's hardly going to have a warm reception in Josan, exiled prince that he is."

Hongbin shrugged. "That was the last thing you said before disappearing. You were very adamant that you won't be able to succeed without him."

The ball of guilt building in Mirae's throat sank to the pit of her stomach, heavy as a stone, as she recalled the last unkind words she'd said to Kimoon, refusing to listen to his impassioned plea that she take his counsel and exorcise the Netherking by any means necessary. She'd balked at his repugnant suggestion then, but now, in hindsight, she wished she'd felt the same urgency he felt, and at least considered the validity of his unsavory plea. Maybe all of this could have been avoided. Mirae didn't know how she could bring herself to ask Kimoon once more to stand by her side. What right did she have to promise him this time would be different?

Because it will *be different*, Mirae told herself, feeling the stone in her stomach settle like an anchor, grounding her. This time, thanks to her switch, she had something she was usually sorely lacking in her fight against the Netherking. Knowledge, the most important weapon she could ever wield against her uncanny foe.

Emboldened, Mirae rose to her feet. "I know our watch isn't over," she said, "but knowing what we do now, I think I should prepare to set out at once. The Netherking has too much of a head start. I can't afford to dawdle."

"You mean *we* need to set out." Hongbin rose to his feet as well and dusted off his hemp mourning clothes. "I'm coming with you, of course."

"No," Mirae said, before her father could. "Hunting the Netherking is extremely dangerous for any magic user, especially one as untrained as yourself. Besides, you're the crown prince. There's no way the Hwabaek will allow you to—"

Hongbin held up a hand, cutting her off. "You know," he said, "for someone so intent on 'following the gods' will,' you sure do like keeping me from doing the same. But I have a destiny, too. I mean, you saw me by your side in the future, right?"

"Yes," Mirae admitted, remembering the stairway of swords up to the heavens, and an embittered version of her brother she wanted to avoid encountering at all costs. "I'm sorry, Hongbin, but I'm not going to endanger you and leave this queendom without an heir. That's final."

Hongbin opened his mouth to protest, his eyes narrowing stubbornly, but Mirae silenced him with a thought, pushed into his mind through their Sacred Bone connection.

I need you here, she insisted, meeting his gaze imploringly. *For Father. He cannot bear to lose us both.*

When Hongbin's mouth closed, his protests dying, Mirae continued. *Father may not have much time left, and there's no guarantee that we'll defeat the Netherking in time to come home and be with him at the end. That's a risk I must take, but you don't.*

Hongbin's shoulders slumped, the fervor in his eyes dimming like a candle burning out as he heard the truth in Mirae's words. After a moment of letting resignation sink in, Hongbin mustered up the will to ask Mirae, voice thick, "You'll keep me updated, though, right? You won't leave me and Father in the dark while you're gone."

"I will soul-walk to you as often as I can," Mirae promised, pressing a hand to her chest, where the connection between them thrummed.

Hongbin let out a shaky breath. "Fine, I'll keep everything in order until you return." His voice was flat, his eyes troubled. He was far from convinced that this was for the best.

"Thank you," Mirae said as she pulled Hongbin and her father into a tearful embrace. Then, before climbing out of the burial chamber, she approached her mother's shrouded body, ghostly white in the darkness. Bowing deeply to the woman whose power pumped through her veins, Mirae whispered a quiet farewell.

"Rest easy now," she said gently. "Feast with the gods, and assure them that their High Horomancer will not fail. Seolla will not fall on my watch, and evil will never prevail." Having delivered her vow, Mirae bowed once more and ascended from her mother's tomb.

Chapter
NINE

Just before dawn, all preparations were finally finished for Mirae's departure. Convincing the Hwabaek to let their queen leave after everything she'd done, and to trust her decision to go after the Netherking despite all the lies she'd told them, was no small feat, complicated even further by the fact that she was suggesting they let their first king regent take over in her absence.

It was a lot to ask, but once her father, the much-adored former queen's consort, who had suffered most deeply from Mirae's lies, had taken her side and emphasized the gravity of everything Mirae had learned in her switch, Sangsin Bada had begrudgingly accepted Mirae's decision to leave. Perhaps a part of her was even relieved to be rid of Mirae for once. And so, she set about helping Captain Hanyoung procure everything Mirae would need on her journey.

The pink skies of sunrise were only just peeping over the horizon when Mirae found herself at the palace gates for the third time that week, preparing once again to do something unprecedented. As usual whenever she left the palace grounds, an entourage of Wonhwa soldiers had gathered to escort her. One of the Hwabaek's stipulations was that Mirae not travel alone into Josan, despite the danger that the Netherking and his pearl posed to magic users. Even though Mirae had repealed the law prohibiting the queen of Seolla and the king of Josan from entering each other's lands, that hardly meant it was safe to do so.

Mirae didn't like the idea of putting the Wonhwa in range of the pearl's devastating spell, but it was faster to compromise with the council than argue with them. And Captain Hanyoung had reassured Mirae that the palace guards were more than willing to take on the risk of death to protect their new queen, as was their sworn duty. They knew as well as Mirae that the only thing worse than losing their lives was allowing the peninsula to fall into the Netherking's hands.

"Your Majesty, your companions are ready for departure." Captain Hanyoung's imperious voice startled Mirae out of her reverie. She turned to see the tan, broad-shouldered captain marching at the head of a small group of people, only one of whom had been asked by Mirae to accompany her.

Kimoon, dressed in a deep plum hanbok, strode just behind the captain, head held high as if in defiance of the hellish night he'd spent with the royal physician. It had been some time since Mirae had seen the exiled prince in daylight, to the point that she'd nearly forgotten what he looked like with some color in his cheeks and sunlight glistening off his silky black hair. Although he'd spent the last several hours having black water purged from his body, he looked surprisingly hale, if a little tired.

Mirae hadn't seen or spoken to him since their parting words in the Deep, but she'd sent a heartfelt message, asking him to return to Josan with her, to finish what they started. She hadn't been sure that he would be willing to face his father, or forgive Mirae for dismissing his ideas. But Kimoon's presence at the gates, chin held high, was his clear answer. An undaunted yes.

Behind him were two uninvited traveling guests. As soon as Areum had heard what had happened to the dowager queen, she'd wrested herself free of the physician to find Mirae and embrace her. They'd cried, and reminisced about Mirae's mother as long as they could, until travel preparations could be delayed no longer. While they talked, Mirae had taken the time to tell Areum about her switch, and what she'd learned about a clan of seers known as the Dark Moon Oracles.

To Mirae's surprise, Areum had heard of this secretive group of women, though she'd been taught at the temple that the offshoot oracles were a myth. Still, she promised to tell Mirae everything she knew about this mystical clan on the road, for she'd decided to accompany her to Josan. When Mirae had protested, Areum shut her up with a simple fact.

You need an oracle with you. Your Sacred Bone connection with the Netherking is a two-way street. You know where he is, but he also knows exactly where you are. If you want any sort of tactical advantage, it'll have to be through the guidance of the gods. Through an oracle like me.

There was no more protesting after that, not when Mirae looked into her friend's eyes and saw something changed in them. Ever since she'd been possessed by Sol, Areum's irises had acquired a metallic cast to them, a silver coating. Mirae wasn't sure if Areum's supplication to become the next shinmyeong had worked, but if there was any chance that the gods did indeed speak through her now, that was a caliber of divine help that Mirae could hardly afford to refuse.

Mirae returned the gentle smile Areum shot her way as she approached, her gaze sliding to the man walking beside her friend. For as soon as Siwon had heard that Areum was leaving the safety of the palace, he had insisted on accompanying her. It was his job to protect the oracles. Under no circumstances was he going to stay behind.

So it was that Mirae's entourage had grown, without her having any say in the matter. Now that everyone had gathered, she took in her companions, Captain Hanyoung, and all the brave Wonhwa with varicolored stone swords sheathed across their backs. Everyone waited for Mirae to lead them toward whatever lay ahead, to Seolla's salvation, or its doom.

One of the Wonhwa handed Mirae the reins to a horse, one of dozens saddled with traveling sacks near to bursting with provisions. Mirae nodded her thanks, mounted the waiting steed, and when everyone else had followed suit, spurred her horse forward through the open dragon gates, the rumble of a small army following close behind.

The steep, hilly road leading away from the palace was one Mirae had traveled many times by palanquin. But now, unconfined by four walls and beaded curtains, Mirae looked around freely at the beautiful landscape between her and the Seollan capital, which was nestled in the valley below, flickering in the light of sunrise like a newly unearthed treasure.

The golden dust beneath Mirae's horse contrasted prettily

with the tumbling, grassy terrain, teeming with sprawling flora and blushing with the redness of dawn. Reins in hand, Mirae took in the scenery, not sure when she'd be able to see it again.

Her quiet study of the world around her was soon interrupted by the voice of someone who had ridden up beside her. "The Netherking has had a good day's head start. I assume you have a plan to shave off some of our travel time as well?"

Mirae turned to acknowledge Kimoon's pertinent question, and was struck by how strange the Josan prince looked with his hair knotted in a bun, in keeping with the Seollan style. Mirae's eyes traced the unfamiliar silhouette of his new hairstyle, unable to decide whether his disguise suited him. It was especially jarring that, for once, his inky tresses were piled onto his head, while Mirae's flowed loosely over her shoulders, as appropriate for someone in mourning.

The moment Kimoon glanced over and caught her staring, however, all thoughts of her companion's ability to pass for a Seollan nobleman were swept clean from her mind. Mirae cleared her throat and answered his question. "You're right, we don't have the luxury of taking the long way into Josan, so instead of heading to the border town of Geumju, we're going to cross over the Josan-Seolla barrier."

"Won't the barrier incinerate us?" Siwon asked from behind, unsurprisingly listening in.

"No, I ended that enchantment months ago," Mirae reassured him. "Its only purpose, if we're honest, was to keep the citizens of Josan out of Seolla. I'd hoped that by eliminating it, the citizens of Josan would consider it an act of goodwill."

"I'm sure they did," Siwon said approvingly, the smile in his voice a warm, much-needed ray of sunshine. "And I'm glad that your foresight allows us to take a shortcut."

"Yes, we need all the advantages we can get," Kimoon said with a sigh. "We have a lot of ground to make up."

Mirae nodded uneasily. "There is some good news on that front. As far as I know, no one has heard anything about the Netherking causing a ruckus in Josan, which means he must be traveling without using magic. Provided we travel just as quietly, the speed of our horses will give us a decent chance of catching up."

"It's wise of the Netherking not to make a scene," Siwon mused. "It's not like he can simply drain the power of anyone who stands in his way, since no one in Josan *has* any powers. If he causes any trouble, he'll have to fight his way through the king's entire army. Even with the Netherking's considerable abilities, he'll likely be overwhelmed."

Mirae nodded, sharing Siwon's relief that there wouldn't be a trail of bodies to follow. No one else would die as excruciatingly as her mother, not if she could help it.

"Do we even know why he's in Josan?" Areum asked. "He must have a good reason for taking a detour, considering what's at stake."

"Yes, he must," Mirae said, turning to Kimoon, who was frowning as he considered Areum's question. As she waited for him to weigh in, Mirae mulled over her own theory—that the Netherking was out to get his long-awaited revenge against the Josan king.

He certainly had reason to despise his sometime ally. Mirae had heard from Kimoon the full extent of his father's betrayal of the Deep. The Netherking had struck a bargain with the king of Josan to bring Seolla to its knees, but the king had gone back on his word, and instead ensnared his liaison with the Deep, the Netherqueen, so that he could seize control of the most important bargaining chip he had—a corrupted Minho. Thus, the Netherking's plan to possess Mirae's brother and use him as a weapon against Seolla had been usurped, leaving the dark lord out in the cold . . . until Mirae unwittingly led Siwon right to the Netherqueen so she could be rescued. In the end, it had been the Josan king who'd lost every advantage he'd stolen, but that didn't mean the Netherking considered them even.

Still, Mirae thought, *now hardly seems like the best time for the Netherking to go looking for payback. If he's good at anything, it's waiting for the right moment to strike.*

When Kimoon finally looked up, his frown of concentration smoothed over and his eyes seemed to gleam with the elation of an epiphany. "Black water," he said, snapping his fingers. "That's what he's after."

When Mirae looked at him quizzically, he explained, "After the fortress on White Spine Mountain was abandoned, my father would have had all traces of black water taken back to the palace, either to keep it under lock and key or to continue his . . . experiments."

Choosing not to inquire about the last, disturbing thing Kimoon said, Mirae nodded at his conclusion, acknowledging the sense it made. She'd seen for herself that the pearl's corruption faded after a while, its milky glow returning if not kept drenched in black water. It stood to reason that, without a supply of that inky liquid, the Netherking's magic-draining spell would be inhibited, rendering his entire plan futile.

And since he'd been driven away from the Deep, he'd also lost his main black water source. What choice did he have but to retrieve what he could from the only other place in the peninsula that had a small reserve of it?

"You're right," Mirae said after a moment. "That must be what he's after. He can't afford to run out of black water, not with what he's using it for."

"Fortunately for you," Kimoon added, looking satisfied, an expression that suited him better than the haggard grimace he'd adopted over the past few months, "I know where my father keeps his collection of black water. If he refuses to cooperate with us, I can simply take us right to it, and beat the Netherking at his own game."

"That is good news," Mirae said, trying to smile. While she wished she could share Kimoon's optimism, she knew better than to underestimate her foe. There were countless things that could go wrong. For instance, what if the Netherking had some-how secured an invitation from the Josan king, his former ally? What was she supposed to do in that case—sneak in while the two kings conversed and assassinate the Netherking unawares, likely inciting the very war she'd fought to prevent?

And even if the Netherking wasn't a welcome guest, and managed to get caught entering Josan, creating the perfect dis-traction for Mirae to steal the black water out from underneath him, could she really allow him to slaughter whoever stood in his path? Despite what Siwon said about the Josan king's army, the Netherking wouldn't go down easily. Even without the pearl, he was formidable. Mirae had seen that herself on the shores of Wol Sin Lake. Was she really willing to sacrifice Josan lives, if need be, to save the rest of the peninsula?

All these questions weighed on her heavily, but there was one that troubled her most of all. *If I have to take the Netherking on directly, am I willing to use black water, as he did, to deliver a killing blow? Am I really ready to let Minho go?*

"Your Majesty?" Areum said gently, the corners of her silvery eyes lined with concern. "We're still days away from the Josan capital. You don't need to make any decisions yet."

Mirae let out a deep breath, unsurprised that her friend had been able to divine her turbulent thoughts. "I know. It's just . . . all this would be easier if the path before me was clear."

"If the path was clear, the gods would have been able to send almost anyone in your stead," Kimoon said with a shrug. "You were chosen to take on the Netherking for a reason, Mirae. When the time comes, you'll know what to do. I trust you . . . we all do."

"And besides," Areum said with mock grandeur, channeling her inner Hongbin, "you've got some pretty amazing friends who won't let you down. If Jisoo and Yoonhee were here, they'd tell you the same thing. You're not doing this alone."

"That's right," Siwon chimed in, his encouragement further brightening Mirae's mood. "There's nothing we can't do together."

Mirae smiled at each of her friends in turn, wishing she could feel as confident as her companions did. Up ahead, the magical boundary between Seolla and Josan gleamed on the horizon like a toothy, glowing grin. Mindful that every second counted in her race against the Netherking, Mirae urged her horse onward, letting the sound of pounding hooves and whistling wind drown out the anxious thoughts still ringing in her head.

They reached the enchanted barrier within the hour. Mirae slowed her horse as they drew near enough to hear the hum and feel the heat emanating off the luminescent wall. No matter how many times Mirae visited the Josan-Seolla border, it was always a mesmerizing sight. The illusion of antlered kirin prancing around the opalescent barrier, gazing out across the land with white-hot eyes, was an impressive one, an enchantment powered by an ancient spell Mirae didn't know the origin of. But now that the incinerating spell had been removed, the wall was nothing more than what it appeared to be—a fancy light show.

And yet, as Mirae paused before the beaming barrier, flashes of memories echoed through her mind, leaving a sharp pang in her heart. Every year, she'd gone with her mother to strengthen the wall's enchantments. Mirae used to love watching her mother embellish the barrier by weaving intricate spells with ease, inspiring Mirae to be just like her someday.

"We're ready, Your Majesty." Captain Hanyoung rode up next to Mirae, followed by all the Jade Witches in their party. Quickly wiping away the hot water pooling in her eyes, Mirae nodded for the witches to begin their work. Obediently, they bowed and raised their hands in unison.

Mirae watched the women masterfully whirl up the air between them, their combined efforts generating a gale strong enough to sweep every horse and its rider up over the wall, while also cushioning their landing on the other side. First, they sent over all the Ma-eum Mages, illusionists who could secure the perimeter before their queen arrived. One by one, they sailed through the beaming barrier, their speed carefully controlled by their sister soldiers. All of them handled the flight with grace, except for one mage whom Mirae could have sworn she heard giggle with glee.

Then it was Mirae's turn to breach the wall. She'd ridden her dragon enough times to feel no apprehension at the thought of flying through the air. Still, her stomach lurched when she felt her body lift into the sky, her horse neighing loudly in protest. Thankfully, they soared quickly over the enormous stone base of the wall and landed safely on the grass of the other side.

Her friends followed shortly after, and then the Jade Witches. Although Captain Hanyoung was flown over last, she was the first to take a discerning look at their surroundings and assume command.

"Which way, Your Majesty?" the older woman asked, inching her horse forward as if ready to get this venture over with.

Mirae looked to the exiled prince who knew the Josan capital best, but he was busy surveying the green fields of his homeland stretching for miles in every direction, his expression unreadable. Mirae wasn't sure what she'd expected him to feel upon his return, but she wasn't surprised when he immediately reached up and unknotted his hair, letting it flow freely down his shoulders. That act, at least, seemed to fill him with relief, his amber eyes for once showing a hint of the warmth that always simmered in Siwon's.

Mirae turned to the other bastard prince in their ranks, a protector who kept his own hair secured in a bun rather than in the style of his homeland. Looking between the two brothers, Mirae couldn't help but notice that, although they were both striking in their own way, the way they carried themselves—one regally, the other gallantly—made their shared blood obvious to the discerning eye.

Siwon, guessing at why she was looking in his and Kimoon's direction, spoke up first. "I spent many months in these rural areas with Suhee during her time as a shaman. If you want, I can be our first guide, while Lord Kimoon takes over once we're near the capital. He'll know that terrain better than I."

As soon as Siwon uttered Kimoon's name, the latter turned and studied the other man. Mirae briefly wondered what Kimoon made of Minho's former servant. Although she had never revealed Siwon's identity to his half brother, she knew Kimoon would have surmised the truth as soon as he saw Siwon's light eyes. As far as she knew, however, Kimoon and Siwon hadn't spoken a word to each other since the events of last year. She had no idea how they felt about each other now.

"I agree with Siwon," Kimoon said after a short pause, his expression as inscrutable as ever. "Let him take the lead for now."

"Very well," Mirae said, gesturing for Siwon to ride at the head of their group.

"As you wish, Your Majesty." At that, Siwon urged his horse to set out first, gesturing for Areum to stick close as he headed deeper into Josan, surging toward the enigmatic path Mirae was none too eager to follow.

Chapter
TEN

As much as Mirae wanted to enchant her party's horses to run tirelessly, she knew better than to break Josan's most rigid law—that no magic be permitted within its borders, on pain of death. There were some traditions even Mirae couldn't challenge. In this case, Josan's surrender to Seollan rule centuries ago had been predicated on the promise that Seollan magic would never tarnish its soil ever again. To be caught breaking that ancient vow would mean an end to the cease-fire, and a united revolt from the kingdom that barely tolerated her rule to begin with.

It eased Mirae's mind a little, at least, to know that the Netherking was similarly keeping a low profile in the magicless kingdom. All Mirae could do was try to make up time by urging Siwon to push their horses as fast as he dared, alternating between spurring forward into a brisk trot and flying across Josan's fields just shy of breakneck speed.

Eventually, Captain Hanyoung called out when it was time to give the horses a well-deserved rest. Everyone slowed their steeds as ordered, dismounting from the weary animals and letting them drink thirstily from a nearby stream.

Even though she rued having to stop when time was of the

essence, Mirae was more than a little happy to finally have her legs in a different position than the one she'd stiffly endured for the last couple of hours. She quickly found a patch of grass off the side of the road and plopped down, rubbing her sore thighs.

Kimoon and Areum soon followed suit, while Siwon remained at the head of the caravan to discuss the upcoming terrain with Captain Hanyoung. Areum collapsed next to Mirae with a groan, but Kimoon retired a little more gracefully, smoothing out his jacket before sitting down. He'd brought a sack of food with him, and began digging around for a bit of refreshment. Moments later he tossed Mirae and Areum a pair of oranges, which they caught gratefully.

Kimoon, on the other hand, selected a peeled carrot packed just for him. As he snapped it in half to consume it more elegantly, Mirae couldn't help but muse at this oddity of his. Shortly after allowing him to find refuge in Seolla, Mirae had learned that the exiled prince refused to eat anything other than foods derived from roots—except for the occasional dollop of honey in his ginseng tea. This habit was something he'd learned from his father, who believed that this diet was the only way to maintain the golden color of their eyes.

According to Josan legend, their kings were descended from Ungnyeo herself, the mythological bear woman who ate garlic and mugwort for twenty-one days to become human. She eventually married a god and gave birth to an extraordinary son. That son, whose golden eyes were a sign of his connection to deity, would later go on to found a nation that his similarly light-eyed descendants would be destined to rule.

But according to Kimoon's family lore, the further removed they became from their divine ancestry, the more their signature eye color began to dull, their connection to the heavens waning. The only way to preserve their divinity was by eating food grown within the earth itself. Mirae didn't fully understand this reasoning, but Kimoon was adamant about maintaining his family's tradition, a harmless enough ideology that Mirae never gave him any pushback on.

As for herself, Mirae was happy to indulge in all the earth's bounty, including delicious fare like the fruit in her hands. Mirae was about to dig her nails into the skin of her orange when Areum, who'd already finished peeling her own, snatched it away and set her swift fingers to work. "You may be roughing it with us for the next few days," Areum said, shaking her head, "but you're still our nation's queen. Besides, you need to preserve your strength."

"Excuse me, this queen is perfectly capable of feeding herself," Mirae said with a sniff, trying to snatch back her snack, to no avail. Areum shot her a don't-argue-with-me look, although the corners of her silver-tinted eyes were creased with a playful scowl.

Mirae grinned in return, despite herself. She knew full well that Areum was purposefully trying to keep the mood light, considering what lay ahead, and the tragedy Mirae had endured a mere two days ago. Normally, keeping Mirae's mental burden light was Hongbin's forte, but at least she still had another close friend keeping an eye on the soundness of her mind.

And Areum was spectacularly fast at peeling. Within seconds, she handed over expertly separated wedges that Mirae hastily devoured, savoring the refreshing, tangy juice with sighs of contentment. As soon as she swallowed her last mouthful, she turned to Kimoon.

"How long until we reach the capital?"

"We've got another full day of riding," Kimoon said after biting neatly into his carrot. "Then it'll be about a half day after that before we make it to the capital's gates."

As much as Mirae's muscles protested that much time atop her horse, it was a different thought that caused her to slowly lower her hands into her lap. "The Netherking had more than a whole day's head start," she said with a gulp. "I guess that means he'll be in the capital sometime tomorrow."

"Yes, very likely," Kimoon said with a shrug. "But don't forget that he doesn't know where, exactly, the black water is hidden. We have the upper hand."

"So we think," she countered, the sticky juice in her throat suddenly difficult to swallow. "He's had plenty of time to consider all the moving pieces of his escape." Something Mirae still didn't know how he'd accomplished.

A hint of something, a glint of emotion too fleeting for Mirae to catch, flashed across Kimoon's eyes before he quickly shifted them to stare down at the ground. "You're right, of course. The Netherking certainly knows how to decimate our best-laid plans."

Realizing that she had probably triggered a memory about what Kimoon had endured at the Netherking's hands, something Mirae hadn't wanted to press him about until he was ready, she quickly changed the subject.

"I told Hongbin that I would keep in touch," she said lightly, wiping small white shreds of orange pith off her hands. "I should go do that now, while we've got some time."

"Good idea," Areum said vaguely. There was a distant look in her eye as she stared at the horizon, lost in thought. "Tell him he's doing the right thing. We need him exactly where he is."

Although she raised an eyebrow at Areum's sudden trancelike state, Mirae didn't want to disturb her meditation. Instead, she lay back on the grass and pressed two fingers to her wrist. As soon as she found her heartbeat, Mirae closed her eyes and tried to follow its thrumming toward her brother, the shared magic in their veins making it so she could soul-walk to him and speak as if they were meeting in the flesh.

But, to Mirae's surprise, the link didn't seem to be working. Try as she might to search for the reverberating line to her brother, which should have been aligned with her own, she caught no hint of it leading back to Seolla. For a moment, she worried that the magicless, stagnant air of Josan was impeding her Sacred Bone connection. And then she feared something even worse.

Mirae's eyes flew open and she jumped to her feet, eyes fixed on the enchanted barrier gleaming against the horizon. *Did the Netherking circle back when I wasn't paying attention? Was I a fool for leaving my family behind?*

To her relief, however, Mirae quickly sensed out the location of the only other man she had a Sacred Bone connection with. The Netherking's heart was beating miles away, far ahead of her and her party, just as expected.

But then, where's Hongbin? Why did we lose our connection?

The only time Mirae had ever lost contact with a Sacred Bone brother was when Minho had been submerged in black water. But Hongbin was safe at home, far from the Deep. She'd never even taught him how to get past the haetae statues that guarded Wol Sin Lake.

There was only one other explanation, Mirae realized with a jolt. If the Sacred Bone link between her and her brother could only be felt here, where she was, then that meant—

Mirae whirled toward her Wonhwa guards. *It can't be*, she thought, a rush of fear and dismay heating her cheeks. *He wouldn't dare.*

"Mirae?" Kimoon frowned. "What is it?"

Ignoring both him and Areum, who looked on silently, Mirae stormed over to the Ma-eum Mages, who immediately stood and lined up at her approach. All except for one of their ranks who was slow to react, too preoccupied with their snack to see what was going on.

"Hongbin." Mirae came to a stop in front of the distracted mage, who froze, refusing to meet her eyes. Without waiting for a response, Mirae reached down and flipped the mage's wide-brimmed hat backward so fast that the string of beads dangling below their chin caught against their throat.

"Ow, that hurts, noonim!" Hongbin scooted away from Mirae's reach, rubbing his neck. "I know you're angry, but that was uncalled for."

Mirae couldn't form any of the words piling up in her throat. The anger within her was too thick, her fury like scalding-hot coals lining her chest.

"I know what you're going to say," Hongbin said, raising his hands defensively. "But I'm supposed to be here with you. I'm following my destiny just like you taught me."

"You're the *crown prince*," Mirae hissed. "The sole heir. And yet you abandoned your subjects, our *father*, in their time of need."

"You mean exactly what you did when Minho was kidnapped," Hongbin muttered. "How is this not what you do all the time?"

Before Mirae could unleash her rage on her brother, Captain Hanyoung rushed over and fell to her knees beside Hongbin. She whipped out her jade sword and held it over her head.

"This is my fault, Your Majesty," the other woman quavered. "I don't know how Seja jeoha slipped past me, but I have failed in my duty. Please, punish me and all the complicit Wonhwa as you see fit."

"Wait a minute, no one is going to be punished," Hongbin said, eyes wide. "It's no one's fault I'm here but my own. I commanded the Ma-eum Mages not to say anything, and they had to listen because you made me king regent, noonim. They had no other choice."

"Oh, I don't blame them for this." Ignoring the contrite captain, and the mages who had also fallen penitently to their knees, Mirae grabbed Hongbin by the ear, eliciting a sharp yelp as she dragged him back over to her friends so she could berate him more privately. Only when they were out of earshot of the guards did Mirae release her brother.

"Noonim, please hear me out," Hongbin started, but Mirae cut him off.

"Siwon, take him back to the palace immediately," she said,

turning to the man who had run over as soon as Hongbin's ruse had been revealed. "Get him to safety."

"I'm sorry, but I can't do that," Siwon said, bowing with regret.

"Kimoon can guide us from here," Mirae said, too angry to do more than dismiss Siwon's refusal. "We're hardly at risk of getting lost."

"It's not that, Your Majesty." Siwon hesitated. "I swore to protect Lady Areum with my life. I cannot turn back unless she is willing to do so as well."

"And I am not," Areum said, folding her arms across her chest.

To Mirae's surprise, her rage wasn't all-consuming enough to mask the additional sting of Siwon's rebuff, or the twinge of annoyance at Areum's abetting of Hongbin's disobedience.

"Look, you really shouldn't send me back," Hongbin said, waving his arms. "I know how the Netherking escaped."

Mirae's limbs froze. "What did you say?"

"I figured it out. I mean . . . I have a theory."

"Well, spit it out," Mirae snapped.

"Okay, okay." Hongbin's arms fell back down to his sides. "Just think about it. Only you can open and shut the passage to the Deep, right, noonim? Which means that, in order to escape, the Netherking must have gotten hold of your power somehow."

"Impossible," Mirae said, her patience thinning. "I never gave him the chance. You know he was locked up in impenetrable chains."

"I do know that." Hongbin began pacing back and forth. "But hear me out. What's the source of the magic you use to keep him contained?"

"It's inside me," Mirae said flatly. "Where is this going?"

"Not just inside you," Hongbin said, gesturing at the left side of her chest, where the link between them thrummed. "It's in your blood."

"What does that have to—"

Mirae's question clotted in her throat as realization dawned on her. Her hand flew to her neck, where a small, fresh white scar, wide as a mouth, hid beneath her collar. "My blood . . . holds my magic," she said slowly.

"Mirae?" Kimoon stared at her, his face looking as white as hers felt. "What is it?"

"It's my fault," she choked out. "I'm the one that freed him."

"What?" Areum and Siwon said together.

Mirae felt lightheaded enough that she thought she might collapse, the world swirling as if everything, every mistake she'd ever made, was orbiting around her at breakneck speed, threatening to crash and explode. "When I last visited Minho, the Netherking . . . bit me."

"He what?" Siwon's eyes narrowed.

Areum gasped, seeming to immediately grasp what Mirae was implying. "He managed to obtain some of your blood . . . *and* some of the black water enchanted to keep him locked away. It would have been on your skin after diving into the lake."

"And with that combination of magical elements," Hongbin said, snapping his fingers, "he had everything he needed to concoct a counterspell."

For what felt like an eternity, all Mirae could do was stand there in silence as the gravity of Hongbin's revelation sank into her like a leaden ball. Although her mouth was open as if to speak, to refute the appalling accusations levied against her, she could make no sound. Instead, all her terrible questions and their equally terrible answers spun in her head, colliding and shattering against her skull in painful bursts.

I'm responsible for the Netherking's escape. The realization brought boiling-hot water to her eyes. *I let him out. I'm the reason Mother died and Minho is lost.*

If Seolla falls, and the peninsula burns to ash, it will be all my fault.

Mirae felt her friends reach out to her, heard the consolation in their voices, but her skin had turned to stone, cold and unfeeling. Her ears attuned to only the roar of her blood, the thundering of her pulse like war drums in her head.

All my fault. Every death, every loss, the end of everything I love—
It will all be because of me.

The tumult inside her whipped around nauseatingly fast, sapping her strength and dizzying her to the point that she didn't even realize she was collapsing until she felt strong arms catch her, steadying her.

"Mirae." She heard Kimoon's voice. "This is not your fault."

It is, it is all my fault.

As if sensing her resistance, Kimoon spoke again, more insistent this time. "You are not to blame, Mirae. The Netherking's chains were flawless. He could not have freed himself, even with the right tools. There is more to his escape than we know. I'm sure of it."

Mirae didn't realize her eyes had been tightly shut until

Kimoon's vindicating words, soothing in their confidence, calmed her enough that she slowly began regaining feeling in her limbs. Soon after, the spiraling thoughts threatening to unravel her mind began to slow. Finally, when she felt steady enough to open her eyes, she looked into the golden gaze hovering just in front of her, steeled with resolve.

Mirae blinked, grateful that the world had stopped spinning, her heart beating at a normal pace once more. A second later, she realized that, based on where Kimoon stood, it wasn't his arms holding her up, bracing her against a chest exuding enough comforting heat to thaw the shock stiffening her limbs. Her embracer was someone taller than her, and broad-shouldered, a man whose heart did not beat in sync with hers.

When Siwon felt her twist up to look at him, he quickly released her, though he kept his arms raised in case she stumbled again.

But Mirae felt remarkably calm, her sense of self restored, because of both Kimoon's bold reassurance and the lingering warmth of Siwon's touch.

"Noonim, I'm sorry." Off to the side, Hongbin's body trembled with regret, his brow creased with contriteness. "I didn't mean to upset you."

Mirae shook her head tiredly. She could hardly blame Hongbin for sharing his epiphany. She *had* facilitated the Netherking's escape, even if the full extent of his schemes eluded her. Although she had regained her composure, her chest felt hollow, an exhausted wasteland no more capable of harboring the will to berate herself than the energy to reprimand her brother.

Instead of sending him away, as she'd intended, Mirae could only muster the strength to walk wordlessly to her horse, striding past the still-kneeling captain and Wonhwa. As soon as she mounted her steed, the rest of her escort silently did the same so they could continue their fraught journey to the heart of Josan.

Chapter
ELEVEN

Mirae's companions gave her a wide berth for the next few hours while they trotted as quickly as they dared across the vast fields and wide rivers of Josan's midlands. Although Mirae was grateful for some space to sit alone with her thoughts, she knew that this was no time to lose herself to guilt. Whatever her part in the Netherking's escape, she had a mother to avenge, a queendom to protect, and a destiny to fight for. She couldn't afford to drown in self-pity, not when it was imperative that she keep her wits sharp enough to cut down the Inconstant Son when they met again. A man she could feel she was closing in on, and who deserved to be punished by her most capable self.

The best way to stay focused, Mirae soon learned, was by focusing on her breaths, inhaling the clean, crisp Josan air while taking in its equally refreshing countryside.

The farther she traveled, the easier that task became. As Siwon led their party past an ever-increasing number of villages, Mirae couldn't help but be charmed by the sights around her, a reminder of all the beauty and precious lives she had yet to save.

Mirae took it all in with wide, curious eyes. The sides of farmhouses paneled with strings of peeled persimmons hanging out to dry; wooden fishing weirs splicing the long gray rivers; and long strips of indigo-dyed fabrics twisting in the wind, their greenish hues gradually deepening into a rich ocean blue. Had Mirae entered Josan under different circumstances, she would have asked Siwon to stop and teach her about all the interesting things she was seeing, and perhaps share stories about his travels with Suhee.

As it was, it was all Mirae could do to remain absorbed enough in her surroundings to block out all other thoughts. Thankfully, the inherent beauty of the sweeping rice fields and glinting streams kept her too awe-inspired to do much more than stare at the world around her.

And she wasn't the only one gawking at an unexpected sight. As her royal convoy sped past thatch-roofed villages and merchant caravans on the road, Mirae caught many a Josan citizen eyeing her and the Wonhwa. Although she smiled and nodded at anyone who met her gaze, not a single soul returned her greeting. Instead, they frowned at the Seollan soldiers and nobles passing by, distrust creasing the lines of their tan, freckled faces.

As the sky began to darken, cooling the air enough to make Mirae's cheeks stiffen from the chilly wind, Captain Hanyoung finally called for their party to make camp for the night. The horses needed rest, and so did their riders. Everyone obediently slowed to a stop and dismounted.

While Mirae groaned as she rubbed her tired legs, the Wonhwa got right to work spreading out bedrolls and whipping out a dozen prepared dishes for Mirae and her companions to eat before retreating to stand guard around their queen and king regent, encircling them like the stiff, sharp petals of a lotus flower.

It felt like it had been days since Mirae had sat down and had a proper meal. Even the humble spread before her seemed like a feast compared to the simple orange she'd had earlier. Mirae settled eagerly in front of the food and threw open the lids of the brass bowls filled to the brim with side dishes—several of which were made out of root vegetables Kimoon could also enjoy. Her friends soon joined her, as eager as she to dig in.

However, knowing that no one was going to touch their food until their queen began eating, Mirae grabbed her chopsticks before anyone else and plunged them into the platter of cucumber kimchi—her favorite—and scarfed down her first, delicious bite.

No one spoke for several minutes as they devoured their meal, hardly chewing in their eagerness to fill their grumbling bellies. Only once they were full, and the bowls between them picked clean, did the silence of the past few hours begin to relax, the tension between them ebbing alongside their gnawing hunger.

Hongbin let out a long, contented sigh and lay back against his bedroll. "I know the reason we're out here is very serious, but man, look at those stars. There's something about Josan that calls to me. It's like I just can't stay away."

Mirae raised an eyebrow. Before she could remind Hongbin that his inclusion in their party was still up in the air, Areum chimed in. "You used to have quite the fantasy about wedding a fair Josan prince," the oracle teased. "A political marriage that ended up becoming a tender love story."

Hongbin chuckled. "True, but that's not what draws me to this place. I mean, I wouldn't *turn down* a love story for the ages.

How about it, Kimoon?" Hongbin turned to face the startled prince, who looked as taken aback as Mirae felt—a feeling that surprised her. "Do you have any gentlehearted brothers who would write quite the romantic tale with me?"

Kimoon cleared his throat. "I'm afraid they're all quite taken in by the need to impress my father, who still hasn't chosen his heir. They're groomed to become cutthroat, cruel, and opportunistic. In my humble opinion, I was by far the 'gentlest' soul in the palace. Well, aside from Soori. He was the youngest prince, and the only one to show the bastards any kindness. You remind me a lot of him, Hongbin. In any case," Kimoon added quickly, "you deserve better than any of my father's sons."

Mirae was surprised that Kimoon had let slip a tidbit about his former life, but she didn't have any time to dwell on that, for Hongbin had already moved on. "I suppose I'll have to search for a fair beau somewhere else, then," her brother sighed.

"Well, I would recommend a certain handsome, kind prince who lives outside the Josan palace," Areum said with a mischievous smile, "but Siwon's heart is already spoken for."

Siwon choked on the water he was drinking out of his canteen and descended into a fit of coughs. Mirae felt a lump form in her throat at Areum's knowing look, a knot of feelings she wasn't prepared to untangle.

"Is it true, Siwon?" Hongbin asked, thumping the other man on the back until his hacking subsided. "Is there someone who's caught your eye?"

"I—" Siwon stammered, avoiding everyone's eyes. "Yes, my heart is . . . committed to the oracles." He took a deep breath.

"And they keep me too busy to think about much else."

The corners of Areum's lips twitched with disappointment, but she said lightly, "And a noble cause it is, too. Hopefully someday you'll have time to think about those other interests you've told me about."

Siwon cleared his throat and quickly turned the conversation back to Hongbin. "Surely there are some Seollan noblemen who would make fine husbands."

Hongbin sighed again. "A few. Not that it matters. Sacred Bone sons don't get final say in who they marry. I'll just have to make sure I don't annoy my noonim too much, so she'll pick a handsome man who will live to dote on me."

"And bring you a basket of sweet, crispy bae every day," Areum said brightly, remembering Hongbin's favorite fruit.

"Yes," Kimoon added, a little too loudly. "As many as you can *pear.*"

His quip was so abrupt that, for a beat, Mirae didn't register what he'd said. But when she and the others finally realized what had happened, they couldn't help but bark out laughs of surprise.

"Did you just make a pun?" Hongbin crowed.

Basking in his friends' delight, Kimoon performed another first; his cheeks pinkened with embarrassment. "Was it really that unexpected?"

"Unexpected?" Hongbin shrilled. "I didn't know you even *had* a sense of humor!"

"On the contrary, I know quite a few jokes," Kimoon said. "I just thought a little levity would be appreciated after our trying day."

"Let's hear them!" Hongbin clapped. "Tell them all!"

But Mirae held up a hand, silencing him. "Look, I appreciate you all trying to lighten the mood, but we've got a long day's ride ahead. We should get some sleep."

Hongbin lowered his arms as he sobered. "When you say *we*," he said cautiously, "does that mean you've decided I can stay?"

Mirae studied her brother, his cheeks rosy and his hair red-tinged with sunset. Backlit by the setting celestial orb that sparked memories of her and Hongbin slicing their hands on a stairway of swords, racing the sun to the heavens. She hesitated and, for a moment, shot her eyes over to Areum, who was staring back at her. Her friend's silvery irises sparkled like coins slyly exchanging hands as she nodded, seemingly assuring Mirae that the gods, who were closer to her oracle friend than ever, hadn't been warning Mirae of Hongbin's future but preparing her for it.

Mirae's gaze fell to her lap as she sighed, hoping she wouldn't regret what she said next. "Yes, you can stay."

Hongbin pumped a fist excitedly and grinned at the congratulatory pats on the back he received from Siwon and Areum. Only Kimoon, who, like Mirae, had witnessed the Netherking's terrifying escape, mirrored her trepidation. Grave danger lay ahead, and another ally at risk of ending up in harm's way was nothing to celebrate.

"Apologies for the interruption, Your Majesty," Captain Hanyoung said, appearing at the edge of the gathering. "I've set up the night's watch. I recommend you all get some sleep."

Mirae thanked the captain as she and the others shuffled over to the bedrolls prepared for them. Mirae eagerly snuggled into the silky sheets atop a thick mat of tightly bound straw, and it wasn't long before utter exhaustion forced her lids closed. Within minutes, she succumbed to the heavy embrace of deep slumber.

Mirae woke to a strange sound, as if someone was hissing into her ear. When her eyes cracked open, the first thing she saw was the distant horizon, bloodred with sunrise. The deep purple veil of the sky was dotted with ruddy clouds that looked like splatters of hibiscus tea. Mirae pulled herself into a sitting position and surveyed her surroundings, looking for the source of the noise that had roused her. Her gaze passed over the two Wonhwa standing guard a few yards away, and then her sleeping friends. Moments later, her eyes flew over to Areum, who was sitting up and staring right at her.

Mirae was about to ask her eonni if the hissing had woken her, too, but the words died in her throat as quickly as they'd formed.

Something was wrong. Areum didn't look like herself. Her body was rigid, as still as a pillar. She stared back at Mirae as if in a trance, not really seeing her, her silvery eyes glowing softly, luminous and round like full moons.

"Eonni," Mirae breathed, unsure what was happening or what to do. A second later, Areum answered those questions for her.

"You are the Unnamed Dragon, High Horomancer of Seolla?" Areum sounded even stranger than she looked. Though she spoke softly, inquisitively, it sounded as if several people were talking at once, their voices vibrating with immeasurable, unknown power. When Mirae didn't immediately answer, too stunned to respond, Areum, or whoever was speaking through her, tilted her head to one side.

"Y-Yes, I am she," Mirae finally mustered, trembling. "Who are you?"

Areum paused before answering. "I am the missing balance," she whispered. "The one who warned, but remained ignored."

Beside Mirae, the others were stirring, pulled from sleep by the quiet commotion. Unsure if this "missing balance" was friend or foe, Mirae timidly inquired, "And what is it you want?"

For a few seconds, Areum stared at Mirae expressionlessly, as if thinking very carefully about her next words. While she sat there contemplating, Siwon's eyes fluttered open. As soon as he saw Areum, he threw off his blanket and sat bolt upright.

"Lady Areum?" He was beside her in a moment. When she didn't respond, he whipped his head toward Mirae. "What's happening?"

"I believe we're in the presence of a deity," Mirae said quietly, even though the entire camp was awake, watching her confront Areum warily. "A new shinmyeong has been called. Now a god is speaking to us through her."

Siwon's eyes tightened with displeasure, blazing golden suns next to Areum's unblinking moons. He knew better than to touch someone radiating divine energy, but he stayed close by as Areum continued, "Fear not, I have not come to harm this vessel, but to offer a warning. After this, you will never hear from me again."

"And what is your warning?" Mirae asked, as eager as Siwon for this heavenly being to leave Areum's body, and soon.

"This ancient conflict you seek to end began with the gods'

folly," Areum said, her voice thundering across the camp. "It cannot end without correcting it."

"And how do I do that?" Mirae asked.

"By edict, I cannot be more direct," Areum said, her conjoined voice humming with regret. "This visit alone may prove disastrous. But I have been watching you, Unnamed Dragon. I have witnessed the limits you put upon yourself, the inherited morals you cling to. I came to inform you that in order to fulfill your destiny and restore harmony to the peninsula, you will have to make a sacrifice you are not yet ready to bear. I must urge you to reassess your commitment to your mission. What are you willing to do, or lose, to save us all—mortal and gods alike? Your answer will determine all our fates."

Mirae's mouth opened to confidently answer the deity's question with a single, all-encompassing word: *Anything*.

But her reply died in her throat, diminished by the rush of thoughts that flooded her mind, proving that her response was a lie. Reminders of when her so-called inherited morals, an instinct to preserve her family and queendom at all costs, as her ancestors had, kept her from making a necessary sacrifice. She had refused to lose Minho, even when his death would have meant the end of the Netherking. When Kimoon offered a repugnant yet viable way of getting everything she wanted, she had refused to tarnish her character by resorting to dark magic. A Seollan queen had to be better than that, she'd reasoned. There had to be lines she was unwilling to cross. But where had that gotten her? Who, exactly, had her morals saved?

No, I am not willing to sacrifice anything, she admitted, heart sinking. *I never have been.*

At that thought, another memory swam to the surface, a deep-sea colossus lurking in the depths of her recollections.

More than a year ago, back at White Spine Fortress, the Deep Deceiver had risen out of her shattered seong-suk to offer a warning similar to the one Mirae had just heard. Scowling, Mirae's murky blue ancestor had reprimanded Mirae for showing compassion to the Netherqueen. An echo of a mistake she herself made long ago when she chose to preserve the life of Prince Dasan and his rebels by casting them into the Deep.

You are woefully unprepared for everything to come. . . . Your naivete horrifies me, the Deep Deceiver had seethed. When Mirae asked what she meant by that, the spirit had insisted that the Inconstant Son could only be stopped by Mirae's most violent side.

No matter the heartbreak, she had admonished, eager to impart as much knowledge as she could before her soul disappeared forever, *no matter the injustice or the unbearable suffering, do not fight this war with your heart. I refused to be a monster, and that has doomed us all. . . .*

"It is not too late," Areum said, the being within her seeming to read Mirae's thoughts. "An impossible choice lies ahead. When it comes, you must not hesitate."

"Tell me what to prepare for," Mirae pleaded, knowing full well she would not get a direct answer. "If you want me to be ready for anything, then tell me what awaits me."

But it seemed Areum's possessor had shared as much as they could. Instead of responding to her demand, Areum turned toward the bloodred horizon. "His dark treachery is far from over," she said quietly. "He, too, will serve his purpose. Balance will come, one way or another, and the folly of the gods will finally be wiped clean. It all depends on you, Unnamed Dragon, and how much darkness you can wield without succumbing to it."

Areum's ominous prophecy reminded Mirae of the last thing the Deep Deceiver had said before her soul dispelled into mist. *They are not broken, those who can embrace both the light and the dark. After all, if the gods' hands are not clean, their servants' can't be, either.*

No sooner had those foreboding words trailed off in her mind than Areum's head slumped forward, the starry glow extinguishing in her eyes. Siwon reached out and caught her before setting her down onto her bedding. He shook Areum gently, attempting to rouse her. But the oracle was locked in a deep slumber, still breathing, but motionless as a corpse. Siwon looked at Mirae anxiously. "What do we do? How can we help her?"

Mirae shook her head regretfully. The expression on Siwon's face pained her as much as her own soul-numbing shock over what had just happened, as well as the troubling promise of a terrible choice lying in wait. Something she had been warned multiple times that she wasn't ready to face. Just as she selfishly began to wish that she, like Areum, had someone's soothing touch to comfort her, she felt something warm rest against her shoulder.

"Are you all right, Mirae?" Kimoon was beside her, close enough that his long, sleep-mussed hair mingled with her own.

Mirae didn't know how to answer his question. Instead, she silently rested her head against his, too weary to do anything more than accept his mercifully wordless embrace.

Chapter
TWELVE

Mirae must have drifted off in Kimoon's arms, because the next thing she knew, she was opening her eyes and staring up at the indigo canopy of the cloudless sky. Worried that she'd overslept, Mirae sat up and looked around at the camp, which had been neatly packed up while she was out. The Wonhwa were standing by their horses while Mirae's other companions—Kimoon, Siwon, Hongbin, and an exhausted-looking Areum—stood just a few yards away, chatting quietly among themselves.

"Why didn't anyone wake me?" Mirae panicked. "What time is it?"

Kimoon, who was the closest to her, raised his hands. "You were only sleeping for about an hour," he soothed, walking over to grab the blanket she'd tossed aside and begin folding it. "We didn't disturb you because we wanted to make sure you and Lady Areum got enough rest. She's only been up for a couple of minutes herself."

Mirae's ire evaporated as she looked over at her friend, whose under-eyes were pink and swollen with weariness, her usually rosy cheeks now as pale as sun-bleached parchment. Mirae swallowed her protests and nodded. "Well, let's not waste any more time."

The Wonhwa moved swiftly, as if she'd barked out a command. Within moments, they'd assisted everyone with mounting their horses. Soon enough, everyone was ready to depart. Except for Areum, who still looked drowsy enough that she might pass out at any second. Siwon, whose horse stuck close beside hers, frowned over at his charge. "Perhaps Lady Areum and I should ride together," he suggested as Areum tipped forward, struggling to keep her eyes open.

"I'm sorry, but I need you at the front," Captain Hanyoung said, shaking her head. "You and I will be setting the speed, so I can't have you worrying about someone else."

"I'll look after her!" Hongbin piped up, eager to prove his usefulness and remain in Mirae's good graces. When Mirae granted him permission with a nod, Hongbin scooted forward in his saddle so Areum could climb up behind him, assisted by Wonhwa who helped lift her into place. Siwon wasn't fully satisfied, however, until the soldiers tied one of their thick sashes around the pair of riders, securing Areum to her guardian.

For her part, Areum was too out of it to protest all the fuss. She smiled gratefully when Siwon draped a blanket around her shoulders and encouraged her to sleep. Only when she obligingly rested her head against Hongbin's back did Siwon finally allow Captain Hanyoung to trot him over to the head of the convoy.

Less than a minute later, the procession began to move. At first, when Mirae urged her horse forward, she made sure to ride close enough to Hongbin that she could be of assistance if he or Areum needed anything. But as they continued riding along, Hongbin began humming happily, and Areum seemed to be resting well, so Mirae gradually stopped hovering, trusting her brother with his obligation while she focused on hers.

As troubling as that morning's visitation had been, Mirae felt that she owed it to Areum to delve back into the urgent message delivered to her, and do her best to internalize it.

But, try as she might to focus on the divine visitor's cryptic warning, and what unbearable sacrifice she would soon be forced to make, another perturbing thought kept sneaking in, distracting her like a snake lurking outside a henhouse.

Deep down, Mirae worried that Areum's daunting new calling as shinmyeong was only conferred upon her because Mirae, in her selfishness, had appropriated the Kun Sunim Trial, abusing its true purpose to help her liberate Minho. *Was Areum always meant to assume this role*, Mirae wondered guiltily, *and I destined to pave the way? Or was a shinmyeong only called because I needed correction? Am I really the gods' chosen champion, or am I only proving to be the arrogant false queen the Netherking thinks me to be?*

"I know that look," she heard someone say, pulling her from her thoughts. Mirae turned toward the sound of Kimoon's voice, surprised that she hadn't noticed him ride up beside her. "I've always found that the best way to get rid of dark, brooding thoughts is by distracting myself with a delicious snack. Care to test my theory?"

Mirae wasn't in the mood to self-soothe, not with the gravity of the accusations she was levying against herself, but something stopped her from rejecting Kimoon's offer outright. The longer she looked at him, the more she realized that there was something different about him. A lightness and a warm gleam to his honey-colored eyes. Whatever was causing this change felt just as sudden and mystifying as the questions Mirae was grappling with.

Interpreting her silence as permission, Kimoon reached into the provisions satchel fastened to his saddle and, after fishing around for a few seconds, procured an onion. When Mirae raised her eyebrow, unimpressed, Kimoon cleared his throat and asked, "Don't you know how to show proper respect to this unsung hero of flavorful cuisine?"

When Mirae said nothing in return, Kimoon tried, unsuccessfully, to hide a smile before bending into a bow as low as was appropriate for a formal greeting, and stated, "The correct thing to say is *onion-haseyo, oh incompara-bulb one*."

As pleased as Kimoon was with himself, Mirae couldn't even bring herself to force a polite chuckle. Instead, her nose wrinkled involuntarily.

"Are all your puns going to be about food?" she asked, trying to smooth out her grimace into a pained smile before Kimoon straightened.

Thankfully, she succeeded. Blissfully heedless of his audience's tragic reaction to his attempt at humor—which Mirae hoped he hadn't spent a long time coming up with—Kimoon flourished the onion proudly in his hand. "I find wordplay comes easiest to me when I make it about things I already enjoy thinking about."

Stopping herself from begging Kimoon to find a new hobby, Mirae instead inquired, "Why the sudden preoccupation with comedy?"

"It's for you, of course."

When Mirae eyed him quizzically, Kimoon's uncharacteristic blitheness faded, and his serious demeanor slid back into place. "I thought I might try something new. Instead of acting as a taskmaster, relentlessly ensuring neither of us forgets the stakes of our mission, I thought our partnership could benefit from a little levity. Something to keep the demons at bay, instead of letting them drive us."

Kimoon looked down at his hands, tightly clutching his horse's reins. Mirae wondered once more what terrible memories he harbored of the Netherking's escape, something she didn't want to probe him about before he was ready. Until then, it seemed natural that he would cling to a coping mechanism. Taking a page out of Hongbin's book was as good a place to start as any.

"There's great valuc in what you do," Mirae said, hoping Kimoon could hear the sincerity in her voice. "I need people by my side who feel the weight of things with me."

"I know," Kimoon said, letting out a breath. "But for so long, I made that my sole purpose. I believed that if I faced the shadows without flinching, I'd help Minho, and you, find the light at the other side of all this. Now I realize that there was a cost to my hubris. It was arrogant of me to push myself so hard, and dismiss the power of a little optimism. Now I know that I should always carry some light with me. For both our sakes. Which is why," he declared, sitting taller in his saddle, "I've made a new goal. I've decided that I'm going to make us both laugh every day we're together. Don't try to stop me, either. You know how stubborn I am when I set my mind to something."

She did indeed. When Kimoon had vowed he wouldn't rest

until he reversed the harm he'd done to Minho, he'd never once strayed from that promise. He supported Mirae's and her mother's work tirelessly, gathering and preparing rare ingredients, reading countless tomes about ancient healing practices, and tending to Minho's body as the only magicless person able to touch him. Mirae had also seen for herself how deeply troubled Kimoon grew day by day as their experiments failed. Kimoon wasn't the type to give up, but he was hardest on himself when failure seemed imminent.

A trait he learned from his father, no doubt, Mirae thought. *Thanks to the vile competition the Josan king propagates among his own flesh and blood.*

To Kimoon, who was waiting for a reaction to his news, Mirae said, "Well, I think you'll make a fine light bringer, and a superb jokester. You just need . . . a little practice."

"Practice, yes." Kimoon narrowed his eyes in determination. "I will exercise my comedic faculties every day, until I become proficient in humor. I estimate that if I practice at least one hour a day, I'll easily be able to elicit a laugh from anyone I encounter within a month."

Somehow, the way Kimoon talked about improving his jokes so seriously struck Mirae as funny. Before she knew it, a small giggle spilled out of her mouth.

That brief slip of sound had an instantaneous effect on Kimoon. He sat up straighter in his saddle, a crooked grin dimpling his cheeks.

"Do my ears deceive me"—he beamed—"or did my lady just laugh?"

Seeing Kimoon like this, utterly changed from his usual stoic self to someone with a silly side, only amused Mirae even more. "Good for you, Kimoon," she chuckled. "You reached your goal for the day."

"One down," he said with a nod. "And many, many years to go."

Though he said those last words casually, the expression on his face suddenly changed, his blushing delight deepening to the crimson of embarrassment. Before Mirae could puzzle over this abrupt shift, Hongbin called over his shoulder.

"Lady Areum wants something to eat!"

Mirae immediately urged her horse forward. Kimoon quickly followed, reaching into his bag and procuring a cucumber, one of Areum's favorite snacks. As soon as he was close enough, he offered it to her, and Areum smiled gratefully.

"Thank you," she said, crunching into the refreshing treat.

"No, thank *you*," Kimoon said, hiding a smile. "I'm actually glad to be rid of it. It was quite cucumber-some to carry around."

Kimoon's eyes shot over to Mirae, checking to see if she might laugh a second time. Thankfully, she didn't have to, for Hongbin let out a loud guffaw that stole back Kimoon's attention. "Good one!" he chortled.

Mirae just shook her head and smiled as the two men struck up a conversation about all the things that cracked them up. Soon, their dialogue turned to other topics, like Josan fashion, classic poetry, and finally back to Soori, Kimoon's younger brother, who, it sounded like, really was a lot like Hongbin. The two princes chatted for some time, leaving Mirae alone with her thoughts, until it was time to stop for lunch and rest their horses.

After a quick meal of rice porridge and the last of the pre-pared side dishes, they set off again, this time with Kimoon taking the lead, for they were finally starting to leave the rural farmlands behind.

Siwon, who seemed relieved to be able to keep Areum in his sights again, immediately began fussing over the tired oracle as he rode beside her, tucking the blanket tighter around her and stocking her lap up with snacks. Seeing him so dedicated to their mutual friend warmed Mirae's heart, but also, unexpectedly, sent a pang through it.

Surprised at herself, Mirae started to shake off the sudden, strange twinge of envy. But before it had quite abated, Siwon turned and caught Mirae staring. Thankfully, he looked away before he could see her face flush, though he himself sat up straighter in his saddle under Mirae's gaze, and squared his shoulders as if that would detract from the dark circles growing under his eyes, nearly as deep as Areum's.

Siwon remained like that, stiff and poised, until Areum finally slipped into a peaceful slumber. Then his posture soft-ened as he let his horse drift back next to Mirae's, sending a thrill of delight through her that she tried, unsuccessfully, to ignore.

For a while, she and Siwon rode side by side in a comfort-able silence, preoccupied with their own thoughts—Siwon likely worrying over Areum's condition while Mirae tried to think of a way to help ease his mind. *Does he blame me for what happened to her?* Mirae wondered as the man stared straight ahead, looking a little tense. *Does he think me a fool for trying to free Suhee with an*

ulterior motive and a terrible plan—one that may end up destroying
another woman he clearly cares about?

As the ruby flush of dusk began flooding the sky, Mirae couldn't stand the silence between them any longer. She cleared her throat, trying to think of something to say to break the ice. Between her and Hongbin, her brother had inherited all their father's social skills.

"So," she began weakly, "how does our brisk ride through the Josan countryside compare to living in a remote oracle monastery?"

For several seconds, Siwon didn't answer. Mirae held her breath, only letting it out in a rush when Siwon finally responded, his voice warm and light, the way it always was whenever he addressed her. "Well," he said thoughtfully, "the food's about the same, but my thighs hurt a lot more."

Mirae was so relieved at Siwon's easygoing tone that she let out a snort despite herself. Her body suddenly felt light enough to fly the rest of the way through Josan. "You do seem to be straddling a particularly barrel-chested horse," she noted.

"Indeed I am," Siwon said. It pleased Mirae that the remaining tension in his shoulders relaxed as they chatted. "While all the other steeds were grazing and taking strolls through the countryside, mine did a thousand push-ups every day."

Mirae chuckled at the ridiculous image. When she saw Siwon glance back over at Areum, however, she obligingly changed the subject, even though it sent a flicker through her heart. "You and Areum have gotten quite close over the last year," she said lightly. "Were you surprised when she was selected as a Kun Sunim candidate?"

"Not at all." Siwon shook his head. "She's incredibly gifted. I might not have any prophetic abilities myself, but having been partially raised by a shaman, my knowledge of prognostication runs deeper than anyone might think. And believe me, Lady Areum is special."

A smile tugged at the corners of his lips until, a second later, he seemed to remember himself, and gestured deferentially toward Mirae. "Of course, my amateur assessment of magical prowess is worthless, coming from someone as unimpressive as myself."

"Nothing about you is unimpressive," Mirae disagreed, surprised at how much she meant that. Siwon seemed a little taken aback by her sincerity as well, and for a moment, they just looked at each other. Then, ducking her head so Siwon wouldn't see the heat rushing into her cheeks, Mirae quickly said, "It's about time to stop for dinner, and rest the horses."

"Yes, I agree," Siwon said, and obediently spurred Himmal onward to relay Mirae's suggestion to the front. Relieved that Siwon had graciously allowed her to change the subject, Mirae thought she had successfully evaded any fallout of her humiliating admission. That is, until Hongbin turned just enough to look back at her and wiggle his eyebrows.

Mirae's face flushed hotter, uncomfortably warm enough that as soon as she slowed her horse and dismounted, she headed toward a nearby creek to splash her face with its crystal clear water while the Wonhwa set out the day's final spread.

Dinner was short, hastily gobbled under Captain Hanyoung's watchful eye. As soon as the last morsel was swallowed, she herded everyone back onto their horses, pushing them onward until the cool, dark blanket of night swaddled the world with frosted starlight.

When they set up camp that night, the mood was somber. Mirae knew everyone was worried about what tomorrow would bring, the day they finally reached the Josan capital. The closer they traveled to their destination, the closer they drew to the Netherking as well.

As Mirae settled into her bedding, eyelids heavy with exhaustion, she couldn't help but feel relieved to bring this slow march toward danger to an end. Although the gods had warned that she may not be ready for what the next day would bring, she never believed that she would be able to defeat the Inconstant Son alone.

Warmed by the hope her companions had filled her heart with that day, Mirae closed her eyes, knowing that Hongbin and her friends would stand beside her through thick and thin, perhaps even being the difference between victory and defeat. She let that comforting thought sit snugly inside her as she succumbed to sleep's welcome embrace.

Chapter

THIRTEEN

Not long after setting out the next morning, Mirae finally saw their destination. Up ahead, she could barely make out the faint outline of a stone wall slinking along the horizon, as well as the pointy, curved tips of the tallest roofs of the Josan capital.

At their current pace, Mirae calculated that she and her entourage would be at the main gates in just a few hours. And, with any luck, they'd arrive before the Netherking managed to acquire the black water they were both after. Even though the sight of the sprawling city, gleaming like a blood-drenched dagger in the heated glow of sunrise, made Mirae more nervous with every step, she took some comfort in the fact that if the Netherking had accomplished his goal, he would have announced his newfound invincibility most dramatically. For now, it seemed, the Netherking was being as cautious as ever, and that meant there was still time to beat him at his own game.

Soon enough, the stone gates of Josan's capital appeared before Mirae, near white in the noonday sun. As she and her companions joined the line of people trying to enter the city, Mirae couldn't help but notice the hostile looks shot in the direction of the Wonhwa, or the low murmurs of the Josan citizens trying to figure out who, exactly, the escorted Seollan nobles were, what they wanted, and, most of all, why there was a Josan prince among them. Kimoon held his head high, allowing his long hair—which he'd tied up halfway in the Josan noble style—and golden eyes to signify his status, a peculiarity that kept the citizens from outright accosting Mirae's party.

That is, until a group of soldiers pushed the crowd back, approaching Mirae briskly. She recognized their armor. She'd seen it before, the full-body bronze mail and purple tunics of the king's royal guard. Of course, last time they'd been filled by mindless soldiers, a part of the dark army the Netherking had promised the Josan king in exchange for his freedom.

Now it appeared that the king's soldiers were regular, unenchanted men in possession of their own minds, their own will, as would be expected in the heartland of a kingdom where magic was forbidden. Mirae barely had time to feel a modicum of relief over this before her "welcoming party" drew close enough for her to see the unrestrained hatred in their eyes, and the knife-deep creases of their scowls.

Captain Hanyoung was quick to intercept the guards, flanked by dozens of Wonhwa. "We come as an official royal envoy," she declared. "Who is your commanding officer? I require an escort to the palace."

"I'm afraid that's impossible." The man addressing Captain Hanyoung had a familiar voice. Detached, and chillingly civil. When he stepped through the parting soldiers, Mirae suppressed a gasp, and noticed Kimoon stiffen on his horse beside her. Captain Keon, who had served Kimoon faithfully at the fortress atop White Spine Mountain, was one of the few members of Kimoon's personal guard to refuse sanctuary in Seolla and pledge to help Mirae extinguish the Netherking's dark army of mindless soldiers. Instead, he'd chosen to return to his king and face his wrath for failing to detain both Minho and the Netherqueen.

Fortunately for him, it appeared his loyalty to the Josan king had paid off. He still wore the feathered military hat he'd worn before, denoting his unstripped rank, and seemed to have a tight leash on the royal guards, who didn't so much as twitch without permission, despite clearly wanting to face off with the equally disciplined Wonhwa.

"I don't believe you understand the gravity of my request," Captain Hanyoung said, her voice just as cold as Captain Keon's. "My charges require an audience with His Majesty. It is a matter of utmost urgency."

"I know who you are. All of you." Captain Keon's gaze shifted to rest on Kimoon, his former master, now a Josan deserter. If he felt any contempt for his sometime liege, however, he didn't show it. Moments later, his eyes flitted over to Mirae, Hongbin, and Siwon, whose faces he also recognized. Every second he spent studying those who had humiliated his king, giving none of his thoughts away, made Mirae's heart race faster. "Give me one good reason why I shouldn't send you all back where you belong."

"Because I bring vital news for my father's ears alone," Kimoon cut in. "You know I wouldn't return unless it was of dire importance."

Captain Keon seemed unimpressed by Kimoon's declaration, prompting Mirae to take a deep breath, resolving to do what she'd hoped to avoid: exert her authority over those who deeply resented her sovereignty.

But time was of the essence. The Netherking could be securing the black water at that very moment. "You do indeed know who I am, Captain Keon," she said loudly, half surprised her voice didn't tremble. "Which means you're also aware that you have no right to detain me. Your High Queen demands to speak with your king. By my own decree, I am allowed to enter your lands whenever I wish, just as your king may enter mine. So, stand down, and let me pass."

Silence fell between the two groups in the wake of her bold command, and yet Mirae could practically hear the sparks of indignation crackling in the air. After a long, tense moment, Captain Keon inclined his head stiffly, as if every fiber of his body was screaming at him to attack rather than obey.

"As you wish, Your Majesty." He said the last two words tightly, as taut as the clenching muscles of his jaw. "You may proceed."

As soon as Captain Hanyoung flicked her reins, however, Captain Keon's head shot up, as quickly as his hands. "I'm afraid you must enter alone, Your Majesty. Your guards are not covered by this new law of yours."

A smug grin twitched at the corners of his lips as Captain Hanyoung opened her mouth to protest, eyes practically flashing with fury. But Mirae spurred her horse forward, cutting the other woman off before she started the very fight Captain Keon was trying to provoke. "Very well," Mirae agreed, ignoring her captain's mutinous look. "My guards will remain here, but my other companions will remain by my side. This is nonnegotiable. Allow this, and we will submit to whatever rules you have in place for those meeting your king."

"Your Majesty," Captain Hanyoung protested. "I cannot permit this."

The look in the other woman's eyes sent a dagger through Mirae's heart. She was struck once again by the similarities between Captain Hanyoung and her predecessor, the ever-loyal Captain Jia, who had begged Mirae not to risk her life carelessly, making it almost impossible to keep her safe.

Praying that she wasn't once again making that same mistake, Mirae offered Captain Hanyoung what she hoped was a reassuring smile. "Wait for me here, and keep an eye out for the Netherking. Send word if you feel his dark magic nearby."

Most of all, stay safe and out of the way, Mirae wanted to add. If there was one thing she was certain of, it was that if she had to watch another innocent, magic-adept soul die at the Netherking's hands, mutilated by the corrupted pearl, she wouldn't be able to bear it. Although Captain Hanyoung looked far from swayed, there must have been something about Mirae's expression that compelled her to nod brusquely, lips tightly pressed to contain the stream of objections she desperately wanted to spew.

Having secured one captain's begrudging compliance, Mirae turned to Captain Keon next, meeting his gaze unflinchingly. Unlike Captain Hanyoung, he didn't appear the least bit surprised by Mirae's refusal to back down. He knew, perhaps better than anyone else in Josan, the depths of her stubbornness. Perhaps that was why, after a moment, he also nodded, and ordered his men to fall back. "Allow Her Majesty to pass," he called out, eyes flickering to Kimoon. "And all those shielded by her protection."

With that, Captain Keon motioned for Mirae and her companions to dismount and follow him. While half the guards remained behind to keep the Wonhwa in check, the rest moved to surround Mirae and her small envoy, leading them past the gawking citizens and through the main gate.

As soon as she crossed into the capital, Mirae felt Kimoon nudge her. When she turned to look at him, he offered her his arm. "We should put our allyship on display," he urged. "It would send a clear message that our two nations can put differences aside and work together."

Despite the sense his suggestion made, Mirae balked at Kimoon's proposal. She didn't know a lot about Josan culture, but thanks to Hongbin, she'd heard a great deal about their courting protocols—which was how she knew that linking arms with someone who was not a blood relative could be misconstrued as a sign of betrothal. As much as Mirae agreed with Kimoon's stated intention, the idea of making a public gesture that could distinguish them as lovers, not just allies, made her cheeks flush, her mind cloudy and flustered.

Before Mirae could form the words to politely decline Kimoon's offer, Hongbin stepped between them, veritably pushing Mirae out of the way. "I'll do it," he said, shoving his arm through the angle created by Kimoon's. "Let's show everyone that the handsome princes of Josan and Seolla are chummy and unafraid."

Now it was Kimoon's turn to decline or accept an unexpected proposition. After a moment, Kimoon nodded and tucked his elbow against Hongbin's. They soon followed Captain Keon together, but only after both of them shot Mirae separate looks. Hongbin's seemed to say *you're welcome*, while Kimoon looked at Mirae as he might a favorite kite that tugged free of its string and drifted miles away.

Mirae didn't have time to puzzle over either man's expression, for Captain Keon and his guards had broken through the main gate's traffic, and all but pushed Mirae forward into the city.

She did her best to keep her feet moving while taking in what she could of the capital. It was difficult to see much of what was going on around her, being tightly surrounded by swiftly moving guards, but the aroma of freshly cooked food wafted far more easily between the horde of passersby than she and her escorts did. The scents of garlicky ox bone soup, spicy kimchi stew, steamed pork dumplings, and the grilling of fatty meat did their best to distract Mirae by prompting hunger pangs to shoot through her stomach.

After what felt like hours of being swept past mouthwatering smells, and shuffling through the crushing swarm of people making their way through the city, Mirae felt that the palace couldn't be much farther away. Her surroundings were changing; the walking path had become less crowded, and the Josan citizens who Mirae caught glimpses of were more and more bejeweled, often trailed by humbly dressed servants.

Even the buildings began looking more exquisite. Where once the road had been lined with open storefronts and merchants hawking skeins of dyed hemp, glass beaded jewelry, and earthenware pots, now richly dressed buyers entered brightly painted shops that touted luxurious silk, lacquered furniture, celadon pottery, and expensive jewelry ornamented with imported gems like sapphire and opal. The aroma of rich, heady incense and floral teas poured out into the street, fragrances heavy enough to give Mirae a headache.

Thankfully, the shopping district was soon left behind as Mirae and her companions entered the residential area of the capital, where the homesteads of court officials and nobles encircled the palace like polished jewels encrusting a crown. Everywhere Mirae looked were elaborately carved doors in thick stone walls, behind which rose spacious houses with latticed screen windows and gracefully sloping roofs tipped with intricate medallions.

Most of the people Mirae passed now were the finely dressed nobles who lived in the walled estates, esteemed citizens whom the guards did not disturb. Trailing them were lines of well-groomed, meek servants who were trained to show deference, never raising their heads to look at anyone but each other.

Still, Mirae couldn't help but notice that some of the nobles stopped and stared when they caught sight of Kimoon. Unlike Siwon, who kept his head bowed, Kimoon held his chin high and gripped Hongbin's arm proudly. Hongbin matched his escort's energy, looking like a true prince despite both their outfits being travel-worn and wrinkled, their hanboks conspicuously unadorned compared to the lesser-ranking men and women around them.

Just as the blue of the sky began to deepen with early hints of dusk, the Josan guards finally slowed to a stop. Ahead, Mirae could see that the labyrinth of houses had vanished. Now the high walls of what could only be the palace stood in view, snaking across a long stretch of grass patrolled by guards who didn't look as if they expected anything eventful to happen.

Mirae took their boredom as good news. If the Netherking had not yet passed through and made a scene, it was possible that he was still figuring out a way inside. Feeling somewhat grateful for her escorts now, Mirae followed Captain Keon and his men to the palace gates.

Mirae gazed up at the enormous doors with awe as she approached. They were similar in scale to the Seolla palace's dragon gates, but given that dragons were a symbol that only Sacred Bone heirs could use, the Josan monarchs had instead chosen phoenixes to signify their power.

The phoenix gates were intricately carved and brightly painted, the craftsmanship of both art forms astounding Mirae to no end, especially considering no one in Josan relied on magic to create their masterpieces. The downy, goose-like silhouette of the gargantuan bird arced as gracefully as any dragon across both halves of the doors, trailing long blue plumes as bright as a cloudless sky. The phoenix's red-frilled rooster head was a deep, rich crimson that blossomed down its long, supple neck, and burst into bright colors as it flowed down the rest of its feathered body, with shades varying from vermilion to jade, indigo, and bronze.

Mirae felt as if she could stare at the magnificent creature for hours, taking in all its ornate details, but Captain Keon jerked her out of her reverie by shouting up to the guards stationed on the palace walls.

"We have brought Her Majesty, High Queen of Seolla, to meet with our king." After announcing her arrival, Captain Keon bowed until the heavy doors began to swing open.

When Captain Keon gestured for Mirae to step past the gates, she hid her surprise that no one was going to search her or her companions for magical items to confiscate, as Kimoon's men had on White Spine Mountain. Glad that her black bell, which she kept in a hidden pocket sewn into her chima, would remain undetected, Mirae took her first step into the Josan palace.

Chapter
FOURTEEN

Mirae was instantly mesmerized by all the dazzling, vibrant colors and glittering adornments beaming at her from every surface and corner. The brassy light of sunset only accentuated the bright red buildings—lined with polished jade pillars and gold-wrought gables—that surrounded the courtyard, which itself was inlaid with perfectly square stones engraved with silver floral medallions. Dotting the wide, paved plaza were hundreds of ministers and officials draped in intricately embroidered robes and gem-encrusted belts perched just below their ribs. Atop their heads were glossy, winged black hats with high domes that curved downward like budding hills.

Even more eye-catching, however, were the flocks of court ladies bustling about with dinner trays and hampers, or trailing important-looking nobles. Even the servants' silk hanboks were expensively dyed, and the jewels flashing in their hair rivaled the ones Mirae had worn as a crown princess. Looking around, Mirae realized that while she'd recently begun considering her own home unnecessarily opulent, the gaudiness of the Seollan palace was nothing compared to Josan's.

Mirae wasn't given a lot of time to stare at the extravagance around her, however. Within moments, Captain Keon gestured impatiently for Mirae to follow him into the courtyard, and toward the buildings beyond.

Mirae obligingly followed, a little surprised when Captain Keon skirted around the tallest structure—a bloodred pagoda that Mirae assumed was the throne room. Instead, the captain led Mirae past all the stately official structures toward what she could only assume was the king's private chambers, a nevertheless impressive, two-tiered structure that was heavily guarded. The building itself was massive, ten times the size Mirae would have expected for a construct that, presumably, only housed a sleeping chamber, a study, and the king's dressing room. Surrounding it was a horde of servants standing still as statues in the dusky, indigo light of the setting sun, faithfully keeping their posts.

As Mirae and her companions walked up the stone steps leading into the king's quarters, Captain Keon showed them where to leave their shoes. After quickly slipping out of their sinbal and placing them neatly beside the glimmering array of at least a dozen other ornate sandals, they allowed themselves to be marched down a long hallway, warmly lit by lanterns glowing through paper screen walls. When at last they reached the entrance to the main chamber, the guards on either side of the doors slid them open and announced Mirae's arrival.

"Your Majesty, the High Queen of Seolla has come to greet you."

A second later, a high, cold voice called back, "Let her approach."

Mirae did as she was bid, her socked feet whispering across the polished mahogany floor of the king's chamber. Her gaze immediately found the man waiting inside, and she was unsurprised to see amber eyes—even lighter than Kimoon's or Siwon's—staring back at her.

The Josan king was quite handsome. Mirae could easily make out the features he'd passed on to his sons, the high cheekbones and sharply tapered jaw. His outfit, however, reminded her more of the Netherking. Sewn from deep purple silk, his outer robe gleamed like a midnight sky, though the circular, embroidered medallion at his front featured a red-and-green phoenix, its long, feathered body set against a golden sun. On his head was a seven-tiered crown shaped like a lotus flower, as glossily dark as his long, oiled beard.

Although Mirae's eyes were fixed on the king's, his moved to stare at Kimoon, and at the Seollan prince hanging off his arm. What the king made of his bastard son's sudden return was impossible for Mirae to guess. His expression was guarded, carefully neutral. A trait Kimoon had clearly learned from him.

The faces of the other spectators in the room, however—thirteen astonishingly beautiful women—were far easier to read. The queen of Josan was easiest to identify. Sitting beside her husband, she alternated between glaring at Mirae, and then at Kimoon. Mirae, for her part, couldn't do much more than gaze back in awe.

The woman before her was achingly lovely, making it clear how she'd stood out from all the other noble daughters in her youth, enough to be hand selected by the reigning monarchs for the highest honor any woman could be granted in Josan—becoming a royal bride to the crown prince, worshipped for her rare beauty and sharp mind.

Lightly lined with age, the Josan queen's face was perfect in every way, her eyes and cheeks softly rounded. Her resplendent silk hanbok, stamped with floral designs in shimmering silver and accentuated by a wealth of jade ornaments, was far grander than anything Mirae had ever worn. By comparison, she felt like a girl playing dress-up, while the woman across from her sat as regally, and impossibly beautifully, as a heavenly maiden.

Mirae was only able to tear her eyes away from the flawless queen when the hot glares of the king's concubines became too uncomfortable to bear. Her eyes scanned the group of scowling women uneasily. They sat in two lines before the king, as if queuing up to meet him. Each of the noble-born ladies was, of course, unparalleled in prettiness and elegance, but it was obvious to Mirae that their gaudy ensembles and flashy jewels were purposefully thrown together to outshine each other, each maiden clamoring to become the king's favorite.

Mirae was brought back to herself and her purpose when Kimoon guided Hongbin to the floor beside him, kneeling deferentially before the silent king. Areum and Siwon similarly dropped into a deep bow, their foreheads pressed against the highly polished floor—thankfully not so reflective that it mirrored back the golden color of Siwon's eyes.

After a long pause, lengthy enough for Mirae to finish studying the room and its inhabitants, the Josan king gestured to the low table set before him, crowded with bronze serving dishes heavy with food. "Have you eaten today, Your Majesty?"

Mirae studied the king's offering, unsurprisingly featuring dishes made from root vegetables. Large bowls of arrowroot naengmyeon had been placed on the outskirts of the main table, while its center sported platters of fresh, grated carrots, radish, and some kind of broth. On a smaller side table was a kettle steaming with an unknown tea, and potato side dishes.

"Thank you for your generosity," Mirae said, ignoring her gurgling stomach, "but our business is too urgent for pleasantries."

"Is that so?" the Josan king asked, his voice cool, carefully treading the line between icy and polite. "And what is it, exactly, that you have traveled so far to tell me?"

Mirae knew she would have to choose her next words carefully. The man before her had no reason to cooperate, let alone admit to the crimes she had helped him bury.

"I have come," she said, hoping the urgency in her voice didn't come across as demanding, "because a villain familiar to us both has escaped my custody. Since we each have reason to fear the Netherking's retaliation, it behooves us to apprehend him quickly."

If the Josan king was shocked to hear any of this, he didn't show it; but when he spoke, his voice was flat. "Are you insinuating that I'm actively harboring the Netherking here?"

"No," Mirae said quickly. "I don't believe you have any knowledge of his whereabouts."

"What is it, then, that you want?" the king asked, narrowing his eyes.

Mirae took a deep breath, gathering up her courage to finally address what he'd done to Minho. "I believe that the Netherking is trying to get his hands on the black water in your possession. I'm asking you to surrender what remains of it to me, lest the Netherking use it to become invincible and destroy both our nations."

Unsurprisingly, the Josan king looked displeased with Mirae's declaration, even more so with her insinuation that he had committed treason. "I'm afraid I don't have any idea what you're talking about," he said stiffly.

"Mirae has not come here to punish you, Father." Kimoon finally lifted his head to lend Mirae his support. "She's telling the truth. The Netherking is out of control. If we don't work together, he will acquire the ability to obliterate Josan. As soon as you turn over the black water, we will depart and take care of the rest ourselves."

The Josan king fell silent, appraising his son from where he sat. His golden gaze flitted over to Hongbin, who'd proudly entered the chamber linking arms with his son, before settling back on Kimoon. Mirae watched the king's face harden, lines of contempt—mirrored by his wife and concubines—flooding his face like a tidal wave that could no longer be contained.

"So, this was your grand plan?" the king asked coldly. "You betrayed your own family to become a consort, instead of a king?"

Unprepared as she was for the sudden shift in conversation, Mirae's breath caught in her throat, her unspoken words as frozen in place as Kimoon appeared to be. He sat there, unspeaking, as his father continued to mock him. "You know what happens to their consorts, don't you? At best, you will be used for breeding more heirs. At worst, well, you've seen what our late dowager queen did to the man she professed to love. Drained him of his life force, turning him into a mere shell of a man."

Mirae's body flashed cold as the king, looking smug at the stunned expression on her face, gestured at her long hair. "Did you come here looking like that to try to blend in, and make it seem like you belong?" He looked Mirae up and down, eyeing her disheveled attire, in sharp contrast to the perfumed beauties surrounding him. "Only men wear their hair like that, Your Majesty. You truly know nothing about us, do you?"

Mirae's fists clenched, her palms growing hot with barely suppressed fire begging to burst out of her, desperate to silence the man scorning her display of mourning, as well as her insistence that the Netherking was going to kill them all.

Thankfully, Kimoon reacted faster than she did, and he, for one, refused to rise to his father's bait. "Slander us all you want," Kimoon said, his voice almost bored. "And parade your dominance however you wish. But the Netherking doesn't care who wears a crown, or a perfumed wig. All are beneath him, and all will submit. Unless you want to lose everything you've sacrificed your soul for, Father, I suggest you take our warning seriously. The Netherking will be far less forgiving of your puerility than our gracious High Queen."

Silence fell in the room. For a moment, Mirae worried that the king was going to leap to his feet and call for the guards outside, but instead, to Mirae's relief, his features smoothed out, his expression becoming unbothered once more. "You are asking me to do something impossible," the king said with a shrug. "There is no black water here."

Before Kimoon could challenge his father's blatant lie, Mirae intervened. "Perhaps not," she cut in quickly. "But if you nevertheless help me track down any black water that *might* be on the palace grounds, unbeknownst to you, I would naturally compensate you."

The Josan king raised an eyebrow. "And what are you prepared to offer me for this courtesy?"

"Something you and your nation have long desired," Mirae said, steeling herself to utter the promise she had prepared herself to say out loud. "I will free Josan from Seollan rule. You will be king of an independent nation. I give you my word."

The silence that followed Mirae's pledge was longer, deeper than the one that preceded it. Mirae could only guess at the Josan king's thoughts, but based on the way his brow creased, he was weighing the benefits and consequences of the two options before him. He could continue his black water experiments secretly, hoping to someday manipulate its dark power to launch an uprising against Seolla. Or he could get everything he wanted here and now. All he needed to do was accept the deal Mirae was offering him, an act that could cause him to be labeled as a traitor to the very kingdom he was trying to liberate.

Mirae stared back unflinchingly into the Josan king's keen amber gaze, praying that he believed the sincerity of her vow, and that he would not regret taking a chance on her. Hopefully he saw in her a queen who would not only keep her word but would also eliminate the Netherking as a threat once and for all. Joining her was the best way forward.

After a long, heavy pause, the Josan king finally spoke. "I will think on your proposal," he said slowly, carefully. "For now, let me discuss this with the queen. I will summon you later when we have come to a decision."

Later? Mirae's breath hitched. *There's no time for later! The Netherking could be entering the palace as we speak!* But, as much as she wanted to press the king to hash everything out now, the urge to extract an immediate verdict ebbed away when Kimoon shot her a warning look and shook his head.

Hoping Kimoon knew what he was doing, Mirae nodded stiffly to the Josan king and allowed the guards to lead her back outside, where the sunless night had cooled the air, its blanket of darkness dotted by lanterns strung across the swooping rooftops.

After allowing them to retrieve their shoes, Captain Keon, more respectful now, bowed. "Your Majesty, I will take you and your guests to royal accommodations while you wait. If the men would follow me, I will lead them to one of the princes' quarters. You and the oracle will be taken to the queen's chamber."

Mirae nodded and watched Hongbin, Kimoon, and Siwon walk away, dimly lit by the torch Captain Keon held high. Moments later, Mirae herself was led to a nearby building similar in size to the king's chamber. The court ladies who guided her and helped her settle into what appeared to be the queen's tearoom kept their heads bowed so low, and moved so quickly, that Mirae never got a look at their faces. They worked rhythmically, their movements fluid as they procured trays of piping-hot tea and various refreshments before scuttling away, leaving Mirae and Areum alone in the wide room teeming with colorful floor cushions and elaborately painted screen dividers.

The earthy smell of ginseng tea, and the sweetness of the finely sliced fruits and tteok placed before her, made Mirae's mouth water. She hadn't had anything to eat since a hasty breakfast of travel-battered vegetables that morning.

Areum, whose silvery eyes were as wide as Mirae's, gulped. "You don't think they'd poison us, do you?"

Mirae shook her head. "Probably not. Though if they decide against helping us, I wouldn't be so sure then."

"But for now it's probably safe to eat what they give us, right?" Areum asked. Her friend looked better rested than she had the previous day, but her skin was still a bit wan, her eyes red rimmed. Although Mirae wasn't eager to break Josan law, she couldn't bear to tell a friend in need of nourishment to refrain from eating perfectly good food. So, cautious of the fact that she couldn't perform any perceptible spells, Mirae hovered her palm over the platters, using Jade Witchery to sense the elemental makeup of the delicacies within them. Finding nothing amiss, she retracted her hand.

"It's all safe," she said, smiling reassuringly. "Dig in."

Areum needed no further invitation. She descended on her half of the food ravenously, but still maintained some semblance of politeness by pouring tea for Mirae as well as herself. Mirae sipped the ginseng and honey concoction, the bitter pairing perfectly with the sweet, as she watched her friend eat her fill, feeling a small sense of satisfaction at the sight, despite the disappointment that sat like a stone in her chest while she waited, uselessly, for the Josan king to do the right thing.

Perhaps I can still find a way to make use of this downtime, Mirae thought, setting down her cup. There was information she hadn't had a chance to gather yet, knowledge she needed to figure out the Netherking's next steps. As soon as Areum seemed to be slowing down, Mirae asked, "Will you tell me what you know of the Dark Moon Oracles while we wait?"

Areum swallowed before responding. "Right, the Dark Moon Oracles. An order of seers that I thought was a myth. Before we left, I took some time to ask the other Kun Sunim candidates what they knew about them."

Mirae nodded appreciatively. "Hopefully you learned something that would explain why the Netherking wants to find them so badly."

"I did, I think," Areum said, setting her teacup down as well. "If anyone knows how to help him reach the heavens, it's them."

"Really?" Mirae leaned forward, but before Areum could say anything else, an unexpected sound diverted their attention. A timid knock that echoed from the far side of the chamber.

At first, Mirae and Areum just stared at each other, as if silently asking, *Did you hear that, too?* When the thudding repeated, they jumped to their feet, looking for the source of the sound.

It was coming from behind one of the silk screens. Mirae peered at the inconspicuous painting of deer frolicking with peacocks under pine trees. It seemed innocent enough. Still, as Mirae began walking toward it, she raised her hands to summon fire if needed, Josan laws be damned.

"Mirae? Can you hear me?"

Her hands froze when she recognized the muffled voice.

Hurrying toward it, she quickly slid the screen out of the way. To her surprise, behind the painting was a door, latched shut.

"Can you unlock it?" Kimoon called out. Mirae hastily did as she was asked, removing the pin that kept the door from opening. As soon as she did, it swung open, revealing three familiar faces peering back at her.

"What are you doing here?" Mirae hissed.

"You know as well as I that we don't have time to wait for my father to make up his mind," Kimoon said, gesturing for Mirae to follow him back outside, or wherever the secret exit led. "Besides, the queen consort is extremely shrewd, and hates Seolla more than anyone I know. Even if my father was swayed by your words, she'll put a stop to it. Trust me."

"So, we're going to steal the black water?" Mirae asked. "Right out from underneath the king's nose? Won't your father be—"

Kimoon waved away her concerns. "We'll deal with him after we save the peninsula. If he still wants to be petty after that, then so be it. Now, are you coming or not?"

Deciding to save her breath for what was almost certainly going to be a whirlwind escape after their daring heist, Mirae silenced her protests and gestured for Kimoon to lead the way.

Chapter
FIFTEEN

The hallway outside the secret entrance was surprisingly short. After only a few steps, Mirae saw the outline of a square doorway, seemingly cut into the outer walls of the queen's chambers. As soon as she slipped outside, followed closely by Areum, Kimoon grabbed a panel of latticed wood, painted bright red like the rest of the building, and pressed it back into place, where it blended in seamlessly with the rest of the ornate wall.

"How did you—" Mirae started to ask.

"Soori and I spent most of our childhood serving the queen consort as her spies," Kimoon said with a shrug. "This was how we snuck in and out, leaving reports for her every morning."

Although Mirae was curious to know more about the strange life Kimoon lived before they met, this was no time for reminiscing. Instead, Mirae looked around for any sign of guards or servants. Thankfully, she and her companions were alone in a dark alleyway at the rear of the palace.

Even more fortunately, there didn't seem to be anything different about their surroundings, except the cover of nightfall dimming all the bright, glittering colors. It didn't appear that the Netherking had torn through, which boded well.

"Noonim," Hongbin hissed, a little too loudly. "Kimoon said the black water is being kept in something called an ice house. It's a cold cellar where they can keep things frozen, since, you know, they don't have magic."

Mirae nodded. "Which way to the ice house?" To her surprise, Siwon turned and started walking down the alley, taking the lead. A split second later, he ground to a halt, as if realizing what he was doing. When Mirae shot Kimoon a questioning look, he shrugged again. "That *is* the right way, though I'm not sure how he knew that."

Wasting no more time, Kimoon quickly took over, striding confidently in the direction Siwon had been heading, while Mirae and the others stole silently after.

Following Kimoon closely, they skirted between the shadows of buildings, avoiding lanterns and patrolling guards with surprising ease. It was clear this wasn't the first time Kimoon had made a furtive crossing, for which Mirae was grateful. She was also glad, in part, that her stockinged feet muffled her steps, since she hadn't been able to grab her shoes outside the queen's chambers. Unfortunately, Mirae's unprotected soles sometimes trod just right on the cold stone underfoot, causing the sharp medallions to dig painfully into her skin. Each time they did, it took all her willpower to wince silently instead of yelping.

Mirae wasn't the only one grimacing as she walked. Siwon's face was also twisted as if he was nursing an invisible wound, one potent enough that he even forgot to fret over Areum. Instead, he seemed lost in his own dark, tortured thoughts.

As much as she wanted to, Mirae didn't dare ask him what was wrong, for fear that speaking might give away their position, but she made a mental note to ask him later why it seemed like this wasn't his first venture into the Josan palace, either.

For his part, Kimoon relied on memory to effortlessly guide them to a remote, unlit corner of the palace that, by the smells of it, was somewhere near the kitchens. When Kimoon finally slowed, Mirae studied the curious structure in front of them, which appeared to be the slightly raised entrance to an underground chamber, fitted with a locked door. Kimoon motioned for Mirae to take care of the latch. She nodded and leaned forward to examine it. Thankfully, it didn't look as if it had been tampered with. Allowing a small ray of hope that maybe, somehow, she had beaten the Netherking to the stash, Mirae touched the padlock, commanding the metal bar inside to slide out. The iron obeyed her, slipping free until all Mirae had to do was pull on the lock for the door to swing open, revealing a narrow, dark tunnel descending into darkness.

"Someone will need to keep watch," Kimoon said, "in case guards wander by."

"It should be you," Mirae said. "Out of all of us, you'll know what to say to send patrols away without arousing too much suspicion."

"Very well," Kimoon said with a nod. "Perhaps Lady Areum and Hongbin would be able to assist by keeping watch at the corners of the nearest buildings, and alert me if anyone is coming. But you and Siwon must hurry, Mirae. If we are caught, there's no amount of talking that will keep us from being executed."

Executed. Mirae gulped at the ominous word and gestured for Hongbin and Areum to do as Kimoon said. "We'll be fast," she promised, and then quickly entered the pitch-black doorway, feeling carefully for the steps that led her deeper underground.

The air around Mirae instantly grew chilly, and she was soon surrounded by darkness, so she held up her palm and summoned a small orb of light to help her and Siwon find their way around. As she took in her surroundings, shivering at the frigid underground air, she was amazed at what she saw: enormous blocks of ice covered in sawdust for insulation, and various pots, bottles, and baskets of food that were best served chilled.

"We should hurry," Siwon said, coming to a stop beside Mirae. His voice shook off Mirae's temporary wonderment, and she lifted her palm high enough to illuminate every corner of the surprisingly large chamber as she and Siwon split off to begin their search. Mirae quickly rounded the first enormous block of ice beside her, looking for any sign of black water hidden behind it. But to her surprise, she saw something *else* on the floor that made her heart pound as quickly as a sprinting rabbit.

A man, dressed as a servant, buried in a blanket of sawdust. As soon as Mirae's palm light hit his face, the man tried to look up at her weakly, but his eyelashes had frozen over.

"Master?" he said pitifully. He looked half frozen, skin blue-tinged.

Mirae fell to her knees beside the man, who looked around her age, and bid her free hand to summon the warmth of the sun. "What are you doing down here?" she whispered. "Who are you?"

"I failed Wangbi mama," the man said hoarsely. "So, she sent me here to die."

The poor servant did indeed look mere seconds away from death's door. Mirae quickly ran her fire over his body, sending heat up and down the length of it until some color finally returned to his cheeks.

"We need to get you out of here," Mirae said. "Can you walk?"

When the man nodded, Mirae helped him to his feet, wrapping her arm around him for support. As his strength slowly returned, so did his lucidity. "Are you one of the court ladies, agassi?" he asked. "They don't usually come down here."

"No, I . . . I just got lost," Mirae stammered, leading the servant quickly toward the exit and hoping Siwon would be able to track down the black water without her.

"You must be new, then," the man said sadly, suddenly resisting Mirae's pull. "If you get caught helping me, it'll be you in here next. I don't want you to be punished."

"It's fine, I'm leaving tonight," Mirae said, impatience creeping into her voice. "Just come with me. I'll take you to safety."

"Your Majesty?" Siwon had rounded the same block of ice, looking for Mirae. When he saw what she was doing, he rushed over and immediately slipped a supporting arm beneath hers, helping her walk the half-frozen man toward the stairs.

"Did you find it?" Mirae asked, grunting under the weight of their shared load.

"Yes, Your Majesty," Siwon said. "I dragged it over to the steps, and then I came looking for you. I was hoping you could enchant the ice so it would be lighter to carry."

"Your Majesty?" the servant asked, confused. His lashes had finally defrosted, so he cracked open his eyes just enough to see Mirae's starry palm. "That light . . . and warmth . . . it's coming from your hand. You're . . . you're a Seollan witch!"

"Yes, one who is trying to save your life," Mirae muttered. "Stop struggling."

"No!" The servant dug in his heels. "I can't let you get away."

"Your master already left you for dead," Siwon said, correctly guessing what had happened. "You don't need to fear what he'll do to you anymore. We can all just leave together."

"No, they'll kill my family if they find out I let you go!"

Mirae could see the glimmering block of frozen black water ahead of them, resting at the foot of the steps that led back out to Kimoon, who would not be happy that they were wasting precious time. "Do you really want us to leave you here?" Mirae asked, exasperated. "Or would you rather live long enough to collect your family and flee to safety?"

"We're offering you a chance to live," Siwon said. With a great tug, he heaved both Mirae and the servant closer to the exit. "You don't have to live like this, under a tyrant's foot. Take it from me."

"No!" The servant went limp, allowing his full weight to drag Mirae's and Siwon's arms down until they lost their grip. Then he sped away from them, running toward the steps. "If I tell my queen you're here, she'll spare me! This is my chance to earn back her good graces!"

Siwon lunged after the servant, but he wasn't fast enough. Mirae shot a gust of wind toward the frozen black water, shoving it right into the fleeing man's path. Caught unawares, and weak from his ordeal, he tripped and fell flat on his face.

"Please don't hurt him," Siwon pleaded, moving to stand between Mirae and the servant. "He's just scared. I can reason with him."

Mirae hadn't even realized that the soothing, warm heat in her hand had blossomed into a fireball. She put out the flames and nodded, holding up her lighted palm instead. Together, they approached the prone man, who groaned as he tried to climb to his feet. "My mother," he sobbed, hiding his face from Mirae's glow. "They'll kill her when they find out what I've done."

"Then we'll just have to get to her before they do," Siwon said. He looked over at Mirae, who nodded in agreement, glad Kimoon wasn't there to cast his vote. "Tell us where your mother lives, and we'll get you both to safety," Siwon promised.

The servant, who had finally pulled himself to his knees, still refused to meet either of their gazes. "Seollan promises mean nothing," he spat.

Before Mirae could extinguish the ire she felt at his ignorant accusation, the servant lunged, an ice pick in his hand. But the thick needle, aiming for Mirae's heart, never touched her. Instead, she felt all the breath get knocked out of her as Siwon shoved her out of the way. Her body banged painfully against a giant wall of ice, and she crumpled to the ground.

Thankfully, her palm managed to stay lit, allowing Siwon to see where the servant was and shove him backward, hard. Then he rushed over to Mirae, shielding her with his body. "Stop!" he begged, holding up his hand. "I don't want to hurt you . . . please stop."

Siwon was injured. Mirae saw the handle of the ice pick protruding from his arm, its metal tip deep in his flesh. Blood soaked his sleeve, dripping onto the ground. She glared at the servant across the room. Before she could stop it, rage built up in her chest, an intense, hot cloud that threatened to fill the room with crackles of lightning.

"What on earth is taking so long?" A low voice, cold as the ice house, penetrated the chamber, intimidating everyone into falling still and cooling Mirae's anger. Seconds later, Kimoon finished descending the stairs, stepping into Mirae's circle of light. As soon as he saw Mirae, who still lay on the ground, and surmised what had transpired, his jaw clenched. Mirae could practically see the white-hot rage flooding his vision, the same fury that had nearly possessed her moments ago.

Kimoon's eyes ran up and down Mirae's body, searching for wounds. "Did he hurt you?" he asked quietly.

Mirae struggled to her feet, lungs and back still burning. "I'll be fine," she wheezed.

Kimoon turned to the servant, who cowered under the exiled prince's imposing golden gaze, as he would any of his masters'. "How dare you touch her!" Kimoon seethed. "You, who are unworthy of the sand beneath her feet."

"But s-she's a witch!" the servant blubbered. "I caught her for you, Daegun, and the traitorous bastard aiding her so you can have them executed! I did it for Their Majesties!"

"Is that so?" Kimoon turned back to Mirae and Siwon. He barely even glanced at Siwon's injured arm before saying, "Hongbin saw torches coming our way. Get the black water out of here now. I'll deal with this fool myself. We cannot allow him to sound the alarm."

Under no circumstances could Mirae allow herself or her companions to get caught; there was no choice but to secure their quarry and get out of there before the guards arrived. With Siwon's help, she stumbled over to the frozen black water, while Kimoon grabbed the servant's arm roughly.

"You made a grave mistake attacking the High Queen," he said, wrenching the servant backward until he threw back his head with a cry of pain. "You should have accepted her mercy before—"

The rest of Kimoon's threat seemed to clot in his throat as he stared, horrified, down at the other man's face. For a second, he seemed at a loss for words, until he finally choked out, "Soori?"

Mirae froze, recognizing the name of Kimoon's younger brother. A prince disguised as a servant, who'd kept his head turned away from Mirae's light so she wouldn't see the color of his eyes. His ruse revealed, Soori dropped his act, and glared up at Kimoon with amber eyes hard as marbles. "Father said you betrayed us," Soori spat, nothing but hatred etched into his face. "I didn't want to believe it, but now I have seen for myself what you've become."

"Soori," Kimoon said again, the only word he could seem to muster as his strength left him. He stumbled back, dropping his brother's arm as if it were a burning-hot iron.

"This . . . this was all a trap," Siwon breathed, gingerly nursing his wound.

"No, it was a test." Soori turned his golden glare onto Mirae.

"My father wanted to see what kind of woman you really are. Someone we could trust to keep her word, or a charlatan spreading false hope just to get what she wants."

"I meant every word that I said," Mirae stammered. "But there wasn't time to wait for your father's cooperation. I had to make my move. The Netherking—"

"So you decided to recant your offer, the very thing we've sought for centuries, by robbing us in the night and spitting on our most sacred law," Soori snarled. "I watched you cast spells on Josan grounds, defiling my home, the very heart of this kingdom, even though you know full well that your ancestors' vow to never use magic within our borders was the highest term of our surrender. You were aware that defying that rule meant an end to the cease-fire, to peace, yet you blatantly disrespected us anyway. Well, you've shown your true colors, *High Queen*."

"No, you cannot tell Father what happened here," Kimoon pleaded. "You don't know what's at stake."

But Soori only smiled at Kimoon's distress. "Oh, I'll tell him everything. I'll spare no details about the High Queen's multiple transgressions, or how you took her side against a loyal Josan subject. Unless, of course," Soori said, smiling cruelly, "you decide to try to silence me."

"What happened to you?" Kimoon asked quietly, flinching at each of Soori's pitiless taunts. "What did Father do to break you?"

"Your Majesty," Siwon interrupted, wincing with pain. "We cannot allow word of our crimes to get out. We need a plan."

As much as Mirae wanted to let Kimoon decide what to do

with his brother, she couldn't deny the truth in Siwon's words. If she merely absconded with the black water, leaving Soori untouched, and able to report back to the Josan king, war would be unleashed on her queendom while she chased after the Netherking, powerless to stop all the bloodshed.

But she could hardly harm a hair on Soori's head, a prince who could become a martyr justifying the very war she had silenced him to prevent.

"There's no use fretting, it's too late," Soori said, cackling at the uncertainty on Mirae's face. "My father already knows what you've done. He's outside with your precious friends. You really shouldn't have left them alone."

Remembering that the two most vulnerable members of her party were waiting for her, unprotected, Mirae whipped around and rushed up the cellar stairs, forgetting everything except the faces of the two people she'd left to fend for themselves. Just as she burst out of the ice house, breathless with worry, she was met with a heart-stopping sight that made her feet freeze in place.

A half circle of royal guards surrounded the entrance, torches raised and swords in their hands. At their center stood the Josan king, and on either side of him knelt two familiar figures, both with daggers pressed to their necks by the soldiers behind them.

"So," the Josan king said quietly, "it appears my wife was right. Now I must decide what is to be done with you. Especially considering," he said, holding up the lock Mirae had enchanted to open, "you seem to have broken Josan's most important law. This, of course, cannot go unpunished."

"Please," Mirae tried, doing her best to meet the king's gaze instead of staring helplessly at the weapons threatening her brother and her friend. "Let me explain."

"That won't be necessary." The king shifted his eyes to look past her, toward the sound of footsteps following her out of the cellar. Moments later, someone shouldered past Mirae, walking over to join his father. Soori fell before his father's feet, pressing his forehead against them in reverence.

"Tell me what happened," the king commanded.

Soori lifted his head, and said the very words Mirae had been dreading. "I witnessed the High Queen breaking our foremost law in order to steal from us. And, as you predicted, Kimoon viewed me as nothing more than pond scum. He has truly fallen far from your grace, Father."

"I see," the king said, sounding pleased.

As much as she wanted to fire off her own accusations, Mirae knew now was not the time to point out that she couldn't technically steal something that already belonged to her—or that the Josan king was being incredibly hypocritical by condemning Mirae for using magic when he himself kept a store of it inside the palace. Neither of those allegations would cool the king's ire, or free Hongbin and Areum.

"He isn't telling the whole story," Mirae said. "About how we tried to help him, because we value Josan lives just as much as our own."

"You accuse my own blood of being dishonest?" the Josan king asked, gesturing for his son to rise and stand beside him. "The new crown prince of Josan?"

With a sinking heart, Mirae watched Soori move to take his

place, head held high with pride. *So, that is what he was promised*, Mirae thought bitterly, *a boon that would make otherwise loving brothers hate each other. Yet another scheme of the Josan king's to punish Kimoon for deserting to Seolla. To break him.*

The pain in Mirae's heart only deepened when she heard Kimoon and Siwon climb out of the ice house, the latter falling into a deep bow that hid his eyes, while the former gasped to see Soori next to their father, realizing exactly why his beloved sibling had turned against him.

The Josan king smiled at Kimoon's anguish and clasped his hands behind his back, looking like a predator who had cornered his prey. "The way I see it," he said, his voice as smug as the look on his face, "there are two options before you, High Queen. The first being that I relay your treachery to my court, and punish you as they see fit. You can, of course, use magic to free yourself, but that will only make things worse. Who knows, someone you care about," the king said, gesturing to his captives, "could even perish in the scuffle."

"And the second option?" Mirae asked, knowing that this was the part where the Josan king made her an offer she couldn't refuse, served at the edge of a knife.

"I could turn a blind eye to everything that happened tonight." The king held his hands out like a forgiving god. "In the grand scheme of things, one small sin for the greater good is nothing. The Netherking must be stopped. We both know this."

"And what must I do to earn such . . . leniency?" Mirae asked thickly.

"Something you were willing to do earlier." The king shrugged as if he was the most reasonable person in the world. "My first stipulation is that you make good on your promise. You have the black water in your possession, and I will allow you to leave with it. In return, you must decree, here and now, that Josan is an independent nation. You will walk over to the throne room, where my court awaits, and sign this into law immediately."

Mirae swallowed back a lump in her throat. "I am happy to sign a statement declaring my intention to liberate Josan," she said, "but I, too, have a council that must back up my decrees. I cannot make such a mandate without their approval."

"I understand that, of course," the king said, much to Mirae's surprise. "I will accept your counteroffer, but only if you agree to leave Crown Prince Hongbin behind, just until you are able to persuade the Hwabaek to make your edict official. You'll excuse me for not trusting you to hold up your end of the bargain without a little motivation. And you needn't worry. Crown Prince Hongbin will be well taken care of. I will treat him like my own son."

Somehow, that sounded more like a threat than a reassurance. Mirae's eyes darted over to Hongbin, who, despite the dagger digging into his flesh, nodded bravely. *Do it*, he seemed to say. *I am willing.* As loath as Mirae was to abandon her brother to the wiles of a man who enjoyed pitting kin against kin, she nodded nonetheless. "I accept your terms."

"Marvelous," the king said, but did not order his guards to release their captives. "Now on to my final condition. This one is a little more . . . sensitive." When Mirae stared back at him stonily, the king went on, "There's just one more, rather large issue we need to address: the matter of public opinion. I, of course, am well aware of the threat the Netherking poses to our peninsula. My kingdom, on the other hand, will be less enthused about you and me forming an alliance. They will think me a fool for trusting you."

Every muscle in Mirae's body tensed as the king prattled on. "If we are to assuage the concerns of my citizens, then we must prove to them beyond any doubt that you are someone they can put their faith in. Someone who will honor our ways in action, not just in words."

"Speak plainly," Mirae said impatiently. "What do you want of me?"

The king bristled at her words, but continued nonetheless. "To gain the trust of my people, it is imperative that you repent for the wrongdoings of your ancestors, and prove that you embrace Josan. You must do this by abdicating, and letting Crown Prince Hongbin rule, as proof that men are no longer going to be passed over. What's more," he concluded smugly, "you must become aligned with us permanently."

It took Mirae a moment to realize what he was implying. But when she did, the palms of her hands began to burn, almost as hot as her reddening cheeks.

"I have a great many noble sons you may have your pick of," the king said. "Noble-born men worthy of your hand. Though of course you could always choose to raise one to the status of legitimacy with a union." He didn't have to look at Kimoon for them both to know who he meant. "If you agree to all this, you will have my full support of your mission to annihilate the

Netherking. Anything you need, you will have. Everyone here will go free, unharmed. All you need to do is say yes to all my conditions."

Before Mirae could respond to the Josan king's preposterous proposition, she felt Kimoon brush past her, and heard his low, biting voice. "You cannot be serious." Kimoon stood in front of Mirae like a shield, confronting his father with eyes that blazed in the torchlight. His long, sleek hair tumbled forward in the evening wind, spiraling like the shadowy arms that had burst out of the Netherking's corrupted pearl. "This is low, even for you."

"I'm afraid my terms are nonnegotiable." Facing off against his son seemed to only embolden the Josan king. A man determined to be known for taming a High Daughter and liberating his people. If he had his way, Mirae would no longer be a false queen, but an espoused pawn under the purview of a king who hated her.

But, if she agreed, she would leave with the black water in hand, her queendom eternally safe from war, as long as she succeeded in apprehending the Netherking. For the price of her happiness, her belief in a royal birthright, Mirae could fulfill her destiny and save everyone.

Her gaze flickered over to Areum as the words of a god echoed back to her. *You will have to make a sacrifice you are not yet ready to bear. . . . What are you willing to do, or lose, to save us all?* To Mirae's surprise, her friend's eyes glowed just as they had that night, bright like silvery moons. Her mouth moved to form a single word, silent but emphatic.

No.

In an instant, Mirae felt as if her lungs had slipped free of a too-tight manacle, her airways no longer constricted. She breathed deeply, filling her body with the courage she needed to do what came next. Something dangerous, unthinkable. An act she was only brave enough to consider because she knew that fulfilling the Josan king's ultimatum was not what the heavens wanted. This was not what they meant by their warning.

This was not her sacrifice to bear.

Still, Mirae hesitated. What she was about to do could very well start a war, if the Josan king was unwise enough to follow through with his threats. Kimoon would lose his home forever. Furthermore, Hongbin and Areum were still endangered, easy targets who would be caught in the crossfire. And if a fight broke out, Siwon wouldn't be able to take much more punishment. His arm needed healing, fast.

Mirae looked at each of her companions, trying to gather strength from them. Hongbin and Areum both gazed back at her trustingly, seeming to support the decision they knew she was going to make. Kimoon, still deadlocked in a staring contest with his father, kept his attention focused on the other man, almost as if daring him to choose violence so Mirae could destroy everyone standing in her way. Finally, Mirae glanced at Siwon, who knelt next to the frozen block of black water he and Kimoon had carried out. The key to saving the peninsula.

Sensing Mirae's gaze, Siwon looked up and read in Mirae's eyes exactly what she required—a distraction, so she could extricate her loved ones safely. Siwon nodded and finally lifted his head high enough to be witnessed by the Josan king, showing his father his golden stare, his striking face, for the very first time.

To Mirae's surprise, the king's sneer slipped away as soon as he and Siwon locked eyes, his mouth falling open, unable to say more than a single word. "Miseol."

Siwon clenched his jaw, either because of the pain in his arm or the agony of holding the king's attention. "Yes, I am her son. The court lady you loved."

As intrigued as Mirae was by this unexpected, mysterious revelation, she had a job to do. People to save. And Siwon's diversion had fulfilled its purpose. While the Josan king's attention was pulled away from his captives, too preoccupied to give a command of execution, Mirae opened up her Jade Witch senses, feeling out the metal in the guards' weapons and bidding them to burn as hot as the sun.

Within seconds, the soldiers began screaming. Hongbin and Areum jumped up while their captors were distracted and rushed toward Kimoon, who pushed them behind him, teeth bared at anyone who dared come after them.

Mirae, on the other hand, wasted no time calling for their ride out of there. It came with a force of wind that seemed to snatch every hue from their surroundings—the red buildings, the yellow firelight, and their bright, travel-worn silks—twirling them all into a rainbow whirlwind that snaked upward into the sky, where the winking colors hardened into scales that interlocked, forming, at last, Mirae's magnificent beast.

As soon as the familiar, looming creature was fully shaped, it let out a bloodcurdling roar. The guards, who'd been howling over their blistered hands, froze in terror, staring up at the horned creature of the elements that seemed to inhale its dappled surroundings. Where it usually shimmered brightly in Seolla and flashed like playful koi, here in the Josan palace, its scales gleamed like burnished metal, armored as if for war.

As soon as her creature lowered its serpentine neck, Mirae and her companions began scampering onto its back, helping each other move quickly. Areum offered a shoulder to Siwon, who clung to her with his uninjured arm, while Hongbin and Kimoon snatched up the block of black water and lugged it aboard.

As soon as everyone had found purchase somewhere on the dragon's ridged spine, Mirae bid it to leap into the air, leaving the Josan palace and its furious king behind.

Chapter
SIXTEEN

They flew through the night, over a land draped in plum and indigo darkness. All that Mirae could see were the winking constellations ahead. But instead of admiring the shimmering, star-strung veil of the sky, or the giant pearl of the moon, Mirae's mind drew in the dark void of night that vastly outnumbered the spots of light.

What have I done? she asked as violent images flashed through her head, horrible events her escape would likely bring about. Captain Hanyoung, caught unawares, ambushed by palace guards. The blazing stone swords of a vengeful Wonhwa army cutting down Josan soldiers who had no defenses against magic. Ma-eum Mages tormenting the king's army with visions of monsters, distracting them with hallucinations so they could be easily slaughtered. Citizens from both nations fleeing burning villages, towing their screaming children behind them.

All while Mirae continued her pursuit of the Netherking, flying through charming, twinkling skies, unable to stop the horrors erupting behind her.

Am I pursuing the Inconstant Son only to come back to a queendom at war? Mirae's stomach churned, its acid burning up her throat.

Have I just doomed the peninsula to remain in a cycle of violence, instead of uniting it? Have I killed us all?

"Noonim." Hongbin had scooted up the dragon's back and now hovered just behind her shoulder. "Siwon needs healing. I could try to help him myself, but I don't want to mess it up."

Mirae turned to meet her younger brother's gentle eyes, reminding her of problems she needed to solve here and now, but let out a gasp when she noticed a streak of red cutting across Hongbin's chin. "What happened?" she panicked. "Are you all right?"

Hongbin swiped a wrist across his face, but the gash quickly refilled with blood. "It's nothing. I just nicked myself a bit on my captor's blade while escaping."

When Mirae reached out to try to heal his wound, Hongbin shook his head and pulled away. "Siwon needs you more," he insisted. "You really need to tend to him first."

Seeing the stubbornness in her younger brother's eyes, Mirae nodded. After instructing her dragon to leave Josan's boundaries quickly and steer them toward Baljin, Mirae pulled Hongbin back to the spot of spine where Siwon lay, nestled between two of the largest ridges.

"Give me some space," Mirae said as she settled in beside her wounded friend. Everyone shuffled backward, letting her work unimpeded.

Although healing magic wasn't Mirae's forte, she knew enough to get the job done. Her command of the elements extended to everything in the mortal realm, be it water, stone, or air. A human's body was complex, of course, but not more so than the materials out of which it, and everything else in the world, had been made.

Closing her eyes to maintain her focus, Mirae placed a hand over Siwon's wound and ordered her powers of Jade Witchery to commune with his muscles, veins, and blood, to empower them to fix what had been sundered. With her help, the veins were compelled to quickly solder themselves back together, his muscles to restitch themselves, and his blood to replenish. As soon as she felt the torn skin beneath her hands close up, knotting into a fresh scar, Mirae removed her hand and opened her eyes.

Although Siwon had cried out several times as his body repaired itself—a process Mirae wasn't skilled enough to facilitate painlessly—he looked up at her weakly, but gratefully. He held up his arm to examine it, still bloodied and marred, but more or less healed. Now it was just another scar to add to the thin ones lightly veining his face.

"Thank you," Siwon breathed. The hair framing his face, curling from the dampening sweat on his brow, peeked out from beneath the silk headband he wore like dark sprouts searching for sunlight. Without thinking, Mirae reached out and tugged the piece of cloth back into place, as she would for Hongbin. The movement made the embroidered bronze moons on the black cloth wink like a handful of tossed coins.

Despite the pain still lingering in his tender, swollen muscles, Siwon managed to shoot Mirae an amused look. "Do I now look presentable enough to be in your presence?"

Mirae smiled apologetically. "I suppose. Though if you wish to remain in my good graces, you shouldn't put yourself in harm's way for me again. I can take care of myself."

"I know." Siwon tried to chuckle, but only ended up wincing from pain. "I seem to have a bad habit of trying to shield women who are sharpened swords. The only time I failed to act rashly was at the Kun Sunim Trial, and look how that turned out."

Mirae tried not to feel disappointed that Siwon had, yet again, turned their friendly conversation into a discussion about Areum. This twinge of jealousy was a strange, ugly pattern that she desperately wanted to shake. Trying to do just that, she leaned into Siwon's regret, hoping to help him heal whatever other wounds he might be harboring. "Why didn't you stop her?" Mirae asked quietly. "You clearly care about Areum, so why did you let her do something so risky?"

"Because it was her decision," Siwon said. He was clearly exhausted. His eyelids were starting to droop, slowly closing like heavy doors swinging shut. "She follows her own moral code, and it's my job to respect that. I meant it when I vowed to protect her, no matter what."

"Doesn't it make it hard to protect people, though," Mirae asked, thinking of the cowardly Josan king, who couldn't seem to understand that the deal she'd offered him was the best thing for everyone, "when they make terrible decisions?"

"Of course," Siwon said sleepily. "But it wouldn't be love if my commitment came with stipulations, if I expected people to submit before I fight for them."

Love. The word sank like a stone into the pit of Mirae's stomach. Swallowing the hard lump forming in her throat, Mirae watched Siwon's lids flutter closed, his breaths evening into the rhythm of sleep. Mirae quietly moved away, leaving him to his rest.

After quickly patching up Hongbin's chin, leaving him with a thin white scar that he insisted made him look like a "dashing adventurer," Mirae noticed Areum looking at her expectantly, sitting a few ridges away. When her friend patted the scales beside her, Mirae obligingly headed over and settled in.

As much as she wanted to ask Areum how she and Siwon came to be so close, hoping to be so charmed by their love story that she could melt away the resentment building inside her, there was something more important to discuss. Something that couldn't be put off any longer.

"I guess it's finally time to talk about the Dark Moon Oracles," Mirae said, trying her best to smile. "Hopefully this time without interruption."

When Areum nodded, the silvery cast of her eyes, though no longer glowing, glittered in the moonlight. *A fine pair they make*, Mirae admitted. *The moon-eyed oracle and the sun-eyed soldier, fighting the rising darkness side by side.*

"I'll tell you the Dark Moon Oracle lore that the other Kun Sunim candidates told me," Areum said, "based on what they've read in our archives."

When Mirae gestured for her to begin, Areum cleared her throat and started her tale.

In the beginning, the gods created heavenly beings to serve as stewards of the mortal sphere. Their descendants were the first humans, who assisted their godlike ancestors in caring for the earth. They sang and danced in tune to the life-giving energies humming throughout the land, reinforcing its rhythm, keeping it strong so that all creation could blossom. These early humans maintained their closeness to the heavens by living off the earth's milk, and joyously integrating her hallowed melodies into every aspect of their lives.

As a reward for their virtuous living, the gods allowed mortals to have supernatural abilities, such as the ability to fly or leap long distances, and live incredibly long lives.

Unfortunately, as the earth's bounty grew and diversified, so did the allure of all the other fruits she grew, plump and lush enough to tempt the first humans to taste their flavors. After discovering the earth's other unique, delicious offerings, early mortals began to abandon earth milk, and, instead of filling the earth with song and dance, they became distracted by all manner of worldly vices, allowing greed and indolence to infest their ranks.

As our ancestors gradually became more and more corrupted, indulging in things that took them away from their stewardship, the earth milk dried up, and the gods closed the gates of heaven, shutting humanity off. Slowly, over time, humans devolved into what they are now—mortals who have lost touch with their metaphysical powers and their original calling.

However, over a thousand years ago, the Go sisters caught the attention of the Samsin after exhibiting exemplary virtue of an almost godlike quality. The Samsin awarded these women with magical abilities, a small taste of the power the first humans wielded; and thus the magic systems of Seolla were created. Along with these new powers, the Go sisters were tasked with a divine mission, that of uniting the peninsula and inspiring humanity to reclaim a golden age where gods and humans could once more mingle and thrive.

This, however, is where the accounts of the Dark Moon Oracles differ from those of the Sacred Bone Oracles. As you know, Seollans are taught that the gift of magic was gods-sanctioned, which makes Seolla the new steward of the peninsula, destined to unite it and bring all people lasting prosperity, provided that they prohibit the rise of the Inconstant Son.

However, the Dark Moon Oracles tell a different story. In their version, the Jade Emperor, ruling god of the heavens, was furious with the Samsin for giving fallen mortals divine power they did not deserve. In his anger, he sought out the goddess of time, demanding to know what calamities would befall creation because of this misstep, and she confirmed his fears—that humans were fated to do what they always did, corrupt the divine gifts given to them. Worse yet, among the ranks of magical men would arise a villain who would not be content with ruling humanity. Should he accomplish his aims, the gods themselves would be in danger.

Thus began a great debate in the heavens. The Jade Emperor demanded that the Samsin rescind their gift of magic in order to keep the heavens safe from the Inconstant Son, and keep mortals in their place until they earned the right to have the heavens, and its gifts, reopened.

The Samsin, however, stood their ground, reminding all the other gods that ever since the heavens had shuttered, their realm had been slowly dying. Their world was inextricably intertwined with the mortal realm, which was why they needed the help of consecrated mortals to magnify the divine energies that kept everything alive.

The other gods couldn't deny that the music of creation had greatly dimmed in the mortal sphere, and that their own kingdom had suffered for it. But they were still troubled by the goddess of time's prophecy about a so-called Inconstant Son. To assuage their fears, the Samsin proposed that safeguards be implemented against the rise of this villain.

Firstly, they would forbid all men from being allowed to wield magic. Secondly, the omniscient goddess of time would be tasked with handpicking three women to wield unprecedented power, equipped to thwart the Inconstant Son, should he still manage to rear his head. If the gods trusted the goddess of time's prophetic abilities, then they should have equal faith in her ability to ensure that the right women were picked at the right time to keep the heavens safe.

Thankfully for the Samsin, the majority of the gods were convinced that this was the best course of action to preserve their home indefinitely. But the Jade Emperor was displeased. In protest, he abandoned the heavens, decreeing that he would not return until magic was removed from the earth. He warned that fallen humans could not be trusted or controlled.

Losing the considerable power of the Jade Emperor meant the gods were unable to travel between realms. Incapable of visiting the earth to communicate with humans, they had to rely entirely on Horomancers to divine their will, and hope that all would go according to plan.

Unfortunately, even the Horomancers themselves soon became divided by the gods' mixed messages. The oracles who trusted the Samsin's reassurances, and later supported the inception of a Sacred Bone line of women who would be powerful enough to lead Seolla, made it their mission to guide their enchanted queens and spread Seolla's influence to every nation. In time, they believed, the divine magic they propagated would permeate the entire peninsula, and restore the mortal sphere to its former glory.

The Dark Moon Oracles, however, heeded the whispers of the dissenting gods who regretted angering the Jade Emperor and ignoring his warnings. In their eyes, magic was a corrupting force in Seollan hands, a weapon used to conquer rather than benefit all mortals equally. At this rate, magic was doomed to lead humanity further away from their calling of restoring earth's divine harmony—just as the Jade Emperor predicted.

But the exhortations of the Dark Moon Oracles were rebuffed, labeled as traitorous ideology. Their persecution became so horrific that they were forced to flee Seolla. Thankfully, they found a new home in the valley of the Chilbyeolsan range, the highest peaks in Baljin. There, they built a safe haven of their own design and called it Sujeongju. The Crystal City became a place where they could preserve the truths Seolla buried and await their chance to correct the queendom's folly.

For the time being, however, they continued to do their best to live worthy of magic by re-creating the lifestyle of the first humans, who were allowed to have open communication with the gods. So it was that, in their community, all were considered equal, and none ruled by virtue of pedigree alone. Most important, knowledge was freely shared so that all in their sanctuary could prepare for the day when Seolla would inevitably bring about its own downfall, and the Dark Moon Oracles' holy tenets would finally come to light.

When Areum's voice trailed off, dawn blushed daintily against the horizon, casting the northernmost region of Josan in a rosy glow. Miles upon miles of pale yellow canola flowers calmly held the pink light of sunrise like cups of hibiscus tea, swaying lightly in the wind. Sprawling homesteads, miles apart from each other, punctured the endless fields, their thatched roofs shining like golden hats in the morning rays that reminded Mirae how long it had been since she'd rested, or eaten a proper meal.

Areum also seemed to be feeling the effects of their harrowing escape. Her head started to nod forward, heavy with exhaustion. Mirae looked around at her other companions, their faces lined with weariness. Hongbin, who had scooted closer to listen in as soon as Areum began her tale, had fallen fast asleep, as if he'd heard the best bedtime story of his life.

Only Kimoon sat away from the others, clutching the block of black water that Mirae had enchanted to remain solidly frozen. She could only guess at the dark thoughts that made his brow wrinkle and fed his brooding glower. There were, unfortunately, any number of things that could be darkening his mood. Grief for losing his homeland. Memories of Soori, a brother once bright and trusting, now a bitter enemy.

But when Kimoon's amber eyes flickered over to where Siwon lay, his lips parting as if considering whether to utter what was in his heart, Mirae wondered if Kimoon was actually troubled because he recognized the name of Siwon's birth mother. There was clearly a story there, one that would rankle any bastard prince who'd done terrible things to be noticed by his father— something another illegitimate son was capable of achieving without any effort at all.

But whatever it was Kimoon wanted to say, he snuffed it out

as quickly as it arose. Catching Mirae staring at him, Kimoon hid his face by resting it against the block of black water, making it clear he wanted to be left alone.

Respecting his wishes, Mirae urged Areum to get some rest before making her way back to the front of the dragon. Then she closed her own eyes, slipping into the numbing embrace of a restless half sleep.

Chapter
SEVENTEEN

Mirae knew the instant her dragon left Josan and crossed into the northern nation of Baljin, not just because the land below had shifted away from sprawling fields to one of azure rivers veining through miles of forested peaks but because of the way the very air felt.

The shift was strong enough to wake her from her light doze and leave her wondering at the strange new world she had entered. While Josan was stagnantly magicless, and Seolla practically vibrated with the energy of enchantments that covered almost every inch of the land, here in Baljin, there was a near-tangible electricity in the air that filled Mirae's body with a heady, freeing rush.

The pull of magic felt loose and wild, determined to follow no rules but its own. When Mirae sent out her senses to interact with the elements, the droplets of water and tendrils of air around her seemed to cackle as they dashed out of reach, cajoling her for trying to manipulate them.

Looking down, Mirae could even see what unfettered magic did to the very landscape below. It was visible in the way trees that normally grew in different climes now thrived side by side, as if it was only natural to get along. She saw that same fascinating lawlessness reflected in the mountainsides themselves, which seemed to mischievously shift out of the corners of her eyes, bulging or thinning when she wasn't looking. Even the direction that lakes and rivers flowed would inexplicably change, almost as if every known characteristic of the earth could be altered or transformed to suit the whims of nature's capricious spirits.

Astounded as she was by the thriving chaos beneath her, Mirae didn't let herself get distracted from her mission. Peeling her eyes away from the wondrous sights below, she peered as far as she could into the distance, searching for the tallest range of them all—Chilbyeolsan, the hidden abode of the Dark Moon Oracles.

Thankfully, she thought she could see it up ahead, towering peaks running along the horizon like the outline of a jagged crown. One that reminded Mirae uncomfortably of the one the Netherking wore.

Realizing it had been some time since she'd sensed any movement from her enemy, Mirae closed her eyes and pressed a hand to her wrist, trying to find the link that connected them. But after a few moments of searching, the only Sacred Bone heartbeat she could feel was Hongbin's behind her.

Perhaps the wild magic of Baljin is difficult to penetrate, she thought, trying to remain calm, and attempted once more to feel out her enemy's location. But, just as before, the Netherking's heartbeat remained elusive.

As sweat began bubbling up on her brow, Mirae was struck with a thought that made her eyes fly open and her heart pound painfully fast, nearly lurching out of her chest. *What if I can't find his pulse because I'm already too late, and he's no longer in this world? Maybe he found a way to enter the heavens, and is preparing to slaughter the gods as we speak—*

"Careful, Mirae," Kimoon said, startling her out of her panic. "If you keep your mouth open too long, there'll be no flies for the rest of us to swallow."

Mirae whirled to face the man who had snuck up on her. The expression on her face melted away the lines of amusement on his. "What is it?" he asked, eyebrows raised in alarm.

"The Netherking . . . I can't feel him. I think he's—what if he's already—"

"Massacring the gods?" Kimoon finished her thought, though his voice was laced with doubt. "Mirae, if the gods were dead, or at war, I think we'd know."

He gestured at the world around them, chaotic but full of life. Untouched by the evil influence of a new, wicked god. Comforted by Kimoon's reasoning, Mirae's cheeks cooled, and her heartbeat slowed.

"You're right," she breathed, trying to expel all the anxiety bundled up in her muscles. "I think the wild magic in the air is messing with my ability to track the Netherking. I'm sure it's nothing to be concerned about."

"Probably not. And trust me, *he's* the one who should be afraid right now," Kimoon added. "The black water is ours, which means he'll eventually be incapable of hurting you with the pearl. Without his abominable weapon, you are more than a match for him."

Marveling at Kimoon's optimism, Mirae was surprised even further when Kimoon pulled an apple out of his pocket and held it out to her.

"Mirae, I know you brought me along so that I could help us get in and out of Josan without incident," he said. "But I failed. Will you please accept my deepest apple-ogies?"

At first Mirae just stared at the red fruit, dumbfounded, until the ridiculousness of the situation sank in. Although she sighed with exasperation, a grin still broke out on her face. "That . . . was terrible. Your worst joke yet."

"Well, you almost laughed," Kimoon said with a shrug. "You have to admit, sometimes terrible works."

Mirae's smile wavered at the flicker in his eyes when he uttered those words: *sometimes terrible works.* He'd said them weightily, as if they were a prelude to what was truly on his mind. When Mirae looked at him inquisitively, bidding him to speak plainly, Kimoon let out a long breath before reluctantly heeding her invitation.

"Last night, I watched you show kindness to a complete stranger," he said. "That man turned out to be a backstabbing impostor, but still, I'll admit you inspired me. I mean, at first I was frustrated at you for losing sight of our objective," Kimoon confessed with a sigh. "Instead of wasting time on a man who was, as far as you could tell, already marked for death, we should have moved quickly, decisively. Maybe we could have even fled before my father arrived. But instead, you risked everything to help someone in need.

"One year ago, I might have lectured you for that," Kimoon

continued. "I would have said that if we keep trying to save everyone, then we may end up saving no one. When the fate of the many is at stake, then the necessity of leaving a few unfortunate souls behind is a kindness that feels cruel. For you to succeed, you must learn to accept a few losses."

As much as Mirae wanted to reject Kimoon's callousness, she could hear it echoing the same warning that Areum's heavenly visitor had tried to impart.

But Mirae still resisted the ruthless call of the unnamed god. And she knew she wasn't the only one. Hongbin always supported her merciful side. And she could hardly forget Siwon, who didn't hesitate to follow her lead in the ice house. He didn't need convincing to help the wretched. It came as naturally to him as it did to Mirae.

But will that be my downfall? Mirae wondered. *Am I doomed to fail if I don't become more thick-skinned? Is there no middle road, a balance between Kimoon's hard-hearted approach and Siwon's compassion? Can I not succeed without losing myself, breaking my promise to Father?*

"I'm not finished yet—bear with me a moment," Kimoon soothed, seeing the conflict on Mirae's face. "As I said, your actions last night inspired me to think a little differently. Perhaps not in the way you'd like, but I still think you should hear me out."

"I'm listening," Mirae said, nodding for him to continue.

"I know you asked me to never bring this up again," Kimoon said slowly, hands raised placatingly. "But after what happened with Soori, I . . . well, I can't stand the thought of you losing a brother the way I did." Kimoon took a deep breath. "I believe that I can help you save the 'one,' Mirae, *and* the many, in one fell swoop."

Although Mirae rankled at what Kimoon was suggesting, she forced herself to listen. She'd promised more than once that she would hear him out, so she waited, letting him continue to tighten the growing tension between them.

"It's not too late, Mirae. Why kill Minho when we can still cure him?" Kimoon asked, referring once again to the dark magic ingredient she'd asked him to forget about. "Let me supply what is needed to exorcise the Netherking from my own body."

"Why are you so convinced this will work?" Mirae asked. Despite her best efforts to listen impartially, her voice was tinged with ice. "Where did you even get this idea?"

"I told you," Kimoon said dismissively, his eyes darting away. "From books the dowager queen kept in her study. They gave me reason to believe that there was truth to seemingly innocent folktales. Dark but effectual remedies we've long forgotten."

"You expect me to believe," Mirae said slowly, "that you became enthralled by the promises of dark magic . . . because of children's stories?"

"Children's stories carry truth, if we're humble enough to dig deeper into them," Kimoon retorted, his voice rising defensively. Loud enough that, to Mirae's dismay, it carried to the ears of someone who'd just woken up enough to start listening in.

"Are you two discussing the virtues of folktales," Hongbin asked, his indignation interrupted by a powerful yawn, "without me?"

Ignoring the warning look Mirae shot his way, Kimoon replied, "Yes, and you're just the person we need to settle our debate. Care to regale us with a story, to prove my point about the power our oral traditions carry?"

"Always!" Hongbin sat up straighter and cleared his throat in preparation. "Do you have any particular one in mind?"

"I do," Kimoon said, finally meeting Mirae's eyes, unflinching in the fierce heat of her displeasure. "How about a classic? 'The Tale of the Rabbit and the Dragon King,' perhaps?"

Hongbin needed no further prodding. As much as Mirae wanted to put an end to Kimoon's manipulation, she didn't dare call attention to why this story made her uncomfortable, nor did she have the heart to deny Siwon some amusement after he'd perked up and voiced interest in a little distraction from the pain in his arm.

Soon after, Hongbin began happily rattling off the seemingly innocuous adventure of a cunning rabbit who was tricked into traveling to the undersea palace of the ailing Dragon King, so the god could eat his liver and be cured of a mysterious illness. While Hongbin's dramatization was certainly entertaining, full of put-on voices and over-the-top facial expressions, Mirae could glean no joy from his performance. Not while Kimoon kept his gaze leveled on her the entire time, silently urging her to give his dark proposal a chance.

He'd done much the same thing the first time he'd brought up the possibility of there being an unexpected interpretation to this innocent story. One that could hold the secret to Minho's freedom. *What if*, Kimoon had excitedly theorized, *we looked at this story literally? The Dragon King had a seemingly irremediable condition, much like Minho, and only a rabbit liver could cure him. It's unorthodox, but what harm could there be in seeing if there's actually something there?*

Of course, Mirae had been quick to ask what led to this sudden, strange hypothesis, but Kimoon had dodged the question then as he did now. Still, Mirae had begrudgingly agreed that there was no harm in testing out his theory. There was some—albeit farfetched—logic to support his idea, given that livers were responsible for purging bodies of toxic matter, and of all the words to describe the Netherking, *toxic* was a top contender.

So, she'd allowed Kimoon and her mother to add rabbit liver to their concoctions, as distasteful as that felt. But when their experiments failed to provide the desired result, Kimoon had been particularly nettled by the Netherking's mockery, and became even more insistent that they were missing something—perhaps the balance was off, or the breed of rabbit was wrong. He refused to give up on his conviction that rabbit liver held the key.

Mirae had indulged his obsession for a while, giving him free rein to postulate as much as he wanted, as long as he didn't try any more tests without her permission. That is, until his wild speculations began to take a dark turn.

One day he rushed at her as soon as she landed in the Deep, eyes red rimmed with lack of sleep, but nevertheless wide and agitated. That was the day Mirae had finally shut down his experiments indefinitely, forbidding him from cracking open any more tomes even distantly related to dark magic. For in their depths he'd found a recipe that called for an unspeakable ingredient that had inspired him to ask a dangerous question.

I figured it out, Mirae, he'd said feverishly. *I know what we were missing. What we would never allow ourselves to consider. Do you know what year I was born? Me and Minho both? That's what made everything click, what made me see. It isn't an* animal *we need to sacrifice. The liver we need must come from a* human, *someone born a very specific year. Do you know what this means, Mirae? We can do it—we can cure him!*

Mirae hadn't listened to any more of Kimoon's ideas, not about harvesting livers from criminals, or those already close to death. She told Kimoon in no uncertain terms that she would never stoop to the Netherking's levels by meddling with dark magic, harming the innocent to get what she wanted. Not even to save someone she loved.

In fact, if Mirae's mother hadn't vouched for Kimoon, insisting that his help was indispensable, Mirae would have sent him away from the Deep. From her very inner circle, if need be. She certainly would never have thought to bring him along in this pursuit of the peninsula's most vile wielder of dark magic, if not for the exhortation of her future self. For that reason alone, she'd allowed him to stay by her side, putting trust in the promise that, without him, her mission would fail.

Hongbin's voice trailed off, finished with his retelling. As Siwon and Areum clapped appreciatively, Kimoon leaned forward and whispered, "Let me do this, Mirae." His dark hair spiraled in the wind, as dark as the plea he refused to rescind. "I want to help you get your brother back, and expel the Netherking. Do not let him win. Do not let him take anything more from you. Let me be the one to end this, and atone for everything I've done."

There was no doubt in Mirae's mind that Kimoon meant every word he said. But after his recent monologue about Mirae's enviable ability to care for everyone she came across, no matter how inconvenient, she was surprised that he thought she'd be so easily convinced to dispose of *him*. Seeing the resistance in her eyes, Kimoon reached out and gripped her arm.

"Don't misunderstand," he said quietly. "I believe you are quite capable of finding a way to preserve my life while extracting what you need. In fact, I'm counting on it. I'm just asking that you give *us* a chance. A true partnership where you and I commit to a cure, no matter what it costs me. It's within our grasp, I can feel it."

Mirae wished she knew what to say to cool the feverish passion that had overtaken her friend. A symptom, she believed, of feeling desperate to finish their mission before he lost anything else that was precious to him. But in her heart, Mirae still believed there was another way to get her brother back, even if she was being hopelessly naive. There had to be a path forward that didn't require her to bend to the call of dark magic instead of eliminating it from the peninsula. She just prayed that the gods would reveal her true path before Kimoon did anything drastic.

"There it is," Areum called out, startling both Mirae and Kimoon. Glad for the timely interruption, Mirae turned to face straight ahead, at the mountains looming in the distance. "We've reached Chilbyeolsan."

The Mountains of the Seven Stars were impressive. Taller

than any other range Mirae had ever seen. Its massive summits were wreathed in trees as thick as fur, and green as the richest shade of jade. Spiraling mist encircled each of the peaks like soaring silver dragons.

"Mirae," Kimoon tried once more, squeezing her arm, more tightly this time. "You promised me once that you would give me something no one else has, a chance to follow my heart and thaw the winter in my soul. This is how—"

Not wanting him to finish that sentence and hold her to a promise she couldn't bear to keep, not like this, Mirae pulled away, silencing Kimoon with a look. "Let us wait and see what the Dark Moon Oracles have to say." Her voice was calm but firm, leaving no room for argument. "If anyone can help us find a more tenable solution, it's them. Until then, I must once more insist that you do not speak of this again."

A flash of anger flickered across Kimoon's face, temporarily muddying the gold of his eyes. But, a second later, he bowed stiffly. "As you wish, Mirae," he said curtly, and fell silent.

Leaving Kimoon to his sulking, Mirae encouraged her dragon to circle the grouping of mountains that formed Chilbyeolsan while she gazed down into the misty crater at the center of the peaks. But the fog was too impenetrable to see through, so Mirae searched for any other possible openings that could lead to the entrance to the Dark Moon Oracles' abode.

Finally, after several rotations, Mirae spotted something peculiar: in the bright, white-hot rays of the early morning sun, she noticed an enormous limestone boulder jutting out of the side of one of the mountains, an anomaly that was perfectly, unnaturally round. The pale, stony orb glittered with crystalline shards that littered its surface like a coat of gems. Moreover, far below it, eternally shadowed by the moonlike sphere jutting out into the sky, was a dark recess that looked very much like the entrance to a cave.

Mirae steered her dragon down toward the shaded opening, hoping that whoever, or whatever, waited for them inside would not immediately turn away—or worse, attack—the Seollan strangers who had flown, unsanctioned, into their domain.

As soon as Mirae landed her dragon, everyone gladly disembarked, stretching their limbs and groaning. Mirae made sure that she and her creation exchanged customary bows before the latter sank back into the earth, coating the ground with a layer of shimmering rainbow dust.

As soon as she released the spell that kept her dragon intact, exhaustion hit Mirae like a wall of stone. She knew it was time to figure out how to enter Sujeongju, the Crystal City, where the Dark Moon Oracles had lived for a thousand years, but she could barely keep her eyes open.

Mirae turned to survey her companions, who looked just as worse for wear. "Get something to eat," she said, gesturing toward the lush landscape around them, where more than a few blackberry bushes and wild yuzu trees surrounded them, and nearby streams sparkled with the silver flashes of fish. "I'm going to rest for a moment."

While her companions started setting up camp—gathering wood so Hongbin could start a fire with his palms, collecting berries for breakfast, and drawing fresh water from the crystal clear stream nearby—Mirae found a soft, mossy patch of earth to sit down on. She closed her eyes for a moment, trying to drown out the noises around her. Before she knew it, her aching muscles melted into the yielding ground, curling her body into itself as her mind drifted away and she knew no more.

Chapter

EIGHTEEN

When Mirae opened her eyes, it was late afternoon. Realizing she'd been asleep for hours, Mirae sat bolt upright and looked around for her companions.

She saw them nearby, each busy with their own task. Hongbin sat by the fire he had created, holding a spitted fish over the flames. Areum was by the nearby stream, dipping her feet into its cold, refreshing water as she rinsed off the various berries she had found in the bushes at the foot of the mountain. Siwon sat near the pebbled shore, crafting a covered pallet made of fallen branches to carry the block of frozen black water. Kimoon had wandered a little ways into the surrounding trees, back bent as he picked what looked to be bushes of herbs.

Despite her alarm at having wasted so much time, Mirae's heart still warmed at her friends' quiet industry, their commitment to helping her see this mission through without complaint. She only hoped that their faith in her would be rewarded.

As soon as everyone noticed that Mirae was awake, they started to gather around the fire, as if they'd been waiting for her to begin their meal. Sitting in companionable silence, they began passing around the food they'd prepared: plump raspberries and a fish skewer from which they could peel juicy meat. Kimoon pulled out his supplies bag, which he'd filled with wild onions and radishes he'd foraged, and began peeling his own meal to be roasted while the others ate.

Mirae was particularly excited about the fish, dripping delicious oil, but just as she was about to take her first bite, a loud voice erupted behind her.

"Stop!"

So startled that she dropped everything she was holding, Mirae whirled around, looking up toward the cave entrance at the foot of the mountain, from which the command had echoed.

A woman stormed out of the opening like a bear protecting its cub. Short and thin, she wielded a staff as expertly as any soldier, her toned muscles bunched and well trained to strike. Nevertheless, the woman's garb made Mirae hold her ground. The woman's linen, sunset-colored robes loosely fit her in a way that reminded Mirae of those worn by the Sacred Bone Oracles; but instead of a bald head, the approaching woman had a long, thick braid of white hair draped down her back. When she finally came to a stop several feet away from the campfire, she stared at Mirae and her companions as if they were snakes stealing chicken eggs from her coop.

Immediately determining who their leader was, she fixed her narrowed eyes on Mirae. "So," she said, "you have come to defile this holy place with your barbarism. The Darksome Lord was right about you."

The Darksome Lord? Mirae thought, stomach twisting. *Is the Netherking already here, turning the Dark Moon Oracles against us? Are we too late?*

Thankfully, Areum swooped in, seeming to understand what had upset the other oracle. She grabbed the fish skewer and threw it into the fire. "My most sincere apologies," she said, bowing deeply. "We did not mean to offend."

Realizing what Areum had concluded, that killing and consuming animals was against their accoster's beliefs, Mirae also bowed in apology. "Please forgive us. We are ignorant about the Dark Moon Oracles' tenets."

But the glaring woman only seemed to grow more offended at Mirae's words. "We are called the Seers of Light," she said coldly. "We do not answer to the derogatory title you Seollans branded us with."

Well, this isn't going very well, Mirae thought sheepishly. Unsure of what to say, or if she should just shut up and stop making things worse, Mirae was almost relieved when the combative seer took over the conversation.

"I am the sentinel of the Crystal City," the old woman said, gripping her staff tightly. "Tell me why I should let you barbaric intruders into a holy place of ancient wisdom."

Mirae took a deep breath, hoping her answer wouldn't inadvertently cause even more offense. "I'm sure you and the other Seers of Light already know why we have come, especially if, as I suspect, the Netherking has already been permitted to enter your city. He probably told you he came here seeking knowledge about the spirit world, but I doubt he's relayed his true intentions. If your people are considering extending your help to him, we humbly ask for a chance to voice our objections. The situation is quite dire."

"He has told us about his mission," the seer confirmed. She

crossed her arms over her chest. "Given that his arrival was fore-told, the council will not dismiss his request lightly."

"The Netherking is a master of lies," Mirae said, bowing again to ensure that her harsh words were not taken as impudence. "I have come to offer information about him that is of great value. Please allow me to speak to the council and tell them all I know."

The seer made a sound of disapproval. "Surely you did not believe we would allow you to enter our sanctuary when you, as a Seollan royal, dishonor our beliefs and our mission. It is bold of you to presume that we need your assistance in determining truth from lie when you are descended from the peninsula's most prolific deceivers."

"I may be their descendant," Mirae said, swallowing. "But I am not like them."

"Oh?" The seer raised an eyebrow and waited for Mirae to explain herself.

As awkward as it felt to sing her own virtues, Mirae knew she had no other choice but to try. "Well, I named my brother as my heir, for starters, and I'm slowly lifting the ban against men wielding magic. When I return to Seolla, I plan to free Josan from Seollan rule. I know I'm still very ignorant about my ancestors' sins, including those committed against your own people, but I'm willing to learn and repent for my country's wrongdoings."

The seer raised an eyebrow at Mirae's heartfelt speech. "Well, the council will hardly congratulate you for finally doing what should have been done all along. All the lives that were ruined or lost over the centuries have not been atoned for."

"Then let me start by protecting all remaining life," Mirae

said. She lowered herself to her knees, and heard her companions do the same behind her. "I don't know what the Netherking has said to the council, but he isn't telling them everything. He isn't baring his true soul. Let me prove that I am different from my ancestors, and that my intentions are pure."

"How?" the seer asked. "How will you convince me to trust a Seollan royal?"

"You could switch, noonim," Mirae heard Hongbin whisper. "Show her that the gods brought you here, and that they reveal unimaginable things to you alone."

Mirae had considered that, too, but rejected the idea. She had a feeling that brazen displays of Seollan power were not going to get her inside the Crystal City; rather, they would reinforce the Dark Moon Oracles' distrust of her. No, there had to be a better way.

Mirae looked back at her companions, who had sacrificed much to stay by her side. An unlikely group of disparate people who trusted Mirae implicitly. When she turned back to face the seer, who was suddenly watching her with great interest, she gestured toward the individuals kneeling behind her.

"It is not my opinion of myself that matters, but rather the people I love and protect. From former outlaws to forsaken exiles, all souls are precious to me. I don't care about the power they give me, or the things they may have done in the past to survive. If there's one thing I've learned over the past few years, it's that people only become their best selves when they are free to do so. That's why I no longer believe that uniting the peninsula means conquering and ruling it, as my ancestors and the Netherking presume, but rather granting everyone self-sovereignty so all may live in harmony. I believe it was a spiritual uniting that the gods spoke of, not the creation of one all-powerful ruling class. Misunderstanding this has led to so much sorrow, and it's time to make it all stop. If you and the Seers of Light agree with me, please let me try to make this belief a reality by exposing the Netherking's true intentions before he ruins our chance to see the world we want to create."

"And then what?" the seer asked, cocking her head to one side. "What will you do after you've thwarted the Darksome Lord?"

"Everything I have said," Mirae said, lifting her chin. "I will liberate Josan, and force Seolla to wield magic altruistically. What is good for one will be good for all."

"And when I am king, I pledge to similarly dedicate my life to making all this a reality," Hongbin said. "My noonim and I will build the world we all want to see."

"You can trust the word of these Seollan royals," Kimoon chimed in. "They had every reason to hate and revile me, and yet they showed me kindness. They are everything they claim to be, and they speak true about the Netherking."

"And they are true believers," Areum added. "Though they have suffered much while walking this path, they never faltered. You can trust them to see their promise through."

"I, too, can attest to their goodness," Siwon said, the last to speak. "The High Queen and crown prince of Seolla are bringers of light, while the Netherking is a sower of ruin. I have seen this firsthand."

The seer stared at Siwon a moment, then her eyes shifted over to Hongbin.

"So, a Seollan king has been promised," the woman said, rubbing her chin thoughtfully. "This is not the first time. Many have tried to assume this honor, and failed."

"They didn't have my noonim supporting them," Hongbin countered.

"That is true," the seer said. "It was always a Daughter of the Sacred Bone who stopped your predecessors, but you have one helping you. That is most unusual."

"We have our hearts in the right place," Hongbin promised. "Things will be different, if you give us a chance."

The seer was quiet a moment before sighing deeply and shaking her head. "I'm not usually one to ignore the wishes of my superiors, but today I woke to the call of a magpie. Very auspicious birds, you know."

Then, quite suddenly, she turned to leave, heading back toward the cave entrance. She stopped when she noticed no one was following her. "Aren't you coming?"

Mirae jumped to her feet. "Of course. Thank you for believing us."

"I never said I did." The seer chuckled as she walked with surprising speed back into the mountain.

Pausing only to give Kimoon and Siwon enough time to grab either end of the covered pallet of black water, Mirae and her companions hurried after, not wanting to lose sight of their guide. As soon as they reached the entrance, Mirae turned to Hongbin. "Will you light the way?"

"Me?" Hongbin asked, surprised. When Mirae nodded, he eagerly summoned a pale blue light into his palms, as if afraid that Mirae would change her mind. Holding his hands aloft, Hongbin lit the sizable entrance to the cave, a stony maw with stalactite teeth.

After taking a deep breath of clean, fresh air, unsure when she'd be able to do that again, Mirae strode forward, leading her companions after the sentinel.

Once inside the cave, Mirae relied on the glow of Hongbin's orb to avoid stubbing her toes on the bases of stalagmites, or brushing against the slick curtains of flowstone stretched across the walls in glistening ribbons. Hongbin's frosty light helped Mirae pick her way carefully through the various obstructions and round the curving walls of the cave, only barely able to keep up with the swift-footed woman striding quickly ahead.

They walked single file through the steep, ascending tunnel for what felt like many miles. Mirae's shins and lungs were burning, her breaths weak and raspy, when the seer finally slowed to a stop. For a brief, panicked moment, Mirae wondered if the seer hadn't been leading them toward Sujeongju after all, but rather into a secret tomb deep in the belly of the mountain.

Fortunately, her concerns were short-lived. Without missing a beat, the seer placed her hand against the wall to her right. Seconds later, a fissure cracked the surface under her palm, lengthening and widening until it became just big enough for one person to pass through at a time. When it was Mirae's turn to squeeze past the opening, she did so quickly, wanting to see what was on the other side. After slipping through, she was surprised to find that the seer had brought them back outside; a few feet in front of her was the enormous limestone orb that had led her party to the cave entrance below.

The sky was starting to darken now, but the stony orb seemed to reflect starlight like a moon tethered to the side of the mountain. Mirae gasped at the striking image, inhaling enough of the chilly evening air to soothe the burning in her lungs.

"Watch your step," the seer cautioned as she sealed the exit behind them and resumed hiking, following a barely visible path. "The earth around here likes to play tricks on the unsuspecting."

The mountain trail was narrow, just like the tunnel they'd vacated. Hongbin, his blue palm light still burning brightly, hurried after the seer, who was disappearing into the darkness. Instead of following in their wake, however, Kimoon stayed put. "I think Siwon needs a break," he said quietly, jerking his head toward the other man.

Indeed, it looked as if Siwon was struggling to catch his breath, and the half of the pallet held up by his scarred arm dipped dangerously lower than the other side.

"I'll take over from here," Areum said quickly, practically pushing Siwon aside. "Kimoon's right, you need to rest."

"I'm all right," Siwon protested, but Mirae shushed him with a look, and he said nothing more as Areum and Kimoon carted the pallet up together, leaving Siwon and Mirae to take up the rear. They stuck close together as they headed higher up the mountain, helping each other step over rocks and roots that, per the seer's warning, seemed intent on tripping them.

After helping Mirae avoid a close encounter with a sneaking tree root, Siwon broke their comfortable silence. "You were very wise not to switch back in the cave, Your Majesty. I don't believe our guide would have been as impressed by your power as I am. It was your heart she was trying to measure, and you showed her your humility. Your goodness."

"She seems rather discerning," Mirae said quietly, for their ears alone. "If she was the one who let the Netherking pass, I'm sure she felt there was something off about him. I think she secretly wanted to let us through, or else we would never have made it this far. The Dark Moon Oracles don't strike me as pushovers."

"Perhaps it would be better to call them the Seers of Light," Siwon said gently. "The name they have chosen for themselves."

"Right, of course." Mirae shook her head. "I'm still getting used to seeing other nations through their own eyes, rather than lenses of Seollan records."

"Well, you've always been good at adapting," Siwon said, bumping Mirae's arm. "And following your instincts. I admire that about you."

Mirae felt her cheeks flush at his compliment. Too flustered to know what to say back, she was relieved when Siwon changed the subject. "Do you really mean what you said? About freeing Josan, despite everything the king has done?"

"Yes," Mirae said. "It's the right thing to do, and it is long overdue."

"It is indeed." The expression on Siwon's face mirrored the near reverence in his voice. "But your people rely on Josan agriculture to survive. . . . What will you do when your queendom inevitably pushes back against your decision?"

"I'll convince them to do what we should have done all along,"

Mirae said. "Create a fair exchange, our goods for Josan's. We will trade as equals. Besides, nothing I've seen shows that a lack of magic has made Josan intrinsically inferior, so why treat them as if they need Seolla's governance, or else they'll perish?"

"But as the class divide between Seolla and Josan closes," Siwon pressed, "your queendom will no longer be much more wealthy or powerful than any other nation on the peninsula. There will be subjects who resist and fear these changes."

"That sounds like a problem for King Hongbin to deal with," Mirae joked, but then cleared her throat, her tone sobering. "You and I both know that our nations will be better off if they start treating each other with respect. It will take time, but soon everyone will come to see things our way."

Siwon nodded. It looked like he wanted to say something else, something stirring from deep inside his soul, but instead he shook off whatever it was and said brightly, "Well, at least King Hongbin won't have to handle all this alone. He'll have you and me by his side."

Mirae smiled. "With what we've both been through, I know we have what it takes to heal this peninsula. We won't let anything stop us."

"We're compatible that way," Siwon agreed. "We always have been."

With those heartfelt words warming the cold mountain air between them, Mirae and Siwon fell into an easy, companionable silence, saving their breath for the rest of the steep climb toward the hidden Crystal City of the Seers of Light.

Chapter
NINETEEN

As soon as they crested the mountain, sunset burgeoned behind the peaks of the rest of Chilbyeolsan like a blooming azalea. The various shrubs and boulders dotting the flat summit were dusted with vermilion and flaxen light, making Mirae feel as if she were wandering between the spikes of an enormous gold-and-agate crown. Shading her eyes from the fiery light, and keeping her gaze fixed on the ground as she walked, Mirae nearly strode right into Kimoon's back before realizing that the seer had stopped their party near the far edge of the mountain.

"Welcome to Sujeongju," the seer said proudly, the only member of the group who wasn't out of breath. In fact, she seemed full of energy as she swept her arms to one side, and then waved them across the view of the valley, as if painting over it with an enormous brushstroke.

The moment her arms cleared the air, Mirae's jaw dropped. The thick mist shrouding the crater at the center of Chilbyeolsan began to disperse, revealing what lay below.

When flying over Baljin, Mirae had noticed that the trees and bushes running down the sides of the ranges were a miraculous mixture of disparate flora that bloomed and thrived no matter the season, or where they were normally expected to grow. Sturdy oak and pine copses grew beside cheery, sprawling cherry blossom trees. Limestone monoliths and diverse undergrowth filled in the rest of the mountainside, teeming with blushing mugunghwa shrubs, blooming indigo plants, and red-dotted wild ginseng.

But what caught Mirae's eye most was the diaphanous lake nestled in the middle of the crater. The surface of the water was a clear, bright blue, even in the rosy light of dusk. But as the water deepened, it lightened in color, for at its center was a gleaming core radiating the palest color of jade. Mirae could only stare at what had to be the outskirts of Sujeongju, a luminous submerged city, the very antithesis of the similarly sunken kingdom of the Deep.

"This is as far as we walk," the seer said, turning to face her followers. "The rest of our journey is for the bitmul to decide."

"The what?" Hongbin asked, extinguishing his palm light.

"The guardian of our hidden city," the seer said, gesturing down at the lake. "No one may enter this valley without her permission."

Before Mirae could ask what this "creature of light" would do to those it deemed unworthy, a gigantic figure burst out of the lake below, shattering its surface into millions of crystal droplets, pink and glittering in the dying sunlight. Long and lithe, the creature twirled through the air like Mirae's dragon, except the bitmul had no horns, and was far leaner. Looking more like a silver-scaled water serpent than Mirae's Sacred Bone creation, the bitmul flew smoothly through the sky, barreling toward Mirae and her party.

Thankfully, the bitmul slowed as it drew near, landing gracefully at the cliff's edge right next to the seer, who was the only one not to take a cautionary step back. Mirae stared up at the proud serpentine creature. The steely armorlike scales running down her body clinked like a hundred swords smashing against shields every time the bitmul moved, causing quite a ruckus as the creature drew itself into a loose coil and studied the humans before her.

Mirae met the creature's gaze, which paused on her in return. Azure eyes, as light as the water of the lake from which the bitmul had emerged, examined Mirae with keen intelligence. A jagged scar, deep enough to mangle the silver scales on the serpent's head, stretched across her face like earth deformed by lightning, bearing testament to the horrors she had endured in her lifetime, as well as to the fact that she was no conjuration, unlike Mirae's dragon. The bitmul was a real beast with a long and heartbreaking story.

"Hello, old friend," the seer said, staring up at the creature fondly. "I have brought more auspicious visitors to help us through this troubling time. Do you agree that they are worthy to enter our precious haven?"

The bitmul took one last long look at Mirae and her party, studying each individual carefully before lowering her head to the ground and shutting her eyes—the same thing Mirae's rainbow dragon did when waiting to be boarded.

"Well, congratulations," the seer said, leading the way once more as she used the bitmul's sturdy metallic scales to climb nimbly up her head and then along her long, lean back. "You've officially been granted passage into Sujeongju. Now hurry; if I miss supper because of you, I'll shave all your heads while you sleep."

Unsettled by the seer's strange threat, Mirae and her companions surged toward the docile beast. However, as soon as the pallet that Areum and Kimoon carried was brought near enough to be hefted up onto her head, the bitmul suddenly opened her cerulean eyes and stared at the bier as if it were the very thing that had given her that unsightly scar. Siwon and Kimoon jumped backward as the bitmul tossed back her head and roared.

Mirae slapped her hands over her ears as the bitmul's ferocious bellow resounded across the mountaintop, echoing thunderously around the hollow crater surrounding the lake. The seer immediately leaped from her perch, landing neatly on the bitmul's head, and placed her face right in front of her closest eye, which had become as gray as the skies in the heart of a monsoon. The seer remained there, calmly meeting the bitmul's darkening gaze until the creature's howls died in her throat and her eyes regained their azure-blue color. Mirae couldn't hear what the seer said to the angered creature, but whatever she whispered thankfully calmed her down. Docile once more, the creature lowered her head as before.

The seer peered down at the pallet and narrowed her eyes at the frozen black water, loosely covered by branches Siwon had bound together. The inky block glittered between the cracks of its cage like a lacquered chest filled with secrets. The seer's jaw tightened as she shook her head. "Not so different from the Netherking after all, are we?"

The seer didn't give Mirae a chance to respond; just as nimbly as before, the elderly woman leaped up onto the bitmul's back and nestled into her ridges. Thankfully, the sentinel didn't urge the bitmul to change her mind and leave the offending visitors there on the mountaintop. Mirae sighed and helped Areum and Kimoon heave the pallet onto the water serpent. Once the pallet bearers were seated, and had their burden securely balanced between them, Mirae, Hongbin, and Siwon climbed up as well. After tucking herself between Areum and their ornery guide, Mirae grasped two of the bitmul's silver scales tightly.

As soon as everyone was on board, the seer called out, "It's time, my friend." At that, the bitmul lifted her head and, without further warning, launched off the side of the mountain.

Mirae would have screamed if the air hadn't been forced out of her lungs by the bitmul's incredible speed. One moment she was on the tallest peak on the peninsula, and the next she was streaking past the verdant, forested walls of the crater, plunging into the jade-tinged water.

Mirae was amazed that she managed to keep her grip when crashing into the lake, but soon panicked at the thought of having to hold her breath for an unknown amount of time; she'd barely managed to eke in even a little bit of air during the brief flight, and wasn't sure how much longer she'd be able to hold out.

Her concern only grew when the bitmul slowed drastically after entering the water, as if relieved to be back in the comfort of her habitat. Mirae clapped a hand over her mouth, trying to hold in what little air remained, until the seer looked over her shoulder at Mirae and said, "Tell your friends not to worry. The lake is enchanted to allow them to speak and breathe."

Mirae heard the seer's words clear as day, and saw the older woman's torso gently expanding and contracting with ease. Mirae took in a tentative breath of her own and found the seer's words to be true—it felt no different from breathing on land, except the air was a little muggier. Mirae immediately turned around and shared the good news with everyone. Hongbin in particular looked relieved. He let out a dramatic breath and inhaled deeply over and over again, as if he'd never filled his lungs with air quite so satisfying.

Finally free to take in her surroundings without worrying about drowning, Mirae looked around at the underwater world she was traveling through, and gazed with wonder at the crystal-line water teeming with life. As with the foliage on the mountain, the fish swimming around Mirae's head seemed oblivious to the seasons, or to the conditions they were originally created to survive in. Here, fresh water and oceanic creatures lived in tandem, silver minnows, spotted skate, and fire-red koi alike. A family of enormous sea turtles with viridian scales floated past Mirae as well, keeping politely out of the bitmul's way. It was as if all creatures, no matter their build or dictated habitat, could live here in peace, including the gill-less like Mirae.

While the bitmul drew closer to the glowing core of the lake, Mirae's attention shifted downward as she tried to catch her first glimpse of the Crystal City, but the thick, luminous barrier surrounding it was practically opaque, too bright to look at for long.

The seer, who had turned to ride sidesaddle along the bitmul's back, suddenly broke the silence without warning. "Just so you're aware, your block of sonsangpi will be confiscated as soon as you arrive."

Mirae glanced over her shoulder at the frozen water, which Siwon and Kimoon had managed to hold in place. What had the seer called it—corrupted blood? "Was the Netherking's pearl confiscated as well?" she asked.

"It was."

Mirae nodded as relief washed over her, as cool as the lake. "I'll happily hand over whatever is required." After a moment, Mirae added, "Thank you for taking a chance on me."

"I did no such thing," the seer said. "I'm just following orders."

Mirae stared at the other woman for a moment, confused. "You mean you were going to bring us here all along?"

"Not necessarily." The seer set her dark, sharp eyes on Mirae. "Like you, I don't always do as I'm told. I just wanted to see for myself if I concurred with the council's decision to grant you entrance, and to see if you were everything the Darksome Lord claimed you were."

Mirae swallowed. "I see. And how did you and the bitmul feel about the Netherking?"

"She sensed a kindred spirit, I think," the seer said. "Collateral damage in a war between the various self-serving powers that be."

"The Netherking is no innocent, whatever he's professed," Mirae retorted.

The seer laughed at Mirae's words as if she were a naive child claiming to see gumihos in the shadows. "My dear, you're going to have to do better than that if you want the council to change its mind about you and your kind."

"I came here to speak the truth," Mirae insisted. "And if the Seers of Light are the seekers of knowledge they claim to be, they will listen."

"To speak the truth, you first have to *know* the truth," the seer chided, raising an eyebrow. "Tell me, have you been told the full history of the Deep Deceiver, who imprisoned the Netherking's ancestors? The very thing he's using as justification for his actions?"

Mirae cleared her throat. "I know all the important parts."

The seer was clearly unconvinced, and Mirae felt her confidence begin to deflate as the old woman continued, "So, you're aware that the Deep is a well of magic that has run dry, and thus how unflattering it looks for Seolla's queen to be here, hunting down the last sacrifice that managed to get away?"

Mirae felt her mouth move, though no sound came out. Yes, the Netherking had told her something she couldn't quite bring herself to believe: the horrendous fate of the nether-fiends, cursed to never leave the cage that not only imprisoned them but slowly stole their magic, siphoning it to be used however Queen Sunbok saw fit. To create dancing kirin in the border wall between Josan and Seolla, perhaps. Or make her hair ornaments sparkle with extra luster. It was a horrific way to die, slowly sapped of something inextricably intertwined with your life force. Mirae had seen this firsthand, but she'd been too bereaved at the loss of her mother to acknowledge that it was hardly any wonder the Netherking had turned the soul-drinking power of black water against Mirae's own family, after losing his daughter to such a horrifying curse.

One Mirae's mother had refused to lift, even to save an innocent child.

"So, even what you do know, you have not yet fully interrogated or accepted," the seer said disapprovingly. "You keep yourself willfully in the dark. I must say, I do not foresee your meeting with the council being very pleasant. Not pleasant at all."

As Mirae floundered for something to say, the seer shook her white-haired head. "I can't believe you came here knowing so little, yet expecting to convince the Seers of Light to change the peninsula's destiny in your favor. Why should they, considering your heritage, and the mission of your queendom that will only take us further from the gods? Although I suppose I shouldn't assume you even know how you got your so-called Sacred Bone powers."

Mirae froze. "What do you mean, so-called?"

The look in the seer's eyes now was one of disdain, and something else—withering contempt. "I could tell you didn't recognize the beast transporting us to Sujeongju, or the evil concoction you've brought with you. Unsurprising, considering what your people did to her kind. She's the last imugi, you know. At least the Darksome Lord's proposal acknowledges the harms his ancestors have done, rather than seeking to maintain their wickedly gained supremacy."

"He seeks to kill the gods!" Mirae blurted out. Her hands clutched the bitmul's scales so tightly she thought her fingers might break. "He'll destroy everything, not just Seolla!"

"Incorrect," the seer said. It was clear her patience with Mirae's ineptitude was running out. "He says he will reverse what should never have been. All that has been built on the blood of the inno-cent, through ill-gotten magic, will be destroyed. The peninsula will be reborn, and all will finally be equal. With the knowledge of the seers, we'll rebuild and live in peace."

"Whatever he's promised, he's lying," Mirae insisted. "He's just saying what everyone wants to hear, when really he plans to steal all magic, killing thousands, so he can have it all for him-self. Think about it—we can achieve everything he's promised ourselves if we use our magic the way the gods intended. There's no need to do things violently."

"Is that so?" the seer asked. She leaned closer to Mirae, her eyes as dark as new moons. "But violence is how your ances-tors got their power, you hypocrite. Do you really believe that your queendom, so reliant on and proud of its elite magic, will level the playing field for the good of all without a fight? Do you really think yourself so mighty that you can single-handedly make your great vision come to life . . . just like the Netherking?"

The seer's final words stole the breath right out of Mirae's lungs, making her feel as if she were drowning in the water around her, as nature intended. The seer shook her head at Mirae's temporary inability to respond; slowly, the ire in the old woman's eyes ebbed away, softening to a look of deep pity. "I'm only saying the words the council will hurl at you. You must pre-pare yourself for the battle ahead. After all, how can you match wits with the Netherking if you don't know his entire plan? How will you prove you can be trusted if you don't fully comprehend the sins of your mothers, something the council will hold against you? The more stubbornly you defend your point of view, the more callous and prideful you will appear. At this rate, I fear you will fail to prevent the Netherking from entering the spirit world."

Breathless from the sentinel's harsh words, ringing with truths that shook her to her core, Mirae sat in silence a moment before finding the will to stammer, "I have to stop him, or countless people will die. I think you believe that, too. Will you help me?"

The seer stared down at the ever-growing glow that housed Sujeongju, the haven of the Seers of Light. "I've already helped as much as I can. I secured your passage and gave you a taste of what you're about to face. The rest, I'm afraid, is up to you and your companions; but for what it's worth, I do believe the gods are rooting for you. Different gods than the ones we follow, perhaps, but that should mean something nonetheless."

The seer's assurances offered small comfort, especially after the baffling things she had said about Mirae's powers and their questionable pedigree. But the other woman had already turned back to the front, done answering questions.

Thankfully, Mirae couldn't sit there and stew on her own troubling thoughts for long, for the Crystal City was fast approaching. As the bitmul—or imugi, as the seer had called her—drew nearer to the massive, beaming core of the lake, Mirae had to shield her eyes until the glaring glow, radiant enough to shine even through her eyelids, finally abated, signaling that she had crossed through to the other side.

Mirae blinked several times before deciding it was safe to look around. When she did, all she could do was stare at the lustrous city nestled in the belly of the Chilbyeolsan range.

All the buildings below, whether they were homesteads, pagodas, or shops in the marketplace, were carved out of gleaming limestone that seemed to grow from the bottom of the lake itself; the stonework was elegant and exquisite, with intricate medallions and sprawling engravings adorning the walls and gables of every structure, even down to the smallest of sheds. All were elaborately beautified, regardless of ownership or purpose.

Even the sloping roofs of the buildings were ornate, whether the tiles were shaped from pale green jade or lined with iridescent pearls. The city streets sparkled as well, seemingly paved with gem-studded sand made out of glittering, sun-bleached shells, and lined with rows of carefully pruned, rosy coral. The sight below, a sea of gleaming white walls, peach foliage, and viridescent awnings spanning the vast lake bed, was truly breathtaking.

Mirae's eye was soon drawn, however, to the enormous pagoda at the center of the city, which had seemingly given the haven its name. Standing almost twenty stories tall, the towering building gave the illusion of transparency, having been forged from a gigantic, cylindrical crystal that made it appear as if the entire pagoda had frozen over. But its walls were thick enough that it was impossible to see anything more than vague shapes and hues inside the crystalline structure. On the outside, contrasting strikingly against the pagoda's paleness, were impressive, tapering golden roofs with swooping edges that arced gracefully, like the fins of a skate.

As the bitmul carried Mirae and her party ever closer to the dazzling city center, it became clear that this was where the council was waiting, where Mirae's final battle of wits with the Netherking was going to take place. Once the pagoda was close enough that Mirae felt she could jump onto one of its golden roofs, the bitmul began her steep descent to the base of the building, twirling her long, lithe body downward until she landed gently on the white courtyard surrounding the pagoda.

Moments later, the creature lowered her head and shut her pale blue eyes, waiting for her passengers to climb off her back. Almost immediately, guards dressed in deep blue robes plated with silver fishlike scales poured out of the pagoda and surrounded the bitmul. The captain at their head strode forward, clearly designated by the golden, wide-brimmed paerangi she wore as a helmet; its warm luster contrasted heavily with those worn by her subordinates, which appeared to be tightly woven from twisted, green-black kelp coated with lacquer.

The captain fixed her shaded eyes on Mirae. "State your name and business."

Mirae stood and called down, "I am High Queen Mirae. I have come with the crown prince of Seolla, two princes of Josan, and an oracle to appear before the council of the Seers of Light in opposition to the Netherking."

The captain glanced at the sentinel who had led Mirae to the Crystal City. When the old woman nodded, the captain turned her attention back to Mirae. "Your arrival has been expected. Follow me, and I shall take you to the Illustrious Hall of the Seven Stars."

Before Mirae could descend, however, her guide grabbed Mirae's arm and whispered something for her ears alone. "Remember that the council will be looking for a reason to dismiss you. You are only here at the Netherking's request, and we both know he does not do anything without reason. Tread carefully, queenling, so you do not fall right into his hands."

At that, the sentinel released Mirae and jumped nimbly to the ground, disappearing into the gathering crowd. Mirae and her companions soon descended as well, though they accepted the help of the soldiers below.

After surrendering the block of black water, Mirae waited for her companions to gather around her so she could look at each of them in turn, gathering strength from the resolve in their eyes. Then she turned toward the entrance to the crystal pagoda and followed the captain inside.

Chapter
TWENTY

The pale limestone of the courtyard continued into the first level of the pagoda, creating a walkway that split the room perfectly in half. On either side were lush gardens of flowering shrubs in full bloom, and trees packed with colorful fruit: golden pears, green plums, bright orange persimmons, dappled yellow yuja, glossy jujubes, and crimson apples. There were also green, bristly chestnuts and vines heavy with magnolia berries. Unsurprisingly, it appeared as if the Crystal City's crops always experienced the never-ending abundance of spring and the harvest-readiness of autumn simultaneously. A land rich in water, light, and magic.

Ahead of Mirae and her companions, flanked by two flourishing, silver-barked peach trees with tinkling jade leaves, was an enormous set of limestone doors that ostensibly led to the Illustrious Hall of the Seven Stars. Etched into the stone were intricate floral motifs that seemed to swirl and flow like the wind and the shifting tides.

The captain slowed once she was close enough to push the doors open. Before she did, however, she turned to Mirae and said, "Only you are permitted to enter."

Unsurprised, Mirae turned toward her companions, but had

hardly completed the motion when Hongbin rushed forward and wrapped her in a tight embrace.

"You can do this, noonim," he whispered fiercely. "The Netherking doesn't have the pearl, so he can't hurt you, and your commitment to delivering the peninsula from danger is a force to be reckoned with. Nothing can stop you—you're bound to be victorious!"

Mirae returned her brother's hug, reinvigorated as always by his unfailing belief in her. "Thank you, Hongbin. I'll try to make you proud."

When she pulled away, Siwon came up to her next, though he patted her arm reassuringly instead of wrapping his arms around her, a gesture that warmed her heart nonetheless. "No matter what happens in there, just know that we've got your back. We'll be right here waiting in case you need anything."

"Yes, we'll stay by your side to the very end!" Hongbin said emphatically.

"And rest assured that the gods are with you, too," Areum said, her silver eyes glittering. "I feel their presence. They'll help you succeed."

"As well they should," Kimoon murmured. "After all, their lives depend on it."

Even though Siwon was the injured one, Kimoon looked the worst for wear. After spending a rough night atop the dragon, his skin was almost as pale as the stone doors, and the reddish bags under his golden eyes were starting to look like bruises. Mirae was almost grateful that they were surrounded by guards, in case Kimoon collapsed while she was gone.

Kimoon must have seen Mirae's concern, for he did his best to smile. "Let's put this skirmish with the Netherking to rest once and for all, shall we?"

Mirae nodded. The sooner she convinced the Seers of Light to accept that the Netherking was a danger to the peninsula, and not its savior, the sooner she could attend to the needs of her family and friends. After giving her companions one last look of gratitude, Mirae turned back to the waiting captain. "I'm ready to address the council now. Please take me to them."

When the captain finally threw the stone doors open for her, Mirae made sure her head was held high, her hands clasped in front of her in a regal pose as she entered and took in the room, while the council did the same to her.

Against the far wall, the twelve councilmembers sat on wide, lacquered thrones with gold etchings of turtles and koi. They wore identical outfits and headgear: flowing, shimmery sea-green robes embroidered with silver cranes, held together by coral-red sashes and square golden belts inlaid with jade. Down their fronts rested heavy, moon-shaped pendants with long, deep green tassels accentuated by elaborate knots. On the head of each councilmember rested an exquisite coronet shaped like a black palanquin adorned with gold and garnet beads, backed by seven layers of glowing, pearly white fabric that winged upward like the petals of a lotus.

Although their ensembles were uniform, Mirae noticed that multiple genders and age groups were represented in that room. From the lines, or sometimes lack thereof, on the council's otherwise unadorned faces, and the amount of gray in their long, straight hair, Mirae guessed that the eldest member was as old as her grandmother, while the youngest looked several years Mirae's junior.

The chamber itself was impressively high-ceilinged, with crystalline walls and floors tiled with mosaiced stone slabs. Behind the council rose a towering statue of a woman in a bustling robe with sleeves as wide as she was tall, intricately etched with constellations. Though her waist-length hair was simply braided and ribboned, the way she gazed elatedly up at the heavens made it clear that she was a holy woman deeply revered by the Seers of Light.

The captain, who had been the first to march into the hall, bowed deeply and broke the silence in the room. "High Queen Mirae has arrived, Your Honors."

"Well met, Your Majesty." The councilmember who spoke sat near the center of the group. As soon as the captain moved out of Mirae's way to stand along the wall with the other guards, Mirae saw that the speaker held the Netherking's pearl in their lap, a pose that reminded Mirae of the mural she'd seen in her mother's burial chamber, depicting Queen Sunbok, the Deep Deceiver. To Mirae's relief, the milky pearl gleamed as brightly as it had before, seemingly purged of the Netherking's magic. The fire of hope rekindled in her chest, for if the seers could cleanse the pearl of the Netherking's corruption, perhaps the same could be done for Minho.

Emboldened, Mirae bowed to the council as deeply as the captain had, her nervousness melting away as she wondered if the gods had indeed brought her here to make everything right. "Thank you for granting me entrance. I am humbled to stand before you."

The speaker, whose eyes looked vaguely blue-black, didn't return the gesture; they remained stock-still, a stance reciprocated by their fellow councilmembers, who all stared at Mirae emotionlessly. After a moment, the speaker said, "I'm sure you are aware that the Netherking has preceded you, and has laid out a detailed plea that we, the council of the Seers of Light, might show him a way to enter the spirit world."

Mirae bowed again. "It is also my understanding that Your Honors are willing to hear my counterplea, which is that you do not grant the Netherking his request."

"We will hear you," the speaker confirmed. "Guards, bring in the primary petitioner."

All the confidence brewing in Mirae's chest dissipated in a single breath. She felt her blood run cold as the doors behind her were opened once more. Slow, self-assured steps rang out, growing louder as they closed in on her until at last a tall, lean figure took his place beside Mirae. Slowly, Mirae turned to face the man she had hunted across the peninsula with no other thought than to annihilate him.

In the light of the Crystal City, Minho's face was nearly unrecognizable. His once full and rosy cheeks had turned gaunt, thinly draped over his prominent bones, and his eyes that once sparkled warmly like maesil tea in sunlight now glittered with a cold, cruel intelligence. Although his hair was still long and silky, it flowed loosely over his shoulders, rather than being swept up into the tidy knot he'd always been so fastidious about. Even the kingly hanbok he wore, which Mirae had never seen in broad daylight, filled her heart with sadness, for gone were Minho's favorite, colorful clothes. In their place was the Netherking's dark ensemble, with an image of bloodred fire-hounds chasing the sun embroidered across his chest. All traces of her brother, it seemed, had been stolen, one by one, by the soul occupying his body.

The man who had killed his and Mirae's mother, and would murder thousands more.

"Your Honors," the Netherking said, his voice—once Minho's—ringing cheerily through the hall. "I am so pleased that our contestation can commence in earnest."

"We have already heard your inquiry," the speaker said, their voice as neutral with the Netherking as it had been with Mirae, for which she was grateful. Even more encouragingly, Mirae noticed that the Netherking's wrists were bound with white mugwort grass. Whether this had been done as a show of penitence from the Netherking, or as a sign that the council didn't fully trust the man in front of them, Mirae didn't know. "We will now hear from your opponent."

The Netherking nodded amiably, his false geniality making a mockery of the man whose personality he was imitating, and of the blood on his hands. "Of course." He turned to Mirae with a smile that suited Minho's face perfectly, a look she and her family had been committed to seeing again, no matter the cost.

Does Minho even know what this man did to our family? Mirae thought, fists clenching. *Or is my orabeoni's soul buried too deeply now to ever be retrieved?*

"The floor is yours, queenling," the Netherking said, his smile broadening; with it came the memory of his maniacal laughter as he mercilessly drained Mirae's mother of magic. His glee over a needlessly violent murder, which he was hungry to repeat in the heavens themselves.

Mirae wanted nothing more than to blast the Netherking with torrents of fire, or crush him with the lake above, but before her was a reminder that he still possessed Minho's body, a fact he was clearly flaunting. Thankfully, before Mirae's growing rage could boil over, the words of the sentinel echoed back to her, reminding her not to act rashly.

You are only here at the Netherking's request, and we both know he does not do anything without reason. Tread carefully, queenling, so you do not fall right into his hands.

As always, besting the Netherking meant keeping her head and anticipating his every move. Right now, he was clearly trying to goad Mirae into seeking revenge, hoping she'd get kicked out of the Crystal City, or be executed by the keepers of lost and forbidden magic, whose spells would be unpredictable and strange. Under no circumstances was Mirae going to allow him to coerce her into doing to herself what she was planning to do to him.

Instead she forced herself to face the council and address them calmly. "May I make a request before stating my case?"

The speaker nodded. Before continuing, Mirae thought back to the sentinel's sobering reproach: *How can you match wits with the Netherking if you don't know his entire plan?* Keeping those words in mind, Mirae asked, "Will you tell me what the Netherking's proposal is, exactly?"

She noticed the Netherking stiffen beside her, clearly disappointed that Mirae wasn't foolish enough to fall into his trap.

The council's speaker, unfazed by the battle of wills between Mirae and the Netherking, responded with a hint of impatience. "As I said, the Netherking has asked that we teach him how to gain access to the spirit world."

"Yes, I know." Mirae looked up at the Netherking, who was curling Minho's lips into a wry smile, curious to see what Mirae was playing at. "But to what end, might I ask? What has he promised to do in return?"

"Must we rehash all this?" another one of the councilmembers asked. Sitting to the right of the main speaker, they appeared to be the oldest person in the room. Mirae couldn't help but be in awe of their white, waist-length hair, blue-tinged and shimmering like distant starlight. "By our own rules, this council must not go backward in deliberations, only forward."

"We already broke our rules when we allowed an unrepentant Seollan royal into our sanctuary," a third councilmember chimed in, the one who appeared younger than Mirae. Although their words were biting, they sounded almost bored. "And for what? I sense a deep love for her queendom in her heart. I move to postpone this hearing until we've rehabilitated this young queen, or else expel her from our midst. There is much that we can teach her that will inform the course of this debate."

"I would be amenable to a postponement, and a reeducation," the Netherking said, bowing. "Whatever Your Honors decide, I will abide by."

Mirae swallowed back her dissent. She had been warned

that, because of the history between her people and the seers, she needed to be smart, not reactive. After taking a few calming breaths, she said, "I apologize if my questions are bothersome. Please instruct me on how to be of use to this court without retrograding its progress."

"Well spoken," a fourth member of the council said. They looked around the same age as Mirae's parents, their long black hair streaked with gray. "I believe the best way to move forward is to ensure that our visitor is brought up to speed. I volunteer to do so, unless there are any objections. My senses are telling me that High Queen Mirae can indeed give us valuable information, and it is against our tenets to turn away new knowledge, is it not?"

Mirae offered an appreciative bow to her unexpected ally.

"Very well," the main speaker relented. "I sense that none of us have any addressable refutations, so you may proceed."

The fourth speaker held out their hand to Mirae. "Come, child." Mirae gratefully strode toward their throne, blinking back tears from the brightness of the glowing stones on their winged coronet. When she was close enough, the councilmember clasped Mirae's hand. "Open your mind, and you will receive the knowledge you desire."

The moment their fingers touched, a jolt ran through Mirae's body, similar to when Captain Jia used to zap her with sparks of lightning during training. Almost of its own accord, Mirae felt her head throw itself back as images and sounds flooded her mind.

At first, everything was hazy and muffled, but gradually, it became clear that she was being shown a memory of the Netherking's first appearance in this very room, though the scene was playing out at a much faster speed, almost as if Mirae was seeing hours' worth of memories in a hundredth of the time. Mirae focused through the pain throbbing up her arm, trying her best to catch everything the councilmember was rapidly showing her.

She saw the Netherking approach the council with the corrupted pearl in hand, but he didn't use it on them. Instead, he allowed them to confiscate it, the price for hearing him out. Then he launched into a long tirade about the many injustices he'd endured at Seollan hands, and what he'd had to do to break free of the Deep. He reminded the council of the wrongs perpetrated against them, too, by the self-proclaimed uniters of the peninsula, who were also its greatest war criminals.

With their monopoly on magic, Seolla's queens had become nothing more than unhinged conquerors, the Netherking had argued. Tyrants who suffocated Josan. It was only a matter of time before they came for Baljin as well. If it wasn't for the way the Deep had valiantly compromised Seolla's queens for centuries, they would have already subjugated the entire peninsula by now. The Deep and the Crystal City were alike in many ways. Both full of exiles who stood up to Seolla, and paid the price for their integrity.

The council had been sympathetic to the Netherking's plight, but were firmly opposed to his proposal that they retaliate against the gods. That was no way to restore humanity to its proper, divine state. And then, right before the Netherking's eyes, the council had purged the pearl, rendering it useless to the

Netherking's violent plan. Mirae was surprised that the Netherking didn't try to stop them; instead, he persuaded them to come up with a compromise—if the council didn't want to hold the gods accountable, they could at least still beseech them to correct Seolla before the queendom rekindled its urge to conquer. After much deliberation, the council came to a decision: the Netherking, absent the pearl, would be assisted in entering the spirit world for the sole purpose of ascertaining the gods' will concerning Seolla's crimes, but only if he first proved that he was taking this great risk out of a sincere, altruistic desire.

That was when the Netherking had insisted that Mirae be allowed to enter the debate. He said that when the council saw how bullish Mirae was, despite everything she'd learned about her queendom's sordid past, they would see there was no hope for peace. Involving the gods, whose names were invoked to justify Seolla's crimes, was the only way.

And, as a show of goodwill, the Netherking vowed to vacate Minho's body, which he'd had no choice but to take possession of in order to escape the Deep. The Netherking said he more or less belonged in the spirit world now, anyway, since he had no body to call his own, and so would remain there after crossing over, dedicated wholly to the task of soliciting the gods' help. He'd then offered to have his hands bound in white grass until the council made their decision about him, as a sign of his repentant nature.

The council had nothing to lose, the Netherking reasoned. They would get a dedicated messenger, and be able to restore a young prince, whom they could rehabilitate before sending home. Everything the Netherking was suggesting would work toward the seers' benefit, so surely this was all set up by the gods, preparing a way to finally make things right.

The council, who had already wondered if the Netherking was the peninsula's hope for a prophesied deliverer, were soon swayed by his honeyed words. So, they had agreed to bring Mirae into their hall and see what kind of Seollan heir she was.

Mirae's vision began to blur around the edges as the memory ended. Once everything finally turned to black, Mirae felt her head right itself; when she opened her eyes, she met the enigmatic, midnight-blue gaze of the fourth councilmember, and knew what she needed to do.

Mirae bowed gratefully to the fourth councilmember before moving back to the center of the hall, her eyes flickering up to the Netherking's as she returned to his side. He didn't seem at all displeased that Mirae had seen what he'd been up to since arriving at Sujeongju. In fact, he looked like he was actually enjoying himself.

"Have you witnessed enough for us to move forward?" the main speaker asked as soon as Mirae was in place.

"Yes, Your Honor." Mirae dipped her head in a brief bow. "I'm ready to present my counterargument."

"Then we will hear you," the speaker said.

Mirae surveyed the councilmembers, looking them each in the eye. "I know you are trying to ascertain my character as a Seollan heir, so let me tell you who I am. I trust your exceptional powers to ascertain my sincerity when I say that I plan to repent for my queendom's wrongdoings. I seek to create the united peninsula that you have dedicated your lives to; one that is not ruled by Seolla, but rather where all are equally blessed by gods-given magic. I will ensure that Josan is released as a sovereign state by the first king of Seolla, whom I have already allowed to train in the use of Sacred Bone Magic. All other magic-adept men will be next. I seek your advice in keeping these promises, as I know these changes will not be met with support by all. But I am determined. I believe that together, with your knowledge and my position in Seolla, a truly united peninsula is not only possible, but inevitable."

The council fell silent, presumably trying to determine whether her passionate declaration could be trusted. Meanwhile, Mirae turned and gestured at the Netherking, whose amusement had blossomed into a full-on smile. "But this man before you is not what he claims to be. He is a warmonger, a usurper, and a murderer."

"He has already confessed his crimes," the speaker said. "We are not in the habit of penalizing those who had to do regrettable things in order to survive, so long as they are willing to make restitution. Those in power who force terrible choices upon the low are the truly evil ones. We must ask you not to bring up that which we have already resolved. This court must only move forward, just as you promised, or you will be dismissed."

The Netherking bowed deeply to the council, hiding the sneer only Mirae was close enough to see. "Your mercy and compassion are immeasurable, Your Honors."

Mirae's arm fell back to her side, trembling at the indignity of not being able to discuss the Netherking's crimes against her family. Mirae was certain that although the council felt the Netherking was amenable to their compromise, something else was putting his heart at peace, fooling their sensibilities. "I'm not asking you to punish anyone," Mirae said, "just that you give me a chance to show you his true colors."

Before anyone else could speak, the fourth seer once again became a surprising ally. "It seems to me," they interjected, "that what we really have before us is a conflict of prophecies."

"I agree," the youngest councilmember said. "Let us talk no more about the virtues or sins of our petitioners. Their pasts mean nothing compared to the vast discrepancies in their self-professed destinies. That is the mystery we must solve here and now."

"Yes, precisely," the fourth speaker said. "According to our doctrine, the Netherking could very well be the Restorer we've been waiting for. However, False Queen Yunseong would probably argue that he is the Inconstant Son she warned us about, which would make Queen Mirae the final High Daughter sent to stop him. Am I understanding this correctly?"

Although Mirae's head spun with all the new names and titles thrown about, she nodded, glad for the shift in the debate; it set the stage for what she was planning to do next. "Yes, Your Honor. It seems the Netherking and I are both prophesied to be either saviors or destroyers. Either your ancestors were correct, or mine."

"If ours spoke true," the oldest councilmember warned, "then you must be willing to accept that you are a false queen, and that all the death you have wrought in your crusade against the Netherking was blood spilled not in the gods' name but your own. Are you prepared for that? Will you respond honorably to the revelation that your birthright is a lie?"

As the seer no doubt intended, their harsh query stirred up

in Mirae's mind all the faces of those who had fallen during her pursuit of the Inconstant Son. Captain Jia. Her mother. Kimoon's soldiers on White Spine Mountain. The Wonhwa guards, perhaps, who had been abandoned at the Josan capital gates. People who would have died needlessly if Mirae was wrong about everything and the Netherking's cause was indeed just.

But that very idea made Mirae's stomach churn, threatening to upend. *No*, she thought, *there is no universe where the Netherking is the righteous one, and I wicked.*

Holding her head high, Mirae declared, "I will accept the council's verdict, just as I ask that you help me deal with the Netherking when his lies are revealed. I know that my ancestors did things that were unforgivable," she admitted. "But that doesn't mean they were wrong about the Inconstant Son, or the need to end him."

The main speaker held up their hand, silencing the room. "I sense that you believe you can prove you are the peninsula's deliverer, High Queen Mirae, and not the Netherking."

"That is correct," Mirae said, bowing again. "For all their flaws, my ancestors were telling the truth about one thing. The gods did speak to them, forewarning of an Inconstant Son. I can show Your Honors that the gods truly did create the calling of the High Daughters, and thus, by default, they also endowed the Daughters of the Sacred Bone with great power and a mission, even if it was misused."

No sooner had those last words left her mouth than nearly all of the councilmembers protested at once, clearly outraged. The speaker raised their hand, silencing the room once more. Then, with a thunderous voice, they demanded, "Are you truly unaware of how Sacred Bone Magic came to be?"

"I—" Mirae swallowed. "Surely it came from the gods. Where else?"

"She only knows the lies her ancestors have told," the oldest councilmember said disgustedly. "Not the truths of her own history, or ours. What can she teach us? Send her away."

"No!" Mirae pressed her palms together. "I have proof of the High Daughters' existence. Let me show you!"

"Let us at least see her demonstration," the fourth speaker exhorted. "If it is but another ruse developed by her ancestors, then we will punish her accordingly."

"It's not a ruse," Mirae insisted. She pointed at the Netherking, who no longer bothered hiding his glee. "If you can lend your trust to a murderer, surely you can spare me a single drop."

"He told us no lies, and we perceive a harmony between his demands and his destiny," the youngest speaker said. "Which is more than we can say for you. We sense that your desires do not lead toward the united peninsula you tout, but to ruin. I vote we send you away."

"We do not turn away knowledge," the fourth speaker warned. "It is against our tenets."

"So is allowing her to even be here," the oldest speaker shot back.

As all the other councilmembers joined in the quarrel, voicing their conflicting opinions while the main speaker listened, frowning, Mirae reached into her pocket and retrieved her black bell. She held it out until all eyes fell on her and the room finally quieted. "I've always been much better at communicating with actions than words," she said. "Please, witness my power as High Horomancer, then decide what is to be done with the Inconstant Son."

With that, Mirae flung her High Daughter relic back and forth a single time. As the bell rang out, its peals echoing like thunder in the vast chamber, Mirae felt the familiar, agonizing sear in her hand race up her arm as darkness closed in and she blacked out.

When Mirae came to, the first thing she noticed was that the pain in her hand had moved to her knees, which throbbed as if she had been kneeling on hard earth for some time. When she opened her eyes, vision slowly returning, Mirae was surprised to see that she was back home, in the courtyard of the Seollan palace.

But everything was different. The sand beneath Mirae was darkly stained and unsmoothed, and the steps leading up to the main hall were sullied as well. Even the building itself had been repainted to a garish red with accents of gold that glittered coldly. The male guards surrounding Mirae reflected that same gaudiness in their uniforms and swords.

Most inexplicable of all was the old man who knelt beside Mirae. The last time she'd seen him had been on a snowy mountaintop, where he'd tried to kill her. He looked exactly as Mirae remembered, his hair mostly gray, and his eyes narrowed with spite. Kimoon, the self-professed Inconstant Son, a man who would someday hate Mirae with all his soul. Hands bound in front of him, he stared up at the main hall with a deranged smile as if he couldn't wait to see what violent fate lay in store.

What is this? Mirae thought, looking around anxiously. *What happened to my home?*

Mirae glanced down at her hands, aged with wrinkles and spots, and saw that they were not bound with rope, as Kimoon's were, but with manacles that reminded her of the Netherking's, meant to inhibit magic. The bits of her loose hair that she could see were as white as her grandmother's. Just like the last time she'd seen Kimoon in a switch, Mirae was in a body decades older than the one she'd left. But the similarities ended there.

Mirae surveyed the all-male guards once more, whose steel swords were heavily enchanted, as were their clothes, signifying that they were magic users. After a quick glance at the stains in the sand and on the steps, which were clearly caused by spilled blood, Mirae turned to her fellow captive and whispered, "Kimoon, stop smiling. We have to get out of here."

He ignored her. Mirae tried again, "Kimoon, please. We have to do something."

When Kimoon finally responded, he kept his gaze fixed on the main hall. "We were promised three voyages, and this is but the first. We aren't going to die today, manyeo. Show a little faith in the Silver Star."

The Silver Star? What is he talking about? Before Mirae could ask that question aloud, their conversation was cut short by the guards shouting in unison, "His Majesty approaches!" The soldiers behind Mirae and Kimoon kicked them forward, forcing them into a bow. Mirae tilted her head up as much as she could to catch sight of this so-called king.

To her surprise, it wasn't the Netherking who stepped out, or either of her brothers. Unless the Netherking had secured another body for himself, this man striding down the steps was someone else entirely, even though his hanbok looked similar to the one the Netherking wore—all-black and embroidered with leaping bulgae.

The king had his dark hair tied up in the Seollan style and wore the tall golden crown that Mirae had only ever seen her mother and grandmother wear. Strings of silver mirrors and leaf-shaped jade charms dangled down the sides of his face, and around his neck was a thick necklace with several layers of garnet beads framing an enormous jade pendant. Rather than the customary rectangular belt worn by members of the court, the king's was forged from intricate plates, from which hung chains dotted with black and red beads.

The king was an intimidating sight descending the stairs, his jewelry glinting dangerously, like unsheathed daggers, and the lines of his face seemingly etched into an eternal glower. He came to a stop at the final step, as if letting his feet touch the blood-soaked sand was beneath him. "Why are you bothering me over these traitors?" he demanded, his voice booming across the courtyard. "Just behead them like all the others."

"The woman is an unlisted magic user," the foremost guard responded. "And she said she bears a message from our Gongju mama."

The king's scowl deepened. "Impossible. The crown princess is dead."

Mirae shot a look at Kimoon, who continued to ignore her. The guard behind Mirae kicked her in the back. "Tell His Majesty the message from Eunbyul Gongju!"

Eunbyul. A name that meant Silver Star. Mirae gasped as she realized where she was, or, rather, *when* she was. Crown Princess Eunbyul, whose name, as it turned out, actually *meant* Silver Star, was almost certainly the First High Daughter, an unparalleled master of Ma-eum Magic. A crown princess presumed dead in this switch. But if Mirae had come to a time when the Silver Star was still on the earth, then that meant she hadn't switched into the future.

She and Kimoon were somehow in the past.

Another sharp kick landed on her back, this one harder than before. "Speak!" the guard snarled.

"I . . ." Mirae had no idea what to say. "Gongju mama said . . . she is very much alive."

The king scoffed. "Returning from the dead, is she? How dare you speak such nonsense? I should have you quartered instead of beheaded."

Mirae shot Kimoon another entreating look. This time he was staring back at her, frowning. After she floundered for several more seconds, unsure what to say, Kimoon cleared his throat and addressed the king. "Yes, our Gongju mama said she is returning, and that she successfully completed the fool's errand you sent her on."

The king looked taken aback by Kimoon's words but recovered quickly. "That's impossible," he growled. "All the dragon pearls were destroyed in the Miri Wars."

"All but one." Kimoon's snide smile returned. "And Princess Eunbyul is eager to show it to you. You see, we are not your prisoners. We were just a distraction."

"And a fine one at that." A new voice, high and cheery as tinkling handbells, rang out from behind Mirae. She couldn't see the approaching woman, but she heard her light footsteps, and those of a whole entourage. It seemed the crown princess hadn't come alone.

"Eunbyul," the king said, taking a step back. He forced a smile to stretch out his lips, which only made his words sound stiff and insincere. "I knew you would return victorious! You are my talented, courageous daughter, after all."

"If I'm your daughter, then why did you try to have me killed?" the Silver Star asked as she continued to draw nearer. "And why have you been beheading all my supporters?"

The king laughed, the sound falling painfully flat. "Those are baseless rumors you should not pay any heed to. I sent you to collect the dragon pearl because only you could. If you encountered dangerous outlaws along the way, that had nothing to do with me. Besides, you clearly handled them. As for these traitors you see before you, they gave me no choice but to—"

"Enough." The Silver Star had come close enough that Mirae could feel her shadow across her back. "They are not traitors, they are my allies. They even carry my signet to demonstrate their loyalty, which has nearly cost them their lives. Now I know *your* loyalties."

"Eunbyul!" the king blustered. "This is all a terrible misunderstanding!"

And yet Mirae could see, even from her low place on the ground, that he was reaching behind him for something. Before he could pull out his dagger, or whatever it was, Mirae felt the shadow on her back disappear. A split second later, a woman landed from an impossibly high jump right in front of Mirae, scaring the king enough that he put his arms in front of his face.

Mirae craned her neck to look up at the Silver Star, who met her gaze with a playful smile. She looked a few years older than Mirae—at least, the body she'd left behind—with deep black eyes and hair, flawless skin lightly blushed on either side of her nose, and a delicate beauty mark on the left side of her chin. What's more, Mirae's stunning ancestor had taken the time to regally dress herself, with the clear intent of putting her usurper father back in his place.

While the king wore predominantly black and red fineries, she was adorned in a teal dangui embroidered with silver suns, and a chima layered with red and gold silks that flowed around her, rustling like wind through a leafy forest. Atop her head was a magnificent daesu bedecked with several beaded ddeol-jam, an ornamented red ribbon around the middle, and several heavy gold binyeo stuck all the way through. Her pure black hair was pulled down from the crown into straight, tight slants that framed her face like a battle helmet, the slightly tipped ends knobbed with bejeweled phoenixes. Her showy ensemble, exhibiting all the symbols of her rank that could fit onto one outfit, made it clear just who this queenly woman was, and what she was not about to let her father take from her.

The Silver Star reached into the pocket of her bustling chima and pulled out a familiar orb—the gleaming pearl that Mirae had last seen resting on a seer's lap. The king gasped and cowered backward at the sight. He knew what it was and the power it held.

"Please, Eunbyul," he stammered, "I am your father. I only wished to look after the kingdom while you were gone. I quelled rising dissent to keep the peace!"

The Silver Star approached her father, who was so panicked that he fell onto his back atop the stone steps. "I think what you meant to say," the Silver Star corrected him, "was you were 'looking after' my *queendom*."

"Yes, of course!" her father blustered. "You know that's what I meant!"

The Silver Star laughed gaily, a sound that made her father flinch. "Be at ease, aba mama," she said spiritedly. "I'm not here to kill you." At that, the crown princess whirled around, facing her father's guards. "Release all remaining prisoners at once, and bring me an accounting of every person you've imprisoned or executed in my absence. Then you will turn in your swords and resign from your posts."

The guards looked to their king, who was growing gradually more and more incensed at his daughter's unexpected return, and the sudden stripping of all the power he'd stolen for himself. Gathering his pride, he jumped to his feet and, while his daughter's back was turned to him, raced up the stone steps toward the throne room, shouting behind him, "Arrest the traitorous princess! Do whatever you must to subdue her!"

The Silver Star's entourage immediately threw themselves at

the king's guards. Mirae struggled against her chains, desperate to break free and help her ancestor defend the queendom against its false, corrupt king, but her bonds held tightly. Not that it mattered; as soon as the king's final words left his mouth, the Silver Star raised the glittering dragon pearl above her head and poured her Sacred Bone Magic into it.

Mirae watched, eyes wide, as the pearl began to burn white hot, like a star fallen to earth. And yet it cast rainbow glints around the courtyard, as if all its untamed light was bursting out of a crystal prism. It reminded her of the dragon bead she'd used in her fight against the Netherqueen, and its radiating power that had seeped out of her very skin.

The pearl's scintillating brilliance grew until everyone in the courtyard had to shield their eyes, including the king, who stumbled back to the ground. As Mirae buried her face into the sand, eyes shut tightly, she heard the Silver Star proclaim, "I did not come here with the intention of killing you, aba mama. Don't change my mind."

"This . . . this cannot be!" the king spluttered.

"What?" the Silver Star asked blithely. "Did you not think that I would be able to wield the Yeouiju of the ones who gave us our power?"

"Please," the king shouted. "What is it you want from me?"

The light from the dragon's pearl did not relent. If anything, it grew brighter, so much so that it began heating the very air with unrelenting warmth; sweat began bubbling across Mirae's forehead and back as the Silver Star said, "I heard that while I was away, you amassed quite the following. So, what I want," the

Silver Star continued imperiously, "is to show the entire queendom whom the gods have chosen to be their ruler. I challenge you, aba mama, to a duel of enchantments. Whoever wins has full claim to the throne, and the loser will be executed for treason. What say you? Will you show the queendom once and for all who its true monarch is?"

"Yes," the king choked out as the heat from the pearl became unbearable. "Let the gods decide what is best for the king— queendom!"

At that, the light of the pearl dimmed, the scorching air cooled, and silence fell across the courtyard. After a moment, Mirae finally, tentatively opened her eyes. What she saw in front of her nearly made her shout with surprise, for crouching before her was the Silver Star herself. Her ancestor smiled, cheeks dimpling in ways that would have made Hongbin jealous. "You're free to go now, my dear halmoni."

Mirae looked down and saw that her manacles had indeed been opened. Mirae let the chains drop to the ground and rubbed her sore wrists. "Thank you . . . Gongju mama."

The Silver Star laughed brightly and offered Mirae a hand up, which she gratefully accepted. Once on her feet, Mirae could hardly believe she was standing face-to-face with the first High Daughter of Seolla. Before her mouth could remember how to form words, the Silver Star turned to Kimoon, who had also been freed and now stood beside Mirae. "Thank you, too, Kimoon, for all your help. As promised, I will now grant you both a single wish. Tell me what you desire, within reason, and it will be yours."

Kimoon bowed deeply. "All I ask, Gongju mama, is to be allowed to witness the inevitable defeat of the False King who has persecuted us and all your followers."

"Is that all?" the Silver Star asked with another tinkling laugh. "Consider your wish granted." She turned to Mirae next. "And what is it I can do for you, halmoni?"

Having no idea what she and Kimoon had gotten themselves into, Mirae smiled and said simply, "My request is the same as Kimoon's. I do not wish to leave his side."

"Then it shall be done. Consider yourselves newly inducted members of my court." The Silver Star patted their arms and then turned to the throne room. She strode proudly up the steps, passing her father by as if he were a mere shrub, before disappearing inside the vermilion building.

Once the king's newly released guards had rushed to their liege and escorted him, fuming, away from the Silver Star's watchful acolytes, Kimoon turned to Mirae. Alone together in the courtyard, he dropped all pretense of being a humble, devoted servant to a High Daughter, becoming once more the seething, bitter man she recognized. "She trusts us now," he hissed. His honey-light eyes gleamed like forged steel cooling with each hammer strike. "Everything is falling into place. Soon I'll have my revenge."

Mirae studied the man before her, wondering what she or the Silver Star had done—what they would yet do—to make him so hateful. Was he really the Inconstant Son, as he claimed? Hadn't the Netherking done enough to earn that title for himself? Unsure of what the gods were trying to tell her, and knowing that her time was running out, Mirae cleared her throat. It didn't seem that Kimoon had realized she'd switched, and somehow, she wanted to keep it that way. "You could have wished for anything," she said quietly. "Why did you choose what you did?"

"Don't ask stupid questions," Kimoon shot back. "You know what we're here to do." His cruel eyes bored into Mirae's. "Don't even think about backing out now. You promised to help me, manyeo."

"And so I will," Mirae said. Whatever it was her future self had agreed to do, Mirae trusted that she had her reasons. For now, she looked around at the garishly painted palace that would someday, hundreds of years later, become her home. The things that had happened in Seolla between now and the time Mirae was born were events she'd learned about in history books; stories the Seers of Light had told her were incomplete, or even outright lies. And now Mirae was here in person, or would be in the "future," seemingly trying to disrupt the narrative. Or was her presence going to ensure that history stayed its course?

Either way, why was she remaining steadfast beside the alleged Inconstant Son? What did this mean for her current fight against the Netherking? As usual, Mirae's enigmatic, unpredictable powers of time travel had only confused her more. It was becoming more and more impossible to tell what was set in stone, and what she was supposed to have a hand in creating, or stopping.

What is the gods' plan, exactly? she wondered. *Is this switch a warning that my current path is wrong, for it only leads to me going rogue with the Inconstant Son? Or are the gods trying to tell me that*

Seolla's past, which I'll perhaps seek to revise or preserve myself, is not to be questioned?

Or maybe the gods are trying to relay that, as in the last time I switched and confronted Kimoon, the Netherking is not who I think he is, and that he must therefore be left alone. What exactly are the gods doing: guiding me, or issuing a warning?

As those confusing, muddled thoughts ran through her mind, Mirae felt the familiar pull of time, summoning her back to the present. She looked at Kimoon one last time, a man who had promised to make her laugh every day, and who now reviled everything she stood for. Wondering what she could do to coax him down a different path, or if she was even meant to save him from this future, Mirae let the encroaching shadows black out her vision, ripping her soul out of this body, this vessel of both the future and the past, and back to the hall of the Seers of Light.

Chapter
TWENTY-TWO

Mirae opened her eyes to a room in chaos. The once impassive, regal councilmembers were now standing in front of their thrones, hands raised in front of them. A shield of blue light, collectively drawing from all their powers, stretched across their half of the hall; the guards, too, had gathered at the base of the dais where the council stood, weapons raised and pointed in Mirae's direction.

Most important, the Netherking was on the ground, wiping blood from his nose and mouth with wrists that were no longer bound, the scorched remains of the white grass once tying them now scattered on the floor. Realizing her hand was stretched out threateningly, palm crackling with lightning, which she rarely summoned, Mirae quickly dropped her hand by her side, bidding her magic disperse.

Thankfully, the strange spell obeyed, fizzling away into nothing. Mirae held her hands up, bare of magic. "It's me, I'm back. What on earth happened?"

The Netherking climbed to his feet, nursing his face dramatically. "You attacked me unprovoked," he cried out. "While pretending to be possessed by a . . . a *madwoman*."

"Not possessed," Mirae said, giving the Netherking's theatrics a disapproving look. "I switched bodies with my future self. It is the power granted to me as the High Horomancer."

Neither the council nor their guards lowered their defenses. Instead, the main speaker proclaimed, "You have indeed proven that you possess a remarkable power. We sensed that the woman who spoke to us moments ago was, as you said, your future self. But how you came by this ability, and what you are meant to do with it, remains to be seen."

"I am here to do just as I said," Mirae said, biting back her impatience. "To stop the Inconstant Son from destroying the peninsula. He is as real as my powers."

"And this Inconstant Son is me, you say? What proof do you have?" the Netherking demanded, still cradling the side of his face.

Before her switch, Mirae would have had the perfect answer by reminding everyone of the Netherking's sins and his true intention behind infiltrating the heavens. But now, having seen old Kimoon again, Mirae felt her certainty falter. The Netherking leaped at her hesitation, pointing at her while blustering, "See how the 'High Horomancer' waffles when questioned about the gods' will? How do we know that they are the ones guiding her? Only I can ascertain that, through the agreement we have already reached."

Again, before switching, Mirae would have spoken instinctively, arguing that the gods *had* to be the ones behind her unique ability, as they had also given her Sacred Bone Magic, but even that once-believed truth had been shattered by both the seers and her switch. What was it the Silver Star had said while raising the beaming pearl? *Did you not think that I would be able to wield the Yeouiju of the ones who gave us our power?*

Mirae bit her lower lip. *What could the Silver Star have meant by that? Is Sacred Bone Magic really a gift from dragons that died out centuries ago, and not the gods? If so, what does that mean for my calling as High Horomancer? Is my ability to switch proof of my connection to the gods, as I've always thought—or is it indicative of something else entirely?*

Realizing that the council was staring at her, waiting for her to say something, Mirae cleared her throat. "There is much that remains a mystery, but this much we do know: granting the Netherking's request without gathering more information about the gods' will would be reckless. After all, he may very well be the monster I, the High Horomancer, say he is. I ask only that you do not help him until we get to the bottom of this, together."

The fourth speaker, ever Mirae's ally, lowered their hand, causing the council's magical shield to dematerialize. "I think that sounds reasonable. Surely we can all spare a few days to explore the questions that have been raised, and ensure our decision is in line with our mission."

One by one all the councilmembers lowered their hands as well. Only then did the guards relax, sheathing their weapons. After the tension in the room had ebbed, the main speaker spoke. "I think an intermission is in order. A lot has happened that we must contemplate."

"Perhaps we could have some refreshments," the fourth speaker said to the approval of all, particularly the eldest councilmember.

The main speaker nodded to the guards, who left their place by the dais. Half of them returned to their posting along the wall while the others left the hall, calling for attendants to bring in some food.

Mirae breathed a sigh of relief. It felt like she hadn't eaten or slept in days; a brief respite to regather herself and plan the next stage of her scheme to discredit the Netherking was exactly what she needed. Moments later, servants in shimmering pink hooded robes with purple sashes came flooding into the room, bearing trays laden with fruit and other carefully plated dishes. They first served the council, who stood speaking softly with each other, before bringing their offerings to Mirae and the Netherking.

Mirae wasn't bashful at all about stuffing her face with the cool, sweet fruit she'd seen in the orchard outside the hall, or the other meat-free delicacies presented to her. She was so absorbed in satiating the hunger pangs that had begun tormenting her at the mere sight of delicious food that she almost didn't notice the last server to approach the Netherking.

Their hood was draped lower than their peers', as if to actually hide their face, and they hadn't served the council upon entering. Instead, they'd made a beeline for the Netherking. Feeling a growing sense of unease, Mirae stopped eating and kept her eyes on the servant. Something about them, their stature and gait, felt familiar.

When they lifted their tray to the Netherking, Mirae dropped the food she was holding and raised her arm, filling her palm with fire; for on the servant's pale hand, clear as lightning across a midnight sky, were veins engorged with black water.

"Stop him!" Mirae shouted. But the fire blazing in her palm, an instinctual move, had drawn the guards' attention to her instead; they charged toward her, weapons drawn, leaving the Netherking free to pick up the dark, gleaming morsel presented to him on the corrupted servant's tray and pop it into his mouth.

The guards surrounded Mirae and, with weapons pointed at her throat, demanded that she extinguish her magic. The council, too, was fixated on her. Their hands were raised against her, shooting blue sparks in warning. Mirae shouted and pointed at the Netherking, but her words were drowned out, her refusal to douse her palm fire seen as the only real threat in the room.

The Netherking smugly chewed on whatever the servant had given him, and when he smiled, black water oozed between his teeth.

His job completed, the servant dropped his tray with a cry and fell to his knees, trembling with pain. As his body shook uncontrollably, his hood fell back, revealing his face. Although his features were rendered almost unrecognizable by the swollen veins across his skin, what Mirae saw took the breath right out of her body.

Kimoon. The man whom her future self had insisted she bring along, and who had been the one to suggest that Mirae go after the black water in Josan. The ally who had been her confidant, her ruthless arm, now a traitor. A servant to her eternal enemy.

Frozen with disbelief, Mirae could almost feel a phantom throb in her neck right where the Netherking had bitten her, obtaining both her blood and droplets of black water. She hadn't known how, exactly, he'd used those two ingredients to create a counterspell to his cage while manacled in anti-magic chains, because it wasn't possible. Not without help.

Looking at Kimoon now, riddled with agony, gasping in pain as he struggled against whatever spell had corrupted him, Mirae couldn't bring herself to believe that he had willingly betrayed her. She could see in his red-rimmed, tormented eyes, and the way he was clenching his fists so hard that his hands bled, that he was desperately fighting whatever was happening to his mind. Fighting and losing to the Netherking's will.

As for the Netherking, who never missed an opportunity to act while his opponents were distracted, he had already turned his attention to the pearl, resting unprotected on the main speaker's vacated throne. With a wave of his hand, a gale strong enough to create ocean waves ripped through the room, throwing the councilmembers aside like dead leaves. When the fierce wind returned, it brought the dragon's pearl along with it.

"No," Mirae breathed, unable to accept what was happening. His villainy on full display, the Netherking spat black water onto the pearl, coating it once more.

"Run!" Mirae screamed, knowing what came next. But the guards, finally noticing what the Netherking was doing, rushed to apprehend him, as was their duty. Only Mirae knew that it was far too late.

The Netherking raised the pearl above his head. Dark tendrils began pouring out of it, finding faces to latch onto, paralyzing each target. Soon, every guard was incapacitated, while a long, writhing arm formed and shot toward the council, who were running to cower behind the enormous statue on the other side of the room. But the shadowy arm was too fast; it barreled into the rearmost councilmember, securing them in its suctioning grip.

"I tried to do things the nice way," the Netherking sighed as the screams of the dying guards and councilmember were siphoned away along with their lives. "But now we'll see if all that disgusting groveling was for nothing. Maybe I can just steal your precious knowledge as well as your magic. Wouldn't that be quite the discovery?"

More tendrils sprouted from the pearl and raced toward the rest of the council, who slapped their hands against the statue and, to Mirae's relief, disappeared, magically transported somewhere hopefully far away. Their safety, of course, would be short-lived, now that the Netherking had been reunited with the pearl.

But what could Mirae do to stop the spread of this indomitable power? Any spell she hurled would just be devoured, and used to bolster the Netherking's magic, just like her mother's life, her brother's body, and now Kimoon's mind.

"Ah, I see," the Netherking said as the shadowy arm gorging on the councilmember retracted, leaving a mangled corpse in its wake. His eyes had become completely black, and dripped ebony tears of joy. "How incredible. All that a person is, their magic, their memories, even their knowledge, is all mine for the taking. Everything, everything, will be mine."

The Netherking turned to Mirae and laughed, his voice echoed by the shadows gathering around him, creating an earsplitting cacophony. Mirae covered her ears but stood her ground. There was nothing she could do now but stare death in the face, refusing to show her enemy the fear he so craved.

"I see now how to break into the spirit world," the Netherking crowed, still enraptured by the councilmember's mind merging with and enlightening his own. As he spoke, the murderous limbs of the pearl's corruption gathered together, becoming one enormous whirlwind of dark magic poised to devour Mirae whole.

But he did not order it to strike. Instead, he took several steps backward until he could press his free hand against the nearest slab of crystal wall. Mirae could only watch as a crack spiraled outward from his palm, causing the wall to crumble away, but instead of leading outside to the rest of Sujeongju, the newly formed hole became a swirling, misty void.

"Farewell, queenling." The Netherking closed his eyes, a shudder of pleasure running through his stolen body. "Consider it a mercy that you will not live to see the desolation of Seolla, and the vengeance of the Deep. At long last, I will be my people's reckoning." With that, the Netherking snapped his fingers, and the monstrous, shadowy formation behind him hurtled toward Mirae.

She shut her eyes and raised her chin, determined to be fearless even in death, until a familiar voice cut through the noise, shattering her composure.

"Mirae!"

Her eyes flew open just in time to see Siwon rush in front of her, shielding her. The Netherking's cyclone rammed into

Mirae's protector before she could so much as scream, engulfing him in a ravenous storm of shadows.

"No!" Mirae was about to dive in after him, but Areum and Hongbin were beside her in an instant, hoisting her between them and dragging her toward the room's exit while dark magic filled the room, hiding them from sight.

"Don't think you can escape me, queenling," the Netherking spat, his words echoing like the hiss of a thousand snakes. "There's nowhere in heaven or earth that you can run."

Just as suddenly as it came, the black mist dispersed, leaving the room clear once more. Mirae gasped at the sight before her: drained corpses littering the room; the howling tunnel to the spirit world fracturing the crystal wall; Kimoon quivering behind the Netherking; and, most of all, a motionless Siwon collapsed on the ground, his back to her.

With a wave of his hand, the Netherking forced cracks to appear in the stone floor, large enough for Hongbin's and Areum's feet to sink into. They floundered in vain trying to free themselves, but ended up falling to the floor, tugging on their legs uselessly.

Mirae stepped forward, holding her trembling arms out. "Don't hurt them. This is our fight, not theirs."

"And who will protect them when you're gone?" the Netherking mused. He still had an arm raised, around which the shadows were swiftly re-forming. "I'm afraid I can't let any Seollan magic users live. They will fight my sovereignty until their dying day."

Mirae lifted her chin. "I will be the one who stops you, make no mistake. It is my destiny. I have seen the future, and you're not in it. One way or another, you will lose."

Mirae thought the Netherking would laugh at her bold, final words before killing her, but instead he stared at her intently, perhaps reading in her eyes that there was some truth to her prophecy. He looked as if he wanted to ask her what it was she'd seen exactly, but thought better of it. He quickly gathered the shadows into a dark blade, long enough to graze the ceiling. "I make my own fate. What you have glimpsed in your switches, queenling, is not set in stone."

"I think it is," Mirae said. "Everything so far has come true. I'm only meant to stop the Inconstant Son, nothing else. And despite everything you've done, my switches have shown me another man whose destiny is intertwined with mine, meaning you're not nearly as important as you think you are; and if you're not the great evil I was sent here to stop, that means you are doomed to fail, just like every other madman who's opposed Seolla. So go on, kill me and enter into the gods' domain. Let's both see what happens next."

Now the Netherking laughed. "Brazen to the end, I see. Just like Suhee. What a nether-fiend you would have made."

With that, he threw back his arm, wielding the magic-devouring shadows like a spear. What he didn't see, however, was Kimoon inching closer and closer to him, dagger in hand, fighting the Netherking's possession with every step. Black water ran from his eyes and nose like blood, and the veins of his neck and face pulsed with poison, but he grimaced through the pain, pulling desperately against the chains of the Netherking's will. Mirae kept her eyes from flitting over to him, hoping against all hope that he, out of everyone, would succeed.

When the Netherking released his shadowy weapon at last, Mirae faced it calmly, praying that her death, Siwon's death, would at least be for something, that Kimoon's last stand would not fail. A split second later, Mirae could only watch, breathless, as Kimoon made his move.

Instead of plunging his blade into the Netherking, as Mirae expected, Kimoon pointed the dagger at himself and stabbed it into his abdomen. Then, wrenching the weapon out of his side, Kimoon lunged forward, screaming as he knifed the Netherking right in the back.

The Netherking howled and stumbled forward, the distraction of Kimoon's attack breaking his concentration, forcing the shadowy spear to dissipate inches away from Mirae's face.

She immediately broke into a run, determined to end the battle before the Netherking could recover. Across the room, the Netherking staggered away from Kimoon, blood mixing with the black water streaming out of his mouth.

"W-What have you done?" the Netherking spluttered. Although he swayed on his feet, breathless with pain, Kimoon wasn't finished. He held something in his other hand, a small glass vial— one of her mother's experimental potions—that he smashed against the Netherking's mouth with the last of his strength.

Kimoon finally crumpled to the ground while the Netherking choked on the concoction spilling into his throat. His eyes rolled back, and his body writhed with agony. Mirae was almost upon him, nearly able to wrestle the pearl from his hand, but before she could, the Netherking regained just enough control of his faculties to hurl the Yeouiju into the swirling portal before collapsing into a motionless heap.

Mirae could only scream as a dark, ghostly form peeled away from Minho's body. Free of its damaged, helpless vessel, the Netherking's murky soul quickly threw itself after the pearl, disappearing in an instant.

Mirae didn't know what else to do except fall beside her brother, who was unconscious, bleeding profusely.

"Orabeoni!" She pressed her hands to his wound. He was losing a lot of blood. Mirae whirled to Areum and Hongbin. "Get a healer, now!"

Released from the Netherking's spell, Areum and Hongbin finally wrenched their legs free of the cracked earth. Areum sprinted out of the hall, screaming for help. Hongbin, however, rushed over to Mirae, placing his hands over her own.

"Hyungnim," he sobbed. "Please, please stay with us. I forbid you to die."

Mirae pressed her forehead to Minho's, repeating Hongbin's plea. They'd come too far to lose him now. He had to live, he had to.

"Your Majesty."

Mirae had been so preoccupied she hadn't even realized that someone else was limping over to her until she heard his voice and felt his hand on her shoulder. Her head shot up, and she gasped. Siwon stood over her, pale and drenched in sweat . . . but alive.

"How?" Mirae breathed. "I watched him kill you."

Siwon fell beside her, looking as if he'd just wrenched his soul back out of the portal to the spirit world. "That spell was meant for you." He groaned, clutching his side. "I don't have magic, so I managed to survive the worst of it."

Overwhelmed with relief, Mirae's head fell against Siwon's shoulder, not caring that it made him give a tiny yelp of pain. A moment later, he wrapped his arms around her as tears slipped out of her eyes and sank into his sweat-dampened clothes.

A shuffling sound made Mirae's head snap back up and turn toward the portal. But it was only Kimoon approaching her now. He'd climbed laboriously to his feet and shed the robe of his disguise; his veins had returned to normal, but his red-rimmed eyes were still near black as he stared at Mirae, and the men she clung to. Then he, too, tore his eyes away, and looked at the portal. Clutching the knife wound in his side, he started dragging his feet after the Netherking.

"What are you doing?" Hongbin cried out.

Kimoon paused and looked back at Mirae, his golden eyes reemerging as the black water faded. In his tortured stare she could almost read his thoughts, his guilt for stabbing the man they'd sworn to rescue, and the anguish of knowing that his betrayal could never be forgiven.

"I'll stop him," Kimoon choked out. "So you don't have to. Stay here and keep Minho safe. You all have to stay safe. This . . . this is my burden to bear."

"No," Hongbin blurted. "You can't do this—not alone."

Kimoon shut his eyes tightly, as if that was the only way to keep in all the words he wanted to say. When he opened them again, it wasn't Hongbin or Mirae he was looking at, but Siwon.

Mirae looked between the two men as Siwon set his jaw and nodded. Wordlessly, he released Mirae from his embrace and walked over to his fellow exiled prince.

"Wait," Mirae said, stunned. "What do you think you're doing?"

Side by side with his brother, Kimoon took a deep breath, seeming to gather courage from his silent companion. "As Siwon said, we don't have magic. We're resistant to the spell the Netherking will use on the gods, but you are not, which means we stand a better chance of getting close enough to finish him off. Don't follow us. Stay and protect this realm."

Hands still pressed to Minho's chest, trying to save his life, Mirae and Hongbin could only watch helplessly, ordering the two heedless princes to stop. But the men turned to the portal without hesitation and ran into the swirling opening between worlds.

Just like that, they vanished. Mirae stared blankly at the doorway that should never have been opened, disbelieving that Kimoon and Siwon were gone, that she let them leave. Behind her, she heard footsteps running in her direction. Foolishly, Mirae turned, half expecting to see Siwon and Kimoon rushing toward her, their stunt somehow failed, but instead she saw a small army of seers in coral-colored robes sprinting across the room, Areum at their head.

Two of the seers sped toward Minho while the rest hurried to the other victims, checking futilely for any signs of life. Mirae and Hongbin leaned back as the healers took over, muttering quick instructions to each other as warm rays flowed out of their hands and into Minho's chest. Mirae scooted backward, praying that the Seers of Light, with their vast knowledge, would find a way to save the man she'd sacrificed so much to recover.

"Your Majesty." Areum grabbed Mirae's hands, not caring that they were slick with Minho's blood. Unsurprisingly, her prescience seemed to have informed her of what had transpired in her absence. "Kimoon and Siwon won't be able to stop the Inconstant Son alone."

"I know," Mirae whispered. "I know."

Areum pressed Mirae's hands to her own chest and looked tearily into Mirae's eyes. "I will stay with Daegun, and save him if I can. But you must go now. Go before it's too late."

Mirae nodded. Areum was right, there was no point in staying to protect the living, not if her hesitation would only result in their deaths. She tore her eyes from Minho, who lay unmoving under the healers' hands. There was nothing she could do for him now except have faith in the Seers of Light.

"Noonim." Hongbin offered an arm to help her up. She accepted, and soon they both stood before the portal, clasping hands. "You've switched into the future and seen the spirit world. I was with you then, yes?"

Mirae nodded, eyes stinging with tears. "Yes, you were."

Hongbin squared his shoulders. "Then I must stay beside you now."

There was nothing more to say, just a silent understanding that everything they'd done and endured had led them to this moment. Clinging tightly to each other, Mirae and Hongbin rushed into the rippling doorway just as the men before them had, leaping into a distant realm never meant for mortal eyes.

Chapter
TWENTY-THREE

As soon as Mirae stepped into the portal, the ground dropped off beneath her feet, sending her plunging into a swirling vortex of blazing light. Brilliant silver and blue beams engulfed her, forcing her to shut her eyes, unfortunately making it that much easier to focus on the way her stomach seemed to be floating up into her throat. If it wasn't for Hongbin's hand clasped tightly in hers, she might have resigned herself to being lost in a luminous void, unmoored in a sea of endless radiance.

But not even Hongbin's grip could distract her from the impact of crashing into the spirit realm. The force of exiting the corridor between worlds felt like dropping hundreds of feet into water, something that should have shattered Mirae's bones and splattered her organs. But she was unharmed; rather, it was everything else that seemed to cease existing—the boundless tumbling, beaming lights, and the earsplitting wind. All she could sense was her own body, which felt as deflated as a crumpled lantern struggling to expand.

Thankfully, there was plenty of air for the taking, even in this sphere designed for the spirits of the dead. Mirae could even feel the pulse of divine energy thrumming around and through her, echoing the beating of her own Sacred Bone heart.

Just as Mirae's lungs finally relearned how to breathe, she felt Hongbin shake her arm. "Noonim, get up . . . you've got to see this place."

The shock of slamming into a new world wore off at Hongbin's touch. Emboldened by her brother's voice, Mirae opened her eyes and looked around.

She was in a grassy field teeming with blushing violets. The flowers, however, were unlike anything she'd ever seen. Their amethyst petals gave off a soft glow, and their yellow centers twinkled like tiny stars. Even the grass itself was a silvery teal, and soft like dense moss. Mirae looked up at the sky, which was completely obscured by purple clouds laced with glints of pink and ocean blue that cast jewel-toned shadows on the world below. In the distance, rolling hills covered in the same verdant and violet flora that Mirae was lying on, spread as far as the eye could see. Every few seconds, rainbow-colored shooting stars streaked past the nebulous clouds like iridescent fingers running through water.

What she didn't see, however, was any sign of the Netherking. Although Mirae tried to sense him out, following the link that connected them, the very air around her thrummed in time to her own heartbeat, making it impossible to try to listen through it, or track someone echoing the same sound.

Wincing against the soreness in her body, and marveling that she was still alive, Mirae carefully pulled herself up into a sitting position. "Where is everyone? And why does everything look so . . . peaceful?"

Hongbin looked around as well. "I'm guessing the Netherking hasn't started his reign of terror yet. If he had, surely we'd hear or see the battle between him and the gods."

"What's he waiting for?" Mirae asked, climbing painfully to her feet.

"More important, *where* on this realm could he be?" Hongbin asked with a frown. Mirae concurred that was a better question. If she and Hongbin hadn't been holding hands when they jumped, who knew where the portal between mortals and spirits would have spat them out? The Netherking could be anywhere on this uncharted plane, and the same could be said for Kimoon and Siwon.

"We need to hurry," Mirae said, hiking up her chima. "We have to find him before he reaches the gods."

Hongbin stood as well, though less certainly. "We have no idea where we are, though. What are we supposed to do, just start wandering around?"

Mirae hesitated. Hongbin was right, she needed a plan. She rubbed her face, wondering how she could still feel so exhausted when she wasn't even technically alive—not that she knew how time, or life energies, worked in the spirit world.

Just then, Hongbin gasped, interrupting her thoughts. "Noonim, look at your hand!"

Mirae lowered her arms, confused, but did as Hongbin said. Then she, too, gasped at what she saw: a thin red thread tied to her smallest finger. The same one that had been guiding her in the starry void she'd switched into at her mother's gravesite. Just as it had then, the string arced in the air in front of her, disappearing just a few feet ahead, guiding her toward a place she had already glimpsed in her own future.

Hongbin stared with wonder. "What is that?"

"The red thread of fate," Mirae said, twisting her hand and watching the vibrant string twirl in the air.

"Isn't it supposed to tether people to their soulmates?" Hongbin asked, raising an eyebrow.

"I don't think that's what mine does." Mirae shook her head, remembering her switch onto the mirrored plane, where she approached a palace at the end of the universe, presumably the abode of her patron deity, the goddess of time. "I think it's meant to guide the High Horomancer to the next step of her journey, wherever that may be."

Hongbin studied his own hands. "Yeah, you must be right, since I don't have one. If the string connected soulmates, mine would be *yanking* me forward." He shrugged. "Or maybe my soulmate is on earth, where he belongs. Yours, on the other hand . . ."

Mirae shot Hongbin a look. "What, my soulmate is dead, that's why I'm being led into the spirit world?"

"No." Hongbin reached down and plucked one of the glowing violets, sticking it innocently into his hair. "He's just here in this world because he'll go anywhere for you."

Not wanting to consider whatever Hongbin was implying, Mirae shook her head and trudged off, loath to waste time on something as frivolous as soulmates; but as she began following the string flowing from her hand, countless tiny orbs of light suddenly surged out of the grass and bobbed through the air, disturbed by her passing. Fireflies, thousands of them, emanating a soft pink light.

Hongbin clapped his hands as he traipsed after Mirae. "Oh, how romantic! If only your soulmate were here with you instead of me."

"Enough about soulmates," Mirae grumbled, striding quickly past the promenading insects. With every step she took, however, more would rise up, encasing her and Hongbin in enchanting, twinkling lights. *It is a pretty sight*, Mirae thought begrudgingly as Hongbin laughed behind her, delighted by the beauty of the spirit world, despite the dangers lurking ahead.

Thankfully, there didn't seem to be any enemies lying in wait for several miles. The land before them was flat, leading to a horizon that sparkled strangely. To Mirae's left loomed a range of mist-draped mountains, and to her right, a thick forest lush with pine trees. When Mirae glanced behind her, all she saw was more flat terrain, and a bright orange glow burning at the edge of the world.

Mirae didn't know what else to do but head in the direction of the red string, so follow it she did, toward the misty mountains to the west, hoping that she would find Kimoon and Siwon along the way.

For now, though, Mirae allowed the heady, blossomy scent of the field's flowers and the balmy breeze winding through it to steady her nerves, refreshing her weary soul with effortless beauty. She was even starting to enjoy the fireflies' light show, when, out of nowhere, the sound of flapping wings rustled through the air behind her, jolting her out of her quiet reverie.

Mirae whirled around and craned her neck upward until she saw what was flying toward them. Her eyes widened at the unexpected sight.

An enormous white bird, the size of ten grown women, was racing toward her. Even stranger, however, was its sheet-pale human face attached to the end of a long, thin neck. Mirae felt Hongbin grab her hand as the peculiar creature shot past them and gracefully landed a short distance away. After settling back on its haunches and folding its massive wings behind its body, it swiveled its elongated neck toward Mirae and Hongbin, so its human face could gaze upon the wary siblings.

Mirae remembered seeing a depiction of this creature in books about mythological beings. The inmyeonjo lowered its pale head in a gracious bow. "Greetings, Unnamed Dragon and fair prince," the inmyeonjo said, its voice low and soothing.

"H-Hello," Hongbin stammered. "It's nice to meet you."

Mirae returned the creature's bow. According to myth, inmyeonjo were sacred and benign, concerned only with keeping the peace and harmony between the earth and the sky. When Mirae straightened, she studied the visitant as it did her, and saw grace and wisdom in its features. Its face, though deathly pale, seemed animated with intelligence. Its keen eyes straddled a long, sharp nose. Small lips, as pallid as its skin, were nonetheless as delicate as its voice, and were greatly outsized by the inmyeonjo's high, full cheeks. Its black hair had been cut to chin length, framing its round face like smooth brushstrokes, while on its head rested an ebony tiered hat with equally dark, flowing ribbons.

Behind the inmyeonjo's extended neck, nearly as long as

Mirae was tall, was a feathered, birdlike frame with a magnificent tail flowing behind it. Each one of the white plumes covering the inmyeonjo's body could have run the entire length of Mirae's arms, and yet she felt no fear standing in front of the gigantic creature. Not when she noticed that its eyes glowed with a soft, silvery light, exactly like Areum's the night of her heavenly visitation.

"Am I right in assuming that a god has sent you to help us?" Mirae asked. "If so, we welcome your aid."

"Yes. I believe you have spoken with my patron once before." The inmyeonjo cocked its head. "As per their instructions, I have paved the way for you. Since the living are not meant to mingle with the dead, I have asked all the spirits in your path to steer clear."

"Maybe you should evacuate them instead," Hongbin said nervously. "The Netherking is a very dangerous man . . . he might hurt them."

"I don't think so." Mirae shook her head. "Since the gods are his targets, I'm sure he's heading straight for the heavens. Besides, it's the living he seeks to rule, not the dead."

"Correct," the inmyeonjo said. "Still, I have cautioned the spirits to stay out of his way, too, just in case. They will make themselves scarce, so have no fear."

Hongbin breathed a sigh of relief. "That's good. Unless the Netherking decides to suck all the magic out of this world and destroy everything in it."

"It would take eons to do that, even with the pearl," the inmyeonjo reassured him. "This place is not just made of magic, but from the fabric of the universe itself. I am also confident that the Netherking will not harm this realm, because doing so would ruin his plan. Everything is interconnected, so if the spirit realm crumbles, so will the mortal realm, and then he'd have nothing left to rule."

"I see." Hongbin nodded. "Well, do you happen to know where the Netherking is now?"

"Of course," the inmyeonjo said. "He is heading toward the black altar."

"Great, can you take us to him?" Hongbin asked, pressing his hands together. "We'll be very good passengers, I promise."

The inmyeonjo shook its head. "I can only approach the peaceful. The evil or warmongering are not worthy of my presence, so to them I cannot go. I'm sorry."

Mirae bit her lip and looked at the red thread of fate knotted around her finger, still leading her west, toward the distant mountains. "Can you at least tell us where the black altar is?"

"Or can you take us to the gods?" Hongbin asked. "So we can ask for their help?"

"Yes, that could work," Mirae approved. "I'm sure they'll be eager to assist us, especially now that the Netherking has left the mortal realm. They won't be breaking the Jade Emperor's rules by interfering on their own domain."

"To that end, I have brought some good and bad news," the inmyeonjo said. "As soon as the gods realized that the Netherking was on his way here with the pearl, and began to believe that the prophecy they'd feared for a millennia was about to come true, most of them fled. I do not know when or if they will return, but you will be hard-pressed to find allies in the heavens right now. Those who remain will likely try to hide until the danger is over."

"What?" Hongbin's voice quavered. "But if the gods aren't willing to fight the Inconstant Son, how are we supposed to do it alone?"

"Do not despair," the inmyeonjo said gently. "There is hope yet. I have already intercepted two of your friends and told them what I will tell you now. There is only one way to cut off the Netherking's access to the gods, but it can only be done from inside the heavens themselves. Which means you must reach the celestial realm before your enemy does."

"Wait, you found Siwon and Kimoon?" Hongbin pressed a hand to his chest. "Are they all right?"

"Yes." The inmyeonjo inclined its head. "They landed quite close to the metal altar, which is where they are currently headed. I suggest you meet up with them there."

Mirae breathed a sigh of relief alongside Hongbin. "So, it's a race, then," she said. "Whoever reaches the heavens first controls the fate of the realms."

"Yes." The inmyeonjo nodded. "There is only one way for a mortal to gain access to the heavens, and that is by obtaining a blessing from each of the altars of the four cardinal directions: the metal altar of the west, the black altar of the north, the earth altar of the east, and the burning altar of the south. Once you have these blessings, you will be granted passage through the celestial gate. From there, you may climb to the heavens and seal it off, preventing the Netherking from following. Although each of the altars is protected by a guardian who will make you pass a test, I'm sure it's nothing that a High Daughter cannot handle."

"Or a ruthless King of the Deep," Hongbin muttered darkly.

"I know you can't approach the Netherking," Mirae said, lowering her head humbly, "but is there any chance that you can take us to the metal altar, to our friends? I fear that traveling on foot will cost us precious time."

The inmyeonjo nodded again. "My patron has commanded me to help you stop the coming calamity however I can."

"Thank you." Keen not to waste even one more second, Mirae grabbed Hongbin's arm and steered him toward the inmyeonjo, who flapped its majestic white wings, allowing it to rise and hover in the air, feet extended. Mirae pushed Hongbin toward one of the inmyeonjo's waiting claws, while she stood before the other. Carefully, the inmyeonjo wrapped its talons around Mirae's and Hongbin's arms and chests until they were securely held. Then it whipped its wings hard and fast, sending them all soaring into the sky.

Chapter
TWENTY-FOUR

The inmyeonjo flew even faster than Mirae's dragon. Each flap of its wings seemed to transport them several miles in just a few seconds, effortlessly shooting them over the endlessly colorful landscape below. At first, the same teal meadow, dotted with violets and fireflies, filled their view, but gradually, the scenery around them began to change, growing rocky and mountainous. The pink and purple clouds overhead thinned, revealing a jade-colored sky and blue peaks veined with brilliant green rivers and foaming waterfalls.

Soon enough, the jagged summits loomed close enough that the spiraling silver mist dissipated, allowing Mirae to see that the mountains were dotted with winged creatures that she at first mistook for more inmyeonjo. But when she looked closer, she realized that they were chollima, flying horses that were fabled to soar as far as a thousand leagues in a single day. While Mirae gazed at the magnificent animals with wonder, the inmyeonjo began its descent, landing on a clearing halfway up the tallest peak.

"This is as far as I can take you," the inmyeonjo said, loosening its talons, "as per the instructions of the white tiger guardian. But I will wait for you here."

Mirae rubbed her shoulders, which were a little sore from being clutched so tightly. After exchanging a quick bow with the benevolent creature that had brought her here, Mirae moved toward the markings of a trail nearby. As she and Hongbin hiked, they kept their eyes peeled for any sign of their friends, who had, reportedly, come this way. Just as Mirae started to pant from the effort of hurrying up the steep mountainside, she noticed a gate up ahead, made of pale, sun-bleached pine. Sitting against one of its pillars was a familiar figure. A man, tall and draped in purple, pressing a makeshift poultice to the knife wound in his side.

Although Kimoon gritted his teeth, trying to hide the pain that caused sweat to bubble up on his brow, Mirae couldn't help but feel alarmed at how wan Kimoon already looked. If it weren't for the magical properties of the very air around them, a place of spirits where death didn't exist, he probably wouldn't last much longer. Not without a healer.

"Ah, you made it," Kimoon said, but his lighthearted quip failed to mask the tremor in his voice. "And even faster than expected. Of course, I never believed you were going to stay behind, but I'm still surprised you're already here."

"Where's Siwon?" Mirae asked, an edge to her voice despite the pity she felt for the mortally wounded man. After all, he'd betrayed her not long ago, and if any part of Kimoon was still under the Netherking's control, he couldn't be trusted not to do it again.

"He's with the white tiger guardian," Kimoon said, wincing with each word. "Trying to earn a blessing from the metal altar."

Hongbin dropped to Kimoon's side, wrinkling his nose at

the garlic poultice Kimoon had clearly made for himself. "You should let my noonim take a look at your wound."

"It's no use." Kimoon shook his head. "The inmyeonjo said our bodies became stagnant the moment we entered the spirit world. This is an unchanging place. I cannot be healed here."

"But . . . that also means you can't die, right?" Hongbin asked.

"Correct. I will just have to endure this pain until we leave." Kimoon tried to smile. "I suppose it's the least I deserve."

"No." Hongbin shook his head. "What happened wasn't your fault."

"I wish that were true," Kimoon whispered.

Mirae's eyes darted away from Kimoon, and the painful injury he had brought upon himself. Instead, she searched for any sign of Siwon on the other side of the gate. She couldn't bear to just stand around uselessly, unable to ease Kimoon's wound or look him in the eye. And she didn't want to hear whatever story he was conjuring up to explain why he'd done what he'd done. She wasn't ready to listen to his excuses. Not yet.

"I'm going to go help Siwon," Mirae announced, turning to leave.

Before she could pass through the gate, however, Kimoon hastily warned, "You can't go in. Only one person is allowed to meet with the tiger guardian at a time. Those are the rules. The rest of us are just going to have to remain here, and put our faith in my brother."

Those last two words, unexpected and soft, tempered Mirae's distress enough that she was able to come a little closer, at least enough to settle down next to Hongbin. The three of them sat in silence for several minutes before Hongbin finally said what needed to be said. "I know it hurts to talk right now," her younger brother said gently. "But I think you owe my noonim and me an explanation."

"I do," Kimoon said tiredly. "I'll tell you everything. In fact, it would be a relief."

Mirae vehemently disagreed with that sentiment, but she had to begrudgingly accept that Hongbin was right. It was time to start piecing together what they could about the Netherking's escape, and the role played by the man her future self had called imperative to her mission. Perhaps because of the things only he knew.

"The Netherking's influence started off small," Kimoon began, his voice a near whisper. "The occasional taunt here and there, or tidbits of vital information that he'd purposefully drop to pique my interest. Of course, at the time I thought I could see right through him. I knew exactly what he was trying to do. But the Netherking has a way of getting into your head. Worming inside without you realizing it. The more I tried to ignore him, the crueler he became. Starting with relaying to me in great detail what he was doing to Minho."

Kimoon paused for a moment, steeling himself. "He told me how he was tormenting Minho relentlessly, trying to splinter your brother's soul so he could seize complete control of Minho's body. Flooding him with delusions that confused his sense of reality, his understanding of right and wrong. Horrible things I couldn't stand to listen to any longer. And it was then, when the Netherking had riled me up, provoking my guilt so thoroughly that I felt I had to act, that he promised to ease up on Minho if I would do one thing for him—fill his days with conversation. Stop ignoring him, and leaving him to rot alone in the darkness. Talk, listen, and spare Minho some misery."

Although Kimoon's breaths were labored while delivering his long report, he pressed on, determined to bare it all. "How could I refuse, knowing what Minho was going through? It seemed a small price to pay, sitting with the Netherking and letting him prattle on, keeping him too preoccupied to torment the soul of the man I was trying to save. I even thought myself lucky for a while. Incredibly sly. Because in time I was able to get the Netherking to admit that he was plotting something new. I learned things he forbade me to repeat to you, Mirae, or else he would torture Minho in even more creative, unspeakable ways."

"You should have told me anyway," Mirae said tightly, appalled to hear what had been happening underneath her nose—her mother's nose.

"I know that now, but in the moment, I thought I had every-thing under control," Kimoon confessed. "I arrogantly believed that if I maintained the Netherking's trust by keeping his secrets, that he would eventually let down his guard and tell me more about his new plan. I truly thought I only stood to gain from this arrangement. After all, the Netherking was chained up. Let him daydream about getting his powers again—his days were num-bered. What harm was there in learning more about our enemy, while shielding Minho at the same time?

"I thought it was working, too," Kimoon said with a sigh. "I thought I was so clever whenever I managed to wheedle more information out of him. And, because words cannot be false in the Deep, I believed everything he told me. So, imagine my utter delight when he eventually let slip that there *was* a way to exorcise his soul out of Minho."

"So, he's the one who told you that 'The Tale of the Rabbit and the Dragon King' held the key to Minho's cure," Mirae said, voicing what she'd already come to suspect. "That's why you were so obsessed with it."

"Yes." Kimoon shook his head at his own naivete. "The Netherking was so good at feigning disappointment in himself for divulging sensitive information that I didn't realize he'd surrendered that bit of truth on purpose, trying to distract me the way I thought I was doing to him. He knew I was getting desperate. The dowager queen's experiments were failing. Morale was low. So, he reinforced my growing belief that we needed to rethink our methods, even if it meant dirtying our hands. I brought my concerns up to you, Mirae, and you listened, at first. But, unfortunately, when mere rabbit liver had no effect on Minho, and you refused to continue supporting my pursuit of this potential breakthrough, I thought I had no choice but to turn back to the Netherking for help."

"So you made a deal," Mirae said, starting to see now where this was going. She shook her head at Hongbin, who raised an eyebrow when Kimoon mentioned rabbit liver.

"To my utter shame, yes." Kimoon shut his eyes. "I was so relieved when the Netherking was willing to tell me what I was missing, how to make the rabbit liver work. Of course, he mocked me relentlessly for pursuing a dead end. After all, I couldn't undo the Netherking's spell without your help, Mirae, and you, he cackled, would never, ever compromise your morals. So, he was happy to tell me what I wanted to know, if only so that I would be forever tormented by knowing *how* to save Minho, but being utterly helpless to do it. In return for this backhanded generosity, all I needed to do was bring the Netherking some of Mirae's blood, and a drop of black water."

"Tell me you were smart enough to refuse," Hongbin said, looking ill.

"I wish I could," Kimoon grieved. "But I was so close to finding a cure, and that made me reckless. I didn't see the harm in doing what was asked of me, because I'd been told that the Netherking couldn't use magic with those manacles on. Magical fluids were useless to him, and what I was getting in return far outweighed any risk. That's what I told myself, anyway."

Mirae's hand reached up to the slightly raised scar on her neck, just a few days old. All that remained of Minho's sudden attack—except for the soiled handkerchief Kimoon had used to sop up her blood. She felt a rush of anguish course through her, realizing now that that intimate, tender moment had actually been a premeditated gesture of betrayal. Kimoon, of all people, should have known better. She'd trusted him to.

Seconds later something else began to blossom inside her, too. A small wave of relief as she realized it wasn't her fault that the Netherking was free. Although Mirae was a little ashamed that she was taking any comfort in Kimoon's confession, it suddenly felt as if her lungs could expand freely for the first time in ages, no longer crushed by the weight of her own guilt.

"Okay, but I still don't understand how the Netherking broke free," Hongbin said. "Because you were right, Kimoon. He couldn't use magic while restrained by those chains."

"Not directly," Kimoon said. He swallowed before continuing his story. "By the time I handed him the blood and black water I'd managed to collect, he claimed that he needed to change the terms of our deal, given that he'd already gotten what he needed on his own, by biting Mirae. If I still intended to get what *I* wanted, then I had to procure something else. That's when he asked to see the pearl." Kimoon took a deep breath, forcing himself to finish. "He said he just wanted to touch something that once belonged to his wife, to feel her presence. He assured me there was nothing to fear. After all, he was magically impotent in his constraints."

"But the pearl was not," Mirae whispered. The blossom of relief shriveled as she finally understood the missing piece of the Netherking's escape. "As soon as you gave him the pearl, he corrupted it with the black water you gave him, imbued with his will from years of manipulating it. Then he flooded it with my magic, my *blood*, and was able to compel it to unlock his chains."

Kimoon stared down at the ground, too ashamed to speak. Hongbin, who looked far more sympathetic than Mirae felt toward the man who'd helped facilitate their mother's death, gently prodded, "What happened next?"

"I don't know," Kimoon said quietly. "I have no memory of anything after I gave him the pearl. The next thing I remember, Mirae was pulling me out of Wol Sin Lake."

"And he did something to you while you were out, didn't

he?" Hongbin guessed. "That's why you turned against us at Sujeongju."

"He must have." Kimoon shook his head as if to knock free all his missing, buried memories. "Even though the royal physician purged me of black water, it clearly wasn't enough. If even a drop remained, the Netherking would still have had his hooks in me. All I know," Kimoon sighed, "is I haven't felt myself recently. I thought I was just overwhelmed by my guilt, and my cowardice in refusing to confess what I'd done. But now I know it was because of something else, something evil taking root inside me, undetected."

"And then in Sujeongju, the Netherking activated whatever lay dormant inside you," Hongbin finished. "He took over your body, like he did to Minho, and forced you to betray us."

When Kimoon nodded, overcome with shame, Hongbin placed a comforting hand on the other man's arm. An unexpected kindness that made Kimoon fall still, a tear forming in his eye. But Hongbin's gesture only further provoked the rage blistering inside Mirae as she remembered everything that had happened after Kimoon had foolishly, inexcusably fallen for the Netherking's tricks. The mother who'd withered right before her eyes, dead because Mirae had trusted the wrong person to be her right hand. A brother in critical condition, harmed a second time by a man willing to stoop to any level to get what he wanted. Each and every time the Netherking crept closer to freedom, Kimoon was central, critical to his plan.

And that was starting to become a difficult thing to forgive.

When Mirae finally found the will to speak, her voice

trembled with all the built-up anger threatening to erupt. "Surely you don't expect me to believe that all of this is the Netherking's fault," she quavered. "It was you who chose to believe that you were above the Netherking's influence. That you were smarter than him. And I can't help but notice that your actions have allowed him to escape my grasp not once, but *twice* in the last few days."

"What happened in Sujeongju wasn't his fault," Hongbin said. "The Netherking—"

"It wasn't the Netherking who directed us toward the Josan king's secret stash of black water," Mirae pressed, not caring that each word struck Kimoon like a barbed arrow. "You're the one who ensured that we acquired exactly what the Netherking needed *yet again*. You can blame some 'undetected corruption' nestled inside you all you want, but it doesn't excuse the things you did of your own free will."

"We're *all* to blame for underestimating the Netherking," Hongbin insisted. "Hell, you can even pass some of the blame onto the gods. We had a living, breathing shinmyeong with us, and they couldn't bother to warn us what was coming?"

"I have my own questions for the gods when we reach the heavens," Mirae acknowledged, waving away Hongbin's protests. "But what I want to understand is why the Netherking can keep counting on you, Kimoon, to be twisted by his promises, and rush toward lines you should know better than to cross. I want to know why your obsession with using dark magic, urged on by vengeful kings, never seems to ebb."

And why you couldn't trust me with your darkness before it spiraled out of control, Mirae continued silently. *Why is it that you're the one I keep seeing in my visions of Seolla's past and future? A cunning, vengeful wretch who embraces the title Inconstant Son. Someone I nevertheless continue to stand beside, across all time and under every moon.*

Although Mirae's accusations seemed to fall like a weighted yoke around Kimoon's already sagging shoulders, he said nothing in defense of himself. He just sat there, quietly accepting Mirae's rage, her condemnation.

Hongbin, however, sighed tiredly. Realizing there was nothing he could say to patch what had been torn, he reached out to them both, gripping their hands tightly. Mirae and Kimoon sat there in silence, Hongbin serving as their link while they struggled to figure out what to say to each other. How to apologize, blame, explain, and forgive. Things Mirae felt she needed years, not minutes, to work out.

But time had other plans. The tension between them was still palpable when Mirae noticed a familiar figure heading back down the mountain path. At his side trotted an enormous, snowy-white tiger with eyes as blue as a sapphire.

Mirae gaped at the magnificent beast, her argument with Kimoon momentarily forgotten as she watched Siwon and the tiger walk slowly toward them, deep in conversation. Siwon kept one hand in the tiger's fur, holding on as a child might to the hem of its parent's clothes. In his other hand, he gripped a gold-hilted sword with a bejeweled scabbard.

Noticing Mirae watching him a short distance away, Siwon raised the sword in a small wave and turned to bow to the tiger, who stopped just before the gate, refusing to cross. Mirae didn't hear Siwon's parting words, but the tiger seemed pleased. Then, as Siwon hurried back to his friends, the black-striped creature turned and headed back up the pass.

"I got it." Siwon beamed, showing off the sheathed sword. "I got the blessing from the metal altar! Now we just need to get the other three, and we'll be able to enter the heavens."

"At last," Mirae said, letting out a breath, "some good news."

As Siwon drew closer, she couldn't help but notice how markedly different he looked after his trek up to the altar. His eyes shone a brighter yellow than before, almost as light as jasmine tea, and his long hair now lay in a silky braid down his back. His cheeks and the tip of his nose were flushed a healthy pink, and his full lips were parted in a relaxed smile.

As curious as Mirae was about what exactly Siwon had encountered at the altar, she never got the chance to ask. A sudden, earsplitting cry caused her to stumble backward and grab the sides of her throbbing head.

He has reached the black altar! the inmyeonjo shrieked, its voice shrill and piercing as it thundered in her brain. *He is about to do the unthinkable. Hurry, Unnamed Dragon—stop him before he destroys the altar, or you will never get all four blessings.*

"What is it, Your Majesty?" Siwon was beside Mirae in an instant. "Is it the Netherking? Is he here?"

Rubbing her forehead, and still reeling from the inmyeonjo's psychic outburst, Mirae turned and sprinted back down the mountain trail, to where their ride waited below. "He isn't here, but I know where he is. We need to get to him quickly."

I cannot take you there, the inmyeonjo reminded her. Mirae was better prepared for the intrusive voice this time, but it still sent a sharp pain shooting through her skull. *I cannot go where the warmongering are. But I will send others who can.*

Before Mirae could ask what the inmyeonjo meant, she heard the answer heading her way. The pounding of racing hooves, the fierce neighs of charging chollima coming to carry Mirae and her friends wherever they needed. When the cloud-white horses finally burst into view, their feathered wings pressed to their sides, Mirae heard Hongbin gasp with delight.

Mirae, on the other hand, felt the urge to jump to the side to avoid being stampeded. But, just as quickly as they raced up to Mirae's party, the proud chollima slowed to a stop and held still, inviting Mirae and her companions to approach.

There was no time to waste, not while the Netherking was doing everything in his power to sabotage Mirae's ability to reach the heavens. She quickly pulled herself onto the closest chollima, straddling its bristly, muscular back, while Siwon and Hongbin lifted Kimoon onto one of the horses before climbing onto a pair of their own. Once everyone had mounted up, Mirae heard the inmyeonjo offer one last, urgent command.

Fly undaunted, Unnamed Dragon, and do not falter. You must acquire the remaining blessings, no matter what.

As if understanding the inmyeonjo's imperious call, the chollima tossed their snowy-white manes and leaped into the sky, hurtling toward the sparkling horizon to the north.

Chapter
TWENTY-FIVE

Perching atop a flying horse was infinitely more comfortable than dangling from the inmyeonjo's talons, and Mirae's shoulders were grateful for the change. The chollima were remarkably swift, too; there was nothing at all leisurely about the flapping of their powerful wings. At times, the wind whipping past Mirae at breakneck speeds was too sharp, too face-chappingly cold, for her to keep her eyes open for long.

Whenever she did try to peel her eyelids apart, she managed to catch glimpses of the landscape below. At the foot of the metal altar mountain grew a vast bamboo forest, the thick, tufted tops of each of the sky-high stalks swaying cheerily for miles. When the forest finally ended, the bamboo trees quickly tapered off, yielding to overgrown grass that slowly browned to a reddish gold sweeping into the distance.

Eventually, the grass began to part, sliced by blue-gray rivers that dampened the earth until the ground was more clay than dirt. It was a stunning sight, countless threads of silvery water winding through grass-speckled mudflats stretching all the way out to a glittering teal ocean that flooded the rest of the horizon. A spectacular view marred by the one thing that didn't belong.

A long plume of smoke streaking upward into the overcast sky, a dark knife splitting the jewel-toned clouds.

Terrified that she was too late, Mirae spurred her chollima down toward the smoldering altar, which rested on one of the few hilly patches of sediment blanketed by red sea fronds. Her flying horse let out a battle-worthy bray before speeding where it was directed. It barely slowed its descent enough to land without sending Mirae tumbling over its head.

As soon as the chollima lurched to a stop, Mirae quickly untangled her fingers from its snowy-white mane. Then she leaped to the spongy ground that immediately gripped her feet. Her heart sank as she approached the altar, fighting the wet, sucking earth with every step.

The black altar, once an impressive monument of antler-like driftwood and seashells, had been scorched beyond repair, the smoke rising out of its remains too thick to see through.

Mirae heard the other chollima land behind her, and her companions' feet squelching through the mushy earth as they came to join her. Hongbin was the first to reach her, the first to speak.

"Nice try, Netherking," he tried to joke, but his voice was too thick to come off as even remotely lighthearted. "You may have destroyed the altar, but we can still talk to its guardian."

"I'm afraid not," Siwon said, pointing grimly through the smoke. The strong ocean winds, bitterly cold and smelling of brine, rushed through the plumes, parting the ashy curtain just enough to reveal the corpse that lay behind it.

Mirae took in the charred shell and withered remains of the

black tortoise guardian. Desecrated and despoiled of magic like her mother. It took everything Mirae had not to fall to her knees in the mud.

We're too late. Mirae pressed a hand over her heart, felt it racing as fast as a chollima in flight. *He killed another innocent, and now I'll never be able to stop the Netherking.*

We've lost, this time for good.

"Hey, it's not over yet," Hongbin said. She could barely hear him over the thundering of her heart, the screams of despair clawing through her head. "Even if we can't get into the heavens ourselves, we still have a duty to make sure he doesn't, either."

"Hongbin is right, Mirae." Although Kimoon clutched his side the way Mirae clutched her chest, he remained firmly on his feet, determined to fight through the pain. "All is not lost. The Netherking managed to steal the last blessing from the black altar, so we're just going to have to take it from him."

"I agree," Siwon chimed in. His concurrence, the last of the three, finally breached Mirae's despair, calming the torrent of horror inside her. She tore her eyes away from the shriveled tortoise, meeting Siwon's bright stare. "The tiger guardian knows what's going on, but the others might not. We have to reach them first, and warn them. Then we'll earn blessings from their altars and take back what the Netherking stole."

Siwon held up his gold-hilted sword, encrusted with glittering garnets and pearls, like a pledge. A reminder that the gods' worthy champions were bound to succeed.

Slowly shaking off the cold, numbing grip of defeat, Mirae nodded, more for herself than anyone else. "Let's go," she said quietly, struck by a deep tiredness that seemed to seep into her very bones. "We've still got two guardians to save."

After bowing deeply to the tortoise guardian's remains, lamenting that she didn't have time to honor its passing, Mirae turned back to her chollima, which patiently waited for her to remount. Before she could command it to race toward their next destination, however, she saw a hand reach up and rest lightly on hers.

"May I ride with you?" Siwon asked. "There's something the tiger guardian wanted me to discuss with you."

Even if she hadn't sensed the seriousness in his request, Mirae would have still agreed. She quickly scooted forward on the chollima's back. After she made room, Siwon climbed up behind her. Then, instead of clinging to Mirae's waist, he reached around to twist his fingers into the chollima's mane.

Appreciating the respectful gesture, but also highly aware of the man's legs and arms pressing into her sides, Mirae didn't hesitate to urge her chollima to begin flying southeast toward the next closest altar, desperately hoping she would reach it in time.

Within minutes of soaring through the air, Mirae noticed the water-spliced clay below firming back into solid land that eventually sprouted a sprawling cherry blossom forest. The bark of the pink-dotted trees was nearly black, in contrast to the pale blossoms snowing onto the ground when Mirae finally turned to look over her shoulder. "What is it you wanted to talk about?"

"I was asked to relay an exhortation from the tiger guardian," Siwon answered, shouting to be heard over the roaring of the wind. "He said that it's not enough to thwart the Netherking by sealing off the heavens. That alone will not rid us of the Inconstant Son."

"What do you mean?" Mirae called back.

"He spoke of your patron deity, the goddess of time," Siwon explained. "She is the one who can show you the secret to defeating the Inconstant Son. Something only she can give you. If you want to receive it, you *must* reach the heavens and visit her."

Mirae wasn't surprised to hear this. She'd already seen the red thread of fate arcing toward the goddess of time's palace, just as it led her toward the earth altar now.

Mirae nodded to show Siwon she had heard and understood his message. Then, preemptively following the pattern of what she now expected to happen in their conversations, she changed the subject to the person who was always foremost on Siwon's mind. "I'm sorry we left Areum behind. I know you're worried about her."

"No more than you are about Daegun," Siwon said. "For what it's worth, I'm certain Lady Areum was able to get Daegun the help he needed. She won't let the Seers of Light rest until he's better. She's wonderfully tenacious like that."

"She is," Mirae agreed. Undaunted compassion was something both her friends had in common. "I'm sure that's one of the many things that made you fall for her."

"Sorry?" Siwon leaned in closer, as if to hear her better over the whipping wind.

The sudden movement caused the encrusted hilt strapped to his side to dig into Mirae's back. She bit back the pain of its burrowing, as well as the pangs needling her heart, as she said, "I'm happy for you two. You're good for each other. But," she said, forcing herself to sound playful, and mostly succeeding, "you better sing my praises to everyone when you announce your relationship. It's only fair since I'm the one that brought you together."

Siwon was silent for a moment. Mirae couldn't see his face, but she heard the confusion in his voice when he finally asked, "You think Lady Areum and I are . . . courting?"

"You don't have to hide it anymore," Mirae said. She loosened her grip on the chollima's mane, worried her anxious clutching might hurt the beast. "It's not like your affection for each other wasn't painfully obvious."

"Your Majesty," Siwon said, seemingly too shocked to say anything else. *Relieved, no doubt*, Mirae thought, swallowing, *that I'm taking this so well, that his relationship with one friend won't cause discomfort for another.*

Mirae felt some relief as well, finally airing out Siwon's poorly kept secret so she could make peace with it. Trying to redirect her attention to her mission, Mirae glanced down at the scenery below to track their progress, and noticed the pink blossoms of the cherry blossom trees were starting to blend in with the prickly green boughs of a sprawling pine forest.

"Your Majesty, Lady Areum and I—" Siwon started to say, but his words were quickly drowned out by the chollima's loud, echoing bray as it shot down toward the earth, so fast that Mirae and Siwon clung to its mane as they would to life itself.

The winged horse landed deftly in a large clearing, a space

framed by astonishingly tall pines with branches that spanned sideways, like arms performing a dance. Golden needles littered the ground, as lustrous as any jewelry Mirae had ever worn. Her feet crunched lightly over the flaxen, straw-like leaves as she turned around, looking for the earth altar and its guardian, or any sign that the Netherking had beat her here as well.

All looked well. The clearing was bright, the earth dappled with the dazzling pink, blue, and purple glow of the nebulous clouds above. Most important, Mirae saw a gateway at the far side of the glade, erected over a path that, she assumed, led to the earth altar. But as Mirae began heading toward the trail entrance, she heard an unexpected sound mingling with the rustling leaves overhead. Low chuckles echoing out of the shadows between trees.

Just as Mirae drew to a stop, raising her palms to summon a defensive spell, the ground in front of her erupted into a plume of crackling blue fire. Gone as suddenly as it came, the brief distraction was all her ambushers needed to leap from their hiding spots and surround Mirae's party, weapons raised.

Dokkaebi. Dozens of them. The tall, horned goblins formed a tight circle, but thankfully made no move to attack. Mirae similarly reined in her magic, waiting for her would-be captors to announce what they wanted. As she studied the creatures of myth, she was surprised to find that they weren't as hideous in person as they appeared in engravings or storybooks. Although they were large in stature—several feet taller than the average Seollan, with muscles as bulging as Mirae's chollima—the dokkaebi grinned at Mirae genially, their fangs as white as their shockingly bright hair. Their faces were fairly humanoid, with strong jaws and wide, shapely cheeks fixed beneath dark, bulging eyes as round as circles. Wrapped around the smiling creatures were common beige hanboks, loosely tied for comfort.

Even the dokkaebi's bloodred fur somehow didn't feel ominous once Mirae realized that the one-legged creatures were raising their spiked clubs in a salute, not in a threatening manner.

Finally, one of the goblins lowered his club, prompting the others to do the same, and spoke, his voice booming. "I am the dokkaebi king."

He paused, waiting for Mirae and her friends to bow. One by one, tentatively, they inclined their heads respectfully. "Well met," Mirae said politely.

Hongbin, on the other hand, could not contain his emotions. Clearly excited to meet his favorite creatures of myth, he exclaimed, "This is such an honor, Your Majesty! Especially since, where I'm from, dokkaebi are extinct."

Thankfully, the dokkaebi king didn't take offense at the outburst. He shrugged and waved Hongbin's words away with his club, which had been painted bright blue like all the others. "Most of our kind are long gone. After the Miri War and the extinction of dragons, many of us magical creations from around the peninsula begged the gods to provide us a safe haven from humans, who we feared would come after our powers next. The gods allowed it, but only for those who had never harmed an innocent. My clan has been here ever since, wrestling with the dead and hearing all their best stories."

"But today we're very bored since the spirits all went into

hiding," another dokkaebi said, hopping on his single leg with excitement. "So you're going to have to play with us!"

"I'm afraid we don't have time for games," Mirae said, shaking her head. "We're actually here to make this realm safe again. Are you the guardian of the earth altar?"

The king shook his head. "No, there is no guardian, not since the last dragon disappeared. However," the king said, his smile deepening, pushing his long fangs farther past his lips, "I do know how to get you the earth altar's blessing, if that's why you've come. I'll show you, but only if you make time to play a quick game with us. If you win, I swear on my club that we will help you get what you came for."

The other dokkaebi cheered at their leader's proposal, but Mirae bit back a groan of impatience. "We really don't have time for this," she said again. "There's a very bad man coming this way. Please, let us through."

To Mirae's dismay, the dokkaebi king and his followers merely laughed at her threats. "Well, this bad man of yours won't get a blessing, either, unless he plays with us. And from the sound of it, he'll be a much more entertaining competitor than you!"

Mirae was about to tell the dokkaebi king exactly how the Netherking would eviscerate them with his corrupted pearl, but a hand on her arm stopped her.

"It's okay, noonim," Hongbin said, his delight over meeting the dokkaebi clearly still coursing through him. "I know how to beat them."

"You don't even know what game they want to play."

"Sure I do," Hongbin said, puffing out his chest. "It'll be what they always ask for—a ssireum match. The same challenge they offered to Jeong-min in 'The Legend of the Go Sisters.' You know, when she managed to trick three dokkaebi into giving her their magical club? All I have to do is tackle my opponent's leg, and they'll fall over. I'll win, easy and simple."

"I know the story, too, but it's just that. A story." Mirae shook her head. "We don't have time for this."

"But it will be fun," the dokkaebi roared, pumping his club into the air. "And you will lose quickly, I'm sure." He guffawed at his own boast, and the others quickly joined in.

"Noonim, please," Hongbin said as Mirae's palm sparked with fire. "I've got this."

As much as Mirae hated to admit it, acquiescing to the dokkaebi king's demands *was* probably the fastest way forward. Without a guardian, the earth altar's blessing could prove impossible to acquire on her own. If the goblin king knew the secret to getting what she came for, then Mirae had no choice but to play along.

Breathing deeply to quell her exasperation, Mirae nodded for Hongbin to name himself their champion. Suppressing a squeal, Hongbin stepped forward and proudly announced, "I will be your opponent, Your Majesty."

"Are you certain, bun-headed one?" the king taunted playfully. "Once we begin, you cannot be swapped out."

Hongbin reached up and patted the ball of hair on top of his head. "I'm certain I can beat you, whether I'm ready or knot."

Kimoon chortled appreciatively, but Mirae swallowed a lump of nervousness forming in her throat as the dokkaebi king nodded at one of his subjects, who hopped back into the trees. When the goblin returned carrying a jar of arrows, Mirae's heart sank as she realized what game the dokkaebi were planning to play. Not a wrestling match but pitch-pot, a throwing competition that Mirae and her brothers had played a lot growing up.

Unfortunately, Hongbin was notoriously terrible at it, and had never won a single game.

Mirae's fists clenched, every muscle taut, but Hongbin seemed unbothered by this unexpected twist, his grin unwavering. Anticipating, perhaps, that Mirae was stressing, he turned just enough to shoot her a wink before returning his attention to the game.

The dokkaebi king waited until his assistant had placed the earthenware jar ten paces away from where he and Hongbin stood. Mirae swallowed as the arrows were handed over to the contestants, her eyes darting nervously to the jar's incredibly slim neck.

Once everything was set up, the dokkaebi king twirled his arrow. "I learned this amusing game from the spirits of this world, and it has quickly become my favorite. I'm assuming you already know how to play, bun head, since this is a creation of your people?"

Hongbin nodded with a confidence that puzzled Mirae. Satisfied, the king continued, "Since you are short on time, I have a proposal. Instead of seeing who scores the most points, let's just say that whoever gets an arrow into the jar first is the winner. What do you say?"

Making this harder is the last thing Hongbin needs, Mirae fretted, her fingernails creasing half-moons into her palms. Siwon, who glanced over and saw the way her nails were digging into her skin, reached over and took her closest hand, gently forcing his fingers under hers to prevent her from hurting herself.

"It'll be all right," he whispered, squeezing her reassuringly, but politely releasing her hand as soon as he felt her muscles relax. "Seja jeoha looks like he has a plan."

"Yes, have a little faith in him," Kimoon said. For a moment, his eyes flickered down to where Siwon and Mirae had been briefly touching, before snapping back to the game that was about to begin. "Hongbin never lets us down."

Although his words were meant to be reassuring, Mirae couldn't help but notice that they were as tense as the muscles in her jaw and neck. Her body stiffened even more when she realized Hongbin had agreed to the dokkaebi king's proposition, and that he'd even allowed the king to make the first throw.

All the breath in Mirae's lungs rushed out of her as the king rolled his broad shoulders before taking up his position, gripping an arrow neatly in his thick, muscular fingers. He eyed the target carefully, as if calculating the exact amount of strength and inflection needed to sink his arrow.

Beside him, Hongbin looked as if he was focusing just as hard. Sweat bubbled up on his brow, which was furrowed in concentration. Just as Mirae was about to resign herself to losing, and having to find another way to get the earth altar's blessing, the dokkaebi king pulled his arm back and made his throw.

Mirae didn't breathe, her eyes fixed on the arcing arrow as it flew through the air. But as it sailed closer to its target, the brief flicker of hope Mirae had tried to hold on to petered out as the arrow found its mark, plunging cleanly into the neck of the jar, scoring the dokkaebi king his first and only point.

Mirae sighed and hung her head, preparing herself to beg the dokkaebi king for a second chance when an unexpected sound made her head snap back up. To her utter confusion, cries of disappointment from the horned creatures thundered across the clearing. For some reason, they didn't seem to realize that their king had won.

"Such good fortune!" she heard Siwon say beside her. "I can't believe he missed, after all that boasting!"

"What?" Mirae turned to look at the jar, at the feathered tail of the king's arrow still sticking out of it, clear as day.

Realizing what Hongbin was doing, his risky but ingenious plan, she shot her eyes over to her brother, who stood there smiling, even as sweat dripped down the sides of his face. He had his own arrow in hand, his arm cocked back. His gaze was fixed intently on the jar, as if compelling it to open wide and secure him the win.

This time, Mirae watched carefully as her brother released his arrow, so poorly aimed that she could tell from where she stood that there was no way it was going to hit its mark. Sure enough, it soared way past the waiting jar, disappearing into the trees.

And yet, the jar clanged joyously, as if Hongbin had scored a point in its depths, and the dokkaebi bellowed again with dismay.

"Incredible," Kimoon shouted over the din, a rare smile splitting his lips. "He did it."

"Yes," Mirae said, a grin tugging at the corners of her own mouth. "Yes, he did."

Thankfully, the dokkaebi king was as unaware as the rest of his followers that Hongbin had deceived them with a simple spell. A Ma-eum illusion that deluded them into thinking their king's arrow had flown wide, and Hongbin's had sailed true. Mirae, naturally, was too trained in Ma-eum Magic to fall for such a trick, but the dokkaebi were not.

No longer needing to maintain a glamour on the king's real arrow, which could now pose as his own, Hongbin released his illusion with a sharp exhale, panting from the effort it took to mislead the eyes and ears of dozens of beings. But his sweaty face beamed from his hard-won victory, both in a game believably won and from an enchantment expertly cast.

"I cannot believe this!" the dokkaebi king howled. "You cheated, you must have! Your posture was all wrong, your aim laughable. I, however, was perfect, my precision impeccable. I am the best pitch-potter there ever was. I beat its creator a thousand times!"

"I guess spirits make poor competitors," Hongbin said with a shrug. "It's been too long since you've played games with beings of flesh and blood. You've clearly lost your touch."

"Hm, perhaps I have," the dokkaebi king said. A split second later, he startled Mirae by breaking into uproarious laughter. "But *aigoo*, was that fun!"

Spurred on by their king's amusement, the other dokkaebi began howling and cackling, creating such a racket that Mirae had to fight the urge to slap her hands over her ears. As soon as the revelry died down enough that she could be heard, Mirae shouted over the babble. "Your Majesty, we played your game and won. It's time you kept your end of the deal."

"Indeed it is," the dokkaebi king said, waving his club until his subjects fell silent. He turned to Hongbin and, with a magnanimous flourish, presented him with the spiked weapon. "Here is your prize, clever mortal. No longer shall you be called the bun-headed one, but *the fleet-fingered trickster!*"

The other dokkaebi let out a celebratory shout before falling quiet as their king waved his arm at them again. "Go on. Use my club to make a wish. And take care not to waste it, for there are limits to what my bangmangi can do."

"A wish?" Hongbin breathed, clearly overwhelmed to be standing in the legendary Jeong-min's shoes, the Go sister who had similarly used a dokkaebi club to save her family. Mirae could practically see the possibilities flashing through her brother's mind. After all, he held in his hands the means of making any number of their current problems disappear. With a wave of his arm, he could ask that the Netherking be banished from this plane, or that the black altar blessing be pilfered from his pocket and slipped into theirs. Or he could solve a more immediate issue, by wishing that Minho be brought back to full health, or that a powerful healing potion would appear, one able to patch up Kimoon's wound.

The possibilities were seemingly endless to a wisher who didn't know any better. But what the mischievous dokkaebi king had neglected to say was that his magic club could only summon things that already existed, a stipulation that Mirae and

Hongbin were both aware of, from stories they'd heard as kids. The bangmangi couldn't create something out of nothing, or grant a wish that was nebulous. No, it would be a waste to ask for something they were not positive the club could grant them.

"Hongbin," Mirae said, hoping her voice would remind her brother what they'd come for, something they desperately needed and could only acquire with his singular prize.

Thankfully, her call worked. Jerked back to his senses, Hongbin shook off the pull of his heart's greatest unspoken desires and raised the club over his head. "I wish to receive the earth altar's blessing," he declared, and smashed the club against the ground. As soon as it struck the pine-needled floor, a burst of blue flame erupted in front of him, gone as quickly as it came.

But it left something behind in its wake. Hongbin reached out and grabbed the earth altar's blessing, holding it up for Mirae to see, a triumphant smile on his face.

Mirae breathed a sigh of relief, and smiled back at her brother as she examined the curious rattle in his hand. Similar in size and make to the ones she'd seen Josan shamans use, the rattle looked deceptively simple compared with Siwon's bejeweled sword. Its smooth mahogany handle fit snugly between Hongbin's fingers, while the dozens of carved wooden bells clanged soothingly, like wind chimes in the rain.

"Congratulations, fleet-fingered trickster," the dokkaebi king said as he snatched back his club. "I must thank you and your useless teammates for today's entertainment, and all the restless nights to come. For I shall not sleep a wink until I figure out how you bested me—this I vow!"

As a sign of his dedication, the dokkaebi king plucked out a single coarse white hair and used it to tie up all his other ones into a messy, frizzy bun, as if he believed that looking like Hongbin was the key to thinking like him, too. Then the king roared for his subjects to move out as he dashed back into the trees, the rest of the dokkaebi hopping after.

"Wait!" Mirae cried. "Don't forget to stay hidden from the Netherking! Do not approach him, under any circumstance!"

To her frustration, Mirae heard nothing but chortles of laughter in response. But her chagrin was short-lived, for her chollima soon nuzzled her from behind, reminding her it was time to leave and secure the last blessing of the four elements.

When Mirae turned around, Hongbin and Siwon had already helped Kimoon onto his flying horse, and Hongbin quickly mounted his next. Siwon, who had left his chollima back at the black altar, turned to ask Hongbin if they could share his steed, but her brother only winked at Mirae before urging his winged horse up into the sky. Kimoon, who looked down at Mirae and Siwon far less enthusiastically, nevertheless followed close behind.

Siwon turned toward Mirae, his cheeks flushed. "I'm sorry to trouble you, Your Majesty, but I seem to be—"

Mirae wordlessly scooted forward on her horse. Bowing gratefully, his face still red, Siwon mounted the chollima behind her and gripped the horse's hair just as before. As soon as her passenger was steeled for takeoff, Mirae clicked her tongue at her faithful steed, who spread its wings and launched into the sky, heading straight toward their final destination—the burning altar to the south.

Chapter

TWENTY-SIX

Mirae and Siwon flew without speaking for several miles, watching the forest of green below them slowly thin into copses of vermilion pines with bark as red as chili peppers, and star-lit boughs that looked as if strings of lanterns were hidden in their leaves. Eventually, the twinkling trees tapered off, the bloodred wood seeming to melt into the ground until the earth turned as bright orange as a tiger's fur. The sunset-colored landscape was soon dotted with boulders as large as palanquins, and silvery green shrubs that stubbornly grew among patches of sun-scorched grass.

Mirae lifted her hand and stared at the red thread of fate, as fiery in color as the earth below, all of which led toward a bright spot on the southern horizon, which she ardently hoped was not the sign of another altar, another guardian, being set ablaze by the Netherking.

As they drew near enough to their destination that Mirae could see the faint outline of a gate up ahead, Siwon finally broke the silence.

"Your Majesty," he called nervously over the rushing wind. "I know this isn't the best time to discuss personal matters, but there's something I wanted to clear the air about." When Mirae didn't discourage him from continuing, Siwon added, "I haven't been protective of Lady Areum because I'm courting her. I just . . . I needed you to know that."

Mirae nodded to show she had heard, and that she understood what he was saying. She knew oracles weren't allowed to have life partners, for they were expected to devote themselves wholly to the gods. She was glad to hear that Siwon wasn't openly courting Areum, lest she get into trouble for breaking the rules, potentially even getting kicked out of the temple. It made sense that Siwon would now fear for the safety of their continued liaison, since Mirae had figured out their secret. "You have nothing to worry about," she called over her shoulder. "My lips are sealed."

"No, Your Majesty, you misunderstand." Siwon leaned in closer, making sure Mirae could hear him clearly. "I've been protecting Lady Areum because I swore I wouldn't let anything happen to her. Her partner made me promise. I agreed because I owe both of them a great debt."

Her partner? Before Mirae could process what Siwon was telling her, her chollima began its breakneck descent, sending a thrill through Mirae's stomach that she wasn't sure came only from the horse's exhilarating dive.

The winged steed slowed just enough to come to a screeching halt in front of the gate Mirae had seen from afar. Unlike the others, this one was colorful and ornate. Bright red pillars held up a swooping roof of golden tiles. Emblazoned on the doors were glowing circles, a red sun and pearly white moon. But what caught Mirae's eye, and held it firmly, was the guardian perched atop the celestial doorway.

A magnificent phoenix, just like the one etched into the Josan palace gates. But this one was no carving. It was a creature of flesh and blood, with eyes that flashed like suns. A guardian that lived and breathed, hopefully for a while yet.

Mirae's eyes flickered over to the burning altar off to the side of the gate, a cairn made out of tiger-orange shale stacked into a chest-high dome. Beaming out of it were two streams of light, one a fiery yellow, the other a soft blue glow.

And the altar was guarded even more heavily than the gate. On either side of it stood two enormous haetae, just as real as the phoenix overhead. Mirae swallowed as the horned, lionlike beasts glowered at her, daring her to try to take what she came for without permission.

But their jagged teeth and hulking silhouettes were not frightening enough to make Mirae turn and run. She knew that their job wasn't to eviscerate the gods' champions, but rather to determine guilty souls from innocent ones, and judge them accordingly. Only the unworthy would be devoured, for no evil spirits could pass the haetae by.

The phoenix guardian, on the other hand, couldn't be pacified so easily. Knowing that the mystical bird was the only being who could grant her safe passage through the haetae, and to the heavens beyond, Mirae dismounted and began making her way to the celestial gate.

But she'd made it only a few steps when she heard Kimoon groan and fall to his knees. Mirae whirled around. "What is it?" she asked. "What's wrong?"

She felt the answer before Kimoon could say anything. A chill like entering a room and realizing a window had been broken in her absence. Dread like a darting figure following her in the darkness. Horror at the thought that she couldn't protect the ones she loved.

Mirae's head turned slowly toward the sky, to the dark spot approaching. The Netherking quickly descended, riding a defiled chollima, its white wings plumed with shadows, its eyes and nose bleeding black water.

"Hello, queenling." The Netherking dismounted, his spirit as corporeal in this world as Mirae's body. Free of his princely vessel, the King of the Deep showed his real face, the same insufferably smug visage that Mirae had hoped to exterminate from this world, and every other.

Mirae raised her hands, ready to summon the elements in defense of everyone behind her, man or beast, but the Netherking held up his palms placatingly, no pearl in sight.

"I'm not here to fight," he soothed, his voice low and oily. "I just want to talk."

"I have nothing to say to you," Mirae spat, keeping her hands raised, knowing that the moment the Netherking drew out his secret weapon, she and everyone else was done for. But he made no move to do so. In fact, he seemed to be going out of his way to make sure Mirae didn't feel threatened. He stayed back, keeping his arms raised, not even flinching when Siwon reached for the golden sword at his side.

But Mirae knew better than to trust his peaceful approach. There was only one reason she was still alive, and that was because the Netherking needed something only she could give him.

"I appreciate you hearing me out," the Netherking said, his gratitude a thinly veiled command. "I'm sure you're aware that if you attack me, I'll have to defend myself. And we both know how that will end."

As much as she hated it, rankled by the power he wielded over her, Mirae knew he was right. "Tell me what you want," she demanded. "And make it quick."

"I'm offering a very simple, straightforward bargain," he replied calmly. "The blessing of the burning altar is not one I can take by force. It must be freely given by the phoenix guardian."

"Good," Mirae said. "I guess your journey ends here, then."

"Hardly," the Netherking said mildly. "I'm disappointed in you, queenling, for not seeing the bigger picture. Even if I am refused entrance into the heavens today, I'll simply return to the mortal world and wreak havoc there. You're hardly ending my campaign by turning me away here and now."

No, this doesn't end here, Mirae thought bitterly, *unless I do as the white tiger guardian says and gain an audience with the goddess of time. Only then will I know how to stop the Inconstant Son for good. But I'll never get there without the black altar's blessing, which the Netherking will not part with unless he and I come to some kind of agreement.*

Even though the thought of negotiating with the man who had killed her mother and twisted her brother made bile rise in her throat, Mirae lowered her hands. "Are you suggesting an exchange?" she asked stiffly. "I acquire a blessing from the burning altar for you, and you give me one from the black altar?"

"If you'd be so kind," the Netherking said, clearly proud of Mirae for finally catching on. "I acquired two blessings from the black tortoise, one of which I'm happy to trade for safe passage through the celestial gate. What's more, I'll even give you a fighting chance of reaching the heavens first, generous as I am."

"How will you do that?" Mirae asked begrudgingly.

"I'll let you pick your path first," the Netherking said. "There are two routes, one of which is much shorter than the other. If you play your cards right, you'll arrive in the godly realm well before me, and have a chance to shut me out entirely."

Mirae narrowed her eyes, knowing better than to take any of the Netherking's promises at face value. But no matter how vile it made her feel inside, Mirae didn't know what choice she had except to accept his offer. If she refused, and tried to steal the black altar blessing from him, there was a high chance that she, and everyone behind her, would be slaughtered.

"I'll see what I can do," she said at last, each word burning like acid on her tongue. Before she lost her nerve, she turned to Siwon. "Keep an eye on him. If things start to go south, take Hongbin and run."

Siwon hesitated, but nodded. "I'll keep him safe. You have my word."

Knowing how seriously Siwon took his role as protector, Mirae's shoulders relaxed as she headed toward the heavenly gate and its bright-eyed guardian.

But as she started to draw close, the haetae snapped their jaws at her, growling with bared teeth. Mirae jumped back, unsure at first why the horned beasts were bristling at her, until she felt something burn against her leg. Like a sizzling coal inside her pocket.

Mirae pressed a hand against her chima, finding the bulge of her black bell, hot to the touch. Encased by a spirit whom the haetae clearly considered unworthy, and wanted to rip from Mirae's body. Thankfully, before the snarling soul-judgers could leap at her, the phoenix flapped its wings imperiously, cowing them. Although the haetae grumbled, they stayed where they were, allowing Mirae to pass them by.

When she finally stood before the celestial gate, Mirae looked up at the magnificent bird, which seemed to be studying her in return with its starry eyes. After a moment, a voice echoed in Mirae's head, deep and feminine.

I have long awaited this day, Unnamed Dragon.

Mirae gulped, unsure how to respond to such a greeting. "It is an honor to stand before you," she said nervously, and bowed to the guardian.

I know why you have come, the phoenix said, its voice piercing but benevolent. *Only the purehearted can acquire a blessing from the burning altar. The unworthy will be killed by its flames. Before letting you pass, I must ask you a question. The answer will make it clear how you should proceed. Do you understand?*

Mirae nodded. Having her consent, the phoenix continued.

The question you must answer is this: Out of everyone who has died in order for you to stand before me today, which individual do you want to bring back to life?

Mirae inhaled sharply, the air as cutting as the censure in the first half of the phoenix's question and the guilt it had purpose-fully stirred up.

But for a second, the briefest flicker of a moment, she felt something else as well. A flutter of hope that the phoenix, a powerful guardian of the spirit realm, was posing more than just a question, but an actual offer to bring back someone Mirae had lost. Before she could shake off that ridiculous, impossible thought, the answer to the phoenix's query flashed in her mind, as well as what it inevitably said about the purity of her heart.

Mirae knew instantly that she would choose one of two peo-ple to save: either her mother or Captain Jia. Women she'd loved and lost. Unfairly cut down by the Netherking's treachery.

But with that realization came an onslaught of shame. Remorse for how quickly she sought to soothe her own grief, without even considering the mourning families of those who'd also loved and lost people because of her. Parents of the oracles whom the Netherqueen had slaughtered. Siblings of the Kun Sunim who had helped Mirae find her way only to have her throat slit soon after. The loved ones of the Josan dignitary, even, who'd been ripped to pieces all because he chose to attend her coronation ceremony. And those were just the deaths she knew about.

So many innocent people had fallen, paving the way for Mirae to ascend, and she didn't even know their names, nor was she haunted enough by their deaths to leap at the chance of bringing even a single one of them back.

Instead, when faced with the possibility of righting a wrong she, or her crown, had some hand in, her heart had immediately passed over the suffering of others, finding hers much more imperative to soothe. More important, even, than clearing her own conscience.

It was only natural, of course, to grieve those she knew and loved. To want them back more than anything. Mirae didn't fault herself for that. But she also knew that she was a queen, the High Horomancer known to the gods as the Unnamed Dragon.

But despite this calling, she was no pure soul. It was still her instinct to put herself, her own loved ones first, preserving them instead of dedicating herself to easing the collective suffering of those her enemies had trampled in her name.

Do you have your answer? the phoenix asked, though by the tone of its voice, they both knew what Mirae had decided.

"I am not worthy," Mirae breathed. "I am too selfish to receive your blessing."

Perhaps, the phoenix said. *But you do not have to walk away empty-handed.*

Mirae nodded, having had the same thought herself. For even though Mirae had faced a brutal indictment of her own soul, she had not come here alone.

Turning back to look at her companions, her eyes rested on her tenderhearted younger brother, who sat with Kimoon, rubbing his back comfortingly.

"Hongbin," she called. Her brother looked up and quickly strode over. As soon as he took his place at her side, Mirae gestured for him to address the phoenix.

At first, Hongbin was confused, until the phoenix's voice filled his head. Mirae couldn't hear what the guardian said to him, but it made his eyes widen, his body fall still. He stared up at the phoenix for a while, nodding every few seconds, or frowning in concentration. Finally, after several long minutes, Hongbin's face cleared of all expressions except joy. He turned to Mirae with a beaming smile.

"I did it!" he cheered. "She said I could proceed to the altar!"

Mirae smiled despite the sinking pit in her own stomach, shame for the things she'd been forced to face in herself. "Well done, Hongbin. I'm proud of you."

After offering a quick, grateful bow to the phoenix, Hongbin made his way over to the sandstone altar, cautiously approaching the haetae until they made it clear that they had no interest in him. Waltzing right past their defenses, Hongbin stepped up to the glowing beams and put his hands into their effervescent light.

As soon as he did, the blue and yellow rays disappeared, leaving in their place two suspended spheres—a shimmery white moon and a bloodred sun, just like the ones painted on the doors of the celestial gate. Mirae held her breath as Hongbin reached out and plucked the orbs out of the air.

They fell into his hands easily, gleaming as brightly as Hongbin's smile as he brought the blessings over to Mirae. She held out her hands to him, and he quickly placed the spheres onto her palms. Against her skin, the moon felt as cool as an autumn breeze, the sun warm like a summer day. Hongbin had done it—they now had all the altar blessings but one.

"Magnificent," the Netherking said as Mirae and Hongbin returned. Although she half expected him to drop his cooperative charade and attack her now that she had what he wanted, the Netherking stayed perfectly still. Which could only mean one thing—there was another deal to be made. Something else he desperately needed that only Mirae could give him.

"Well, are we making the trade or not?" Mirae demanded.

"Soon enough, queenling," the Netherking said. "Just as soon as you hold up your end of the deal." When Mirae glared at him mutinously, the Netherking shrugged. "You promised to help me get past the celestial gate, in exchange for the black altar blessing."

"What more do you need?" Mirae snapped.

The Netherking's face creased with mock regret. "Unfortunately, the haetae are a bit of an issue, for they will certainly judge my soul as evil and try to eat me. I could try to obliterate them, I suppose, but even if I managed to get past them, evil spirits cannot enter the heavens. Ancient, magical protections, and all that. There is something, however, that would make all my problems go away."

"And that is?" Mirae prompted impatiently.

"Why, to be a spirit no longer," the Netherking said, as if it was rather obvious. "The haetae can only devour the evil spirits of the *dead*. They and all the gods' safeguards cannot stop me if I'm alive. But in order for that to happen, I will require a new body."

"A body?" Mirae didn't understand what he was implying until he glanced over at Kimoon, still on his knees and fighting the pain of whatever the Netherking was doing to him.

"This one is already half mine," the Netherking said lightly.

"It would be easiest to simply finish what I started with him. But I will leave the decision to you, queenling. As a kindness."

Mirae just stood there, staring, as a rampage of emotions stormed through her, chief among them the urge to strike the Netherking down, faster than he could reach for his pearl. But out of the rush of chaotic thoughts in her head, one stood out sharper than the rest. *I'm not giving him a single soul. I will not surrender anyone else to his endless torment.*

But her conviction was immediately shattered by a voice quavering behind her.

"I will do it," Siwon said, stepping forward as he began unfastening the golden sword around his waist. "I will be your vessel."

"Siwon, no," Mirae stammered, pressing her hand against his chest. "You're not going anywhere."

"It's all right," he said, though his hands trembled, unable to fully loosen the scabbard. "The rest of you are important, but I'm no one. We all know I'm the obvious choice."

"You are *not* no one," Mirae shot back. "Not to me."

"I appreciate that, Your Majesty," Siwon said, his voice hollow, his eyes already dull with acceptance of his horrific fate. "But someone has to do this."

"Maybe," Mirae whispered. "But it isn't going to be you."

"Then who will it be, queenling?" the Netherking asked. He stood there calmly, hands clasped behind him, as if he didn't already know what she would do. What she had no choice but to do, despite her conviction moments ago.

For the truth was, there was no way out of this. Not without sacrificing thousands more by turning the Netherking away, sending him back down to the mortal world, where he would bring nations to their knees. Even if Mirae refused him here and now, nothing was stopping him from whipping out his pearl and annihilating everyone in his way, taking the body of whoever was left standing. But allowing Mirae to help him by turning on one of her own was the easier path, one where he had the added benefit of watching Mirae make an unforgivable choice.

As much as Mirae wanted to spare the others, she knew that surrendering herself was impossible. She had divine work to do, and a power she could not allow to fall into the Netherking's hands. And she was never going to let herself lose another brother. Sending Hongbin into harm's way was out of the question, that much everyone seemed to understand.

But between the men who remained, Siwon and Kimoon, the choice was, as the Netherking had already said, practically made for her.

"No, Mirae," Kimoon gasped, still bent over with pain. He craned his neck to look up at her and shook his head at whatever he saw in her eyes. "Please, you can't do this."

No, she admitted, letting out a breath. *I can't*. It was too awful. She may have failed the phoenix's test of her heart, but she was no monster. No traitor to her friends.

Mirae fixed her gaze on the Netherking, who listened to her next words with disbelief. "Both our paths end here," she said quietly, barely loud enough for everyone to hear. "Someday we will meet again in the mortal sphere, and we will end this eternal struggle. But today, we both walk away with nothing."

"Your Majesty," Siwon protested, grabbing her arm that still held him back. "What about the tiger guardian's warning? You can't just—"

"None of us will go any further," Mirae repeated, even though she saw the red thread of fate fluttering in the air, tugging her toward the celestial gate. "We're at an impasse, neither of us able to proceed without the other. So, let's just cut our losses, and leave the heavens out of this."

"Oh, queenling." The Netherking shook his head. "I called you a lot of things when I was locked up in the darkness, cursing your name. But never once did I consider you a coward."

Mirae bit back a retort, refusing to be baited. "Just leave and accept that the heavens will never be yours."

"Apparently you need a reminder about what, exactly, is *mine*," the Netherking snarled. Shedding his mask of cooperation, he reached into the pocket of his shimmering black robe and pulled out the pearl, deep purple with his foul corruption. "If you do not give me what I want, I will *take* it, and then drain that pretty little prince you love so much, just to show you what happens to those who defy me."

Hongbin took a step closer to Mirae, who didn't take kindly to threats against her brother. But before she could jump to his defense, the Netherking raised the pearl, compelling its shadowy tendrils to start licking outward, rearing to find a target. "Give me what I want," he said menacingly, "or I'll kill everyone."

Mirae knew the only reason the Netherking wasn't making good on his threat was because there was a chance, a very small chance, that he would lose a head-to-head fight against all the powerful magical beings facing him. And the Netherking was not one to take chances, to start battles he didn't know he could win. Not if there was another, more manipulative way.

Mirae wasn't keen on making a deadly gamble, either. If she took the Netherking to battle, someone, if not everyone, would die. That much was certain.

"Make your choice, queenling," the Netherking sneered. "One man, or all these deaths. Which terrible decision can you live with?"

His taunt echoed the words of the gods themselves. A warning that Mirae would have to make an impossible choice. A sacrifice that would determine everyone's fate.

It all depends on you, Unnamed Dragon, and how much darkness you can wield without succumbing to it.

Mirae looked down at Kimoon, into his golden, pleading eyes. He was the one her future self had said to bring along, claiming that her mission would fail without him. The yellow gleam of his gaze flickered like a candle about to go out, unable to fight off the Netherking's influence much longer. As if reading her thoughts, the Netherking chimed in again, his voice softer now. "I swear I will take good care of him, queenling, as if his body were my own. Besides, he's a dead man anyway. If you do the right thing, he'll live far longer with me than he would have on his own. This is the only way to keep him alive."

"Don't listen to him, Mirae," Kimoon begged. "I know what he does to the souls of his vessels. He hates me for taking Minho from him—he will not show me mercy."

Mirae's fingers curled tightly over the celestial orbs, both the heat and the cold making her hands go numb, the way she was trying to make her heart feel. It was the only way to steel herself to do what the gods had already ordained, what they had tried to prepare her to do. Their exhortations, messages voiced by her friends, rang through her head.

It's not enough to thwart the Netherking . . . you must *reach the heavens.*

What are you willing to do, or lose, to save us all?

Mirae dropped to her knees beside Kimoon and lowered the orbs into her lap so she could reach out and cup the sides of her friend's face. "I have seen you in my switches, Kimoon," she said softly. She looked into his eyes, hoping he could see the truth reflected in hers. "Someday, you will define my future, my purpose and world entire. This is not the end. We will meet again, and when we do, I will never, ever leave your side. I will earn your forgiveness, I swear on my mother's grave."

"Mirae," he whispered, pressing his face against her palms as if he could force her to hold him tighter, to drag him with her to the ends of the earth. "Don't let him do this. Please." But Mirae stood, resisting Kimoon's pleas. Growing desperate, he reached out to grab her, but his body was too racked with agony to do more than brush his fingers against her ankle.

"Mirae," she heard Hongbin sob, "you can't do this. He's our friend."

Vision blurring, Mirae wiped away her tears before grabbing the orbs that had fallen to her feet. When she straightened, she looked the Netherking in the eye, hoping her hateful gaze blistered him to the core. "Give me the water blessing," she said coldly. "And I won't stop you from doing what you must."

The Netherking inclined his head and, with his free hand, reached into his hanbok and pulled out a piece of the black tortoise's shell, its underside flashing his reflection onto its mirrored surface. "Move away from my new host, and I'll toss you your prize."

Stifling a rise of white-hot rage, Mirae did as her vile nemesis instructed. For every step the Netherking took, she took one away from Kimoon, closer to the celestial gate. Siwon and Hongbin backed away alongside her, the latter clinging to her arm, echoing Kimoon's pleas. But when she continued to ignore him, Siwon stepped in, holding Hongbin tightly, his own face racked with torment.

As soon as he reached Kimoon, the Netherking smiled and, true to his word, tossed the mirrored scale in Mirae's direction. It landed with a thud at her feet.

"There," he said. "Now, hand over the phoenix's blessing, if you please."

"Mirae, this isn't right," Hongbin tried one last time. "This isn't worth the cost."

As much as it killed her, Mirae leaned down and grabbed the shard of shell she'd traded Kimoon's life for. Then, with her party in possession of all four blessings, Mirae raised the sun orb, the path she always knew she was going to take because of her switch, and watched the celestial gates swing open.

On the other side glared a brilliant light, too bright to stare into. Mirae shielded her eyes, contemplating rushing into the heavens, leaving the Netherking without a means of following. As if sensing the direction of her thoughts, the Netherking shouted, "Do not test me, queenling. Give me the key to the moon path, or I will do far worse things to your handsome friend than I ever did to Minho. Unspeakable things. Keep your word, and I will put him under, into a merciful, peaceful sleep. It's the least you can do for him, don't you think?"

Slowly, tearfully, Mirae let the moon orb slip from her hands, denting the earth right outside the gate. Then, without looking back, she stepped into the bright light, away from the growling haetae, and the sound of Kimoon's screams.

Chapter
TWENTY-SEVEN

As soon as the brightness of the doorway faded, Mirae fell to her knees on the other side. She took several shuddering breaths, trying and failing to slow her racing heart. She'd made it. She was in the heavens, right where her switches had prophesied she'd end up on this nightmarish journey. But the gods hadn't told her what the unbearable price of getting here would be.

"Your Majesty." She felt Siwon grab her arms and help her to her feet.

Mirae looked around, her breaths ragged. She, Hongbin, and Siwon stood on a cutout of earth tapering down into a cliff's edge. It was hard to see much more than that, for the air around them was thickly shrouded in cool, silvery mist, but she could make out the silhouette of two pillars on either side of the platform, one engraved with the sun, the other the moon.

"Are you all right?" Siwon asked, brow creased with concern.

"No, I'm not." Mirae could almost still hear the echoes of Kimoon screaming her name, begging her to come back. She squeezed her eyes shut, trying to block it out.

"You did what you had to," Siwon said softly. "Let's hurry and finish this, so we can find a way to rescue my dongsaeng."

"Rescue him?" Hongbin's voice drifted between them, sharp and chilling. "Like the way we *rescued* Minho from Josan, only to trap him inside the Netherking? Tortured out of his mind, neither dead nor alive?"

When Mirae looked over at her own dongsaeng, the expression on Hongbin's face was one she'd never seen before, not on him, and certainly not directed at her. He stared at her almost exactly the same way Kimoon had in his last moments.

"Hongbin," she said hoarsely, "there was no other way."

"You're the High Horomancer," Hongbin said, lifting his chin defiantly. Mirae couldn't help but stare at the scar on his skin that her recklessness in Josan had put there. "You are sworn to save everyone on the peninsula, to *find a way* when everything is stacked against you. But when your loyal friend needed you, you left him. You just . . . walked away."

"I had to." Mirae pressed a hand to her mouth, holding back a sob. "I had no choice."

"Didn't you?" Hongbin took a step back, as if he couldn't stand to be anywhere near her.

"As long as the Netherking has the pearl, he holds all the cards," Mirae said helplessly. "Only the goddess of time can tell me how to defeat him. I have to do whatever it takes to reach her."

"So, you played right into his hands," Hongbin said coldly. "He presented you with a deal, and you just took it. Which was exactly what he was counting on. That's why he keeps winning, noonim. We're just predictable little fools. It's starting to feel like our whole mission is to bumble around, slowly being manipulated into fetching the Netherking everything he needs."

"That's not fair," Siwon interjected. "Making the best of two bad choices isn't the same thing as choosing to support evil. The Netherking is vile and manipulative. Bending people to his will is what he does best. Despite this, Her Majesty has taken far more from him than she has been forced to give him."

"Tell that to the fresh supply of princes my noonim keeps tossing him." At that, Hongbin turned and, just as Mirae had minutes ago, walked away from the person begging for a second chance. As her brother retreated, Mirae hung her head, swallowing back the apologies she knew would never be enough.

"Don't worry, he'll come around." Siwon let out a breath. "Deep down, he knows as well as I do that you meant it when you said you'd never turn your back on Kimoon again. You'll find a way to save him. I know it."

Mirae wiped away the tears pooling in her eyes and sniffled. "Thank you, Siwon. I'm grateful that you're here. More than you know."

"I'm glad to hear it," Siwon said, but there was a hitch to his voice. "Unfortunately, this is where we'll have to part ways. At least for a little while."

When Mirae's eyes snapped to his, he quickly explained. "As horrible as our last encounter with the Netherking was, we both know it could have gone a lot worse. The Netherking clearly has another trick up his sleeve, or else he never would have risked letting us leave alive, let alone take the quickest route to the heavens. Something made him feel confident enough to settle for a deal instead of slaughter, and I want to know what that is. If I can, I will sabotage whatever he's planning."

"What are you proposing, exactly?" Mirae asked uneasily.

"After you and Seja jeoha activate the sun path, I will retrieve the orb so the Netherking cannot sneak up behind you. Then I'll hide here on the platform." He inclined his head toward the thick pillars of the gate behind them, thick enough to conceal him. "When the Netherking comes through, I'll follow him down the moon path."

Mirae shook her head. "No, I won't allow it. It's too dangerous."

"For you, yes," Siwon said, doing his best to smile. "But I'm impervious to the pearl's worst spell, remember? Out of everyone, I'll be the safest. Besides, we have to find out what the Netherking is up to. We can't afford to let him outwit us again."

Not waiting for Mirae to change her mind, Siwon gently pushed her toward Hongbin, who stood forlornly by the sun-engraved pillar. "Go on. You know I have to do this."

This time, Mirae didn't try to stop him, because he was right. Siwon wasn't meant to climb the stairway of swords with her and Hongbin, for she hadn't seen him there in her vision of the future. "Promise me you'll be careful," she said, voice trembling. "Do not confront the Netherking. If you see anything amiss, come back immediately and report."

"I will, I promise." Siwon looked as if he wanted to say something else, a thought that made him step a little closer. But he quickly shook off whatever it was, choosing instead to gesture once more to where Hongbin waited for her.

Mirae reluctantly turned to join her brother at the edge of the cliff. He said nothing when she arrived, refusing to even look at her. Leaving him to his brooding, Mirae silently examined the thin stone pedestal engraved with a beaming sun. Seeing a shallow bowl carved into the top of the pillar, Mirae placed the celestial orb into its grooves. As soon as she did, a thin archway of golden lights shimmered in the air in front of her, a sheer, twinkling veil. Before Mirae could so much as marvel at the beautiful sight, she felt Hongbin push past her and glumly enter the gossamer gate.

Heaving a sigh, Mirae silently followed, turning around just in time to see Siwon reach out and pluck the sun orb from the pedestal, blocking the Netherking from also taking the shortest route to the heavens. Although the golden, lucent archway began to dissipate as soon as the orb was retracted, the reassuring smile that Siwon shot through its fading glow warmed Mirae's heart until her friend, too, vanished from sight.

Emboldened, Mirae swiveled back around to face what lay ahead, and noticed that the heavy mist on the platform had parted just enough to reveal an endless expanse of sky in front of her, and a sharp drop-off to endless depths. Even though her switch had already shown her what lay below, Mirae couldn't help but peer curiously over the edge.

Rising slowly out of the bright abyss was a ball of radiant light. Though it was small with distance, Mirae could already feel the heat emanating from its core. Her and Hongbin's race with the sun was about to begin.

Conscious that there was no time to waste, Mirae still closed her eyes and tried to summon her dragon, hoping that the brutal climb to the heavens could be avoided with a little magic. Unsurprisingly, the elements refused to heed her call, bound by the ancient, magical protections that the Netherking had spoken of.

Undeterred, Mirae searched the vast, cloudy sky before her, looking for the sword bridge that she knew was there, and saw the glint of steel right in front of her face. Had she stepped forward even a few inches more, it would have sliced her nose in half.

Mirae turned to explain to Hongbin what came next, but he had already crouched down, examining the staggered blades hovering in the air. Seeing that they were placed sharp-side up, he carefully pressed his fingers against the flat of the nearest blade and pushed until the sword flipped onto its side, making it safe to step on.

"You first, noonim," he said, avoiding her gaze. "As always."

Mirae bit back yet another urge to beg for forgiveness, even though she knew in her heart that Kimoon's fate had been decided long ago, and not by her. Still, Hongbin resented her for not stopping what was meant to be, and as Siwon said, only time, if anything, would change that. So, after quickly tying the tortoise's reflective scale into the knot of her jeogori ribbon, she wordlessly placed her foot on the sword Hongbin held for her, keeping it in place as he reached out and secured the next step. When it was ready, Mirae moved her next foot onto the second sword, and marveled, briefly, that she was standing suspended in the misty sky.

Then Mirae reached down and flipped the next sword over. She waited until Hongbin's foot sidled up next to hers, keeping the lowest blade from shifting back into its point-up position, before she took another step, climbing higher into the air.

Working together, Mirae and Hongbin soon found a rhythm, both rotating the sharp footholds in front of them, or for each other, and cautiously balancing on the blades arcing upward into the heavens. As the sun grew closer, urging them onward, the hazy clouds around them warmed from silvery blue to a rosy pink, laced with flaxen beams that were far hotter than they looked. Mirae quickly learned that if she wasn't careful, and left a bit of arm exposed to the light for too long, it started to burn, flushing her skin bright red.

As long as she was mindful of that, the going was relatively smooth. That is, until she heard Hongbin gasp behind her. Mirae wanted to spin around, but she knew better than to make any sudden movements in such a precarious position. "What happened?" she called down.

"I cut my finger." Mirae could hear the frown in her brother's voice. "I guess our bodies aren't stagnant in this liminal space between the spirit world and the heavens. Lucky us." Grumbling under his breath, Hongbin resumed reaching out to flip swords for Mirae, though this time his fingers left a small streak of blood.

Soon enough, Mirae, too, sliced her fingers and stockinged feet more than once as the heat from the rising sun goaded her and Hongbin into picking up the pace, the blades beneath them growing uncomfortably warm from the celestial body chasing them. Even the metal bell in Mirae's pocket seemed to absorb the sun's radiating heat, practically searing its designs into the flesh of Mirae's thigh.

This just urged her onward even faster. Thankfully, her and

Hongbin's bodies didn't seem capable of tiring in the heavens, though there was no telling how far into the sky they still needed to climb. All Mirae knew for sure was that at some point she would switch, and find herself back in Noksan, while her past self spoke with an embittered Hongbin. Now that Mirae knew what she had done to anger him, she couldn't help but wonder if her upcoming switch might be a chance to fix things, to warn the past of what was to come.

Even as she had that thought, however, the Kun Sunim's warning from years ago echoed back to her: *You must change* nothing *except the rise of the Inconstant Son. . . . If you use these switches for anything else, your power, along with all hope of destroying the Inconstant Son, will be ripped away.* Smoothing over a sibling feud certainly didn't seem to count as "stopping the rise of the Inconstant Son," and part of the reason Mirae was journeying to the heavens was to prevent the loss of her switching powers. No, she couldn't afford to let anything about Noksan change, not if it meant undermining her mission here, in the realm of the gods.

But it wasn't too late to try to patch things up right now, in the present. With that thought, Mirae cleared her throat. "You know, there's one good thing that's come of all this."

When Hongbin said nothing in response, Mirae took a steadying breath before continuing. "Minho's finally free, and he's with the most knowledgeable healers on the peninsula. I'm sure they'll find a way to save him, and then he can finally go home."

Just when Mirae thought Hongbin wasn't going to respond to that, either, he suddenly said, "Yes, we might have saved him. But at what cost?"

Mirae's hand hesitated on the next blade, causing Hongbin's shoulder to bump into her, unaware that she had stopped climbing. "What do you mean?" she asked. "I thought getting our brother back was something we were both dedicated to. We always fight for the ones we love, across all time and under every moon."

"That has been our pattern, yes." Hongbin nudged Mirae's leg, prompting her to keep moving. "But we should never have let things get this far."

"We didn't *let* the Netherking do anything," Mirae said.

"Didn't we?" Hongbin let out a breath. "We had it within our power to prevent all this from ever happening. But we didn't . . . because we love Minho too much."

Similar words, a taunt uttered by the King of the Deep, echoed back to Mirae. *All monsters loved someone once. Love is the greatest calamity, and it will be your undoing.*

Mirae shook off memories of the mocking laughter that followed, a sound that rankled her, and made her voice sharper than she intended. "So, you're saying I should have killed Minho on the shores of Wol Sin Lake? Is that it?"

"What I'm saying is that our tradition of treating family members as indispensable is what got us into this mess." Hongbin sighed. "Maybe that's why it all keeps going wrong. Like how quickly you changed your mind about sacrificing Kimoon when the Netherking threatened to hurt me instead."

Mirae's first instinct was to challenge Hongbin, to defend her right to protect her loved ones, until she remembered that she'd failed the phoenix's test over those same thoughts. Her younger brother, however, had passed the very same trial.

"We're not special," Hongbin continued, voice shaking. "We should be willing to die, to lose each other for the sake of the peninsula. Like Captain Jia. She loved Minho, but she would never have gone after him if it weren't for us forcing her to, and look what happened. We fell right into the Netherking's hands, and she died. But you know what? The people who lend us their aid just because we're Seollan royals, even when we're being self-serving, are not any less precious. I mean, if we keep sacrificing others so we can fulfill our destiny, does that really make us worth saving?"

"I wasn't just choosing you over Kimoon," Mirae argued. "It isn't that simple. I've seen the future, remember? It had to be you and me on this bridge, not me and Kimoon. It didn't matter what I wanted; it was fate."

"Right, fate. Well, do you ever wonder how much of the Inconstant Son's rise is occurring because of these things you've seen, and what you do with your visions? What if all this is only happening because of the choices we *think* we have to make?"

"Look, I've seen Kimoon in the future, when I'm old and gray," Mirae said tiredly. "He isn't gone forever. This is not the end of his story, I promise."

"And when you see him again, how is he? Did you save him? Does he have the same chance at a happy life as he did an hour ago? Or did you ruin him forever?"

Not forever, Mirae thought. *Though it may take decades, I will keep my promise to him, that much I know.* What Mirae wasn't so sure about, however, was whether Hongbin was right about her greatest fear, that she was only creating the Inconstant Son by trying to stop him. After all, didn't Kimoon claim to be the High Daughters' sworn enemy, years into the future? Was her ill-fated promise to remain loyally by his side the reason she wouldn't try to stop him?

Mirae sighed, wishing her switches were as instructional as Hongbin expected them to be. But her glimpses of the future never seemed to give her a clear sense of direction. Rather, they were more like dim lanterns along a dark road, helping her avoid wandering off the path of her true destiny—the one where she was the uniter of the peninsula, not its dismantler. But exactly where that path led, and what she would encounter along the way, were still a mystery.

Realizing she was taking too long to answer Hongbin's question, she finally replied, "Don't worry about Kimoon. I won't abandon him, I promise."

"Promise me this, too," Hongbin said quietly. "The next time our mission requires us to choose between each other or sparing someone else, someone who doesn't have the responsibility we do to atone for our ancestors' mistakes, you'll do the right thing."

Mirae swallowed, unsure if the sudden burst of heat in her cheeks was from the sun below, or Hongbin's criticism. "Even if that means sacrificing you?"

"Yes." Hongbin's usually cheery voice was grave. "If that's what it takes. Even if it means breaking the hearts of those who love me, or making them hate you forever."

"Hongbin," Mirae said, nearly losing her balance. "You don't mean that."

"Yes, I do. More than I've ever meant anything." From his tone, it seemed that he, at least, believed that to be true. "It would have been better to let Minho ascend to the peace of the spirit world than to make him suffer like we did. Most importantly, the Netherking would be dead. Your mission fulfilled. Seolla and the gods would be safe. Mother would be alive. Kimoon well and free." Hongbin took a deep breath. "I'm not saying this is all your fault, noonim. Of course it isn't. But if we could do it all over again, if you find a way in one of your switches, please do the terrible, impossible thing. Stop all this before it happens, even if no one, including me, ever understands."

Mirae was silent for a long time, processing Hongbin's harsh words, his plea. Thankfully, he didn't press her for a response. So, Mirae climbed in silence for a while before eventually gathering her thoughts enough to voice what was in her heart.

"I don't regret a single thing I've done," she finally said. "And I don't think you realize what you're asking. If I had let Minho die for the greater good, you would have begged me to go back in time and spare him, whatever the cost, not knowing what that meant. But the truth is, it doesn't matter what I do; this calling was always meant to be devastating. The only way to make it all worth it is by following my destiny to its bitter end, and making sure everyone's sacrifices mean something. I may not know what lies ahead, but I do believe that our current road is leading us to the best possible outcome, even if it doesn't seem like it right now. That is why I cannot change what has been, or what must be, for fear that it would only bring about something worse, or make me powerless to stop what's coming. What I can promise you, Hongbin, is that when the time comes, I will not hesitate to make the Inconstant Son pay for what he's done. His reign of terror will end with me."

"I hope so, noonim," Hongbin said softly. "I really do."

Just then, as if echoing Hongbin's wistfulness, the clouds around them fully parted, revealing the ocean blue of the eternal sky. As the mist that had sheltered them from the heat and brightness of the sun melted away, the glare of the fast-approaching celestial orb flashed off the metal swords, searing Mirae's eyes.

"The sun is coming!" Hongbin cried. "Go, noonim, climb!"

But Hongbin's frantic voice faded away as something else thundered in Mirae's ear—the pounding of her heart, loud as drums. Her vision, too, began to blur and darken despite the radiance emanating from below. It was happening. She was about to switch.

Mirae pressed her hand against the fixed, flat side of the blade in front of her, bracing for the imminent pull into the past. Her palm burned fiercely, from both the heated sword and the mark of a switch; so did the black bell pressing into her side, scorching her like a brand marking its victim. Mirae heard a piercing scream split the air, close enough to hurt her ears, even though she felt herself being ripped out of her body, no longer in control of it.

Then the world turned black, but the bloodcurdling scream followed Mirae into the lightless chasm between the present and the past, the void where travelers could slip involuntarily through time. Even when she felt herself grounded once more and the darkness faded away, the scream persisted.

Mirae tried to slap her hands over her ears, but her arms refused to move. As the heart-wrenching, relentless keening threatened to tear through Mirae's eardrums, she fell to her knees, losing the ability to do anything more than just try to endure the sound.

"Shaman Suhee!" Mirae barely made out another voice, warbled against the shrill reverberations in her mind, but sharp enough to cut through the noise. "What are you doing? Stop this ridiculous act!"

As if startled by the sound of another person speaking, the screaming inside Mirae's head abruptly ended. Mirae's eyes opened of their own accord, and she saw a familiar sight before her, a scene from her past; but everything in front of her was blurred, as if she'd rubbed her eyes a little too hard. Only because she'd been to this place before could she make out the vague, golden outline of the kut arena just outside of Noksan, where Mirae had been delivering a kongsu until everything went wrong.

Standing at the edges of the sandy square were tangols in white hanboks, holding a medley of instruments: janggu, bamboo flutes, two-stringed haegeum, handheld cymbals, and bells. The smell of ash, peppers, fish, and incense lingered in the air. As her vision slowly began to clear, Mirae saw the fan in her right hand, the black bell in her left; the sand before her was dotted with chestnuts, reminding Mirae of who the woman standing nearby was. Noonsol, the glaring shaman who had called Mirae's bluff.

"Guards, arrest this fraud!" Noonsol gestured imperiously. "She is no kangsin shaman, but a Seollan *impostor*."

For some reason, the guards hung back, even though their swords were drawn, their intent to apprehend Mirae unmistakable. Something was making them hesitate. Mirae wanted to turn and see if there was something behind her that was frightening them, but her body refused to listen. It was as if she could only watch what was happening through her own eyes while someone, or something, else controlled her body . . . as if she'd been possessed like Minho.

What is this? a voice hissed inside Mirae's head, startling her. It echoed in her mind the same way the scream had, afflicting her alone. *Where am I?*

Mirae couldn't answer, or demand to know who was in control of her body. All she could do was stare blankly out at the crowd of people gathered for the kut, their features barely discernible as her vision still struggled to return. Not even her heart seemed to heed her wishes, for it didn't thunder the way it usually did when Mirae was afraid.

This . . . this is Josan, the voice continued. Its timbre was low and rich. Familiar. *Why am I here? Where is the queenling? I . . . I must kill her! Her and the traitorous bastard!*

The more frantic the voice became, the easier it was for Mirae to recognize where she'd first heard it, the bitter cries of a woman once imprisoned in a basin of black water. *Suhee?* Mirae thought, incredulous. *Is that you?*

But it didn't seem as if the Netherqueen had heard her. The voice in her mind raged on. *How dare they try to trick me, to turn my own son against me? I'll flay the skin from their bones and pry the nails from their fingertips. I'll make that ingrate watch, and learn to savor the screams of his enemies, the false rulers who murdered his own—*

Suhee, who clearly didn't remember her demise on White Spine Mountain, finally noticed that the man she spoke of was standing there, off to the side. Siwon, who was desperately trying to hold Captain Jia back from attacking the guards and escalating the situation. *No*, Suhee hissed, fixing Mirae's eyes on the captain. *I killed you. I gored you with my spine, you vulgar Jade Witchling.*

Mirae stared, along with the Netherqueen, at the captain who had been her mentor, her friend. A woman unfailingly loyal, whose powerful shoulders had borne the weight of training a naive princess, falling in love with a prince, and trying to protect them both from the nefarious machinations of a dark king. Captain Jia had also been the first person to die for Mirae, a sacrifice she didn't think she'd ever forgive herself for.

How is this possible? Suhee murmured. *Why is she still alive? And where is the queenling?* Suhee managed to piece things together faster than Mirae expected, suddenly exclaiming, *They must not have reached the fortress yet. But that means this is the past. How can that be? And if what I suspect is true, then that means I'm still—*

Just then, Captain Jia managed to wrestle free from Siwon, and shoved him to the ground. The Netherqueen screamed, flooding Mirae's head with skull-splitting pain. *How dare you touch him, witchling! I will obliterate you, and every soul in your wretched queendom! Today, you will all die like the vermin you are!*

Suhee roared again with a frightening fury, powerful enough that Mirae felt her mouth open, releasing the Netherqueen's howls, her frenzied words: "I will annihilate all you vile servants of the False Queen, murderers and thieves, defenders of Seolla's lies and unspeakable evils. I will burn your depraved queendom to the ground!"

The Netherqueen stretched out her neck, as if expecting it to tear away from Mirae's body. "*I will be your reckoning.*"

But nothing happened. No head pulled free of its body, unsheathing a razor-sharp spine. Suhee grabbed Mirae's neck, stunned and confused about why her transformation had failed. The guards, meanwhile, finally shook off their trepidation and began to charge. Captain Jia and Siwon moved to intercept them, slowing the soldiers down while Suhee grappled with Mirae's throat, as if to yank it free herself. Her fingers tangled with the strings of the satchel hanging beneath her clothes.

What is this? Suhee tore open the bag. *Noeul's beads? Why do I have them?* She fished around inside the small pouch until she found the small vial of black water. She gasped and held it up to the sun, where it sparkled like melted ebony. *Ah, this is just what I need—this will renew my power!*

She unstoppered the lid and began to tip the vial's contents into Mirae's mouth. As soon as the black water touched her lips, Mirae felt its energy run like a jolt of lightning through her body, a source of amplification that she realized, with a burst of hope, might be her only chance of wresting back control. She couldn't move her own body, but she still felt her connection to magic, as inseparable from her soul as stone from a mountain.

While the effects of black water flooded her body, Mirae summoned all the willpower she possessed, and bid her powers to absorb the amplifying spark coursing through her. Remarkably, it worked—she felt a stirring, a heat deep in her core, like a fire on the brink of blazing to life.

The Netherqueen seemed to notice it, too. She dropped Mirae's arm, lowering the vial. But it was too late. The drop of black water had revitalized the dormant magic inside Mirae's body, which Suhee finally realized was not her own.

"No," she hissed. "No, you will not stop me, queenling." Quickly, while she was still in control, the Netherqueen fell to her knees, tossed away the fan, and reached for one of the shamans' swords cast off to the side of the arena. "I will bleed you for the sins of your mother!"

Realizing what Suhee was about to do but still unable to fully free herself from the Netherqueen's possession, Mirae desperately summoned the only thing she could think of that would throw Suhee off until the switch ended, and shield Mirae's companions from the guards. A spell she'd known all along she would cast when she returned to this place.

"Today will be the end of Seolla's line!" the Netherqueen shouted triumphantly, gripping the sword tightly. "The downfall of this peninsula's vile oppressors and—"

The Netherqueen's ferocious vows were suddenly drowned out by the overwhelming drone of squirming brown insects rising from the earth. Millions of chirping, leaping pests instantly coated the ground, and everything on it, an illusion perfectly executed to inspire terror. The spectators and shamans screamed, fleeing as if they were being eaten alive. The guards, startled by the swarm, were easily knocked out by Captain Jia and Siwon, who were immune to Mirae's spell at her behest. The former immediately ran to Hongbin, who was staring at the cricket-covered world with wide eyes, and shook him, shouting at him to run.

Siwon, however, stared at Mirae, at the words the Nether-queen was saying to him, even though he couldn't possibly hear her over the high-pitched humming. "We are forever tied together, you and I," Mirae felt herself mouth. "I love you, I will always love you. But please save me, Siwon. You have to save me."

Mirae felt a familiar sear in the palm of her hand, signaling the end of this disastrous switch. Her vision blackened as her soul prepared to return to a bridge made of swords, similar to the weapon that fell from her hand. Then she and the Nether-queen were ripped away from the slumping body they'd fought so fiercely over, and back through the tides of time.

Chapter
TWENTY-EIGHT

The searing pain in Mirae's palm followed her back to the present, refusing to diminish even after she returned to her body, still precariously balanced in the sky. When Mirae opened her eyes, she realized why; she had been gripping one of the swords on the bridge so tightly that her hand had sliced open. But that hardly mattered once she realized that Hongbin had his arms wrapped tightly around her legs.

"Please, noonim," he whispered. "You have to let him go."

Mirae was taken aback by his show of affection, the same kind he used to give her before the Netherking entered their lives, but the sadness in his voice broke her heart. Mirae reached down to console her tormented brother, but instead of patting him soothingly, she cried out as the Netherqueen's voice raged in her head again.

What have you done to me, queenling? Where's my body? Where's my family? What did you do with my son?

"Enough!" Mirae clapped her free hand over her ear. "Leave me alone!"

Alarmed, Hongbin pulled away. "What? What is it, noonim?"

Release me this instant! the Netherqueen howled.

"Oh, believe me, I would," Mirae shot back. "If I only knew how."

"Noonim, what are you—"

Mirae didn't hear what Hongbin said next, not over the Netherqueen's continued barrage. *What happened after you and the bastard ganged up on me? Where is Siwon? Why didn't my husband come back for me? Why are we in this horrible place, where my skin feels like—*

"It's not your skin, it's mine, and if you don't shut up," Mirae swore, "I will find a way to hurl what's left of your soul into the sun. Understood?" For good measure, Mirae tipped her face down at the fiery orb that was getting uncomfortably close, its surface red hot and bubbling like magma. Even just turning toward it scalded her flesh like steam over a boiling pot.

"Noonim?" Hongbin repeated. "What's going on?"

"I wasn't talking to you," Mirae said, righting herself. Thankfully, the Netherqueen took her threat seriously, and resorted to seething wordlessly. "I'll explain later. Come on, we have to hurry, the sun's almost upon us."

Mirae followed her own advice, climbing as speedily as she could. The going was trickier now that blood ran freely out of her palm, but there was no time to waste nursing a wound.

"We're almost there!" she heard Hongbin shout. "Just a little farther!"

Mirae didn't look up; she needed every ounce of concentration to maintain her balance on the increasingly slick blades. Although she slipped a few times, she always managed to remain upright, never slowing for long, and even felt Hongbin steadying himself by grabbing her legs when he lost his footing. It seemed like they were going to make it, until the wound on Mirae's hand split open even wider. The blood gushing out of it coated one of the swords so swiftly that when her foot stepped on it, it skidded right off.

Mirae yelped as her body tipped sideways, careening off the sword bridge. It happened so quickly, she didn't get a chance to grab one of the blades to save herself, nor did Hongbin react quickly enough to right her from below. Mirae flailed as she toppled, looking for something, anything, to latch onto, but there was nothing but air. For a split second, she feared that this would be the end of the road, the end of her mission and the peninsula, until a hand shot down from above, grabbed her wrist, and hauled her up to safety.

On firm ground once more, a cliff's edge jutting out to meet the sword bridge, Mirae clung to whoever had saved her as sobs burst out of her.

"You made it," she heard her rescuer say, hugging her tightly. "I knew you would."

Mirae recognized her rescuer's voice, and the strength of her embrace. Mirae pulled away just enough to take in the face of the woman who was somehow always beside her when she needed her most, even in death. The familiar sight of her friend's rich brown eyes and defined cheekbones only made the tears flow more freely from Mirae's eyes.

"Captain Jia," she breathed, her surprise quickly waning as she took in her friend's sublime regalia. "I should have known the gods would exalt you."

"Yes, you should have," Captain Jia said. "I was pretty amazing in life."

The captain's words made Mirae laugh instead of cry, as they were no doubt meant to. "You were the most amazing woman I've ever known," she said, glancing over the former captain's attire, so different from what she usually wore. Instead of her typical uniform of a thick tunic, scale armor, and a red sash embroidered with gold peonies, she wore sunny yellow robes with green trim, her flowy sleeves almost as long as she was tall. Her hair, which had always been simply braided, now rested atop her head in a bun composed of artful loops and swirls. Mirae's friend was no longer a mere Wonhwa captain, it seemed, but an elite guardian of heaven.

"I can't believe you're here," Mirae breathed. "How did you find me?"

Captain Jia raised an eyebrow. "Where there is trouble brewing, and a divine realm to be sealed off from encroaching evil, that is naturally where you will also be."

Mirae snorted despite herself. "Speak for yourself, Captain. You're as guilty as I."

Captain Jia gave a small laugh before reaching around Mirae to help Hongbin up as well. His jaw dropped at the sight of their old friend, and he quickly wrapped her in a tight embrace. "It's so good to see you, Captain!"

"You as well, Gunju. Or, should I say Seja jeoha?" Captain Jia asked warmly. Mirae felt she was already accustomed to her former captain's new, flowy attire, but the loss of her rigidity, and this new comfortableness with showing affection, were still quite a surprise.

One thing, however, remained eternally unchanged about her friend. "I see you didn't flee the heavens with the gods," Mirae said. "You stayed behind, brave as always."

"More like I didn't trust you to seal off the heavens properly without me," Captain Jia quipped. When Mirae shot her a playful glare, the captain smiled in return, but turned the conversation back to the matter at hand. "So, tell me, is the Netherking hot on your trail?"

Mirae shook her head. "He took the longer moon path."

Captain Jia looked relieved, but only slightly. She knew as well as Mirae that when it came to dealing with the Netherking, no advantage should be taken at face value. "Good, the moon path dips into the underworld. To get up to the heavens from there, the Netherking will have to convince the gods of the dead to reveal their secret passage, which will be difficult considering they delight in tormenting evil souls like his. Still, it's always best not to underestimate our old foe, especially since he can always threaten the gods with his pearl."

Mirae nodded. "What do we need to do to seal off the heavens?"

Instead of answering, Captain Jia looked between Mirae and Hongbin. "Where's Siwon?"

Mirae heard the Netherqueen breathe deeply at the sound of her adopted son's name, whom she hadn't realized was traveling with Mirae. Thankfully, she still seemed to remember Mirae's threat to hurl her into the sun if she made another peep. Head still free of the Netherqueen's distracting voice, Mirae quickly explained that Siwon was following the Netherking, and that he would hopefully be along shortly to report back.

"Why didn't the gods cut off access to the heavens themselves, instead of just running away?" Hongbin asked after Mirae finished.

"It's not something the gods can do alone," Captain Jia explained. "The mortal realm, spirit world, and the heavens are inextricably connected. To cut off one would mean permanently severing the energy that flows from each into the other, dooming them all to erode and decay. Hence, the Jade Emperor made it so that the only way to separate heaven from its subservient realms is through the unified efforts of representatives from all three spheres, to make sure sealing off the heavens is only done under the direst of circumstances."

"Well, our current situation certainly qualifies," Mirae said.

"Indeed, this is the first time in heaven's history that such a thing has ever been attempted," Captain Jia said. "We can only hope that once the Netherking is out of the picture, the gods will find a way to reattach the worlds before too much damage is done. All we need now is for our final representative to arrive."

Just then, as if summoned by Captain Jia's words, Mirae heard Siwon's voice echoing from the sun path behind them. She scrambled over to the cliff's edge and, shielding her eyes against the glaring light, saw her friend clinging to the sword bridge, scrambling up it as fast as he could. He still had quite a ways to go, and his palms were bleeding profusely.

Mirae stretched out her hands, trying to summon a gust of wind to sweep Siwon back to her side, but remembered too late that her powers didn't work in the chasm between realms. Moments later, a shadow drifted across her face, cooling both her flushing skin and the worry firing up inside her. Mirae looked up to see Captain Jia standing over her, raising her own arms to the sky.

With a twirl of her wrists, the proud celestial being conjured up a blast of sun-heated air, powerful enough to make the sword bridge quiver and carry Siwon swiftly up to the edge of heaven.

Flailing with surprise, Siwon reached out as soon as he saw Mirae, and clasped her waiting hand. With a firm tug, she whipped him free of the torrid storm and steadied him as he landed beside her. Other than the nicks and cuts on his hands, his panting breath and bright red cheeks, he looked none the worse for wear.

Siwon, Suhee breathed. Mirae could feel the same affection lacing the Netherqueen's voice coursing through her own body, though the former's had an edge of anger to it. A bitterness lingering from her son's betrayal.

When Siwon finally caught his breath enough to speak, he immediately launched into his report. "The Netherking has managed to convince an underworld god to grant him passage to the heavens—we need to seal everything off *now*."

Captain Jia sprang into action, gesturing for everyone to gather around her. "It appears that we'll have to not only sunder the heavens from the spirit world, but also from the underworld. We must work quickly."

"Wait, I thought you said all the realms need to be represented in order for this to work—mortal, divine, and spirit," Hongbin said. "But you're an exalted being, aren't you, Captain? Not a spirit?"

"That's correct, but there's no need for concern; there is a spirit among us." Captain Jia looked pointedly at Mirae.

Mirae, who hadn't thought she'd have to reveal her strange predicament so soon, swallowed as she reached into her pocket and retrieved the black bell. She held it out, allowing everyone to see that it was no longer glossy with the Netherqueen's soul. After clearing her throat, she reluctantly explained, "The Netherqueen and I are currently . . . cohabitating my body. I think the magic of the heavens may have triggered some kind of synthesis. I'm not sure. Anyway, Captain Jia is right. There is a spirit among us, so we can proceed."

"Is she willing to help us?" Hongbin asked, clearly having trouble processing this unexpected news. Siwon, too, looked taken aback by Mirae's revelation.

I will never help you, the Netherqueen said. *You may as well cast me into the sun, queenling. If you can.*

Mirae ignored the scathing woman as she returned the bell to her pocket. "Suhee is in my body, so her opinion doesn't matter."

"Her presence alone should be enough," Captain Jia said. She gestured to Hongbin. "Now, are there any other questions, or can we begin?"

Once everyone shook their heads, Captain Jia knelt and pointed at a stone medallion in front of her, set into the ground near the cliff's edge. "To begin, each of you must place your hand on the element that represents your soul's heavenly energy."

"You mean our zodiac sign?" Hongbin asked as he and everyone else knelt around the stone inlay. Mirae studied it, quickly deciphering its symbology, and recognizing the layout as a simplistic map of the spirit world. The emblem was divided into five parts, four curved slabs surrounding a golden center. Each slab was engraved with a symbol for one of the four elements and the cardinal direction that corresponded with it.

"That's correct," Captain Jia said in response to Hongbin's question. "I'll go first. Since I was born the year of the wood dog, the wood element is mine." With that, she put her palm on the curved slab pointing east, mirroring the location of the forest where Mirae had acquired the mahogany rattle.

"I'm a water goat," Hongbin said, slapping his hand against the northernmost slab.

"Fire rat," Siwon declared before pressing his palm against the segment pointing south.

"And I'm a golden snake." Mirae placed her hand on the remaining piece of stone, representing metal. As soon as she touched it, the center of the medallion began to glow.

"It's working!" Hongbin said. No sooner had those words left his mouth, however, than the sun began to peek over the edge of the cliff, searingly bright and unbearably hot. Mirae felt as if her flesh were melting as she jerked her face away from the fiery orb, squeezing her eyelids shut.

"Soak in as much warmth as you can!" Captain Jia yelled, barely audible over the waves of heat billowing around them. "You'll need it where we're going!"

As the sun's scorching brightness pierced even through her eyelids, Mirae wondered how she could possibly survive this onslaught when her stomach suddenly began to flip inside her and air rushed past her as if she were riding her chollima once more. The sun's heat and incinerating blaze diminished as everything around Mirae dimmed and cooled.

Mirae opened her eyes once she deemed it was safe and gasped as she realized she was being carted away from the intolerable sun. The platform at the cliff's edge, where she and the others were kneeling, appeared to be rotating, eclipsing the blazing celestial body and shielding her from its infernal radiance as she was flipped upside down into a second, rayless world.

Mirae's stomach gave another leap as the precipice beneath her completed its flip, blocking out all traces of sunlight. Now that she and her companions were encased in darkness, Mirae looked around, feeling disoriented at the idea that she was now upside down from where she'd been kneeling before. Here, in the underbelly of heaven, the sky was inky and vaulted, the air frigid. Mirae shivered, understanding now why Captain Jia had said to enjoy the sun's warmth while it lasted.

This cold, dark realm was dimly lit by floating stars as big as Mirae's head. Their scattered blue and pink glows were laced together with shimmering lines that formed constellations Mirae had studied before—from much farther away—as well as others that were completely new to her. There were far more undertones to the otherwise midnight-black sky than Mirae was used to as well. Nebulous, prismatic clouds of every conceivable color swept across the expanse, swirling like floral tea spilled from a thousand cups.

But the most bewitching feature of the underworld was the pearly, waxen moon descending from above. Its milky face with silver marbling slowly gravitated toward Mirae, slipping down the same track as the sun, though it existed as its opposite in all things. Its luminous halo emanated a soft, flickering white shimmer, although the moon itself gleamed with a cold, secretive beauty, as aloof as a sleeping deep-sea dragon.

"Is this the underworld?" Hongbin gazed around with wonder.

"The highest peak of it," Captain Jia confirmed. "The rest is far below. Now, let's seal it off before the Netherking finds his way out of here."

"Right," Mirae said, tearing her eyes away from the starry sky and the falling moon. "What do we need to do?"

Captain Jia pointed at the stone medallion in their midst, a little different now from the one they'd touched in the heavens. This one was etched with designs featuring the four guardians: a dragon, a phoenix, a tortoise, and a tiger. Beneath each was the name of one of the four seasons, and at the center was a silvery dome. "All you need to do is touch the same piece of stone as before, which is still representative of your heavenly energy, and our job will be complete. Simple enough, for those who manage to get this far."

Mirae and the others obeyed, acting in the same order as before. As soon as Mirae's hand pressed against the white tiger engraving, and the symbol for metal beneath it, the silver dome began to glow like the approaching moon. Then the earth shifted as before, turning over on its side until it had flipped completely around, transporting its passengers back to the heavens.

As soon as the world righted itself, Mirae breathed a sigh of relief. The sun had climbed past them into the sky, high enough now that, while the world was still as warm as the hottest day of summer, she didn't feel as if she was about to be incinerated. "We did it," she breathed. "The heavens are safe."

Her companions all let out a sigh as well. They'd succeeded; the Netherking's plan to become a god was forfeited. Of course, he could still wreak plenty of havoc on the mortal realm, but the gods could now return to their rightful place, and Mirae was right where she needed to be to beseech them for guidance.

Siwon fell back into a sitting position, shoulders slumped with exhaustion, though there was a smile on his face. "So, what next? Please say we can take a long nap and wake up to a magnificent feast prepared by the gods."

Mirae returned Siwon's smile, but shook her head ruefully. "I'm afraid there's no time for rest, at least not for me. We may have bested the Netherking this time, but he's still at large. This will never be over until we figure out how to end him."

"Yes, that's true," Siwon sighed. "So, we're off to find the missing gods?"

"Just one goddess, and she's not missing." But instead of dragging herself and her companions to the next part of their mission, Mirae took one look at the exhaustion on Siwon's and Hongbin's faces and decided a bit of a breather was in order. "Tell me what you saw when you followed the Netherking," Mirae said to Siwon, giving them all a chance to sit and rest.

Siwon suppressed a shudder. "As soon as the Netherking exited the moon path, he was greeted by one of the gods of hell. They seemed to be on friendly terms. Apparently while Daegun daegam was possessed by the Netherking, his soul was suspended between life and death, which created a channel to the underworld that the Netherking was able to exploit. While conversing over the past year, the Netherking and the underworld god came to an understanding, which was why the god agreed to help him reach the heavens. I don't know much more than that, unfortunately. As soon as I saw that the Netherking had a way in, I rushed back to tell you."

As Siwon finished his report, a slow web of horror tightened around Mirae's body as she remembered what Minho had said when the Netherking allowed him to rouse for a few minutes: *I was trapped in a starry void, with no warmth or food. All I could see or hear . . . was* him.

Not quite dead, not quite alive, Minho's soul had been buried in its own body, with one foot firmly planted in the afterlife. A liminal state that allowed his possessor to tap into the world of the dead, and do what he did best—strike a deal with someone powerful enough to keep his evil plans alive. While Mirae sat overwhelmed with what her brother had endured, horrified at the diabolical link she'd allowed the Netherking to find, she heard the Netherqueen stifle a low chuckle, gleeful over her husband's infuriatingly clever subterfuge.

"This is grim news indeed," she heard Captain Jia say. "With such a powerful ally at his side, we need to prepare for the possibility that the Netherking has more than one backup plan. We sealed off all the known entrances into the heavens, but that may not be enough."

Mirae climbed to her feet. There was no more time to rest, not after what she'd just learned. "I'll head off to see the goddess of time. Even if we can't anticipate the Netherking's every move, that won't matter once we know the secret to defeating him."

Everyone else jumped up, too, but Mirae shook her head as Hongbin and Siwon moved to follow her lead. "I want all of you to work together to track down the gods and bring them back. If anyone can stop a god of hell from consummating his betrayal, it's them. Stick together and stay safe. If you see the Netherking, do not engage."

"What about you, noonim?" Hongbin protested. "Who's going to keep you safe?"

"I should come with you," Siwon said. "Your mission is most important, and the Netherking will be hunting you down. Let me shield you from his abominable spell, if I can."

Before Mirae could object, Captain Jia chimed in. "I agree with Siwon. Seja jeoha and I will seek out the gods ourselves."

Siwon nodded as he gripped the golden sword around his waist. Hongbin, too, ignored Mirae's protests as he wrapped her in a tight embrace. "Be safe, noonim. I don't want our prior conversation to be the last words we say to each other."

Finally softening to the plan everyone had made without her, Mirae pulled away and cupped her brother's cheeks. "I'm glad we argued. Your opinion matters, and you did nothing wrong by telling me how you feel, so let's not part with any regrets. Besides, it's impossible for my amazing, handsome brother to make a mistake, or so you've always said."

Hongbin stroked an imaginary beard. "Yes, that's true. It's about time you acknowledged my absolute perfection."

Mirae gave her brother one last squeeze. "You are *more* than perfect."

Hongbin smiled, but the corners of his eyes were creased with sadness. "Promise me we'll see each other again soon."

"I promise." Mirae patted her brother's back until he released her. After that, he moved aside for Captain Jia.

"To reach the goddess of time," Captain Jia said, getting right to the point, "just follow the cliff's edge until you reach the end of the heavens. That's when the bridge to the cosmos will appear. Walk along it until you reach the eternal plane. From there, you must walk straight ahead until you reach your destination. And take care, for if you don't keep your wits about you, you may never find your way back."

Mirae nodded, understanding why Captain Jia had issued that warning. From what she remembered in her switch, the infinite expanse of the eternal plane had few guiding points, and no landmarks. Without a clear head, she would easily lose sight of which direction she was walking in, or even just wander around in circles. Thankfully, she had the red thread of fate to keep her on track. "Thank you for sticking around to help," Mirae said, clasping her friend's hand. "I don't know what we would have done without you, Captain Jia."

"Please," the other woman said with a smile. "Up here, I'm just Jia."

At that, the two women embraced, squeezing each other so tightly it became hard to breathe. After she pulled away, Jia walked back over to Hongbin. They both bowed in farewell, smiling brightly before they turned and set off to track down the missing gods across the jewel-green grass of the heavens.

Only when Jia and Hongbin began to fade from sight did

Mirae finally tear her eyes away from them, setting her gaze on the cliff's edge running along the sun's chasm, jagged and unpaved. Then she turned to Siwon, whose shoulders were squared.

"Ready?" she asked.

"Ready."

With that, they set off, striding briskly side by side along the outskirts of heaven.

Chapter
TWENTY-NINE

They walked in companionable silence for a while, just taking in the sheer beauty of the picturesque realm of the gods. The heavens were sprawling and colorful, like something out of a painting. Growing intermittently out of the teal grass were copses of tall pine trees with bright red bark and lofty green needles bundled in cloudlike bunches. Nestled between them were jade-green bamboo groves, and bursts of red, spiraling mushrooms.

The chattering rivers running swiftly across the land were filled with golden water, frothing white where they brushed the shore. Along their banks were hundreds of jewel-colored cranes, standing regally over happily splashing turtles. There were flocks of other birds, too—pheasants, ducks, and peacocks—soaring in the air, chirping in the red pine branches, or wandering with golden deer under the heavy boughs of peach trees.

Mirae plucked one of the low-hanging fruits as she and Siwon passed by, admiring its dainty white skin and puckered pink tips. When Mirae bit into the heavenly peach, its juicy, summery sweetness made her eyes close involuntarily as she savored the rich nectar that dribbled down her chin. As she devoured her treat, she felt Siwon's eyes on her. She snuck a glance at him and realized he was staring at her, smiling.

"What?" she asked over a mouthful of pulp.

"Nothing, it's just nice to see you like this," he said, eyes darting away.

Mirae swallowed, a little confused. "Would you like a bite?"

For some reason Siwon looked even more embarrassed. "No, I'm all right, thank you."

Shrugging, Mirae was about to continue eating when she heard the return of a familiar nettled voice. *I forbid you to speak to my son again. If you dare to disobey me, I'll torment you endlessly until you go mad.*

Mirae polished off her peach and tossed the pit into the grass. Then she heaved a deep, exasperated sigh and said, "Siwon, your mother says hello."

To his credit, Siwon took Mirae's declaration in stride. "Tell her I miss her," he said, "and to stop threatening you, which I'm sure she's already done repeatedly. Remind her that if you hadn't had compassion for her back at the fortress, her spirit would be tormented in the underworld right now, instead of traveling with us in this beautiful place."

The Netherqueen was silent a moment. *You preserved my soul, queenling? Why?*

"Because Siwon loves you," Mirae said, knowing that Suhee's soul, pressed up against her own, could feel the truth of what she was saying. "And you deserved a second chance. One where you were free of the Netherking's manipulations."

"Free to be with me," Siwon added softly. "And find redemption. Now, maybe, we'll find a way to put Sol's spirit to rest, so we can both see her again someday."

Suhee was quiet for a long time after that, while Mirae and Siwon continued trudging toward the edge of the heavens. The distant, misty green mountains ahead, faceted to gleam like crystal monoliths, were close enough to block out most of the sky before Mirae heard another peep from the woman sharing her body.

Will you ask Siwon something? the Netherqueen asked, her voice resentful but far less hostile. Mirae waited for her to continue, which she did hesitantly. *I want to know why he is so devoted to you. It goes against everything he has fought for, and I . . . I just need to understand why he turned on his family.*

After a moment of deliberation—for Mirae was not keen on striking up a difficult, private conversation about someone else's family—Mirae nudged Siwon's arm. "Suhee feels betrayed by you. Can you explain to her why you and I are no longer enemies?"

"Of course," Siwon said easily. Touring the beauty of the heavens alongside Mirae seemed to have done a lot to lighten his heart. "It's because you were the first person who saw who I really am. Not who you thought I could become, or how I could be useful to you, but who I've always been. You believed in me, and because of that trust, I will never be the same. No one ever gave me what you did—self-sovereignty. That is what you are the patron of, Your Majesty, and what you will deliver to the peninsula. It is a gift that you have given my mother as well. Although she may not possess her own body, she, too, can now choose what her own soul will become. Now nothing can stop her from embracing her true destiny."

I am not free. I'm trapped here against my will, the Netherqueen spat. *And there is no such thing as destiny. We decide our own fates.*

When Mirae repeated those words to Siwon, he shook his head. "That's the beauty of Her Majesty's power. She is the High Horomancer, but she is also Queen Mirae, the champion of choice. Everything she's striving for is to give everyone on the peninsula equal access to life, magic, and opportunity. Why wouldn't I want to follow her?"

Because she is a Daughter of the Sacred Bone. You cannot trust the promises of those with power. She is not trying to improve the penin-sula, she's trying to protect her birthright.

"Let me guess," Siwon said, studying the look on Mirae's face. "She thinks I'm a fool for trusting a Seollan royal?"

When Mirae nodded, he leaned in close, as if to convey the importance of what he was about to say. "Look inside her soul, Mother. See for yourself that Queen Mirae is merciful, but not to a fault. She is a forgiving monarch. The queen who spares."

"Not always," Mirae said quietly. She remembered the sound of Kimoon's screams, and his final, vehement plea. "I don't know if I could have spared Kimoon from his terrible fate," she said. "I've failed at so much and made so many mistakes."

"Have you?" Siwon countered. "You prevented the war my netherparents were instigating, and spared everyone who had done you and your family wrong. You gave them all a second chance, and some of them wasted it. Now that you've resumed your divine mission, you've been settling the score while saving the peninsula. The way I see it, you've freed Daegun daegam and foiled the Netherking's plan *again*, just as you said you would. Now it's time to find out how to punish the Netherking for his sins, as is your destiny. Honestly, if I was the Netherking going up against you, I would run away while I still could."

"But I've lost a lot, too," Mirae said. She wanted to see what Siwon saw when he looked at her, but the weight of her mistakes still weighed on her, especially when coupled with the Netherqueen's bristling agreement. Perhaps Siwon was right, and there was no way to accomplish everything she had without losing a single life. All things considered, everything could have gone a lot worse. But was that justification for allowing good women like her mother and Jia to die for her? For sacrificing Kimoon against his will?

You are right to question your own integrity, the Netherqueen cut in, her voice mocking. *Siwon's sense of reality is clearly distorted by his naive admiration for you, but I can read the thrumming of your soul, and I see why you abandoned the bastard prince. You let him go because you didn't need him anymore, simple as that. You brought him here to serve you one last time. You have become ruthless, just like me.*

Mirae could say nothing in response to the Netherqueen's accusation because she wasn't sure she could argue against it; after all, Mirae had disposed of Kimoon almost as soon as he became more of a liability than an asset. Worse yet, Mirae's future self had specifically requested that Kimoon be brought along, knowing full well how his time in the spirit world would end. What kind of benign "champion of choice" did such a thing?

Well, queenling, the Netherqueen taunted, *are you going to tell your starry-eyed disciple what dark thoughts you've harbored in your heart—who you really are?*

"Your Majesty?" Siwon's brow furrowed. "What is my mother saying?"

"It's nothing," Mirae said, forcing a smile. "She's just going to take a little more convincing, which is understandable."

"Don't worry, she'll come around," Siwon said. "As my mother travels with us, I know she'll learn to trust me the way I trust you."

No, I will not, the Netherqueen scoffed. *I'm the only one here who is not an utter fool.*

"I think it's my turn to ask a question now," Mirae said, eager to change the subject.

I'm not interested in edifying you, the Netherqueen said shortly.

Once again seeming to read Suhee's mind, Siwon said, "Tell my mother that if she answers your question, we will take her to see Sol when we leave the heavens."

You'll do that anyway, weakhearted as you are. But the Netherqueen did not repeat her refusal to hear Mirae out. Having walked far enough to fall under the cooling shadow of the jade mountains, Mirae suppressed a shiver as she finally gathered enough courage to disclose the troubling question that had been weighing on her since her audience with the Seers of Light. "There's something . . . disturbing I've come to learn about the Deep. Something I don't want to believe, but I also can't turn a blind eye to it, either."

"What is it?" Siwon asked.

"I heard that the Deep is not just a cage," Mirae said, "but a well of magic."

"Ah." Siwon let out a deep sigh, his breath rattling. "You want to know the full extent of the Deep Deceiver's curse on the nether-fiends."

"So, it's true?" Mirae asked, heart sinking. "Many of the wonders of Seolla were built by leeching magic out of the prisoners of the Deep?"

Siwon nodded, his face grim. "It's true. The Deep Deceiver didn't just imprison magic-adept men and their sympathizers. She fashioned a cruel cage by enchanting the black water above them to drink their magic, leading to an agonizingly slow death. Then she would routinely collect the siphoned power she'd stolen and use it to strengthen Seolla and expand its influence. Some of the things you credit to your ancestors were actually stolen from the Deep."

"So that's why she didn't kill the nether-fiends," Mirae said, her stomach churning. "Not out of mercy, but to exploit them."

Mercy? the Netherqueen spat. *She trapped men, women, and children down there, and deliberately gave them a long, excruciating death as punishment for challenging her—and you dared to even consider that an act of mercy?*

"I thought she just couldn't bring herself to kill them," Mirae said. "I thought maybe, in her heart, she—"

There were hundreds of people, entire families, who died by her hand. Tortured to death while their magic was stolen to make your palace oh so pretty, your barriers dazzling. Meanwhile the nether-fiends dwindled in number, racked with endless pain. And what was their crime, exactly, that demanded such torment across generations? Daring to protest the coronation of a clearly unhinged queen.

Mirae didn't want to believe it. But in her vision of the Nether-king's speech in the Hall of the Seven Stars, the council, keepers of lost knowledge, had been aware of the horrors enacted in the Deep, and had deplored the unjust extinction of the Netherking's people. They had sympathized with him—the last of his kind, and the nether-fiends' final chance at obtaining justice, which had become the Netherking's only, unflinching purpose. The Seers of Light hadn't even batted an eye at how he'd slaughtered the Queen of Seolla by draining her of magic—an atrocity his family, too, had endured, but more slowly, more agonizingly, and for the sole benefit of those whom Mirae was trying to protect.

"Why didn't anyone tell me this?" Mirae asked shakily. "My mother, the oracles, the Netherking, or even you, Siwon?"

"By the time we met, the Netherking was already the last of the nether-fiends," Siwon said sadly. "And there's nothing you can do now about the Deep Deceiver's curse, so I didn't see any point in dredging it up when it had little to do with our mission."

Little to do? the Netherqueen fumed. *You're trying to stop my husband from reclaiming what has been stolen from him, and finding justice for his people. But all that has "little to do" with the queenling's entitled, self-righteous sense of duty?*

"It isn't justice he's after," Mirae insisted, though she wasn't even sure she believed the defensive words that came, almost unbidden, out of her mouth. "He wanted to murder the masses . . . he thought himself worthy of becoming a god."

And why shouldn't he be one? Is he any less worthy of governing the peninsula than those egomaniacal, self-indulgent deities you wor-ship who gave magic to an exclusive group of believers on a whim, and then ran back to their palaces with impunity? My husband, at least, would have annulled that reckless decision, and done what your petty gods should have done all along—distribute magic responsibly, and rule with accountability.

"Maybe he claimed to want that once, but I know he's no longer interested in governing fairly," Mirae argued, more confident about this assertion. "He's become obsessed with retribution. He would have made Seolla become the next Deep, even though my people are not to blame for what their queens have done."

You don't care about what's fair, the Netherqueen hissed. Not if you think your people's suffering is unethical, but the nether-fiends' torment is just an unfortunate thing of the past.

"I don't think that," Mirae said. "I don't think that at all."

Then what will you do, queenling? The spiteful edge to the Netherqueen's voice shifted to one of long-abiding grief, a pain that had nowhere else to go. Since he was a child, my husband has carried the immense burden of being his people's savior. He was the last healthy babe to be born among the nether-fiends, for years of magic-draining had left them emaciated, increasingly barren. Those who could used what little magic they had left to shield him from the Deep's curse, so that he could grow powerful. They knew he was their last chance of breaking free, their only hope, so they gave him their all. Imagine growing up and watching everyone around you hastening their own deaths so you can be their vengeance.

"I can't," Mirae said. "It's too horrible." She let the Netherqueen continue her story, listening without interruption. It was the least she could do.

Before my husband, the nether-fiends tried everything, for

generations, to free themselves. They kept their wretched population going, refusing to die out in oblivion. Those who were of the Sacred Bone line taught their children to combine forces, inflicting madness on the minds of the false queens, but it was all to no avail. Their fight was futile as long as their magic kept getting stolen from them. But that all changed when my husband was born.

They knew he was different the moment his magic began to manifest. He was a true Son of the Sacred Bone, as powerful as the queen herself. From the moment he could conjure a simple spell, he dedicated himself to mastering his magic, learning everything that his forebearers had passed down. Eventually, he grew strong enough to torment the queen himself, to the point that she was too afraid of his power to come near Wol Sin Lake anymore. Thus began the season of hope in the Deep. No more magic was siphoned for some time, so the nether-fiends began to live longer, fuller lives while my husband devoted himself to developing his power and plotting his people's release.

It was around that time that I stumbled into his domain, and became his wife. I gave him a child, too, upon whom his entire world began to revolve. But Noeul, who never forgot her encounter with the Deep, and had to watch as her own mother's mind became rapidly warped with madness, grew paranoid about the Netherking's growing power. So, despite the toll it took on her, she resumed the evils of her ancestors, draining and collecting magic from those imprisoned in the dark lake.

My beautiful daughter, who had a smaller store of magic to be depleted than the others because of my Josan blood, was the first to fade. But Noeul had no mercy even on the innocent half-cursed. She was too afraid of the Deep's long-brewing thirst for revenge to allow even a drop of cursed blood to leave that ungodly prison. The nether-fiends rallied around Sol and their king, sacrificing themselves to keep their leader strong, just as before, and allowing him to experiment on their bodies to perfect his black water concoctions, which he touted as the key to turning Josan into their deliverers. But Sol's impend-ing death made him reckless. His once careful plan, aided by all those who believed in him, including myself, became an obsession that only eradicated our people faster. When the last of them died, Sol's chance of survival disappeared as well.

And when she took her last breath, my husband alone remained—not as his people's savior, which he had so desperately wanted to become, but as their last hope for vengeance.

But then, of course, in a cruel twist of fate, destiny decided to play yet another malicious hand on the already wretched, for the High Horomancer was awakened, and unleashed to counter the Nether-king's righteous claims for retribution with a mission of her own. My husband's carefully seeded plan was laid to waste, leaving him no other choice but to free himself the only way he could. You were the one who decimated all his other options, and then had the gall to dedicate yourself to punishing him for the choices you forced him to make.

And now, betrayed by even the gods who sent you to cut him down, is it any wonder, queenling, that he has come all this way to punish them for the unforgivable things they allowed? Is he the wicked one for putting an end to the dereliction of the gods, and seeking to lead the heavens in a new, fairer direction? Would you not, in his shoes, do the very same thing?

"Perhaps I would," Mirae admitted, clutching the sides of her chima so tightly, she thought it might rip into pieces, like the very fabric of her beliefs about her birthright, her calling. "I'm sorry, Suhee, for everything you endured. Your abandonment at my mother's hand, the loss of your child, the despair of the people you treated as your own family. None of it was right, and every victim inside the Deep deserves justice."

I'm aware of that, the Netherqueen snarled. *What I want to know, queenling, is what* you're *going to do with the truth you've unburied.*

Mirae swallowed, unsure how to respond. There were too many emotions and thoughts whirling in her mind, maddeningly loud and discordant—the convictions passed down to her by her ancestors clashing with the stinging truths festering in the Deep. And, at the center of it all, the Netherqueen's inescapable question burned bright as the sun overhead, overshadowing all of Mirae's other, anguished reflections.

"Your Majesty." Siwon, who had waited patiently for Mirae's exchange with the Netherqueen to end, brushed the side of her hand with his own as softly as he uttered her title. "Talk to me. You don't have to figure all this out alone."

Siwon's touch melted the tension in her muscles. "I know," Mirae sighed. "But in the end, the fate of everything will fall to me, won't it? The Netherking wants to destroy and rebuild, but I seek to protect and repair a broken system. Who's to say whether I am the true moral champion or he is? Who will history say should have won this ancient, convoluted game of perceived good versus evil? I thought I could answer those questions once, but I've since learned that there are two sides to every moon. What you see depends on where you're standing."

"I think history will tell you that the answers you're looking for are not that simple," Siwon said gently. "Stop beating yourself up and remember why we're here. If you really want advice, then who better to consult than the goddess of time herself?"

Siwon's logic worked like magic. Mirae breathed easier, her mind clearing. He was right. The whole point of this last leg of her journey was to find answers to her burning questions, hers and the Netherqueen's. The time to choose the peninsula's future was not yet at hand, not until she consulted the patron goddess who had enabled her switches to begin with. If anyone knew Mirae's true purpose, her destiny, it would be her.

"Thank you, Siwon," Mirae said as her shoulders relaxed and the pressure in her chest dissipated. "I'm glad you're here, that you were the one fated to be with me at the very end."

"I'll always be wherever you want me to be," Siwon said, his eyes gleaming like twin stars. "Call, and I'll always come running."

"I'll hold you to that," Mirae said, even though she had already seen that she alone would cross over into the endless plane, led by the red thread of fate, and that Siwon was nowhere beside her in the future where she and Kimoon would somehow end up traveling through time together. "You are the only companion I've seen in my switches who never resents me. Promise me that will never change."

Siwon slowed to a stop and took her hand. Mirae's breath caught in her throat as Siwon turned her toward him, staring into her dark eyes with his warm golden ones. "My feelings for you will never change. That I promise you."

Mirae's face flushed as if the sun had returned with its bright blaze, heating what little air remained in her lungs. Then, as Siwon leaned in closer, her heart burst into flight, like a bird flitting around a room. He paused a few inches away, waiting for her to stop him, if she wanted. When she didn't, he closed the space between them, his lips pressing softly against hers.

The second he began kissing her, sweetly, almost reverently, the world around them seemed to slow, lulling time to a stand-still as it seared that blissful moment in Mirae's memory forever. But then, like a butterfly briefly cupped and then released, the instant passed as soon as the kiss ended, and Siwon pulled back to look shyly down at Mirae.

Elated and breathless, Mirae could only smile as Siwon cradled her face, his heart pounding fast enough that she could feel it through the palms of his hands, racing as joyously as her own. With a gasp of wonder, Mirae realized that their pulses were beating as one in that moment, mirroring the divine rhythm of the heavens. It was as if she, Siwon, and the world around them had all merged into a single endless soul.

When the utter exhilaration of that thought finally subsided enough that she could regain her composure, Mirae cleared her throat and said, "Now I'm *really* holding you to your promise."

Siwon laughed. "Good, I'm glad you finally believe me, Your Majesty."

"That's Mirae to you," she said, grabbing his hand. "And only to you."

"All right . . . Mirae." Siwon's cheeks blushed as he called her by name for the first time. Mirae felt her heart warm at his bashfulness, his undeniable happiness at the gift she'd given him.

Mirae cleared her throat to keep from grabbing his face and kissing him again. "By the way, you really meant what you said, right? About you and Areum just being friends?"

"I would never lie about that," he said, squeezing her hand. "As I mentioned, Lady Areum and her lover helped me out of a bind several months back, and I owe them a great debt. When Lady Areum was chosen as a Kun Sunim candidate, her secret partner, one of the other oracles, had a premonition that things would go terribly awry, so she begged me to watch over Lady Areum. Of course, I told her I would protect her with my life."

"I see," Mirae said, breathing a sigh of relief. "Well, you certainly took that assignment very seriously. The two of you seemed so close, I couldn't help but assume you were . . . very close."

Siwon chuckled. "We're close enough that she knew I had developed feelings for someone last year. A compassionate, courageous woman utterly out of reach. For what queen with as many impressive titles as you, Mirae, High Daughter, High Queen, High Horomancer, and elite dragon rider, would ever fall for a lowly servant who's terrified of heights?"

"You do seem to be getting better at handling your fear of flying," Mirae chuckled.

Siwon snorted. "Tell that to your poor chollima's mangled hair. I tried to be brave for you, Mirae, but in reality, my eyes were shut the entire time."

As much as Mirae wanted to stand there and laugh with the handsome man whose kiss was still making her heart flutter, she knew she didn't have that luxury. Not until they completed their mission. Eager to make that happen as quickly as possible, Mirae squeezed Siwon's hand and started walking along the sun's chasm again, pulling her lover along. He followed elatedly, matching her stride.

Their hands never let go as, together, they continued walking along the edge of heaven.

Chapter
THIRTY

As Mirae and Siwon trekked along the outskirts of the gods' abandoned realm, time seemed to pass them by meaninglessly. The sun and the moon swapped places in the sky several times, but Mirae and Siwon only paid attention to each other, moving as one, inseparable. When the world burned too brightly to endure as the sun rapidly approached, they took shelter together behind enormous jade boulders, fanning each other. When the air grew icy in the cold moon's wake, they instinctively huddled without having to say a word, warmed by each other's presence as much as any embrace.

Most of the time, however, they talked about everything and anything, from their favorite types of precious stones to theories about how, and why, magic worked. Thankfully, the pain in Mirae's cut-up feet ebbed the longer she stayed by Siwon's side and, perhaps even more important, the Netherqueen predominantly let her and Siwon be, only interrupting their conversations occasionally with a snide remark. But for the most part she stayed quiet, as if, having said her piece, she was waiting with bated breath for the answers to her questions: What would Mirae do with the things she'd learned about the Deep? What fate awaited the peninsula, if left in her hands?

In time, the colors and refulgence of the heavens slowly began to fade, as if a veil of deepening shadows was being draped across the world. Mirae knew that the end of the realm must be close now, the place where she and Siwon would have to part ways so that she could enter the eternal plane.

When the ground beneath their feet finally cut off, giving way to the darkness beyond, Mirae searched for the bridge Captain Jia had told her about, turning her head every which way until something strange caught her eye. Pitch-black in color, the camouflaged path would have been almost impossible to discern from the shadows had she not been looking for it, and had it not been trembling in the vast nothingness ahead, rippling like boiling ink.

"The bridge to the cosmos," Mirae breathed. She stared nervously at the undulating passage. "Jia said it will lead me to the eternal plane."

"Then I suppose this is where I leave you," Siwon said. When she turned to him, surprised, he chuckled at the look on her face. "I always suspected that you were planning to visit the goddess of time alone, and I know better than to try to get in the way of your destiny. But rest assured, I'll be waiting here for you, Mirae, until you come back to me."

Mirae smiled at how timidly he still spoke her name, and his unflinching trust in her choice to finish this journey without him. "I'll be back," she promised, remembering the Festival of Heaven she would one day attend with a man wearing a silver snake mask. "I've seen a glimpse of our future together, and I wouldn't miss it for the world."

Siwon smiled even brighter. "I'm happy to hear you say that. And remember, Mirae, if you run into any trouble, just call and I will come, no matter what stands in my way. I will travel across all time and search every moon until I find you."

Mirae leaned in and kissed Siwon one last time. "The place I want you most is right here. You are the one I want to see when I return."

"As you wish," Siwon said softly, brushing the side of Mirae's face. "I won't move a single step from here, even if the heavens around me begin to crumble."

"Don't worry, I won't let it come to that," Mirae assured him. "When you see me again, I will have the power to restore all that is, or has been, broken, including the heavens. You'll see."

"I know I will." With that, Siwon gave Mirae one final embrace before letting her turn to face the bridge of the cosmos stretching out into oblivion. Taking a deep breath, Mirae gathered her courage and took her first step onto the pitch-black platform of shivering ink.

No, not ink, she realized as her foot sank into something soft and downy. Feathers, millions of them fluttering together, overlapping tightly across the abyss to form a quivering path that arced upward into the darkness, to a place that lay higher, even, than the heavens. Mirae took another step, then another, until she was confident enough to quicken her pace, striding eagerly up toward the wilderness of stars that awaited her on a distant, endless plane.

· ❖ ·

She knew the instant she reached the otherworldly realm of the goddess of time. It looked just as she remembered it, an infinite mirrorlike surface reflecting the expansive dome of stars around her. Crystal clear water splashed across her shoes, cooling the throbbing cuts on her feet and dampening the hem of her chima, though the plane itself was motionless and quiet, barely rippling when she moved. The whole world felt, just as it had before, as if time itself had been suspended, here in a starlit place that Mirae hoped was a vault of destiny's greatest secrets waiting to be opened.

As she strode onward, following the red string around her finger, Mirae shivered against the growing cold of the sunless void, and soon found the eerie serenity of the starry plane a little unsettling. She even began to miss the Netherqueen's combative company, which was perhaps why the other woman said nothing, leaving Mirae alone with her trepidation. Still, Mirae pressed forward. The goddess of time was waiting.

Mirae quickly lost track of how many hours had passed, unsure, even, if she'd been walking for several days, when she suddenly felt the black bell begin to burn through her pocket. A familiar sear rushed up her arm. *It's time*, she thought, struck by a sudden, deep sadness. *Time to go home, just for a little while.*

She wasn't sure what she would say to her family when she saw them, knowing all that she knew now. All Mirae could do was close her eyes and let her soul get swept away, barreling back into the not-so-distant past where her mother's death was still as fresh as the grave her family kept watch in.

This time, when Mirae felt that she had returned to her body, she immediately fluttered her fingers and her eyelids, ascertaining whether she was still in control. When her eyes opened on command, Mirae breathed a sigh of relief. The Netherqueen was still with her. Mirae could feel her like a moth on her shoulder. But this time, Suhee seemed content to merely watch and listen, utterly silent in the tomb of her onetime friend turned bitter enemy.

Mirae, too, was silent for a moment as she took in the sight of her family. Her mother's shrouded body, her exhausted father, and Hongbin, who stared up at her with red-rimmed eyes.

Hongbin was the first to speak. "Did it work, noonim? Did you switch?"

Mirae nodded at her brother, a version of him who had not yet become bitter with resentment, and pulled him into a hug. Startled, Hongbin patted her on the back, and nervously asked, "What, am I dead or something, wherever you're from?"

Mirae shook her head. "No, not dead. I would never allow that."

"Okay, good." When Mirae pulled away to stare at Hongbin's face—bereaved, but still kind and guileless—he said, "I'm sure you know why we summoned you here. Can you tell Father and me whether or not we should let you chase after the Netherking, after he . . ."

Hongbin's voice trailed off, heavy with the words he wasn't yet ready to say. Mirae glanced over at her mother's shrouded body, and felt the Netherqueen's soul stir again at the somber sight, before fixing her gaze back on Hongbin. "I'm in another world, getting the answers to every question we've ever had about the Netherking."

"Another world?" Hongbin asked, wide-eyed.

"Yes," Mirae said. "Somewhere high above the spirit world and the heavens, in a place that doesn't have a name. That's where the goddess of time, my patron deity, lives. She's going to tell me how to fulfill my mission as High Horomancer."

Hongbin nodded, clearly impressed. "And do you know what the Netherking is planning? Can you tell us?"

Mirae inclined her head. "Yes. And, in answer to your question, you *should* allow me to hunt him down before his new plan comes to fruition."

"Why, what is he going to do?" Hongbin asked.

"Something unthinkable," Mirae said. She looked her father in the eye, the one who needed the most persuading.

"What is it, Mirae?" her father asked, his voice a near whisper, eyes glistening. "What is so terrible that I must risk losing the rest of my family?"

Mirae shut her eyes, unwilling to watch her father's face crease with sorrow as she relayed what everyone needed to know before her switch ended, a summary about the Netherking's diabolical plan, and how the Jade Emperor's absence meant the gods were defenseless. Then she explained that Hongbin needed to tell her past self that there was a way for the Netherking to reach the heavens—through the Dark Moon Oracles of Baljin.

As Hongbin listened, trying to memorize every word she said, Mirae briefly considered exhorting her brother to head straight to the Crystal City, bypassing their stint in Josan, until she remembered that if they hadn't retrieved the block of frozen black water, Kimoon would never have been able to betray them, prompting a string of events that led to Minho being released, and Mirae—hopefully—reaching the heavens in time to cut off the Netherking's access to the gods.

She remembered Siwon's recent words, too. He believed that, all things considered, the path she had ended up following was painful but triumphant. The best possible outcome. Changing the course of things now would not only go against the strict instructions the Kun Sunim had given her about altering the past but would also jeopardize the impending victory against the Netherking that Mirae had fought and lost so much for.

So, instead Mirae forced herself to say, "There's one more thing you need to know. Make sure you bring Kimoon along. We won't be able to succeed without him."

"Kimoon?" Hongbin asked, surprised. "I thought he was still recovering from—"

"He is," Mirae said thickly. "But we can't do this unless he's by our side."

Mirae forced herself to look into her father's eyes, which were welling up with tears. She knelt before him and pressed her hands together. "I know you want to keep me safe, but no one will be safe if I don't do this. Please, give me your blessing, Father. Only I can stop him. I must stop him."

Mirae felt Hongbin kneel beside her, joining her entreaty. Before she could hear her father's answer, Mirae felt the palm of her hand begin to burn, signaling that her switch had come to an end. But she was at peace with that, for she had given her family the knowledge they needed to proceed, information with a predestined role in leading her back to that very moment. So,

Mirae closed her eyes as darkness clouded her vision, knowing that when they opened again, she would be standing before the pearlescent palace of the goddess of time.

Mirae returned to a quaking plane, still reverberating with the echoes of a thunderous thud. Her eyes flew open, but she saw no sign of danger, nothing but the same starry void as before. Puzzled, but unsure what else to do, Mirae held out her hand and, seeing that the red thread of fate was arcing over her shoulder, swung herself around, back toward the palatial building she had been expecting to see.

The palace was just as she remembered it, an immensely high, sharply peaked pagoda with seven disclike levels made out of iridescent blue stone. The glowing walls of the structure looked as if they were drenched in liquid pearl, thinly veiled by the silvery mist that coiled around them. The string around Mirae's finger had grown taut, leading her directly toward the hollow opening at the peak of the palace's snow-white, half-moon steps.

Mirae climbed the stairs without faltering until she finally stood before the dark opening. Then, bracing for whatever lay in store for her, Mirae stepped into the shadowed doorway.

She found herself in a short, dark tunnel. A pale blue light emanated from the far end of it, so Mirae walked forward until she stepped out into the heart of the palace. The inside was similar to the exterior, built out of the same effervescent blue and white stone, but there were no furnishings, no goddess. Instead, at the center of the room, was a pearly, spiraling staircase leading up to the highest reaches of the palace.

Mirae moved without hesitation, approaching the milky, glinting steps and making her way up them as swiftly as she could. As before, when traversing the sword bridge to the heavens, Mirae's body didn't tire while climbing, so it didn't take her long to ascend all seven levels of the pagoda until at last, she reached the very top.

Had she been in any other realm, the dizzying height of the palace's highest peak might have made Mirae's stomach flip inside her. But here, surrounded by eternal night, where stars and darkness had no beginning, no end, Mirae felt as if she was merely floating through the cosmos, just another celestial body, one of billions drifting listlessly.

But Mirae quickly reminded herself that she was not an aimless star meant to remain here, trapped in a floating expanse. She shook off the ceaseless wonder that had diverted her, and the peaceful, numbing draw of the unfathomable void distracting her from her mission. Once her mind had cleared, Mirae spun slowly around on the highest platform of the pagoda, taking in her surroundings.

The roofless chamber she stood in was a bone-white disc, both the floor and spiraling pillars seemingly forged out of glossy ceramic, much like unadorned sun baekja pottery. Draped across the top of the pillars were billowing, gossamer linens, pale as a shroud but embroidered with bright gold threads. As Mirae wandered beneath them, staring up at the softly curving bellies of the shimmering fabrics, she marveled at the intricate murals embroidered on the starlit cloths, tales from history, across all time.

As Mirae strode forward, something just as enthralling came into view on the far side of the platform. Steps leading up to a low dais, atop which a woman was perched, gazing out at the universe. As she approached, Mirae studied the motionless, oblivious goddess, the first deity she'd ever seen. Her face was turned away, so at first all Mirae could take in were the goddess's clothes. A sheer, starry gown draped across her impossibly tall form, surrounding her like a veiled galaxy of which she was the glorious center.

When Mirae was close enough to climb up the steps to the dais, and around the goddess of time's backless throne, she finally saw the divine being's immaculate face.

She was the most beautiful woman Mirae had ever seen, her features perfectly smooth and softly rounded, as impeccably shaped as the finest vases money could buy. Her black half-moon eyes stared out at the cosmos as if caught up in a deep meditation, one that had seemingly arrested the goddess's attention for eons, for every inch of her skin was waxy and deathly pale, like she'd been carved from flawless limestone and then left here to bask in the universe's beauty, marooned in a palace dedicated to containing a priceless treasure. In a similar fashion, her long, satiny hair fell heavily across her narrow shoulders, seemingly having nothing to do but grow aimlessly, spilling down the back of her sheer gown like an endless midnight river, pooling like skeins of dark silk onto the stark white floor.

Overwhelmed by the exquisiteness of the being who had summoned her from the farthest reaches of time, Mirae fell to her knees, prostrating herself before her patron goddess.

"Yeosinnim," she called out reverently. "I have come to beseech you for your guidance."

When she was met with silence, Mirae peeked up at the goddess, who hadn't moved. "I am the High Horomancer, your foreordained servant."

Again, there was no response. The goddess of time's unblinking eyes continued to stare out at the universe, heeding nothing that Mirae said. Puzzled, she climbed to her feet and approached the divine being cautiously. "Yeosinnim?"

Unsure what else to do, Mirae glanced out at the celestial expanse, searching for whatever had captivated the woman beside her. Stars burning and dying, comets streaking across the sky. Ringed planets twisting around their suns, and moons loyally coursing after. Nebulas and black holes expanding and devouring everything in creation.

It was a mesmerizing sight. Hypnotic, even. But hardly more pressing than what Mirae had come there to do. She tore her eyes away from the ever-shifting cosmos and waved a hand in front of the entranced goddess's face, but was not rewarded with a reaction.

Oh, queenling, did you really think your problems would be more important to the gods than all the mysteries waiting to be explored out past the reaches of our existence? The Netherqueen, who had roused herself from her silent watch to taunt Mirae, cackled. *Of course, entitled as you are, you believed you were the only thing on your patron goddess's mind. Her sole concern. You probably thought she was waiting with bated breath for your arrival, didn't you? That she'd prepared a gala in honor of her bravest, most cherished servant?*

Mirae ignored the Netherqueen. Contrary to the other woman's belief, Mirae knew that the task before her was probably a test, not a slight. If the goddess of time was distracted, then Mirae simply needed to figure out how to draw her attention. She needed to say or do something compelling enough to draw her patron's depthless eyes. Something that would startle her, amuse her, or even provoke her. An act, perhaps, that would give the omniscient deity, who saw past, present, and future as one, something she rarely ever experienced:

A moment where time stood still.

Mirae remembered sharing that very feeling with Siwon, when their first kiss had made the world around them freeze, just for a second, as if it was stamping that moment eternally into the stars. Holding that precious memory close to her heart, along with what it foretold about the masked man at a heavenly festival who would one day remind her that love could shatter unbreakable chains, Mirae leaned forward and pressed her lips softly against the goddess of time's frosty cheek. As soon as she pulled away, she saw that the spot of skin she'd kissed had begun to warm, turning a rosy peach.

Then, slowly, that delicate pink started to spread, as if the rest of the goddess's body was beginning to thaw, from the bloom on her cheek down to the bare tips of her toes.

Once the goddess's ghostly pallor melted down to her neck, she turned her flawless head and rested her gaze on Mirae, her dark, all-knowing eyes taking in the mortal before her as if ascertaining who, exactly, had disturbed her out-of-body venture through the stars.

Mirae fell to her knees and prostrated herself again. "Yeosin-nim, I am your faithful servant, the High Horomancer of Seolla. I have come seeking your guidance."

For a moment, the other woman gave no response. Then, in a voice both aloof and cutting, reverberating as if a thousand of her were speaking at once, the goddess finally uttered her first words.

"Hail, Unnamed Dragon. We have much to discuss."

Chapter
THIRTY-ONE

Mirae thought she would know exactly what to say to the woman before her, what questions were most pressing. But in the presence of such resplendence, and faced with the very being who had both given her a noble calling and knew the truth of every event in history that had been buried by her ancestors, Mirae surprised herself by forsaking her purpose to ask, "Are you not lonely up here, knowing all that you do, with only stars to keep you company?"

The goddess of time looked puzzled by the question, her head tilting slightly to one side. "Stars can be rather haughty conversationalists, I suppose, proud as they are of being the pivotal centers of their systems, but planets have many diverse opinions, and engage in the most wonderful debates. Comets and asteroids are tireless nomads who have seen countless wonders that they are always eager to talk about. I could never grow weary of my companions, not for another million years."

"They do sound marvelous," Mirae admitted, even as she shuddered each time the goddess spoke. Bumps bubbled up across her skin as she was barraged by the chorus of voices that sounded as if every iteration of the yeosin was speaking to Mirae from across all time. "I'm sorry I interrupted your dialogue with the cosmos, but I think you know why I've come."

"Of course. I preordained your arrival." The goddess of time finally stood, towering over Mirae, taller than anyone Mirae had ever seen. Her sheer, glittery gown billowed behind her like effervescent mist, while her hair spilled down her shoulders in a sleek black train. "Walk with me, Unnamed Dragon. There isn't time for me to tell you everything you wish to know, but I can share enough to illuminate the path before you."

Mirae bowed gratefully before moving away from the pedestal throne. When the goddess of time moved, Mirae followed, keeping pace with the other woman's slow, unhurried gait, and taking care not to tread on her thick, flowing hair, unspooling on the ground with every step.

"It is not my duty to chronicle the events of the mortal sphere," the goddess began, gesturing at the gold-threaded curtains suspended above, depicting some stories familiar to Mirae and others that remained a mystery. "But some moments capture my fancy enough that I render them here, that I may never forget the noteworthy feats of your world. I hope they'll be remembered, someday, when I am long gone."

Although the goddess said those last words emotionlessly, Mirae wanted to ask why the woman next to her thought her divine reign would ever end. Before she could, the yeosin pointed at one of the embroidered tales, and her thunderous, reverberating voice rattled all other concerns out of Mirae's mind. "This tale should be of particular interest."

Mirae stared up at the gauzy covering, its flaxen threads

weaving a troubling image of women commanding the elements, pitting their magic against each other while dragons and imugi twirled through the sky, maws snapping at each other. As Mirae's eyes trailed down the mural, the flying beasts and women dwindled until only two figures remained. The last dragon lay bleeding on the peak of a snowy mountain, its pearl raised triumphantly in the hands of a queen wearing Seolla's tall golden crown.

"Is this the Miri War?" Mirae breathed, eyes riveted on the elated woman.

"It is." The goddess lowered her head, presumably in respect of the countless lives lost in a conflict that Mirae had only just learned about.

"I heard that it was in the aftermath of the Miri War that the Sacred Bone line was created," Mirae said, no longer certain she wanted to know the truth about how her ancestors came to power. "Is it true that my rare ability to command all three of Seolla's magic systems was not a gift from the gods, but rather something woman-made?"

"It's a little more complicated than that," the goddess said mildly, "but no, your unique power was not originally a part of the Samsin's design."

Mirae took a sharp breath, though the frigid air of the surrounding cosmos did nothing to cool the heat blossoming in her cheeks as she remembered the scorn of the Seers of Light when they realized she knew next to nothing about the extent of her ancestors' sins, beginning with their very inception. "Tell me everything," she said. "I want . . . I need to know it all."

"There isn't time," the goddess said, a hint of regret in the echoes of her voice. "I urge you to return to the Seers of Light someday and beg them to impart their knowledge. It will not be complete, but it will be sufficient to abet your final quest."

My final quest? Mirae had seen only one other journey in her switches, one where she walked side by side with a man who claimed to be her worst enemy. Recalling the vitriol in his eyes, and the betrayal at the burning altar that put it there, Mirae tore her eyes away from the gossamer linens above, spangled with unsettling truths, and craned her neck to look up at her patron deity instead.

"Will you tell me who the Inconstant Son is," she asked, "and the secret to ending him before he destroys all that is good?"

Instead of giving an answer, the yeosin gestured for Mirae to follow as she padded over to another one of the sheer tapestries and pointed at the three women depicted in its low-hanging belly. Mirae reluctantly looked where directed, fervently hoping it wouldn't reveal yet another cryptic piece of the puzzle that darkened her path, instead of illuminating it as promised.

But as soon as she realized whose stories she was seeing, Mirae couldn't help but study the fabric above her intently, the histories it depicted sparkling with gems and glittering beads as well as the typical lines of bright gold thread. Mirae immediately recognized the playful smile and resplendent, helmet-like headdress of Crown Princess Eunbyul, the Silver Star, first of the High Daughters and unparalleled master of Ma-eum Magic. She stood before her proud, snarling father serenely, unbothered by the diamond-encrusted spear he hurtled at her chest.

In the next canopy, Queen Sunbok, the Deep Deceiver and Seolla's most celebrated wielder of Jade Witchery, stood before the familiar banks of Wol Sin Lake, its water rippling with deep red garnets, while its bone-white shore gleamed with unpolished shards of the same cold ceramic that coated the floor beneath Mirae's feet. Behind the Deep Deceiver, hundreds of ghostly faces, half-submerged in the lake, peered out at her with ebony eyes glittering with hate.

As for the final embroidered covering, the one that portrayed Mirae's own unfinished tale, all that had been sewn in so far was the faint outline of an old woman embracing a weeping man. The rest of the skein was empty, offering no clue as to where Mirae and Kimoon had ended up on their mysterious journey, or what sorrowful deed they had resolved to do.

Mirae turned away from the threadbare fabric just enough to look at her patron deity. "Do you not know how my story ends?" she asked, her breath hitching.

The yeosin didn't meet Mirae's gaze. "I see many possibilities," she said, her voice echoing uncertainly.

"Please tell me how to achieve the best possible future," Mirae pleaded. "I need to know the secret to succeeding where the other High Daughters failed."

"Failed?" The goddess raised an eyebrow. Then she pointed back at Crown Princess Eunbyul's tapestry. "The Silver Star succeeded in curbing the Inconstant Son she faced. It was the Deep Deceiver who failed by creating the Deep. This Netherking who plagues you is a product of her dereliction, a long-festering mess that was left to you to wipe clean."

Mirae blinked up at the goddess, her mind slowly processing the significance of what she'd just said. "Are you telling me that there are three Inconstant Sons, one for each of the High Daughters to destroy?"

The goddess of time nodded. "Three corrupters, and three champions."

"So, the Netherking," Mirae said slowly, heart pounding louder than the yeosin's reverberating voice, "is not the Inconstant Son I was fated to defeat, but rather a remnant of the Deep Deceiver's, whom I must destroy in addition to my own?"

"That is correct."

Mirae was too shocked to do more than listen as the goddess continued, "It is a pity that the Deep Deceiver's weakness created so many complications. Had she succeeded, her descendants would not have been tormented by the nether-fiends, and you, Unnamed Dragon, would not have been forced to enter the trial of the gods so young. You would have ascended to the throne later in life, and unlocked your switching ability when you were more prepared for it, eventually learning to master it. Instead of these random traipses through time, you would have been able to self-direct your switches, making your power more intentional and effective as you parceled out the various futures you could manifest, or avoid. Unfortunately, this was not to be, because, instead of defeating one monster, the Deep Deceiver instead created thousands more."

It took every ounce of Mirae's strength not to stagger backward. "Why didn't I know any of this?" she stammered.

"When the Deep Deceiver realized the magnitude of what

she'd done, she was too ashamed to admit that she'd made a terrible mistake." The goddess shook her head, sending shivers down her black river of hair. "So, on her deathbed she told everyone that the Inconstant Son, a singular enemy, was safely locked away, thanks to her, but could only be destroyed by the fated last High Daughter. Then, in front of all her adoring followers, she shifted her soul into her seong-suk, vowing to return when Seolla needed her again."

"But in truth," Mirae said hollowly, "she intended to bury her secrets with her until the High Horomancer was called. She hoped that she could make a show of helping me to succeed and be heralded as a hero once more."

The goddess nodded. "Now you understand the reason I brought you here."

"You couldn't interfere with anything happening in the mortal world," Mirae said wearily. "So, you had to bring your 'champion' here in order to correct the path that the Deep Deceiver's lies were leading me down."

"It is as you say." The yeosin inclined her head, rippling her cascading hair again, as dark and glossy as Mirae's black bell. "But now that you are here, I can offer you one last gift to help you end this conflict between Sons and Daughters for good."

At last, the moment Mirae had been waiting for. "I'm ready to put all this to rest."

The goddess swept her sparkling gown behind her and headed back toward her throne. Mirae followed, wondering how her patron goddess could, with a single boon, help Mirae fulfill both her duty *and* the Deep Deceiver's. When the yeosin came to a stop beside the low seat she'd once used to gaze out at the universe, the golden shimmers of her gown brought a lump to Mirae's throat, for they matched the eyes of the man she now knew was indeed the Inconstant Son she was fated to face. A tragic vessel unwillingly bound to the Deep Deceiver's disastrous legacy. It was an ill-fated union that nevertheless presented Mirae with the chance to fulfill her two-pronged destiny in one fell swoop—as long as she was willing to destroy the friend she'd betrayed rather than save him.

"We are almost out of time, Unnamed Dragon," the goddess said, her voice echoing ominously across the chamber. "So do not think too long about what I'm about to offer."

With that, the yeosin raised her arm, holding her hand flat as if bracing it against an unseen wall. "I will grant you one jump through time, anywhere you wish, for as long as you want. This is not a switch," she clarified. "You will not swap bodies with your future or past self. You will go as you are, to wherever or whenever you desire. Choose wisely, and you will strike a final blow to this ancient threat and deliver all the realms from an unspeakable fate."

A fate one of my own doomed us with, Mirae thought darkly. And now it was up to Mirae to pick up the pieces, shattered across generations.

"So, what is your wish?" the goddess asked, bringing Mirae back to the choice at hand. "Tell me where you see yourself fulfilling your destiny."

Mirae knew better than to ask her patron to make the decision for her. If she'd been willing to do so, she would have done it instead of staring blankly down at Mirae with those dark, unfathomable eyes, expecting the High Horomancer she'd chosen to use what she'd learned to foresee the exact moment when her twofold calling would come to a head. A rare opportunity that the goddess of time had more or less spelled out for her already.

Knowing full well that this last mission, one she'd only ever seen herself face alone, could lead to a future where she grew old on a wintry mountaintop with an old friend who'd grown understandably cruel, instead of returning to the edge of the heavens to reunite with the man destined to be her lover, Mirae cast her teary eyes down to the spotless floor as she mustered the will to say, "Send me to a time and place where the men I must destroy will be together, and most vulnerable. The Inconstant Son I was born to annihilate, and the vile Netherking, a blight upon this peninsula who must come to an end."

The unblinking goddess nodded. "It will be done."

No sooner had she finished speaking than wisps of light began to form on the surface of her palm, gradually thickening into winding beams that twisted together, forming a churning, radiant vortex. A portal to the very moment Mirae had described, where the unsuspecting villains of both her and her ancestors' creation would be thrown together by the threads of fate.

"Your wish is fulfilled," the goddess said, stepping back from the luminous doorway, clearing Mirae's path. "The rest, Unnamed Dragon, is up to you."

As Mirae stared into the swirling portal beckoning for her to step inside and unravel the mysteries of the future she'd only ever caught glimpses of, she steeled herself for the fight to come. The final battle between her and those twisted by revenge.

Feeling the eyes of the goddess who'd made all this possible boring into the back of her head, Mirae nevertheless hesitated to stride into the portal, even though this was the moment her quest had led to. The culmination of everything she'd lost, the sacrifices of those who'd believed in her. Now was her chance to make it all worth it. And yet, something was holding her back.

What's the matter, queenling? the Netherqueen asked, no longer remaining a silent observer. *Don't you want all this to end?*

Of course I do, Mirae thought. She didn't know what was making her hesitate. A premonition, a fear? Reluctance, perhaps, to risk never seeing anyone she cared about ever again, leaving them behind in the present while she potentially died in battle somewhere far away from anyone who'd ever loved her, vanishing forever out of the reach of those who, if given the chance, would have crossed the universe to remain by her side.

But Mirae knew that this was a sacrifice she had to be willing to make. She could not afford to falter as the Deep Deceiver did, for if the last High Daughter failed, the consequences would be catastrophic. Worse than the fallout of her predecessor's blunder, which she'd seen with her own eyes.

Taking a deep breath and uttering a fervent prayer that she would be able to strike a blow, quick and true, to end the threat of every Inconstant Son, and return victorious to the people and place to which she truly belonged, Mirae prepared herself to bury whatever selfish urge was arresting her resolve, and force herself to do what needed to be done.

Just as she was mustering the will to take a step forward, she felt the platform beneath her tremble. Just a small quiver at first, but then, after an earsplitting crack thundered through the air behind her, the ground began to shudder more violently, nearly enough to knock Mirae off her feet. The pristine white floor started to fracture, hairline fissures veining into the surrounding pillars and the goddess's throne. Waving her arms to keep her balance, Mirae tried to search for the source of the disturbance, but it wasn't until the earth fell still and her vision stabilized that she saw him.

At first it was just the top of his head as he ascended the spiral staircase. Kimoon, his purple robe whispering over the steps as he climbed. As soon as he stepped foot on the platform, he turned and found Mirae standing beside her patron deity. Then his amber eyes flickered to the churning, radiant doorway.

"I see I'm a little late," he said coolly. "My apologies. A rather tenacious young man tried to confront me on my way here, which delayed me."

Mirae's fists clenched, both at his words and at the horror of confronting what she'd done to Kimoon. What she allowed him to become. "Where's Siwon?" she demanded hoarsely. "What did you do to him?"

The Netherking merely waved away Mirae's indignation. "You know, my wife was very fond of him once. I suppose that made me feel a bit nostalgic as well, so I spared his life." Mirae let out a breath and heard the Netherqueen do the same as the Netherking continued. "But I did leave him rather . . . indisposed. You should go to him, queenling, if you want him to make it out of here alive."

"No, Unnamed Dragon," the yeosin urged. "You must complete your mission. Go through the portal and fulfill your destiny."

"I suppose you could do that," the Netherking said with a shrug. "Go on and leave me here to drain the goddess of time. With her power, I'll easily be able to hunt down the rest of the gods one by one." The Netherking started walking toward Mirae slowly. "What will you do without your patron's power? I wonder. How will you get back here if she's gone? How will you save all those people who will fight on in your name, never knowing why you disappeared, leaving them here to rot?"

"Ignore him, Unnamed Dragon." The yeosin gestured toward the portal.

But indecision gripped Mirae's legs like a web ensnaring a fly. The Netherking was right—if she left, the goddess of time was doomed. And if her patron died, so did her way back home. Mirae would be trapped wherever she was, forever.

But if she stayed here, there was no guarantee that she would manage to escape the Netherking again. Either way, the goddess next to her would die, paving the way for others to follow. No matter what Mirae chose, the Netherking would win.

The Netherking stretched Kimoon's lips into a mocking smile as he retrieved the pearl from his robes and held it in front of him like a cup of exquisite wine. The Yeouiju sat like a new moon in his hand, reflecting its dark master with glints of purple and yellow flickering across it.

"Go, now," the goddess of time urged one last time. "As awful as it is, you must make this sacrifice."

"Yes, sacrifice them all, queenling," the Netherking laughed as twilight tendrils began to form on the surface of the pearl, twisting to form one long, dark arm. "Run away and let everyone else die. That is your destiny, False Queen."

Fool Queen, more like, the Netherqueen murmured. *He's doing everything he can to stop you from taking that leap because he's afraid. Terrified of you and what you'll do. He always has been. You're the only one who's never understood that.*

Mirae didn't see any fear in Kimoon's eyes, however, as the Netherking shot the arm of magic-draining mist forward, aiming it not toward Mirae or the yeosin but the goddess's portal. But just as the tendril surged forward, the goddess of time stepped right into its path and raised her palm, shooting a beam of radiant golden light to intercept the Netherking's spell.

The two shafts collided, spears of midnight and noon equally met, neither advancing nor retreating. But the Netherking's magic was set to devour, not repel. The dark, writhing arm began to swell as it gorged on the yeosin's tremendous power, and slowly, her divine shield began to dim.

"No!" Mirae started to run forward, but the goddess turned to look at her one last time, grimacing with pain as she shook her head. "Escape," she thundered. "Save the realms."

"I can't," Mirae gasped. "I can't just let him—"

"It's all right, Unnamed Dragon." The goddess of time managed to soften her face into a tender smile. "I never intended to be endless."

But watching the goddess fall to her knees, crying out in agony as her formidable magic was ripped from her body, Mirae could almost hear the screams of her mother, the battle cry of Captain Jia. Women she couldn't save, who'd died horrendously.

No, I can't watch this again. Mirae raised her palms, ignoring the Netherqueen's screams that she was going to kill them both. *I will not stand by. Not this time.*

Taking advantage of the Netherking's concentration on the arduous task of killing a goddess, Mirae summoned flames into her palms and, just as she had the last time she'd chased off her mother's killer, hurtled her fireballs directly at his pearl-wielding hand.

Just as before, she hit her mark dead-on. The Netherking howled and whipped toward her, his eyes widening as Mirae strode out from behind the goddess, shocked to see that she hadn't run off to save herself, deserting her patron as she had the man whose body he was wearing.

With the element of surprise on her side, Mirae shot fireball after fireball, some consumed by the magic-leeching tendril, others finding their target until at last, the Netherking screamed in pain and dropped the pearl.

A thrill of elation shot through Mirae, a tempest of triumph that shot forward in a burst of wind that caught the Yeouiju into its embrace and sent it sailing out into the starry void.

The Netherking roared with rage and rushed to the edge of the platform, but it was too late. The pearl, along with its devastating spell, had disappeared, swallowed up by the universe.

Mirae wanted to let out a scream of her own, a victorious battle cry, until she saw the goddess of time double over and fall to her knees. To Mirae's horror, the yeosin's body was starting to fade, nearly as transparent as her sheer gown. The portal was flickering, too, as dim as a lantern about to go out.

Mirae rushed over to the yeosin and grabbed the goddess's arm. "Do you have any magic left?" she asked quickly. "Can you heal yourself?"

To her relief, the goddess nodded and weakly raised her arms, filling the space between them with an orb of shimmering golden light. Faint, but growing more radiant with each passing second. Her healing spell hadn't fully formed yet, however, when the Netherking whirled around and strode back from the edge of the pagoda, his face twisted with fury.

Even without his corrupted instrument, Mirae knew he was a formidable enemy. Powerful enough to challenge the divine and perform unprecedented acts of evil. If it wasn't for the help of Sol and her gwisin army a year ago, Mirae would never have been able to overpower him and shackle him inside the Deep.

Thankfully, she wasn't alone now, either. Furious as he was, the Netherking was no match for a High Daughter and a goddess. But the dying yeosin was struggling to conjure her cure, which seemed to be costing her almost as much magic as it was meant to restore.

Determined to protect her patron, Mirae stood and cast fireball after fireball, trying to stave the Netherking off just long enough for the goddess to join their battle. But the Netherking swatted away all of Mirae's attacks as effortlessly as a swarm of gnats. No longer needing to put all his focus into maintaining his abominable spell, the Netherking rebuffed Mirae's onslaught easily with one hand, while conjuring an orb in the other. A sickly green ball of mist crackling with lightning.

"You think you've won, queenling?" he spat as power coursed down his arm, imbuing the insidious sphere with all his rage, his will to destroy Mirae. "This is as far as you go in one piece, False Queen. Today, you will break."

He cocked back his arm and pitched it forward with a snarl, sending the soul-shattering orb hurtling toward Mirae, large enough to engulf first the goddess and then her protector in one killing blow. Mirae tried to send the Netherking's curse off course with the strongest gale she could summon, but his frenzied, maniacal will propelled his spell forward, as if her wind was little more than a summer breeze.

Just as Mirae feared all was lost, the yeosin raised her golden orb and pressed it against Mirae's chest.

Mirae had no time to react before the Netherking's sparking ball of magic crashed into the goddess, dissolving her into a cloud of glittering stardust. A second later, it slammed into the yeosin's final spell. As soon as the two conjurations collided, they exploded into a realm-shaking, searing blast and the ear-splitting claps of white-hot lightning.

Mirae cried out as she was thrown backward, the force of the competing magics ripping through her, one obliterating, the other healing, as she flew into the portal just as the last of its light finally flickered out.

Chapter
THIRTY-TWO

Tumbling into the stream of time, Mirae could do nothing but scream as the two spells blended devastatingly, continuously tearing and repairing her, body and soul. Every nerve was alight with fire. She could practically feel her joints trying to burst out of their sockets, her skin prickling as if being stabbed by a thousand blades. Her organs swelled, just shy of bursting as all the air was ripped out of her lungs.

And yet her mouth still parted in a silent shriek as she plummeted toward the fulfillment of her final wish—to a point in time when her enemies would be as vulnerable as she.

Suddenly, just as quickly as the skull-splitting agony began, it mercifully fell away, leaving Mirae lying face up on cold, hard earth.

When Mirae finally mustered the strength to open her eyes, she squinted against the dappled sunlight streaming through leafy boughs, peacefully illuminating a forest thrumming with cricket song and the twittering of birds.

I'm alive, Mirae thought, half surprised that, despite the Netherking's vow, she was still in one piece. She lifted her arms, her legs, and took several deep breaths. Everything seemed fine now that she wasn't falling to her death, barraged by insidious magic.

As soon as she felt ready to risk even more movement, Mirae carefully sat up, giving her head a moment to clear, her vision to unblur. When she looked around, the forest she'd plunged into seemed serene, no sign of the men she'd come here to battle. The trees swayed lightly, their leaves rustling. Several yards away, Mirae saw a rabbit darting through the underbrush.

Did I come to the right place? she wondered, climbing stiffly to her feet. It didn't seem like the kind of location where an Inconstant Son and a would-be ruler of the realms would come across each other. But she couldn't imagine that the goddess of time had made a mistake sending her here. This had to be the spot, or somewhere close to it.

Just then, a noise made Mirae whirl around. Someone was singing, their slow, sad song carrying easily through the sparse trees. A woman who clearly had no idea that someone had traveled across time and a great distance to finish an ancient battle in her own backyard.

Mirae followed the sound of the gentle, lilting voice, assuming that where one person could be found, others would be also. She trod as quietly as she could, wincing with each step and being mindful of branches that would prick her damaged feet and snap loudly. She couldn't afford to lose the advantage of surprise. It would take everything she had to combat two villains at once in a fight she couldn't afford to lose.

Too many have died, she thought, eyes brimming with tears as she strode determinedly toward the singing woman, clenching her jaw and fists to keep from losing her nerve as she thought back to the goddess's final moments, spent protecting Mirae instead of herself. *I will finish this, and I will do it for Mother. For Jia. For the Yeosinnim who bet everything on me. For Siwon and Hongbin, who I will find my way back to, somehow, someday.*

And for Kimoon, she grieved. *The one I betrayed, but can yet save.*

As the singing grew louder, Mirae saw a clearing through the trees, a humble homestead at its center. Clay walls and a thatched roof over a short stone platform. A small courtyard with various earthenware jars, baskets, and a covered dais for eating and gathering. As Mirae drew closer, she saw the woman she was looking for sweeping the stone foundation beneath her house, completely absorbed in her task and her melancholic song.

Mirae searched for any sign that the woman wasn't alone. Finding none, she crept closer. Mirae made it all the way to the edge of the clearing without being spotted, but before she left the cover of the last tree and made herself known, she was struck with a thought. *What if she attacks? I should be ready for anything. I have no idea what year it is, or even what country I'm in. She could have magic, or a weapon. This could be a trap, if either of my enemies has somehow become powerful enough to know I'm coming.*

Loath to leave anything to chance, Mirae hid her hands behind her back, not wanting to be immediately confrontational, and bid her palms to summon a small ball of fire. When nothing happened, Mirae tried again, assuming her exhaustion was just getting to her. But all she could manage was a small lick of flame, a few sparks that immediately disappeared.

What is this? Mirae held her hands in front of her face as her heart began to pound. *What happened to my magic? What did the Netherking do to me?*

Too late, Mirae realized that the woman's song had ended. Footsteps were fast approaching, and she heard a familiar voice call out, "Who's there?" A second later, the woman spoke again, her voice high, hopeful. "Hongbin? Is that you? I can sense your Sacred Bone blood. You don't have to be afraid. Whatever he did to you, I'll never—"

As the woman rounded the tree Mirae was hiding behind, she froze, and Mirae couldn't help but do the same.

Staring back at her was her own face. Many years older, but still unmistakably hers. Apart from a few threads of gray in her dark hair, and cheeks that had lost their plumpness, the matron of the homestead was Mirae's spitting image. They stared at each other, speechless with disbelief, for several moments before Mirae's older self finally managed to whisper, "Who are you? Is this another one of the Netherking's tricks?"

Mirae had been wondering the same thing, but from the look in the other woman's eyes—utter confusion and shock that mirrored her own—Mirae couldn't help but feel that this woman was no illusion. No ruse. Mirae could feel in her core that she was facing another version of herself, someone real who felt like a missing half. Mirae's older self could feel it, too. She reached out slowly, unsure, and grabbed Mirae's hand.

The instant their fingers touched, Mirae gasped as a burst of visceral images and emotions—a decade's worth of them—exploded into her mind, missing memories bridging the gap of time between the two women:

A flash of light as the final spells of the Netherking and the goddess of time collided. This version of Mirae flying backward, but landing on cold, hard ground; her summoning a world-ending ball of fire and hurtling it at the Netherking as she screamed with rage over the yeosin's death, sending her enemy flying out into the starry void; the pagoda trembling violently and beginning to crumble as Mirae fled; wandering in the endless plane without the red thread of fate; Siwon's voice calling to her from the edge of the heavens, an anchor for her to follow. . . .

Mirae's heart raced as the memories continued, showing her everything that her other self had done after fulfilling their destiny:

Finding Siwon and weeping in his arms, relieved to see him alive; reuniting with Captain Jia and Hongbin to celebrate the defeat of the Netherking and the Inconstant Son, while mourning the loss of their friend Kimoon; witnessing the return of the grateful gods who reconnected all the worlds, giving Mirae, Siwon, and Hongbin a way home; choosing to explore the heavens with Siwon a little longer, and even attending the Festival of Heaven.

The next flashes of memory made Mirae's lungs deflate as she watched her other half live the life she'd imagined spending with the man she loved:

Returning to the mortal world with Siwon to be greeted by Minho and Hongbin, both alive and well; negotiating the return of the Wonhwa held captive in Josan by finally liberating Seolla's sovereign state; officiating the marriage between Areum and her lovely wife after changing the nuptial rules of their order; weeping over her father's grave while wrapped in the arms of her brothers; hugging King Hongbin goodbye as she left Seolla in his capable hands; marrying Siwon in a quiet grove, in a beautiful ceremony that perfectly melded both their countries' traditions; Siwon cooking a delicious dinner while she sang and swept their remote, humble home, her belly swollen with child.

As tears formed in Mirae's eyes, the flashing memories suddenly took a devastating turn, forcing Mirae to watch her older self's life begin to unravel:

Falling to her knees as Areum warned that the Netherking had returned from the void and was raising another dark army; arguing with Siwon about whether to stay in hiding to protect their child or rush to Seolla's aid; Mirae screaming as a war-weary Areum tells her that the Netherking slaughtered many of her relatives and friends in battle and captured King Hongbin; soul-walking to her younger brother and watching the Netherking torture him with black water; arguing bitterly with Siwon, who believed that Mirae and their child, the last Sacred Bone heirs, should remain hidden until the day that they can finally strike back. . . .

When the connection ended, Mirae stumbled backward, overwhelmed by all she had seen, experiences both sweet and horrifying, snapshots of a life that was taken from her the instant that two imploding spells cast at the same time—sunder and save—had combined strangely, obeying both commands the only way they could: a splintering. The creation of two whole Miraes, severed from each other; one who remained behind in the heavens, and one who split off first, reaching the dying portal just in time. Two women totally unaware of each other's existence until now.

Mirae's older self looked as if she, too, was reeling from the transference of memories. But instead of succumbing to the immeasurable sadness Mirae felt, grieving the loss of a life she would never have, and the devastating knowledge of what the Netherking's return would reap, the other woman's eyes widened as she stammered, "If the Yeosinnim brought you here, then that means—"

Before she could finish, she and Mirae both turned toward the sound of running feet. A man burst into the clearing from the other side, chest heaving, golden eyes round with fear.

"Mirae!" he shouted, searching frantically for his wife. "He's found us—*we have to run*."

The woman he called to grabbed Mirae tightly and pulled her out of the shadows, lugging her toward the man, who, like the woman clinging to her, had aged many years since the last time she'd seen him.

Siwon, whose curly hair was loose, cut short enough to brush the tops of his shoulders. A headband drenched with sweat sat on his brow over familiar yellow eyes that stared at Mirae as if she were a ghost. As much as Mirae wanted to rush into his arms and feel the comfort of his embrace, she knew this Siwon both was and was not the man she'd kissed. The sweet, young lover she'd left behind was someone she was never going to see again, still waiting in the heavens for a woman who wouldn't be her.

"We always knew he would track us down eventually," Mirae's older self said, pulling everyone's attention back to the matter at hand. "If he's on his way, then it's already too late. We have to stand and fight."

Fight? Mirae swallowed. Although this was what she'd come here to do, she didn't know how she could possibly be of any use without her magic. "I don't understand," she faltered. "The yeosinnim said she'd send me to a time when the Netherking and Kimoon were together and most vulnerable. But based on what I've just seen—"

"The Netherking is more powerful than ever," her other self said darkly. "I was a fool to think that the goddess of time had sacrificed herself to motivate me to unleash my full power, and that I had truly destroyed my Inconstant Son while cleaning up the Deep Deceiver's mess with one terrible spell. My arrogance caused me to fail. This . . . this is all my fault."

"That's not true, yeobo," Siwon said, gently but urgently. "The only person to blame is the monster coming to kill us and our child. Please, we have to go *now*."

But instead of listening to her husband, Mirae's older self took a step back, her mouth falling open with horror. "A time when Kimoon and the Netherking would be together," she whispered, "and at their most vulnerable."

Siwon's eyes widened, round as gold plates, as his wife reached out and grabbed Mirae's arm, her nails biting painfully into her flesh. "My child," she implored, surprising Mirae with her vehemence, "you have to save him. Promise me."

Taken aback, Mirae suppressed a yelp of pain as the older woman's nails dug in deeper. "You did not bear him," her splintered self blurted, her voice fast and panicked. "But he is yours all the same. You will understand when you see him." She shot a look at Siwon, whose shoulders squared with determination as she continued. "We will hold off the Netherking as long as we can, but you must swear that you will save our child. *Swear it.*"

Although Mirae balked at the idea of running away from the very fight she'd come here for, the grave, pleading faces in front of her softened her resistance. *I'm useless to them anyway,* she thought bitterly. Mirae could sense the powerful enchantments and protective wards surrounding the homestead. It seemed Mirae's older self, who'd been fortunate enough to live many happy years, had also kept the majority of their powers. There was no question which of the two Miraes would be more useful next to Siwon, who could resist the Netherking's magic-draining spells.

I came all this way only to be too shattered to get my revenge, Mirae agonized, hot tears blurring her vision. *But if there is an innocent child to be saved, then I must help him, at least.*

To the relief of the anxious parents, Mirae nodded and, leaving the fulfillment of her destiny to more capable hands, hurried toward the house, quickly slipping inside.

It took her eyes a moment to adjust to the dim lighting of the cool home, but her ears immediately picked up the sound of a baby gurgling in one of the nearby rooms. Mirae skirted around the tables of soaking vegetables and herbs in the middle of the main area, careful not to trip on the piles of carefully folded bedding pushed against the walls. Following the giggles, Mirae quickly found which of the chambers housed the child she'd agreed to protect.

The nursery was small but well lit. An open window let in a refreshing breeze and warm sunlight. In the middle of the room a fine satin quilt was laid out, the only luxurious decor Mirae had seen in the modest homestead, and atop the blanket rested a chubby baby boy, old enough to babble happily at Mirae as soon as he saw her but not yet big enough to crawl.

Mirae stayed by the door for a moment, overcome by a flood of emotions, both at seeing the gold irises of a baby born to the family she'd thought would be hers and at the name embroidered on the blanket in shimmering thread that matched the child's eyes.

Kimoon. A name that explained why Mirae had been brought here, where her path had always been leading. And why the babe's mother outside had begged Mirae to spare him.

This tiny boy in front of her would someday grow up to be a hateful old man, a self-professed Inconstant Son. Her very own child, innocently named in honor of the man who'd sacrificed everything in order for Mirae's other half to live a fraction of the life she'd always dreamed about. A babe the goddess of time had sent Mirae to extinguish when, as requested, he was most vulnerable.

This baby, *her* baby, was the one she was meant to destroy all along.

As Mirae stood there, too shocked to move, or to even begin comprehending what all this meant, she heard a commotion outside. The blast of protection wards exploding, the crackle of fire, and the roaring wind of Jade Witchery at war. Siwon uttering a battle cry just before the sound of steel clashing against steel reverberated through the courtyard.

The child fell quiet, startled by the noise. He didn't cry, but Mirae knew it was only a matter of time before the baby unwittingly gave both of them away. Still, as much as she wanted to scoop up the innocent infant and flee, as she'd promised, her limbs were stiff with mortification, her mind spiraling with the revelations she couldn't bring herself to comprehend.

Mirae's body froze further still when she heard the sound she hated most in the world. The Netherking's low, oily chuckle drifted into the house, chilling her to the bone. From where she stood, Mirae could see only a piece of the courtyard outside, framed by one of the nursery's open windows, but it was enough to witness the horror unfolding there.

Mirae watched her older self and Siwon brace for battle against the figure slowly approaching them, who'd easily thwarted all their defenses. The same dread that flickered across their faces flooded Mirae as well, like ice water engulfing her body, pulling her into dark, inescapable depths.

"I have searched a long time for you, queenling," the Netherking said, spitting out the last word. "Is this where you've been all along, hiding like a lowly rat in a gutter?"

When the Netherking came fully into view, Mirae barely managed to avoid gasping at the sight of him, at the state of the man whose body he wore. Where Kimoon had once dressed himself in rich purple silks, his hair tidily swept away from his face, his tall, lean frame was now draped in a sleek, deep green robe that trailed several feet behind him, emblazoned with a snarling gold dragon arcing all the way from Kimoon's neck to the bottom of his hem. His hair was pulled up into a high pony-tail long enough to slink halfway down his back, held together by a small coronet dotted with jade beads.

Mirae's older self lifted her chin. Although her skin was pale with fear, she put on a brave face and calmly shot back, "It took you long enough to find us. Awfully embarrassing for someone who calls himself the Eternal Emperor."

The Netherking smiled dangerously. "I'll admit it's a little more difficult to hunt Sacred Bone traitors without their blood pumping through me, but that hardly stopped me from dis-patching the False King and seizing what was rightfully mine."

Hongbin. Mirae's hands flew over her mouth, holding back a sob at the thought of what her brother had endured at the Neth-erking's hands. If he was even still alive.

Just then, the baby let out a soft whimper. Horrified, Mirae watched the Netherking turn his head, fully exposing Kimoon's face, and the deep, nasty scar splitting it in half. His sallow skin was a corpse-like gray, the deep shadows in the hollows of his brow and cheeks making him look more skeletal than alive. His once golden eyes were now bloodred, and his veins bulged with black water, engorged like leeches. Before he caught sight of Mirae through the window, Siwon quickly grabbed his attention back with a taunt. "I heard the True King has been quite the handful. Did he not escape some time ago, and is now leading a surprisingly hardy rebellion? How humil-iating that must be."

The Netherking whipped back around, his ire clearly piqued. Not wanting to risk the baby making another sound, Mirae crouched out of sight and crawled over to the child. Thankfully, while Siwon kept the Netherking distracted, no one but her could hear the baby's coos as he looked up at her adoringly, thinking her his mother.

But Mirae wasn't charmed in return. How could she let herself feel anything for someone she'd been sent here to destroy? Looking into the child's golden eyes, she found herself briefly wondering if both Kimoons were the same person somehow, but quickly dispelled that notion. The Kimoon who was her friend had become little more than a decaying vessel, the soul of the man inside probably long devoured by his possessor. His scarred face was nothing like the one she'd seen in her switches, either. No, the Kimoon she'd once called a friend would never grow old, never live long enough to exact his revenge. He was someone who, despite Mirae's fervent promise, could never be saved.

This infant in front of her, however, smiling and innocent, would face a differently horrifying fate altogether. One that was still an utter mystery to her.

Mirae's other half, the woman who had birthed and loved this child, had begged her to save his life. But Mirae hesitated, knowing that she couldn't afford to fail like the Deep Deceiver, and leave another ungodly mess that no one would be able to clean up, for Mirae was the last High Daughter. On the other hand, she also couldn't bring herself to hurt this innocent baby who reached for her, seeing only its mother with those golden eyes it got from its father.

I don't have to be the one to do it, Mirae reasoned desperately, searching for any way out of this terrible choice. *I could just coax the Netherking into destroying the cabin, and everything in it. I could flee and find a way to help Hongbin, dedicating the rest of my life to finishing off the sole remaining threat to the peninsula, fulfilling my duty. The sacrifices of my mother, Jia, the Yeosinnim, and Kimoon need not be for nothing.*

As if helping her find the courage to enact her plan, several voices echoed back to her from the past, urging her to do this unforgivable deed as the clamor of battle erupted outside.

If you find a way in one of your switches, please do the terrible, impossible thing. Stop all this before it happens, even if no one, including me, ever understands.

I came to warn you that in order to fulfill your destiny and restore harmony to the peninsula, you will have to make a sacrifice you are not yet ready to bear.

This was her calling, something only she could do, for this child's mother had made it clear that if she survived the brutal fight in the courtyard, she would never hurt her son, not to save the world. Mirae wasn't even sure *she* could find the will to harm a hair on the head of the baby who was, in some way, her child as well. As she reached down and cradled the infant in her arms, she racked her brain for any other solution. Perhaps she could raise Kimoon to be good, to never become the Inconstant Son. But in Mirae's heart, she knew it was no use defying the goddess of time's instructions. She either killed Kimoon now, or she failed the peninsula. There was no alternative.

Just as Mirae wondered, again, if she could ever force herself to do the unthinkable, a familiar voice rippled through her head.

Are you really going to kill an innocent babe?

The Netherqueen, whom Mirae had presumed dead after the splintering, spoke sharply, unsurprisingly rising to the defense of her grandchild. But her cutting reprimand was all Mirae needed to make up her mind, for hearing the horrible deed she was contemplating spoken aloud while she looked down at the face of pure innocence made the answer to Suhee's question reverberate throughout her body.

No, she decided, pulling baby Kimoon closer. *I won't. I can't.*

A bloodcurdling scream suddenly rent the air outside. The battle, it seemed, was coming to an end, and her other half was losing. Soon, the Netherking would storm inside the house and find out about baby Kimoon, whom he'd either kill or seize for his own purposes. Outside the window as his wife cried out in agony she heard Siwon beg, "Help us, *please*."

She knew he wasn't talking about himself. He was beseeching her on behalf of his son. The desperation in his voice, a final plea from the man she loved, gutted Mirae to the core.

Committed to her choice, to the promise she'd unthinkingly made, Mirae gathered the blanket on the floor around the child, wrapping Kimoon into a thick, warm bundle. Holding him close, she crept back out to the main room and toward a side exit leading to a second porch. Sneaking quietly in her stockinged feet, she slipped outside, well out of sight of everyone in the courtyard, and headed back toward the trees. Once she was safely in the shadows, too far away for the rustling of underbrush to be overheard, Mirae broke into a run.

You know that if you do this, the Netherqueen said as Mirae raced through the forest, *if you choose to save this child, then no one, not even the Deep Deceiver, will have failed the gods greater than you.*

"I know," Mirae panted, clutching the baby to her chest. "Am I out of my mind?"

No. To Mirae's surprise, Suhee sounded as if she was in awe of her choice. *What you are doing is brave and honorable, unlike the beings who created you to do their dirty work. I'm with you on this, queenling. Tell me what you need, and I will help.*

For the next few days, Mirae stuck close to the trees, keeping to their shaded depths to avoid encountering anyone on the road, especially the patrolling soldiers with steel armor and dark green tunics, marching in uncanny unison. Their faces were expressionless and their eyes dull, hollow men fully under the Netherking's control.

Mirae did her best to avoid villages, too, and other refugees fleeing their burning homes, except once or twice to trade whatever jewels or strips of silk she could part with for apples and pears to mash and feed the baby, who grew heavier in her arms every day. She even traded Kimoon's luxurious blanket for a more sensible one, and a pair of shoes for her bleeding feet.

After a week, her toes and ankles were covered in blisters, and her stomach grumbled so loudly at times that Kimoon would jolt awake and cry. She'd soothe him with more of the fruit she saved for him, while she survived on the sparse weeds and wild mushrooms she foraged as she walked, whatever the Netherqueen told her was safe to eat.

Finally, on the eighth day, Mirae spotted the outskirts of the forest surrounding the Seollan palace. Knowing better than to go anywhere near the heavily guarded walls where the Netherking had no doubt set up his vile seat of government, Mirae kept to the woods, making her way carefully toward the Garden of Queens. Just as the chill of evening fell, she finally stepped into the clearing where her ancestors lay.

Every other time Mirae had entered this sacred place, she'd offered proper obeisance to the women who'd paved the way for her, and dedicated their lives to preserving her birthright. Now, however, Mirae did little more than weave her way through their silent tombs, heading straight for the shadowy doorway she hoped was still there.

To Mirae's relief, the dark portal was still exactly where she remembered it, though it looked as if the Netherking had done everything in his power to destroy it. Scorch marks riddled the ground, and the haetae statues Mirae had erected were nothing more than shattered pebbles. Thankfully, the ancient magic that had created the doorway to the Deep was so strong, not even the Netherking's tremendous power could undo it.

After checking to make sure the coast was clear, for it was imperative that no one know where she'd gone, Mirae took a deep breath and clutched the sleeping baby to her chest before stepping into the swirling circle of darkness.

It was somewhat of a relief to see that the wintry trees and bone-white sand of the Gwisin Forest were largely unchanged. As she limped down the pale path, missing the days when she could just summon wind to carry her, Mirae kept an eye out for any sign of Sol, or her gwisin army. But the sparse trees remained empty, no one disturbing their stillness but Mirae and the companions she carried.

Quite the party we make, Mirae thought wryly, licking her chapped lips. *Me, the splintered queen who shouldn't exist; Suhee, a twisted spirit bound to her former enemy; and Kimoon, an ill-fated child shrouded in a dark, uncertain destiny. All hiding from the same villain who doesn't know they exist, heading toward the one place he will never go.*

When Mirae finally broke through the forest, she was glad that Wol Sin Lake also looked untouched. Neglected. Spiderwebs sparkled between the dry branches of the surrounding trees, and seaweed littered the ghostly shoreline.

No one had been there in quite some time, exactly as Mirae had hoped. Cradling baby Kimoon, Mirae walked up to the inky waters of the Deep and stepped into the shallows. She waded slowly, cautiously, calling for the bohoja in her mind.

Thankfully, it heeded her summons, even though the Sacred Bone Magic within her was weak. Sensing what she needed, the green hand expanded, doubling in size until it was large enough to create an air pocket to transport both her and the child in her arms.

Still, Mirae hesitated, agonizing over her decision. *Do I really think I can find a way to protect this baby* and *the peninsula? Am I really going to defy the gods by giving this child a chance to break his curse, and rewrite both of our destinies? Or is this all a huge, horrible mistake?*

As her hands shook, the burden in her arms suddenly doubly

heavy, Kimoon cooed in his sleep and cuddled into her, trusting and innocent. She could feel the Netherqueen soften at the sight just as her own heart melted and her mind steeled with resolve.

Holding the infant tightly, Mirae settled into the giant green hand, and together, the High Daughter and her Inconstant Son, the last of their kind, sank into the waters of Wol Sin Lake.

ACKNOWLEDGMENTS

First, I want to thank my amazing agent, Holly; my editors Alice, Liz, and Clare; and the rest of my team at Harper for helping me to bring my books to life.

Next, I'd like to give a huge shout-out to my amazing *And Break the Pretty Kings* street team, with special thanks to Michaela, Luchia, Christina, and Alys for being incredible superstars. You are magnificent human beings who deserve all the cozy socks and unlimited book hauls in the world! The same goes for you, Kristin. I cannot thank you enough for all your support, you beautiful, hilarious, talented goddess.

Also deserving of my unending praise is my sanity-preserving, morale-boosting support system. I'm grateful to Na-Young for all the brainstorming sessions, and to Tricia, who's the most incredible writerly friend a reclusive, socially awkward debut author could ask for.

To Aaron, I will always love you across all time and under every moon. Thank you for all the matcha lattes, neck massages, and for being endlessly patient with my writing-frenzy-induced absentmindedness. I love you too, B and Y, you sweet and beautiful puppies.

Last, I of course wish to give the warmest of thanks to you, dear reader. You're wonderful and beautiful in every way.

사랑으로,

Lena